Storm

Storm

Kim Pritekel

P.D. Publishing, Inc.
Clayton, North Carolina

ISBN-13: 978-1-933720-43-2
ISBN-10: 1-933720-43-3

9 8 7 6 5 4 3 2 1

Cover design by Linda Callaghan
Edited by: Kay Porter / Linda Daniel

Published by:

P.D. Publishing, Inc.
P.O. Box 70
Clayton, NC 27528

http://www.pdpublishing.com

Dedication

Mo anam cara:

We've had an incredible past, and may we have just as an incredible a future.

Ta gra agam duit

"Realizing what a deadly disaster had come to them, the people quickly drove the Italians from their city. But the disease remained, and soon death was everywhere. Fathers abandoned their sick sons. Lawyers refused to come and make out wills for the dying. Friars and nuns were left to care for the sick, and monasteries and convents were soon deserted, as they were stricken, too. Bodies were left in empty houses, and there was no one to give them a Christian burial."

~ Anonymous

Part 1
Europe, 1349

The woods were smoky and dark, entirely too quiet. Devoid of birds, the numerous ancient trees had tops that reached out to the Heavens, branches spread before God in prayer. Perhaps they were praying for the safe keeping of His people. Perhaps they were raising fists, damning a god who'd punish the land with such merciless fury.

A lone figure moved through the maze of trees. A pale hand clasped together the ends of a brown cloak in an attempt to keep the chill of the air, and the unknown enemy, at bay. Unseen green eyes watched ever vigilant from beneath a large hood which kept the feminine face in shadow. It wasn't wise for a woman to travel alone, especially on foot. A small dagger was gripped in Cara's unseen hand, fingers sweating as they flexed against the wooden handle. The cool metal of the hilt brushed against her skin.

Hearing footfalls in the fallen leaves of the forest floor, the girl pressed her body flat against the trunk of massive oak. The hand, once clasping the cloak, reached up and pushed the hood back slightly. She heard many footfalls — heavy, as if made by boots. That would mean knights or nobles. They were often worse than any highwayman.

Scanning her surroundings, Cara saw that she had little chance of remaining hidden. There were only trees — no caves, no rock overhangings. Sucking in her lower lip and squeezing the handle of the dagger in her palm, she waited.

"I see a body, my Lord," John shouted, his voice echoing throughout the woods. Grimacing, he put a cloth to his mouth and nose. A disgrace. From the distance of three horse lengths, the gender of the corpse couldn't be determined. The skin was mostly black and eaten. The eyes were open, but only one stared out. The other appeared to have been dinner for a small forest creature.

"Well, stay far from it, man!" Lord Avery, Third Duke of Cornwall, shouted back. "We steer around these woods. Forward!"

Cara's heart began to beat again as the noise of the small army receded, their booted footfalls and clanging armor becoming distant, soon only an echo.

"Thank ye, my Lord," she whispered, eyes flickering Heavenward. Not waiting a beat longer, she pushed off the tree, making her way through the woods that she knew so well, the weight of her pouch bumping against her hip as she darted from tree to tree. She, too, had seen the body the soldier had spoken of, and she knew these woods were cursed.

She must hurry.

"Bugger," Merryn growled, tossing the rotten piece of fruit aside. Let the vultures add it to their enormous feast. Crouching as she made her way through the carnage, she stopped, kneeling beside the body of a child. His blue eyes stared up at her, silently begging for help that never came. "Dona look at me, lad," she hissed, throwing a piece of cloth over the child's face.

It had stopped bothering her long ago; now it just annoyed her. The girl never liked to be looked at or noticed by the living, let alone the dead. Even so, the dead offered so much more than the living. Noting the child's hand still clutched around something, she pried his fingers open, wincing at the sound of breaking bones. Damn the stiff ones.

Though it was grotesque work, the treasure inside was worth it. Merryn's blue eyes opened in surprise at the gold that winked at her. Three gold coins had been kept shiny by the child's sweaty palm; that is before the body dried out.

Plucking the precious metal pieces from the dry, gray palm, she quickly wiped one on her cloak before bringing it to her teeth. Satisfied by the small mark made, Merryn pocketed the money then moved on.

"Get out! Flee, ye savage!"

Merryn looked up to see an old, grizzled monk picking his way through the layers of the dead, an angry fist raised in her direction.

"Go back to yer monastery, Father. There's nuthin' here fer ya," she said, tucking a dagger into her belt.

"How dare ye steal from the dead!" he bellowed, grunting as one of his turnshoes was sucked into a badly decomposing body. Unable to hide his disgust, the priest lifted his foot, balancing on the other foot and his walking stick as he leaned down to grab his captured shoe from the mess.

Merryn chuckled, all the while shoving the few valuables she had found into her cloak.

The priest finally reached her, panting heavily after his journey through the street which, from necessity, was now a lane of the dead.

"Go back Father, before t' blackness gets ya, too." Merryn didn't even spare a glance at the old, rotund man. She continued picking through the bodies, shaking out the rags that had once been clothing to see what would fall out. Most in the tiny village were dead, so Merryn had the pick.

"And ye, young boy, thief!" He hobbled over to the cloaked figure, grabbed her by the arm, and swung her around. Merryn glared at him as her hood fell away, exposing a tanned, dirty, and decidedly female face. "God have mercy, a girl!" His glance took in her torn, dirt-encrusted tunic, a belt at the waist with a goodly length of coiled rope and several daggers tucked into it, and a baldric across her chest with a sword dangling from it. His mouth fell open in shocked disgust as he saw her breeches and booted feet.

The old man was about to admonish her when his eyes flickered up. He choked on his words as he looked down the blade of the very sword he'd just spotted. At the other end stood a very unamused young woman.

"Leave it be, Father, or I'll send ya ta yers."

"Burn in Hell, ye will, child," the priest said quietly, yet with great earnestness. Merryn grinned, nodding as she put her hood back in place.

"So 'm told. If'n 'tweren't me, would be some other lad. Leave me be." She lowered her sword, smoothly easing it back into place.

"Damned Celt," he muttered, knowing there wasn't anything he could do. He was no match for the girl and her blade, so instead he turned and blessed the dead, freeing their souls to rest in Heaven. Turning back, he was stunned to see the girl was gone. Nervously he tucked one hand into his robes, grasped his walking stick in the other, and moved on.

Cara sighed with relief when she saw the split stump she knew so well. Just a hundred paces beyond would be the entrance to her village. She began to run now, no longer worrying about being seen alone wandering through the woods.

Her hood flew off her head, allowing her long, golden hair to flow behind her as she ran. The young woman — just fifteen summers old — ran faster the closer she was to town.

"No," she breathed, hand coming to her mouth as she quickly stopped. Her eyes widened in stunned shock and dismay at the bodies that littered the landscape. She wasn't sure which face to linger on longest; many were no longer identifiable. Taking slow, careful steps, the girl made her way through the sea of bodies, waving off masses of flies and the awful stench.

She was too late.

"Mother!" Panic setting in, Cara ran as best she could, whimpering as a fear greater than any she'd known before, gripped her heart. She saw the shack she shared with her mother and younger sister, Grace. The plank door was open, the windows dark.

Slowing, Cara tried to distinguish any inside movement. She knew in her gut what she'd find inside, and she really didn't want to see it.

"Oh, Mother," she cried, rushing to the prone figure on the dirt floor. Her mother's skirts rode up over the blackened skin of her swollen legs. Falling to her knees, the girl gently turned the body over. A quick, shrill cry escaped her throat when she looked upon the face of the only parent she'd ever known.

Cara could feel the lunch of berries and bread she'd eaten earlier threatening to rise once again, but swallowed it down. Raising a trembling hand, she brushed dark blonde strands away from her mother's nearly unrecognizable face — eyes open and bulging, a silent scream frozen on the swollen mask. Numerous sores littered the face, the pus that had leaked out in life, dried and smeared in death.

"Oh, mother. I failed ye. Forgive me," the girl cried, hugging the stiff body to her, rocking gently.

"My child," said a soft voice. Cara looked up, her grief so profound she was almost unable to make out the image of the priest standing in the doorway of the shack.

"I was too late, Father Steffen. Too late." New tears began as the young woman buried her face in her mother's dress, almost choking on the smell of death that clung to it.

"No, dear Cara. The Lord had plans for Mary and Grace. Do not blame yerself." The priest walked into the hovel, his walking stick making soft clicking sounds on the dirt floor.

Wanting badly to believe his words, Cara released her mother, laying her gently back onto the floor. She wiped her eyes, but to no avail, as new tears quickly fell. With her shoulders slumped in defeat, Cara untied the thick rope from around her waist, removing it and the bag that hung from it.

"I brought the medicine as quickly as I could." She laughed ruefully, the irony lost neither on her or the priest.

"Keep it for yerself, child." Father Steffen grunted as he lowered himself to his knees, pulling the girl he'd known all her life, into his warm, fatherly embrace. "Ye must go far from here, Cara. Those who lived have gone. Ye must go, too."

"Do ye think I'll go ta Hell, Father? Fer killing my mother and sister?"

Father Steffen looked down into the eyes he'd known for so long. He smiled down at the child who was growing into a lovely woman. Shaking his head, he brushed a few strands of hair from her tear-streaked face.

"Nay, child. Ye have been blessed with life, survivin' the blackness that walks the land. Death came to us, stalkin' our every move." He grabbed the bag, filled with hard won herbs and roots, including rose petals, that would be mashed into a mixture that would relieve the pain and suffering of those who caught the plague. "Go now. Ye've beaten death; do not stop here. Heal those ye find and bring 'em peace with yer lovely smile." Steffen smiled as the very smile he spoke of shone on him.

Cara nodded, giving the priest one last hug before picking herself up, taking the bag he handed to her before he gruntingly got to his feet, also.

"Go, child. Survive this darkness with the light God has given ye." Father Steffen watched the girl leave until she was out of sight. He had always known that someday that girl would be so much more than the peasant life she was born into.

The fire was burning bright, warming a cold, lonely night. Merryn wrapped her cloak around her shoulders a bit tighter, then rotated the rabbit carcass that hung above the fire.

The night was quiet, very quiet. So many had died. Merryn tried not to think about it, knowing that it would do her no good. Death was part of life, just as breathing was.

She'd been wandering for so long now, it seemed. Long before the sickness had scorched the land. Looking down at her pack, she dragged it over to settle it between her booted feet. Pulling her pack open to peer inside, all the goods she'd found over the past few days glittered in the firelight. She'd be able to do some good trading for much of it, using the rest for herself — weapons, clothing, and the blankets that made up her bedding.

Pulled out of her reverie, Merryn realized her dinner was beginning to burn. Leaning over to the fire, she poked at the meat with a dagger, but stopped mid-stab. She scanned the inky forest around her, ears perking up, to determine what exactly she just heard.

Slowly rising to her feet, she turned in a small circle, trying to determine which direction the noise was coming from, and what exactly it was. There were footsteps, hurried, not careful or stealthy.

Then she heard a scream.

Snatching her sword from the baldric, she ran headlong into the dense foliage in the direction the scream came. Up ahead she heard the whimpers of what sounded like a young girl, the muffled words of a man, and lots of thrashing.

As she entered a clearing, Merryn saw the glint of steel in the moonlight, bringing her attention to two dark figures becoming clearer as she got closer. A young girl was pressed against a tree; a man held her there with his body and a blade to the girl's throat, as he loosened the ties of his breeches. The girl was breathing hard, her chest heaving against the rough material of his shirt.

"Please! Help me!" the young girl begged, as she spied Merryn approaching. Merryn grabbed the man by his long, unkempt hair. He howled in pain as he was tossed onto the forest floor, dead leaves and twigs the only things padding his fall. In what Merryn knew would be a brief respite, she grabbed the girl, yanking her away from the tree by the front of her dress, then pushed her behind her own larger body.

"Ye jus' made a big mistake, girl," the man growled at Merryn as he got to his feet. Again, there was the glint of steel as he brought his dagger up, eyeing Merryn's sword, which she held in a slightly trembling hand.

"Run away 'n ya will only lose yer pride," Merryn said, sounding far more confident than she felt. The man laughed, whipping his head back slightly to toss the dark, greasy locks out of his eyes.

"Slit ye from gullet to that pretty mouth of yers, I will, wench. I say ye walk away and leave me to me business and maybe I'll let *ye* live." He shifted his weight from foot to foot, waiting and watching to see what the girl would do. Maybe he could have fun with the both of them.

"Try it and tell yer tale to Satan, himself, lad." Merryn could feel the girl behind her, clinging on to her cloak with claw-like fingers, her breathing fast and erratic.

"Ye've go'a big mouth on ye, lass. There are far better things for it than this rubbish." With that, he attacked, using brute strength against the smaller girl.

Merryn hadn't been prepared for the attack and was knocked to the ground, the other girl backing out of the way and screaming in frightened surprise. Within moments the man was on top of Merryn, trying to press his advantage of surprise and size.

Merryn's head hit the forest floor with a resounding thud that echoed through her brain as he grabbed a handful of her long hair, using it to pound her head into the ground a second time. She swore she saw stars flying in front of her eyes, as the second pounding made her teeth clash together, nipping her tongue in the process. The warm, salty taste of blood filled her mouth. She knew she had to do something and quickly, before this thug got the upper hand and knocked her out. If that happened, neither she nor the other girl would be safe.

With a mighty grunt and heave, Merryn leveraged the thug by pushing with her feet against the ground. The movement she used caused them to reverse their positions. Now sitting astride the man, she used the pommel of her sword, slamming it into his jaw. A resounding crack filled the night, followed closely by a cry of pain. Blood leaked out of the man's mouth, oozing black in the moonlight.

"Nasty wench!" he shouted. Bringing a fist up, he connecting solidly with Merryn's own jaw, throwing her head to the side. A hot flash of pain filled the right side of her mouth as something very hard was loose against her tongue. Spitting her tooth to the ground, she bared her remaining teeth, using every ounce of strength she had to pummel the fool silly. His head whipped this way and that, crashing again and again into the hard ground beneath him.

"Stop! Ye'll kill 'im," a soft voice said from just behind and above Merryn. She glanced briefly behind her to see the other girl, huddled in her cloak, her face the picture of worry and fear.

"If'n I dona, he'll kill us," Merryn said, turning back to the man whose eyes, half-hooded, showed the world closing in around him until finally his head stopped moving, as blackness enfolded him.

"Is he...?" The girl with the blonde hair couldn't bring herself to say it, after seeing so much death lately.

"Nay. He's out o' his head." Merryn got to her feet, her head pounding, her jaw badly hurting and bleeding.

"Ye're hurt," the girl said, hurrying over to look up into Merryn's face with the kindest, gentlest eyes. Merryn pulled her face away from exploring hands.

"'M fine." Turning back to the man, she knew she'd have to do something with him. She could leave him be, but, when he awoke, he'd want to find the wench who'd done this to him. She couldn't very well kill him just like that. "Go ta my campsite back yonder, grab ta rope inside ta pack. ... *Go!*" she shouted when the girl hadn't moved. As she ran off into the darkness, Merryn turned back to the man. Maybe she could run him through while the girl was gone? "Bloody hell," she growled, knowing she couldn't do that.

Sooner than she expected, she heard the girl's voice again, "Here's the rope."

Merryn took it from the shaking hands of the girl.

"Now get out o' here," she growled, turning to the man who was starting to come round. "I said go!" she yelled over her shoulder, heaving a mighty kick at the man's head. He grunted then was out again like a snuffed torch.

The girl gasped, covering her mouth with her hands, her eyes huge as she looked at the panting Merryn.

"I tol' ya ta go," Merryn growled as she knelt, using the rope to tie the man's hands and feet. The girl said something, but it went unheard as the man's head fell to the side as she moved him. Leaning in a bit, she hissed, jumping to her feet. Behind his ear and down the side of his neck were the telltale marks of the sickness. "Bugger me."

Without another word, she grabbed the man's dagger, which he had dropped, planting it firmly in the soil next to the man's unconscious body. He could cut himself free, if he had the strength.

Ignoring the girl, Merryn went back to her campsite, where she began to pack up.

"What are ye doing? What's happened?" the girl asked, not sure what to do or where to go.

"Ya've brought death ta my campsite," Merryn said, pointing an accusing finger at her.

"What? I do not understand..."

"Ta lad has got ta sickness," Merryn snarled, roughly gathering up her pack. The remaining rope was not coiled since the whole thing had toppled over. "He'll be dead by mornin', most likely," she muttered absently, tossing a few things back into the pack.

"What is this?" Quick as lightning, the girl was kneeling at her side and reaching into the pack. The girl's hand glittered in the firelight as she brought out gold coins. "Stealing from a child, are ye?"

Merryn looked at two of the three gold pieces she'd taken off the boy. "He was dead! Hardly needs 'em anymore." She reached to snatch them away, but the girl was too quick, jumping to her feet.

"I gave these to that boy," Cara whispered, looking at the shiny gold resting in her palm. "He's dead, ye say?"

"Aye. Quite," Merryn smirked, the smile fading quickly when she saw the deadly look aimed at her. Clearing her throat, she stood. "Give 'em here." Holding out her hand, she stared into narrowed green eyes, made golden by the firelight.

"No." Cara closed her fingers around the coins, holding her fist close to her chest. "Where's the third?"

"There were only two," Merryn lied, hoping she could at least get good use out of the last piece. It was obvious the girl didn't believe a word she said, but she didn't care. You had to survive any way you could.

"Thief," Cara muttered, slipping the gold pieces into the pouch tethered to her waist. The girls stared each other down, a battle of the wills showing in their eyes.

As Merryn stared into those deep, soulful eyes, she was stunned by the way they seemed to be looking into her very soul. She began to squirm, worried about what the girl saw there.

Clearing her throat again Merryn turned away, pretending that breaking up camp was far more important than some silly game. Once everything was bundled and hidden under her cloak, and her weapons were in place, she began to kick dirt onto the fire. She kept her eyes off her unwanted guest, but knew the girl still stood nearby. Out of the corner of her eye she saw a hand reach out and grab the badly burnt rabbit from the fire.

"We'll need this fer the road," Cara said softly, wrapping the meat in a cloth.

"You are not coming with me, lass," Merryn said, walking over to the girl. As she reached out to snatch the food, it was promptly moved out of reach. She sighed. "Dona play wit' me, girl. 'M in no mood."

"My name is Cara, not 'girl'. And ye owe me."

"I owe ya not one thing! Fine. Keep the damned meat. 'Tis burnt anyhow." Like a child, Merryn stomped on the dying embers and set out into the dark forest. Cara quickly followed after, mindful that her skirts didn't drag through the red pit.

"Ye stole from me," Cara said, having to hurry to keep up.

"Ya lie," Merryn tossed back over her shoulder.

"I gave those coins to David, and ye stole 'em from 'im." It took everything Cara had to keep her voice steady, and not give in to the emotion she felt in her throat. She knew she had to stay strong, especially around this girl. She wasn't entirely sure she was successful.

"No time for tears now, lass. Ta boy was dead, and he certainly wouldn't need 'em ta get through Heaven's gates, now would he?"

Cara sniffled, trying to swallow the growing sadness that welled up inside her. "Ye still shouldn't have taken them. 'Tis disrespectful." Cara yelped in surprise as she nearly ran headlong into the other girl, who had turned on her.

"Respect dona keep ya alive, lass. Remember that." Standing toe to toe, they looked into each others eyes, one looking for a weakness of any kind, the other looking to see how she could exploit the other in the quickest way and get rid of her. Finally Merryn broke the silence. "If'n yer gonna follow me around like a dog, keep yer trap shut. These woods are no' a safe place, if ya hadn't noticed."

Cara grudgingly nodded her consent. They traveled in near silence for what seemed like days, but was actually a few hours. Cara was starting to wobble on her feet.

"Wait," she said, slowing to lean against a tree. "I need te stop."

Merryn turned, looking back to see the girl leaning against the tree, hand on the trunk, head bowed.

"Sick, 're ya?" she asked warily, keeping her distance. Merryn was fine with the dead ones, but had trouble watching the live ones die.

"Nay. Jus' tired."

Merryn sighed, looking up at the sky, trying to determine what time it was. It was very late, and as much as she didn't want to admit it, she was exhausted herself.

Without a word, she struck deeper into the wood, trying to find a good place to camp for the night.

Cara noticed that her companion had picked out a suitable location. "I'll gather some wood," Cara offered, starting off, though keeping her hand near the dagger at her side.

Cara had been walking all day, trying to find life somewhere, *anywhere*. She had found wanderers like herself, everyone afraid to stay with their homes. The dead were piling up faster, the stench of burning and rotting flesh everywhere, making Cara nauseous. The man in the woods had taken her by surprise, grabbing her from behind and slamming her against that tree. She shivered at the thought of what would have happened had her dark companion not shown up.

Making her way back into the circle of their camp with her load of wood, Cara asked, "What 'tis yer name?"

The other girl looked up from where she'd been laying her bedding on a cleared spot and answered, "Matters not."

"Does. I dona want to call out 'what 'tis yer name', and I want te know who te give my gratitude to."

The other girl sighed, stood up, and took the armload of wood from Cara. "Merryn."

"Merryn." Cara tasted the name, deciding she liked it. "Well, thank ye fer what ye did, Merryn. I owe my life te ye."

"Ya owe nothin'. And dona thank me, Cara, because this time tomorrow, ya will be on yer own," Merryn said as she placed the load of wood by the fire.

Cara was silent as she bent over and readjusted a few sticks in the fire circle, helping them to catch. The fire began to illuminate their surroundings, sending shadows over everything the light of the flames didn't lick.

"'Twould be safer for us to travel together, Merryn," she said, her voice soft. She glanced at the other girl who stood by the fire, feet planted wide apart, arms crossed over her chest.

"I dona need ya with me, lass. If 'tweren't far ya, I'd be sound asleep by now." Merryn's eyes were cold as she stood there, unmoving, both body and soul. Without a word, Cara nodded, dropping her eyes as she untied the pouch around her waist.

"'Tis yer choice, Merryn. Let me have a look at yer mouth."

"'Tis fine—"

"Sit."

Merryn landed on a log with an "oomph" as Cara stood above her. Glaring up at the girl, she stayed put. Cara knelt before the stubborn girl, raising gentle, warm fingers to examine the damage and to see what would be needed.

Merryn watched, fascinated, as the girl pulled out a small bowl, carved from a single piece of wood, and sprinkled various herbs into its depths. Setting the bowl aside, the girl tore off a sprig of something Merryn had never seen before. She put the weed into her mouth, chewing for a few moments before spitting the newly-made mush into the bowl.

"Have ye any water?" Cara asked, raising her eyes to the confused look of her temporary companion. She smiled softly when the girl nodded dumbly. Merryn reached to her small pile of belongings and handed over a small animal bladder.

Pouring a little water into her mixture, Cara pulled out a small, thick stick from her pouch and began to mix it all together, making a strong-smelling paste.

"Ya look a bit young to be an apothecary," Merryn said quietly, her eyes never leaving Cara's movements. The other girl smiled.

"Because I am not."

"Yer da, then?"

Cara shook her head, meeting Merryn's gaze. "Since I was a small child I've understood what would help those who were ill." She shrugged. "Father Steffen used to say I was a chosen one." She smiled shyly. "I dona believe that, but 'tmight have saved my life. A man in my village was struck with the black sickness, so I left to gather what would help 'im. I was gone but a few days, and at my return..." her voice broke.

Merryn cleared her throat softly, guilt consuming her. "How did ya know those gold pieces belonged to the boy?"

Cara quickly swiped at her eyes. Now was not the time to mourn. She finished mixing, moving closer to her patient.

"Because I gave 'em to 'im. A soldier had passed through our village. He had been hurt in battle, his leg growing dark with sickness. I helped 'im," Cara said, a slight smile of pride spreading across her lips as she cleaned Merryn's bloody mouth. "I'm sorry. I'm being as gentle as I can," she said when the other girl winced.

Merryn did her best to not react as the gentle fingers touched her. She focused on Cara's face as the girl continued her story. She was a beautiful thing. Merryn wondered what wondrous colors would jump from the girl's expressive eyes come the light of sun.

"So grateful was he that he gave me the three gold pieces." She glanced up briefly to meet Merryn's eyes. "I knew they were the ones that belonged te the boy because we're so near my village and gold pieces are rare around here, pieces of gold like that aren't laying around just anywhere."

Again, Merryn felt a stab of guilt and looked away. A gentle touch on her chin told her not to move. She kept her patience as the paste was applied to her face with the stick and tapped down lightly with a fingertip.

Merryn was stunned as the pain began to recede. Her jaw was sore, indeed, but the cuts and bruises seemed to shrink under Cara's care.

As if reading Merryn's mind, Cara spoke, "I've made ye a bit extra so ye can take it along with ye." She sat back on her heels, looking at her handy work. "Within a day or so yer wounds will be healed."

"What is in this?" Merryn asked, taking the bowl and holding it up to her nose before quickly jerking back. The smell was not unpleasant, but potent.

Cara smiled. "'Tis secret."

"Oh?" Merryn raised a brow, letting the bowl be taken back from her hand.

Cara nodded. "'Tis." She scraped the remnants of the paste onto a cloth, wrapping it before handing it to Merryn, who was adjusting her jaw.

"Like magic," Merryn murmured. She could have sworn the lad had broken her jaw.

"Dona breathe that too loud, Merryn, or get me hunted, ye will."

Merryn smirked, then stood, walking over to her sleeping rags. Without another word, she made herself comfortable and fell asleep.

Cara watched her go, a sense of sadness washing over her. Yet alone she'd be again. Sitting by the fire, the girl brought her knees up, wrapping her arms around them and staring up into the Heavens.

For her whole life she'd been surrounded by those who loved her, and those she loved. Her father had died many, many years ago, but her mother and Grace... Cara felt tears chilling her skin as they fell silently. She wished she'd been able to give her mother a proper burial. At least she'd been able to say goodbye, which is more than she could say about her sister, Grace. A mere child, Grace had been the light of Cara's life.

Forehead resting against her knees, she really began to sob, unable to keep it in any longer. She was devastated and filled with a profound sadness. What now? Where would she go? What would she do?

Startled, Cara looked up as her fingers found the rough material of the cloak that had just been wrapped around her shoulders. She brought the warmth closer around her. She tried to curb her emotion, thinking that Merryn was not likely to be the crying type, but she just couldn't control it. Glancing up over her shoulder, she saw Merryn heading back to her bedding. As she sat down upon the pile of rags, she met Cara's gaze for a short moment. A brief smile, and she lay back down, cocooning herself in the rags.

Cara sighed, grateful for the kind gesture. She decided to try and get some sleep. She curled up within the cloak, which was bigger than her own, allowing her to create a bubble of warmth around her. Her own cloak served nicely as a pillow.

A deep breath. Then another. And another. A green eye opened. The sideways world showed a fire crackling, and a small, iron pot sat on a few flat rocks in the flames.

The world righted itself as Cara sat up, running a hand through her hair. A deep rumbling in her stomach reminded her that she hadn't eaten since midday the day before. Movement behind her caught her attention, and she watched as Merryn tugged on leather twine between her teeth, repairing one of her bracers, which were simple brown leather with no decorations or ornamentation.

"Stir that, will ya, lass?" Merryn asked, not looking at Cara as she set the bracer aside, grabbing one of her boots.

Without comment, Cara made her way to the pot to stir the contents, using the wooden spoon that rested on a rock outside the fire ring. Leaning over the wonderful-smelling stew, she was mindful of her sleeve and the licking flames as she stirred the concoction, roots and wild potatoes bobbing in the mix, along with chunks of cut up meat. Bringing the spoon to her lips, she blew over the broth, made of mostly water, and the few juices left over from the rabbit the night before.

"'Tis just about ready," she said, setting the spoon back on the rock. Standing, she stretched her arms high over her head, balancing on her toes for a moment to stretch out her calves and arches. A day full of walking was torturous on the body.

Merryn did not reply. She tugged on her boot, which Cara could tell was slightly too large for her. Boots were rare, and Cara's curiosity got the best of her.

"Where did ye steal those?" She neatly folded Merryn's cloak, which had been put over her shoulders the night before. Blue eyes twinkled up at her.

"Who knows? Let us say that there's a soldier out there wit' cold feet."

Cara grinned, shaking her head as she gently set the heavy garment atop Merryn's belongings. Seeing the cloth filled with the remains of her herbal mixture, she walked over to Merryn. Squatting in front of her, she raised a hand.

"Let me have a look at yer mouth," she said quietly.

Merryn held still, allowing Cara to do what she needed to. She focused on the girl's face, seeing the skin, surprisingly smooth considering the hard life the girl had already endured. Slightly arched, dark blonde brows drew slightly as the girl's concentration deepened. Merryn looked at her eyes, such an unusual color. They were green, but it wasn't the color that caught the attention. There was a depth to them, a wisdom far beyond the girl's maybe sixteen years.

Those eyes glanced up to meet her own for a moment. Cara smiled encouragement before she returned to her task.

"Ye've healed well, Merryn. One more day and ye should be fine. Perhaps a bit of a bruise, but nothin' more."

Merryn nodded her acknowledgement of the news, sitting as still as she could as Cara applied a second layer of the paste.

"How long have ye been alone?" Cara asked, surprising her companion with the softly spoken question.

"Many a year, lass," Merryn said just as softly, as Cara gently wiped away a smudge of the paste she'd accidentally spilled onto her patient's cheek.

Cara sat back on her heels, looking up at the girl who sat upon a large rock. "Don't ye ever get lonely?"

Merryn shrugged, suddenly feeling shy. "Sometimes. 'Tis the way of things, and I move forward."

"Where are yer parents?"

"I know not. Was left on the steps of the nuns, and I ran from that place."

"I'm sorry," Cara whispered. She was amazed at the pain she could see in those incredibly bright, blue eyes, which shone even brighter from the dirty face they looked out of.

"Do not. 'Tisn't worth pity, Cara. I'm alive and no longer anyone's whipping boy. Nor will I be again."

Cara nodded her understanding.

"How have you managed to avoid the black sickness, lass?" Merryn asked, putting voice to a question she had been wondering about since the day before.

"Father Steffen said 'twas because I was blessed, but I think 'tis more because I found that cleanliness is next to Godliness." She smiled sweetly, standing.

"What does that mean?" Merryn also stood, walking over to the fire, using her knife to hook into the iron loop on the pan, tugging it from the fire.

"The sickness seems to live in the dirt, the mire, and dung. Since I was a small child, I wash nearly every day—"

"Ev'ry day! Are ya out of yer mind, lass?" Merryn cried, stopping mid-scoop when she heard the outrageous boast. "Man nor beast needs that. How have ya got any skin left?" She looked at the girl's face and arms, shocked.

Cara laughed. "Ye won't lose yer skin, Merryn. 'Tis better fer ye and, from the looks and smell of ye, a trip to a river would be a good idea."

"Not on yer life."

The lake was cold. Very cold.

"Tell me again why I didn't let that bugger do away with ya last eve?" Merryn growled, eyeing her companion, who was clearing the water out of her eyes. Cara grinned.

"Because deep down ye want someone ta travel with ye, and the moment ye laid eyes on me, ye knew I could be yer very own troubadour."

"That *must* be it." Merryn rolled her eyes before dunking herself under the surface of the cool water, rinsing off the last of the herbs Cara said would clean her hair. Running her hands down the rope of wet strands, she squeezed some of the extra water out of them. She had to admit, though it would never be to Cara, that she felt much better and liked the feel of a clean body.

Cara grinned, ignoring the sarcasm in her new friend's voice. She swam around a little to stretch her arms and legs before deciding she was cold enough. Walking out onto the rocky shore, she quickly grabbed her clothing.

"Wait, lass," Merryn said, wading to the shore. "Ya may not die from the black sickness, but ya'll catch yer death if you make your garments cold and wet."

Cara watched as Merryn quickly got a fire started, right there on the shore, seemingly unconcerned with her nakedness. She looked away, wanting to give her friend some privacy.

"Come here, lass. Warm yerself." Merryn laid herself down on her cloak, her hands tucked behind her head. It was a beautiful day, and the sun was shining down to warm their skin. For the first time in — she couldn't remember how long, Merryn was enjoying herself. She glanced across the dancing flames at Cara, who lay in almost the exact same position.

"So where are we going?" Cara said, eyes twinkling. Merryn smirked.

"*We,* lass?" she asked, with her brow raised. Cara smiled sweetly, but said nothing. Merryn shook her head, incredulously. She was filled with guilt once again, as her thoughts turned to where she was off to next. Yes, she should take Cara with her, and yes, they had fun in the lake. Perhaps this washing thing isn't so bad, but would Cara drive her crazy as time went on? Merryn was a loner, always had been, always would be. "I'll take ya to the next town, maybe London if ya're lucky. But at that, lass, we part ways."

Cara looked at her friend, her heart dropping, but she nodded in agreement. She would have to be grateful for what she could get.

"Are ye a character in the Bible?"

"Nay," Merryn said absently, looking around as they made their way through the forest. The snow had fallen heavy and brutal, and their breaths and words immediately crystallized in the air. She worried they wouldn't be able to find any dry wood for a fire.

"Dead or livin'?" Cara asked, brows furrowed as her mind brought up image after image of possible candidates for their game.

"Dead."

"Dead. Alright." Cara stopped for a moment, head cocked to the side. Merryn had heard something, too. "What is that?"

Ignoring the question she had no answer for, Merryn struck off toward the left, hearing the sound get louder. Soon she was running, her cloak fanning out behind her, and her boots crunching in the snow.

Cara waited, but ran towards the sound when her name echoed through the wood. Out of breath yet grateful for the warmth that spread through her body from the exertion, she burst through the trees into a clearing, stopping suddenly.

Merryn slammed her sword into the frozen ground with a grunt. "Give me yer rope," Merryn shouted, seeing Cara over her shoulder.

Cara gasped at the site before her. The noise they had heard was a horse that had fallen through the ice of the river.

"Now, girl!" Merryn shouted, desperation in her voice as she threw her cloak to the ground, stripping herself of all her weapons. Acting purely out of instinct, Cara untied the rope with trembling fingers, her eyes never leaving the beautiful horse thrashing in the ice, desperately trying to keep its head above water.

Merryn took the rope thrown to her and quickly tied one end to the cross-guard of her sword and the other around her ankle.

"Hold on to my sword, lass," she said quietly over her shoulder as she edged toward the ice. Cara hurried over to the blade, fell to her knees, and wrapped her cold-reddened hands around the grip. She flexed her fingers before lacing them, making a stronger hold. Her heart was beating fast as she watched Merryn make slow but sure progress across the ice, her boots sliding, her arms out for balance.

Cara listened as Merryn murmured calming words and sounds to the terrified horse. Then a sharp crack rent the air. Merryn stopped in her tracks, her eyes huge as she tried to find the source of the crack. The horse was making things worse, the cries of terror and distress almost deafening.

Realizing that the horse would tire soon and then it would be too late, Merryn continued, sliding faster across the ice until she reached the animal.

Cara's hands flew to her mouth as Merryn fell into the water with the animal. Remembering what she was supposed to do, she quickly wrapped them around the grip again, her heart stopped cold in her chest.

Merryn's breath was stolen from her lungs as she was immersed into the frigid water. Going under, she quickly forced her way back to the surface, reaching down to untie the rope from her ankle. She had to be very mindful of the frightened animal's movements, as the horse could easily kill her in its frantic state. She jumped onto the horse's back, a death grip on its neck.

Cara watched as Merryn fought to get the rope tied around the animal's neck.

"Tug on the rope, Cara!" Merryn cried, her lips barely able to get the words out, so frozen they were.

Jumping into action, Cara wrapped her hands around the rope, using her body weight to pull. With her eyes squeezed shut, her teeth bared, and as an echoing cry erupting from her throat, the horse began to move.

Another crack, then another, and another. Cara's eyes opened in time to see a spider web of cracks rush across the ice, the horse following as the ice parted.

"Pull, lass! Pull!" Merryn cried, half in desperation and half in laughter, as the horse broke its own way out of the river. But the laughter was cut short when the horse reared up, throwing Merryn and sending her crashing through the ice, disappearing under the surface.

"Merryn!" Leaving the sword, Cara ran toward the ice as the horse jerked forward, running toward her as it broke through the last of the ice. Getting out of the galloping animal's way and wading her way into the water, Cara continued to cry out, "Merryn!"

Seeing movement, she sent thanks to the Heavens and hurried forward, gasping as the water rose until she had to swim.

"Merryn," she panted, seeing the darkness of long hair. Hurrying over to it, she grabbed at her friend, startled, but immensely happy when Merryn gasped loudly, taking in a long breath. Cara grabbed her, tugging quickly, knowing she had to get them both out of the frigid water as soon as possible. "I've got ye," she panted, kicking her way toward the shore in the open waters created by the horse. "I've got ye."

Finally able to touch the bottom of the river, Cara dragged the coughing, shivering girl toward the shore. "'Tis all right, Merryn," she encouraged, helping the girl to the ground. Looking around, she saw a long, deep trail in the snow and realized it was from Merryn's sword. The mare had pulled the weapon out of the ground and had dragged it behind her in her haste to escape her terrifying confinement.

"I'll be back quickly," she said, gently squeezing Merryn's shoulder.

Hearing heavy breathing and snorting, Cara scurried through the trees, ignoring her own shivering as she stepped carefully around the trees, not wanting to frighten the animal. When she finally found her, she saw the horse was lying on its side, ribs heaving. Each hot breath managed to melt a bit of snow at its head, forming a small trench. The rope was still around the horse's neck. She was finally able to see that this was a beautiful mare. So as carefully as she could, and conscious of a big brown eye watching her, Cara untied the rope from around the sword, which lay not far behind the horse, and tied the rope to a nearby tree.

"I'll be back, girl," she murmured, kneeling at the animal's head and gently running a hand over the mare's nose.

She ran back to Merryn, who lay where she'd been left, huddled in upon her own body, which was shivering violently. Ignoring her own chills, Cara made quick work of searching through Merryn's belongings, tugging out her sleeping blankets.

"Here, Merryn. Sit up," she said, her voice soft and soothing. Merryn did as she was bidden, her lips almost as blue as her eyes. Cara untied the laces of Merryn's shirt as quickly as her trembling fingers would allow. Once the shirt was removed, she wrapped the blanket around Merryn's icy shoulders.

"I'll make a fire," she said, rubbing her hands frantically up and down her friend's arms, trying desperately to put some warmth back into her. Merryn nodded, still unable to say anything.

The wood was damp, causing her to cry out in frustration several times. Cara was desperate to get a fire lit, knowing it was the last hope for the two of them. Finally, she got it started.

"Thank ye, Lord," she whispered, hurrying over to her friend. "Come, Merryn. Let us warm ye." With a groan, Merryn stood, shakily, and walked the short distance to the fire.

"Ya need to warm yerself, as well, lass," Merryn said, looking at the shivering girl.

"Soon," Cara said, hurrying back through the woods to the mare. She found the horse on her feet, still too exhausted and cold to put up a fight. Cara untied the rope and led the weary animal back to camp, tying her to a tree near the fire. The mare immediately went about nosing the snow out of the way, finding grass at the base of the tree.

Finally out of energy as the cold took over, Cara collapsed next to Merryn. Quickly, she untied her cloak which was heavy and water-logged.

Both girls absorbed the warmth that finally managed to permeate the layer of ice on their skin. As feeling returned to Merryn's body, she turned to Cara, who was staring into the flames.

"Ya saved me, lass," she whispered. When green eyes met hers, she smiled. "Ya saved my life."

"Then we're even," Cara smiled back.

"We are."

"'M alright, lass," Merryn said, though the last word was interrupted by another violent coughing fit. Cara rubbed small circles across the heaving back, her brows knitted in worry. It had been two days since they had rescued the horse from the icy waters, and Merryn's health was faltering quickly.

"No, Merryn, ye're not. Ye've gotten worse."

"Nay." Merryn waved off her words of concern, determined to go on. She'd been sick before and could beat it this time, too. She didn't need to be pampered as if she was a child. "'M fine."

Cara said nothing more to the stubborn girl, but kept an eye on her as she led the mare, yet to be named, through the trees. They traveled down the path they had been following since starting out that morning, toward London.

Merryn's pace slowed more and more as the day passed, and she finally agreed to stop for the night. Cara tried to get her to eat the soup made of a few roots they'd been lucky enough to find during the day. They really needed to get to London soon, so that Merryn could get out of the cold.

"Please eat, Merryn," Cara pleaded, bringing their one bowl to her. The steam from the food warmed Merryn's face, but the smell made her nauseous. Turning away, she brought a hand up, tucking the other against her stomach.

"I canna, lass," she groaned, the bile rising in her throat. Sighing, Cara looked down at the food, uncertain what to do. Merryn hadn't eaten more than a few spoonfuls of food in two days. She was weak and unable to travel for long lengths of time.

"Please, Merryn?" she tried again. "Fer me? Just a couple bites?" Cara's green eyes looked into the sunken blue ones of her companion. Merryn nodded, accepting the bowl.

Not long after, she helped Merryn to bed. That is, as much as the proud girl would allow.

"Stop yer fussing," Cara gently admonished, her patience being tried. She grabbed the heel of one of Merryn's boots and gave it a mighty tug while keeping her balance so she wouldn't fly back into the fire once the boot came loose. Setting it aside, she pulled off the second one, noticing the sole was beginning to wear. "We need to get this repaired when we get to London," she said absently, setting the boot aside and grabbing Merryn's cloak.

"A bit breezy," Merryn whispered, her voice hoarse, just before she was racked with another coughing fit.

"Shhh," Cara cooed, moving up to the girl's head. Cara looked down with concerned eyes, bringing a hand up to gently brush dark hair away from a sweaty brow. She thought for a moment, then began to sing, her voice soft on the cold night air. She wouldn't be London's next minstrel, but her voice wasn't unpleasant, either. It helped to calm and lull Merryn into an uneasy sleep.

Exhausted herself but knowing what must be done, Cara grabbed her pack, sifting through until she found what she sought. Pinching a few of the dried leaves between her fingers, she moved back over to the sleeping Merryn, gently parting her lips before placing the leaves on her tongue. Merryn's brows drew for a moment, and her lips briefly tucked inside her mouth as the dried leaves tingled against the soft flesh of her gums and tongue. Finally with a soft sigh of contentment, Merryn was still, her breathing even.

"Sleep well, my friend," Cara whispered, placing a gentle kiss on Merryn's clammy forehead. She swept mahogany locks away from Merryn's face, usually so beautiful, but now pale and sickly.

Merryn's fevered mind wandered through the trees, under the surface of the river, ice bumping into her face, giving her the shivers. This caused the fear of flame to lick at her body, causing a great sweat that turned into a small glacier, which she stumbled over. Her blue eyes widened in terror as the deep brown mare turned into a raging beast, a dragon of old. Fire, flaring from its dilated nostrils, hit her with a wave of heat, making her cry out as it singed her mind.

A voice. A sweet, lovely voice. "Merryn? Come back to me, Merryn." The voice echoed, bouncing around between her ears, like a ball of string she once had. The string now unwound, tugs at a litter. The dragon pulled the litter, tugging her with the unwound string. "Merryn? Are ye hungry?"

Food. What food comes back to life to snap at you? Crazy lass gave her food that bit at your throat, stung the inside of your mouth, and made your tongue tingle like so much ale.

Cold. So cold. So very cold.

Softness. Do the clouds fall from the skies? Lie upon the land like so much dew? Warmth and softness are found along her body and in her mind. The wool keeping her ears apart had grown soggy, capturing her thoughts into tiny little caves where spiders crawled in and out of them.

Warmth.

Her blue eyes slowly fluttered open, blinking several times before becoming focused. Quickly Merryn squeezed them shut again, her head pounding, her temples pulsing.

"Shhh, 'tis all right, Merryn. I know it hurts," a soft, warm voice said to her right. Turning her face in that direction, Merryn kept her eyes closed as she felt coolness spread across her forehead, and a small, calloused hand take her own. "The pain will pass, I promise."

"Where am I?" she whispered, her voice as scratchy as her throat after little use.

"The nuns at St. Michael's were kind enough to allow us respite," Cara explained softly.

"How..." Merryn cleared her throat, trying again. "How long 'ave we been here?" She attempted to open her eyes again, squinting in the dim light of a single candle that rested in its holder upon the small table next to Cara's chair.

"Three days," Cara said, her head cocked slightly as it was tilted down to look at her patient.

"Why does my head hurt so badly?" Merryn blinked again, grateful to feel the pain beginning to ease.

"'Tis the comler root I gave ye. 'Twill break yer fever, as it seems to have done."

"To what horror," Merryn groaned. She saw a small smile briefly cross Cara's lips.

"I'm sorry, Merryn, but a pounding head is more welcome than the raging fever of a week in age." Cara removed the damp cloth, the coolness sucked right out by the wicked heat of Merryn's skin. She dunked it in the wooden bowl, filled with cool water that the sisters had provided her with. Wringing out the cloth, she reapplied it, gently wiping away the few beads of sweat that remained. Merryn closed her eyes once more at the cooling sensation, which helped to ease her headache. "Other than a hurting head, how do ye feel?"

Merryn paused before she answered that question, taking stock of her body and all its moving parts.

"I'll live, lass," she whispered, pleased at the soft chuckle that received.

Part 2

Merryn couldn't help but get the shivers as she walked the halls of the giant cathedral. Where others saw beautiful windows made of colorful glass depicting the saints and Bible stories, she heard cruel words and saw a fist flying through the air, nearly knocking her, as a young girl, off her stool as she tried to please the sisters with her washing skills.

Her eyes scanned the windows which bled red, blue, and yellow onto the floor of the sanctuary. She looked up to see Christ looking down at her, his eyes half-hooded as he blessed his faithful, only to be nailed to a cross in the next pane.

As onlookers marveled at the finely carved wood and beautifully sculpted saints, Merryn saw a confused child, forever wondering what she'd done so wrong to deserve the wrath of the nuns who swore to protect her.

"A worthless whore like your mother!"

The words still echoed in her mind, as her boot steps echoed upon the fine marble of the cathedral floor. The smooth beauty had been pilfered from the ancient statues and palaces in Rome, where they had been bought after being scavenged and sold for a pretty price.

Moving further into the sanctuary, Merryn studied the rows of highly polished pews dotted by bowed heads and heard the soft sobbing of a woman near the front.

As she scanned the parishioners, Merryn saw a familiar blonde head, bobbing slightly as its owner rocked. Walking down the center aisle of the nave, she quietly scooted into the pew next to Cara. The girl's eyes were closed, her hands clasped together, and her lips moving in silent conversation, but with whom?

She waited patiently for Cara to finish and her eyes to open. As she waited, she remembered Sister Marie, the only woman who had been kind to Merryn as a child. Sister Marie had actually sat with the young Merryn two pews ahead of where Merryn now sat with Cara. The nun would teach the young girl to read, insisting that some day Merryn would become a nun, herself, and would need to be able to read Latin.

Cara seemed startled to find Merryn sitting next to her.

"Who were ya speaking ta, lass?" Merryn asked quietly, eyes twinkling. Cara looked away, embarrassment coloring her young face.

"No one."

"Ya lie. 'Tweren't it the job o' ta Father ta be doin' yer talking fer ya?" Merryn asked, nodding her head toward the priest at the altar. Cara followed her indication, then looked down at her hands, which fidgeted in her lap.

"I cannot tell the priest what I need to tell God," she softly explained.

"And why not?"

"They'd call me a witch and do away with me," Cara answered, fear coloring her eyes. Merryn studied her for a moment, knowing the truth of those words. She nodded agreement. After considering what she'd been told, she looked to her friend again.

"What do ya tell Him?" she asked, her voice soft. Cara studied her for a moment, trying to make out the sincerity of the question. Seeing nothing but honest curiosity, and feeling that she could trust her friend with what she was about to say, she looked around, making sure no one was nearby.

"I hear a voice in my head, Merryn," she whispered. Merryn's first impulse was to laugh, but when she saw the earnestness in those deep, green eyes, her mirth died in her throat.

"What does it say?"

"It tells me what I must do, te help someone. 'Tis almost as if," Cara thought for a moment, trying to get the right words, "as if a picture of the root or herb, or combination of them floats before my eyes, and then I know what I must do. It guides me, Merryn," she said, her voice growing even softer. "It guides my hand. Am I mad?"

Merryn looked at the young woman for a moment, contemplating this question for long minutes. Finally she smiled, shaking her head. "Nay, lass. Seems ya're blessed."

Cara's gratitude was palpable. She'd never been able to tell anyone of her gift. Not even her mother or Father Steffen knew the full scope of it. She looked at Merryn.

"Thank ye."

"Nonsense, 'tis I who should thank ya." Merryn grew serious for a moment, holding Cara with a piercing gaze. "Ya saved my life yet again, lass. How did ya get me here?"

"Brogan pulled a litter I built fer ye."

"Brogan? My native tongue," she said, then smiled with a nod. "She is a sturdy one, 'tisn't she?"

Cara beamed, pleased her friend understood. "Aye."

Merryn looked around the church again, noting some of the sick being brought through the doors.

"Can we leave this place?"

"Do ye feel strong enough, Merryn? We can stay..."

"We should go," she said, standing. "Ta black sickness spreads ta this place. I can feel death crawlin' around here." Her eyes scanned the cathedral, almost as if she were looking for death herself.

"God be with you, child," Sister Agatha of Renault whispered, hugging Cara close. Pulling away gently, she looked into her eyes. "You're certain you can't stay awhile? The ill could use such a friendly face and kind word." She smiled, her plump face seeping from her habit. Cara smiled in return.

"I'm sorry, Sister, but I must go."

"I understand." Turning to Merryn, the nun took the somewhat resistant girl into a gentle embrace. "I'm sorry we weren't able to outfit you properly, child," she said, eyeing the girl's masculine clothing. "'Twas good your brother had clothing for you to wear."

Merryn said nothing, briefly glancing at her friend, then smiling with a curt nod. "Aye. 'Twas lucky."

As the two left, Merryn glanced over at Cara, a question in her eyes that she need not speak. A bout of coughing caused her to pause for a moment, hand resting on a wagon they were passing. Cara was immediately at her side.

"Are ye alright, Merryn?" She rubbed the girl's back, under her cloak. Finally Merryn nodded.

"Fine, lass. Just pushin' ta rest out." Taking Brogan's reins from her, Merryn hauled herself up onto the mare's back. Looking down at Cara, she held her hand down to her. "Come up, lass. 'M too tired ta be walkin'."

Cara took the proffered hand, feeling herself being nearly yanked off her feet. Once on the horse, she hugged the massive animal's body between her thighs as she tried to get secure on her back.

"Settled, then?" Merryn asked, glancing over her shoulder. Getting a weak nod, she clicked her tongue and nudged the horse into motion.

They rode on in silence, Cara's arms wrapped around the waist of the girl sitting before her. It had been frightening, watching her friend become so ill and weak. Merryn had more pride than any king's soldier the girl had ever seen. She had fought hard for the freedom she prized above all else. And for her to become a slave to sickness... Cara knew Merryn had not been in her right mind since she could care for her so completely. Merryn never would have allowed Cara to rock her to sleep, her fevered head in Cara's lap and a soothing lullaby frosting the air.

Though Cara was not afraid to be alone and, in fact, oft craved isolation, she had always had her mother and sister close at hand. She had always taken for granted that no matter what happened, they'd be there for her to go home to. Her mother and Grace loved her unconditionally, as she loved them. She never worried about judgment or doubt in her abilities. The fact was, more than once Mary had tried to talk her daughter into taking her healing abilities outside their small village. Shy and unwilling to leave her people, Cara always refused.

Now she felt so far away. Her village, her people, her family, all felt like a lifetime ago. Cara knew herself to be a different person now. Yes, she had Merryn, but one thing the strong girl had taught her was to rely on herself, never on anyone else. The help of others was like smoke — it looked thick and smelled strong, but the slightest shift in the wind would cause it to float away.

Cara turned her head, resting her cheek against Merryn's back, needing to feel that wisp of smoke for just a moment. She felt a chilled hand brush against her own, which made her smile. Just the briefest of contact, that she had no doubt Merryn hadn't even realized she'd made.

Nothing more had been said about parting ways, and Cara didn't think there would be. If nothing else, she'd managed to prove to Merryn that she could serve some purpose, even if it was the ability to save Merryn's life from time to time.

"Cara?" Merryn said later that night, as they both lay on their separate bedrolls. Cara, lying on her back, turned to meet Merryn's blue eyes made gray from the fire. Merryn lay on her side facing her, hands tucked under her chin. Their blankets and cloaks covered both girls completely; only their faces were visible. "Tell me about yer mother 'n yer sister."

Cara turned to look into the Heavens again, swallowing hard, then nodding. She began her tale, her voice soft and hushed.

"My mother, Mary, was a kind, loving woman. She could be tough as nails, if need be." She smiled at random memories parading through her head. "But all in all she was tender. Oh, she loved Grace and I," she whispered the words with vehemence. "She would do anything fer us. And she did."

"What did she look like?" Merryn whispered, her eyes scanning her friend's profile, seeing the way the firelight danced along the bones in the girl's brow, outlining the shape and shadowing her eyes. The straight nose, a golden tip in flames. She watched as Cara's mouth moved, lips forming the words, her tongue peeking out from time to time in the formation of a sound, or to absently lick dry lips or rid them of stray spittle.

"Her hair was darker than mine, though not nearly as dark as yers." Cara glanced at her friend, seeing she had her full attention. She smiled at that, quickly returning to her story and her study of the stars. "Her eyes were so sad. Always sad and tired. A hard life she had. Had the chance to marry a Duke, ye know." She shook her head with a sigh. "Flat refused because Grace and I were not te be part of her new life. She could have got out of the squalor, out of the dirt, the cold, and the sickness," her voice trailed off, lost in thought and memory. Oh, how she'd fought with her mother, trying to convince her that she could take care of Grace.

"A brave soul, lass. I now see where ya get it." Merryn smiled softly at the surprised look she received. Cara looked down, suddenly shy and embarrassed.

"And then there was Grace." It almost hurt more to talk about her small sister, than it did about her mother. "What troubles she caused our mother." The sad look was replaced with a smile that lit up Cara's face brighter than the firelight. "Oh, what a villain she was. Her hair, so blonde, so thick. We once sold her hair for a gold piece. It was cut and used to stuff a mattress." Cara laughed quietly at the memory. "Less than a season and it was long again."

"Healthy child."

"She was." Cara nodded in agreement. Sighing, she turned onto her side, grunting softly as she got herself settled and mirroring Merryn's position. "I didn't get a chance to say goodbye to Grace," she continued. "She was not with our mother when I found her dead in our home." Sighing, she looked at Merryn. "I miss them."

"I know ya do, lass. I know ya do." To the surprise of them both, Merryn reached out her hand and gently wiped away a single tear that had escaped one of the beautiful green eyes. Cara smiled at the tender gesture, and Merryn smiled in her turn. The hand remained placed gently against Cara's face, her eyes closing as she absorbed the touch. The loss of affection from her life bothered her almost more than anything.

When Sister Agatha had hugged her, Cara had wanted to cry. She needed to be hugged and found it more and more difficult to not attack Merryn, insisting on a daily hug.

Her eyes opened as the touch slowly drifted away.

"Ride, lass! Ride!" Merryn cried, her long legs pumping as fast and as hard as they could, her cloak flying out behind her along with her hair.

Clicking her tongue, Cara got Brogan moving, her own hair flying away from her face as she ducked under branch after branch, heart pounding like mad.

Cara tied the mare to a tree just outside the entrance of their cave and was gathering wood from the pile they made the night before, when she heard Merryn's heavy footfalls and erratic breathing noting her arrival.

"Ye're going to get us killed, Merryn," she said, partly scolding the girl, partly laughing at her as Merryn followed her back into the cave.

"Nonsense." Merryn panted as she tossed her goods to the stone floor. Bending over at the waist with hands resting on her thighs, she attempted to catch her breath. "He was a fast bugger, though," she conceded, taking the water skin Cara passed to her.

"Indeed, his belly like a bowl of animal lard te boot," Cara teased, earning a glare as Merryn tied the skin shut.

"Alright then, I'll take those back ta him," she admonished, as she pointed to the boots she had been carrying.

Eyes opened wide, Cara hurried over to the stolen goods, her fingers touching the fine, rich leather of the boots; she'd never owned her own pair before. "Thank ye, Merryn," she squealed, rushing over to her friend and crushing her in an enthusiastic hug. Though Merryn did her best to look annoyed, she couldn't help but be pleased by the reaction.

Cara lugged the heavy boots with her to a rock near the cold fire ring, forgetting all about the lack of warmth for the moment. She tugged off her own turnshoes, which were badly worn and in need of repair — or destruction. She'd dismantle them and find a new purpose for the leather. Tugging the boots on, her eyes closed in pleasure at the instant warmth.

Merryn chuckled at the pleasurable sigh that echoed in their stone hideaway. Kneeling next to the fire ring, she soon had new flames coloring her features orange. She smirked as Cara clomped around the cave, nearly falling on her face in the oversized, unfamiliar footwear.

To Cara, it felt so strange having something fit so snugly against her calves and not feel the constant breeze on the tops of her feet. When she wore the turnshoes, the heaviest stockings she could find were the only covering for her feet. Cara looked over her own shoulder down at the new, full leather boots. Cara watched as the firelight gleamed off the brown leather heels.

Merryn was amused at the girl's antics. "Don't fall and smash yer face in, lass. 'M afraid ya'd have to stay smashed. I dona have ta healin' touch ya do."

Cara glared at her friend, making her way over to the pouch of goods that had been dropped with the boots. Digging through them, she was pleased to see Merryn had managed to get everything she asked for — suet, flour, and nuts. She already had raisins and spices.

Ordering Merryn to fill the pot with water, she turned to her own pack and pulled out a small, thick piece of cloth, as well as the rest of the ingredients needed for their Christmas meal.

"How long, how long, how long?" Merryn asked excitedly from behind her, chin almost resting upon Cara's shoulder. Cara grinned, shrugging the taller girl away.

"Have the virtue of patience," she said.

"That, I do not possess, lass."

"I hadn't noticed," Cara gave her friend a mischievous grin. Stuffing the cloth full of the ingredients, she pulled the cloth to form a bag, tying off the neck tightly with a length of rope. The water in the pot was just beginning to warm, so she gingerly sank the bundle into the depths.

"I got us something ta go with supper," Merryn said with a grin. She opened her cloak, unhooking a wine skin from her baldric.

Cara's eyes lit up; she had tasted wine but a few times in her short life. She made her way over to her friend, trying not to trip over in her unfamiliar footwear. "Let me have a breeze of that," Cara said after reaching Merryn and sat next to her, having enough of her boots for the time being.

Merryn handed over the wine skin, after taking her own long, satisfying draw. She sighed in contentment and relaxed with a smile. With hooded eyes she watched her friend sip cautiously, Cara's face screwing up as she tasted the bitter drink.

"Wuh," Cara shivered as the drink singed down her throat, boiling into her stomach. She handed the skin back to her friend.

"'Tis good stuff," Merryn sighed, capping the skin. It was their only wine and it was not for wasting. Cara looked at her friend as though she had just grown into a dragon.

"Good?"

"Aye. 'Tis." Merryn nodded, glancing over at her friend as she rested her head back against the cave wall. Cara smiled at her.

"Thank ye for the boots, Merryn."

"Merry Christmas."

"Ye don't celebrate Christmas," Cara said softly.

"Aye, 'tis true, but ya do, lass," Merryn said equally softly.

Not knowing what to say, so pleased was she, Cara continued to stare at her friend. She searched Merryn's eyes, such a rich blue, bright and inviting, filled with the fire of her heritage. Her gaze moved around her friend's face, seeing the high cheekbones and a strand of hair, so dark, starkly contrasting with those eyes. She reached over, running her fingers across the smooth forehead, smoothing the strand away.

"How are ye feeling?" she whispered, noting that Merryn hadn't had one of her coughing fits in days.

"Fine as wine."

Cara smiled. "We have a poet in our midst."

"Far from it, lass. More like a wanderer with no place ta wander to." Merryn smiled a sad smile. Her eyes fluttered closed when she felt Cara's fingertips drift along her arched brow, gently sliding down along her temple to her cheek.

Cara watched as the long lashes trembled a bit just before they lifted and Merryn's eyes opened.

"There is such strength in ye, Merryn," Cara whispered, her fingers running along one of those cheekbones, following down to the proud jaw line. "Ye can do anything."

"Nay..."

"Shhh." She rested a finger on Merryn's lips. "'Tis true. I have faith in ye. A strong leader, ye are." Cara smiled sweetly. "I know I'd follow ye anywhere."

"And I'd take ya, Cara." Merryn shook her head. "Won't leave ya behind."

Cara sighed in contentment. How was it that the most profoundly painful time in her life was quickly changing into the most wondrous? With that thought, the sound of boiling water claimed her attention.

She crawled over to the fire, using a dagger to poke at the bundle gently enough to not rip the material of the makeshift bag.

"Almost ready."

"'Tis good news. 'M just about ready to feast on those new, shiny boots o' yers." Merryn smirked, tapping the boots in question with her sword. Cara glared at her over her shoulder, making Merryn laugh outright.

"Christmas dinner is served," Cara said, lifting the bag from the water, carefully lying it on the stone floor. She cut the steaming rope, using the dagger to slowly peel the material away from the prize inside. "Lovely, lovely," she whispered, seeing what lay beneath.

Merryn watched as she laid the food on a flat stone, slicing it with her dagger. She cut into the hard, fatty meat that had once encased the kidney of a sheep, and the good things inside spilled out.

Cara licked the sweet sugar-nut mixture off her fingertips. Humming in pleasure, she placed a large piece of pudding in their one bowl and handed it to Merryn who raised a brow, Cara placed a hand to her hip.

"Tell me ye've had plum pudding before?" she asked, incredulous. Merryn shook her head, leaning in to sniff. "Well, then you are in for a treat," she said, joining her friend by the wall again, her own portion balancing on a cloth.

"Lucky for ya 'm hungry enough to eat anythin'."

"Lovely," Cara said dryly, her eyes closing in utter pleasure as she took the first bite. She chewed slowly, savoring each taste sensation that exploded in her mouth. Merryn sniffed one last time then took the hunk of a piece, ripping at it with her teeth, cheeks rounded with the mouthful. A sip of wine helped it to go down even better.

"Not bad, lass," she finally admitted, tearing another hunk off.

"Thank you. I must agree."

Cara stopped, her head tilting slightly as she listened, trying to hear above the sound of the cold water around her.

"These, Mother?" a child's voice asked. Sounded like a little boy.

"No, child. Fall over dead, ye will."

"Like Da and Samuel," the child reasoned, resigned sadness in his voice.

"They're askin' fer trouble, being so loud," Merryn grumbled from the shores of the tiny stream. She capped their water skin, tossing it to the shore before beginning to fill the second.

"True, that." Teeth chattering, Cara made her way from the icy waters, wringing her long, stiff hair out and gasping at the half frozen water released down her back and bottom. Merryn smirked.

"Crazy as a loon, you are."

"Yes, but c-c-c-clean," Cara shivered, quickly drying herself with a few rags and stepping into her dress. She sighed in pleasure as the dry material surrounded her chilled flesh. The addition of her heavy cloak touched off another contented sigh. She almost outright moaned as she slipped her boots on.

"I won't never understand," Merryn muttered, still thinking Cara was mad for bathing every time they came upon water. Cara always made sure the water wasn't tainted with what she called "the squirts". *Strange lass.*

The pair heard more of the mother and son's conversation further in the forest. They spoke of everyday things and of the village they'd left, especially the black sickness. The epidemic was coming back with a vengeance from the reprieve of the winter, as spring came upon them.

Cara was most interested in this correlation. It was almost as though the source of the black sickness either died or was halted during the cold months. She had been thrilled that the horrible death had finally left the land in peace. But when they had approached the last village in search of supplies, the odor of the rotting dead had met their noses before the daily noise of the village had.

"Perhaps we should invite them to midday meal," Cara mused as she gathered the wet rags and stuffed them in her pack, from whence she brought out her comb.

"Bad idea, lass," Merryn said absently, slinging both water skins over her shoulders as they started away from the water. Cara carefully combed out her tangled locks, which had partially frozen together.

"But why? You heard them — they have little."

"As do we, Cara." Merryn looked the girl deep in the eye as they headed back toward the cave that had been home for the past three months. "And our supplies grow ever thin, lass," she added.

"But..."

"Shhh," Merryn hissed, her body becoming stock still. She held a hand up to ward off anything else Cara might have to say. Had she been a wolf, her ears would have been perked.

"What 'tis it?" Cara whispered, trying to listen for anything out of sorts.

"Bloody hell," Merryn muttered, grabbing Cara by the arm. "Let's go, lass, and be quick about it." She began to move through the trees, making little to no sound save for the swishing of the water in the skins upon her back. Cara followed. She had learned the trick of the stealthy, and was often the one to get their supplies nowadays.

Cara gasped as she now heard what had engaged Merryn's attention so thoroughly. Far off in the trees, though getting closer, was the sound of the clanking of chain mail, heavy boots, *lots* of heavy boots, and swords banging against greave-covered legs.

Merryn prayed the regiment had no dogs with them or they'd be lost.

"You there!" a man's voice boomed, scaring the birds from their perches in the trees.

Cara's heart froze in her throat. She felt Merryn grip her arm again then heard her breath in her ear.

"Run, lass, like you've not run before."

"But—"

"Don't argue with me, Cara!"

Two water skins fell to the forest floor as they began their flight. Cara ducked between and around trees, arms and legs pumping as fast as they would go. The chilled air ran through her still partially frozen hair, making her teeth chatter even as the rest of her body burned.

Grabbing Cara's hand, Merryn turned their direction. They ran through a thick patch of undergrowth, the better to cover any prints left in the new soil of spring.

The cave gaped with a welcoming maw, and they both threw themselves inside, panting in the darkened shadows.

Far off in the woods two screams rose, one begging for the life of her child and the other crying for his mother.

"We must help them," Cara whimpered, lunging toward the daylight again.

"No!" Merryn caught her and held her tight, turning her own back to the light of day, protecting her.

"Let me pass, Merryn. They'll die..."

"And so will we!" Merryn hissed. She shook Cara by the shoulders until Cara looked at her. "You can do naught."

"They'll kill them," Cara whispered, her eyes filling with tears as shrill screams filled her head. She buried her face into Merryn's chest, clutching her for all she was worth.

"I know, lass. We are no match fer 'em," Merryn whispered, one hand on the back of Cara's head, the other pressing against her back. They remained that way until everything was peaceful again and life in the forest had returned to normal.

Sniffling softly, Cara stepped away from Merryn, her green eyes bright from the tears. She used the end of her cloak to wipe her face. She was quiet as she turned away from her friend, before whirling round with angry eyes. "You just let them die!" she accused.

Merryn was taken aback, staring for a moment at Cara, unsure what to say. It didn't take long for her anger to build. "Do not put their fate in my hands, Cara!" she shot back. "If ya want to shout, lass, that's yer bid. But shout at them!" She pointed to the day behind her, her eyes on fire as she glared.

Cara said nothing, just stared at her. Cara's blood boiled mainly out of guilt, which she knew she was directing unjustly at Merryn but couldn't take back. Instead she turned away, toward the fire ring. She was still deeply chilled and needed to warm.

Growling softly to herself, Merryn turned, storming out of the cave.

"Where are ye going?" Cara asked, hurrying after her.

"We need supplies, lass," Merryn hissed, leaning in close to Cara's face. "I'm going to see if those bastards left anythin'. Is that alright with ya?"

"No, 'tis not." Cara didn't flinch as Merryn's eyes narrowed and her body stiffened. "If ye go and pillage from their bodies, Merryn, it makes ye no better than they."

"We..."

"It's called having a heart, Merryn," Cara explained, her voice softening with the passion behind her words. "Only that separates us from King Edward and his thieving, raping soldiers." She took Merryn's hand and placed it over her own heart. "This," she said passionately, squeezing the larger hand, "is what makes us strong and not like the animals. Not like *them*." She looked deeply into Merryn's eyes. "Please don't become like them."

Merryn found herself lost in Cara's eyes, in the passion of her words, and in the feel of the breast beneath her hand.

As Cara looked into Merryn's eyes, she saw something wash through them — a softening. Her face relaxed, then became pensive again. Cara was very aware of the heat from that hand, which emanated through the thin material of her dress, warming her entire upper chest, her breast on fire. She realized that her heart was pounding almost painfully in her chest. She was able to feel it all the way into her temples.

Taking a small step back, Cara was able to breathe again as Merryn's hand fell back to her side. Neither woman said anything, both confused by the swarm of heat and unrecognizable feelings.

"I'm going to get more wood," Merryn said quietly, quickly leaving before Cara could stop her. Cara, for her part, was in a daze. She looked down at her chest, seeing that the nipple of her left breast stood in stark relief against her dress. It was almost painfully erect. Sensation was shooting between her legs as she covered her own breast.

"What on earth?" she breathed in confusion.

Merryn walked for a long time, mindful of her surroundings in case the soldiers weren't gone. She needed time alone and space to breathe, to think.

Stuffing her hands inside her cloak, she wandered back toward the stream where she'd dropped the water skins.

"Blast," she muttered, seeing they were gone. Kicking at a few stones that lay about, she raised her head to the Heavens, feeling the sun's warmth upon her face. She strolled along and glanced at the nearby stream. She smiled as her mind allowed her to see Cara again, as she stood washing herself at the deepest point and freezing, the water coming no further than her armpits.

"Crazy, lass. Ya truly are," Merryn whispered as she moved on. She knew there was a village not far, and she and Cara were running very low on supplies.

Whistling softly to herself, she tucked her hands inside her cloak. It wasn't long before she stumbled upon the results of the violence of minutes before.

Slowing her pace, Merryn brought her hands out, lightly resting them on the trunk of a tree.

"Lord have mercy," she whispered, looking on at the carnage. The child, no more than six summers old, lay on his side curled up, his eyes closed. For him it had been quick, the red fire of a blade trailing through his middle. The blood was already freezing as it seeped from his young body.

The woman didn't fare so well.

"Oh, lass," she whispered, slowly folding to her knees, one ear tuned to all that was around her. The mother was not much older than Merryn, herself. Her skirts were torn and bloodied, her sex exposed. Her throat had been slit, and her face was forever frozen in horror and pain. It was obvious that in life the girl had not been healthy; her frame was painfully thin.

Merryn had seen such scenes before, but suddenly the face of Cara flashed before her eyes. What if it was she lying here in a pool of her own fear and misfortune? A rage filled Merryn that could neither explain nor contain. Never before had she felt anything but luck at finding bodies before anyone else did. Now, any thoughts she'd had of pilfering from the mother and her son were gone. She began to feel the bitter taste of vengeance on her tongue.

Swallowing it down, Merryn gathered all the belongings of the pair. The soldiers had no doubt found the simple sword and empty leather pouch not good enough to bother with. One whiff of the bag told Merryn that it had once held food for the pair. They were trying to find a meal when attacked and senselessly murdered.

"Bastards," she muttered, pulling out one of her own daggers, using it to dig a small hole in the still winter-hard ground. She placed the meager belongings in the hole and quickly pushed dirt over the top, patting it down.

No one else was going to steal from these two, either.

Turning back to the bodies, Merryn pulled the woman's skirts as much into place as the tattered shreds would allow. Placing the woman's son in her arms, she bowed her head, closed her eyes, and murmured a small prayer.

"May Arawn take vengeance for you," she finished, opening her eyes and standing. Brushing her knees off, Merryn tugged her cloak around her shoulders and set off for the nearby village.

Cara raised the torch, looking closely at the paintings. Bringing up a hand, she traced the faded lines of what looked to be an animal of some sort — big and brown, with horns.

"What on earth," she murmured absently, squinting and tilting her head to the side as the firelight bounced off the stone walls.

"Drawin' purty pictures, are ya, lass?"

Cara yelped at the voice in her ear, whirling around to see her friend standing there. "Don't *do* that, Merryn!" she exclaimed, hand held to her rapidly beating heart.

Merryn smirked, raising an arm to ward off a flying hand. "'M sorry, Cara." Merryn laughed as she headed back to their fire and placed her bundle down.

Cara took several deep breaths to get her pounding heart under control then followed her friend, curious about what prizes she'd brought with her.

Merryn sat next to the fire and brought her hands to the warmth, sighing softly as she began to thaw. "Summer be swift," she said quietly.

"'Tis a cold night," Cara agreed, sitting across the fire from her. Her eyes glanced at the large stitch bag, filled with unknown prizes. She shook her head slightly, a smile on her lips. Merryn hadn't had that bag when she'd left earlier in the day.

Merryn saw the inquisitive face across the fire. "What?" Cara's eyes strayed to the bag, then met her own again. Merryn chuckled, nudging the bag toward her with a shove of her boot.

Quickly like a child on Christmas morning, Cara grabbed the bag and tore open the thin rope that held the mouth together. The bag would be useful as they traveled, and she began to unpack it: a bag of lard, vegetables of just about every type, bread, and a wooden bowl.

"What's this?" she asked, bringing out something long and slender wrapped in cloth. She glanced over the fire at a grinning Merryn. Unwrapping the object, she found a simple wooden flute.

"I thought as ya whistle enough, lass, perhaps ya c'n make music."

"Thank ye!" Cara threw herself at Merryn, wrapping her arms around her neck, clutching the flute tightly.

"Ya're welcome, Cara," Merryn whispered, thrilled that the spontaneous gift made her friend so happy.

Pulling back, Cara sat back on her heels, turning the flute over in her hands.

"Well, come on, lass. Play!" Merryn encouraged, relaxing against the wall of the cave.

"I've not played one before," Cara said shyly.

"Practice while I make supper."

Cara took her prize into a corner, turning it this way and that in her hands, and inhaled the smell of the rich wood.

Merryn watched surreptitiously as Cara took careful, quiet, and tentative toots on the flute. Thinking she was basically alone in her little world of music, she continued, fingers pressing over various holes as she tried to see what notes would come out.

Smiling to herself, Merryn filled their pan with water, chopped up some of the vegetables and some meat, and added a small chunk of lard for flavoring. Soon enough the stew was cooking, so Merryn sat back to enjoy what she had brought for her own amusement.

Pulling out the last of her daggers, she took hold of the thick piece of branch she'd cut from a tree before coming into the cave. Turning the wood round and round in her hands, she chewed on her lip as she tried to decide where best to begin. Finally she began to peel the bark from the branch.

"Merryn?" Cara asked, some time later. She sat on her bedding, looking into the dying fire.

"Yes, lass?" Merryn answered, her brows knit as she studied the thus far shapeless wood creation.

"Were they both killed?"

Merryn looked up, seeing only her friend's back as the girl wrapped her arms around her drawn legs.

"Yes, Cara. They were." Returning to her whittling, she missed the small sigh of resignation from her friend.

Cara's eyes snapped open, a scream of fear locked into her throat. She tried to struggle against the hand that was clasped over her mouth.

"Quiet!" Merryn hissed, close to the girl's ear. "Wake up, lass. We must go. Now!" With that, she disappeared into the darkness that swamped the cave, the fire long ago burnt out.

Her sleepy mind coming into focus, Cara heard the sound of yelling men and barking dogs echoing out in the night.

"Oh, Lord," she whimpered, quickly gathering her bedding, shoving it into her pack.

"Grab only what you can, Cara. We must go!"

Cara nodded unseen by her friend. She heard the scraping of a blade being dragged across the stone floor before it was fastened to Merryn's baldric. Cara's wide eyes felt as if they would pop out of her head, as she tried in vain to see through the molasses-thick darkness.

She yelped as a hand grabbed her arm and another hand returned to her mouth. She could feel the hot breath of her friend against the side of her face.

"I need ya to listen to me, lass, and listen fast." Cara nodded at the whispered words. "The soldiers are climbin' through these woods, lookin' for anythin' alive."

Cara felt the hand lift from her mouth and her face cupped between two warm palms. Though she could see nothing, she *felt* those intense blue eyes on her.

"Let us go," Cara whispered. She felt Merryn's warm breath on her face.

"Whatever happens, Cara," Merryn said, her voice soft, yet deeply earnest, "if we get separated, I'll find ya. I swear it ta yer God, I'll find ya."

Cara nodded, swallowing the tears of fear and love that swelled in her heart. Her eyes closed as instinct told them to. She was not surprised when she felt the softest touch against her lips, feather light and brief, but it touched her to the core of her heart.

"Now run."

Part 3

Merryn felt the cold night air on her face, the hood of her cloak having long ago flown off her head. She looked around the tree she leaned against, the sliver of moon above casting no light onto the darkness. She closed her eyes for a moment, letting her sense of hearing take over what her eyes couldn't do.

The soldiers were near the cave. Brogan whinnied at the unfamiliar guests. Merryn hated leaving the mare, but there was no other choice. Trying to ride her through the trees in near blackness would have been suicide. Leading her would have slowed them down and proclaimed their presence to the soldiers.

Opening her eyes, she glanced to where she thought Cara was, though she didn't dare speak out to her. It sounded from Cara's heavy breathing that she was one tree over.

Listening to the night again, she heard some of the soldiers talking — their voices clear in the still night.

"Not long ago. They got ta be here somewhere."

"Search these woods. The King will be happy to have 'em healthy."

"Yes, sir."

"Take the horse, too."

The men spread out with the clamor of armor.

Merryn pushed off the tree and reached for where she thought Cara was. She was relieved when she felt the rough cloak of her friend. Giving a light squeeze to let Cara know she was on the move again, Merryn was off.

Trying desperately to remember the lay of the land, she ran in the direction she thought would lead to the village, where she'd been but two days ago. She felt her lungs begin to burn as she broke out into a clearing, legs pumping as fast as humanly possible.

"Bloody hell!" she gasped as she heard the vicious sound of the royal hounds, hot on her trail.

"Merryn!" Cara cried out, her voice far behind. Merryn glanced behind her, only able to see a darker figure against the dark background of night.

"Cara! Come on!"

"I can't," Cara gasped, her voice desperate as she heard the dogs getting closer, followed by the soldiers, their clanging armor almost deafening.

"Ya have ta, lass!"

"No! Run on, Merryn! Leave me!"

"No..."

"Go!" the vehemence in Cara's voice struck Merryn.

"Cara!!" she cried when she heard a scream that was cut off by the savage barking of a swarm of hounds. Her own voice echoed in her ears as time seemed to slow to a crawl for a brief moment of complete desperate fear.

"Get the other one!" one of the soldiers yelled.

Blinded by her tears, Merryn ran on, her heart shredding with guilt and fear of her friend's fate. All she could do was press on, just as Cara told her to do. She'd expect the same if their positions were reversed. She could do Cara no good dead.

Merryn could barely make out the glitter of water and was upon the stream before she realized. Pushing on, she splashed through its depths, wading until she had to swim. The dogs ran to the edge of the water, barking furiously, with the soldiers following close behind. Maybe those little bastards would lose her scent. There was no way the soldiers could follow her in their armor— they'd drown within minutes.

Barely registering the call for her pursuers to return to the camp, Merryn ran on after reaching the other side. Her soaked clothes clung to her; the water-logged cloak slowed her down. Out of breath, she fell to her knees, grunting in pain as her hands skidded against the harsh, rock-bestrewn soil.

She reached up to push her sweat-soaked hair out of her eyes. Looking around her, she saw the teasing flicker of lantern light.

"Made it," she gasped, slowly getting to her feet with a groan. Every step she took sloshed from her late night swim. She followed the distant flicker, needing to find a place to rest for the night. At first light she would begin her hunt.

Frozen flesh stung against the blow against the hard wood of the door, but Merryn brought her fist up again to pound the door.

"Wha' ya want?" a deep, gruff voice boomed from the other side of the plank door. As it was yanked open, a dim triangle of light fell through the doorway. A man stood frowning at the sight of the shivering girl on his doorstep.

"Please sir," Merryn begged. "Might I stay a night? 'Twon't be a bit of trouble, be gone by first light."

The old man stared at the girl wondering what sort of trouble such rabble had got into. Looking out into the night beyond his most unwanted guest, he roughly pulled the girl in by her cloak.

"Lord above, yer wet!" he grumbled, brows drawing in further as he continued to frown, nearly covering his gray eyes.

Merryn nodded. "Chased, I was." She slid down the rickety wall, landing on the dirt floor with a thud.

"I want no trouble..."

"A highwayman, he was. Out for blood," she said quietly, knowing it would do no good to let the old peasant know she was being chased by the King's men.

"Well, stay there if ya want, girl, but I've not got food for yer mouth!" he boomed, waggling a sausage finger at her.

Merryn nodded, exhaustion beginning to overwhelm her. "Aye."

The old man stomped back over to the tiny log table where he had been sitting. He was using a thick, wooden needle to mend a torn garment. His work was lit by the lantern she'd seen flickering through the single window.

Merryn watched him with hooded eyes as exhaustion and grief began to weigh on her, almost making her feel that she could drown in either. Tearing her gaze away from the old man, Merryn took in the sparse shack. To the right was a small cot fashioned of planks covered by layers of rat-eaten rags. Next to the table was a small stack of wood for the fire ring, which was to the left. Above it were a few cupboards lined with wooden bowls and two mugs.

Merryn considered that the man's wife must have recently died, since seconds were still around. Once the man had stopped grieving, he'd likely sell or trade the excess.

She looked up to the thatched ceiling, which had a hole bored in it to allow the smoke to drift out.

Merryn was sure she heard the cries of hounds echoing into the night causing her fingers to curl into a fist. Squeezing her eyes shut, she forced her tears to stay behind the closed lids. She wouldn't allow herself the release of crying. She should be hanged for letting Cara be caught by those bastards. She had to forcibly shut her mind off or it would conjure up the myriad of things that could be happening to her friend at that moment.

I'll find ya, lass. I swear it.

"Break camp! We leave within the hour!" cried a booming voice. Merryn watched, as she lay flat-bellied on the bluff above the camp. The rising sun bounced off the armor of the men below who bustled about, emptying pitchers and bladders, and barked orders.

Merryn scanned the tents, looking desperately for any sign of Cara. She didn't have to wait long. She spied a man walking toward one of the tents, hand resting on the pommel of his sheathed sword. As he disappeared between the flaps, a cry rent the air.

"Get up, wench," the man snarled. There was another cry.

"Cara," Merryn breathed, fists clenched in the dirt. "Ya'll pay, ya bastard." Backing away stealthily, she was soon running back toward the village she'd left much earlier that morning.

Hiding among the trees, small leans-tos, and shacks, Merryn scanned the area. She breathed a sigh of relief as her gaze lit on what she sought. There, in the middle of a small pasture, was a massive black horse, happily munching the grass.

Merryn's fingers dug lightly into the tree she stood behind as she looked in every direction. The village was beginning to come alive; she could hear hushed voices and the hacking coughs of the sick. She had to make her move, but care was needed. This crime would be punishable by stoning.

Running like the wind and launching herself over a waist-high make-shift fence, Merryn got herself into the pasture with the horse, which raised its head to study the visitor.

Merryn took another look around, turned back to the horse, then raised her hands to calm the animal, which was beginning to lightly stomp her back hooves.

"Calm, girl," Merryn said softly, taking a step toward the horse. "'Twon't be hurtin' ya; promise." She looked around her again, knowing she had to be quick, and took several steps toward the horse. She grimaced as the mare reared up and whinnied as she rested a hand on her flank. "Bugger me."

Whipping herself up over the mare's back, Merryn grabbed the horse's brown and white mane, kicking hard into her flanks.

"Ha! Ha!"

"Hey!" someone yelled, running toward the flying mare, but he had to jump out of the way or risk being trampled.

Merryn rode hard, needing to put as much distance between her and the village, yet she had to stay on the trail of the soldiers.

Not surprising, the soldiers' camp had been completely struck, leaving behind dying embers and debris. Landing in the mud with a grunt, Merryn began to scan the area, looking for clues. With brows drawn in absolute concentration, she walked over to the closest fire ring. Kneeling down, she breathed in deeply, taking in the acrid smell of ashes not long ago abandoned. Slowly passing her hand over the area where the fire had once been, she guessed the men had left a half hour ago.

Rising to her feet, she looked all around her, seeing where the ground had been torn to shreds by the hooves of a hundred horses. "I'm comin' fer ya, lass."

London was bustling with activity and life, yet the telltale stench of death and sickness hung heavily in the air and in the hearts of the Londoners. The London sky was gray, the color of a winter yet to let go, as well as smoke from both individual fires and funeral pyres.

Merryn led her horse down the streets, careful to keep her face and female body covered by her cloak. She felt anger burn deep inside each time she saw a soldier walking the streets or leaning against a building watching those that passed. Each time she saw a soldier her deep anger rose closer to the surface until it felt like a river of lava running just beneath the surface of her skin.

The vengeance that boiled her blood also kept her calm. She knew that she'd never stay alive long enough to find Cara if she didn't keep her cool.

From the looks she was getting from those she passed, Merryn knew she must look like Death with her black cloak hiding all but her black boots as she led her huge, black horse through their streets. She was certainly causing a stir.

The shadows were getting long and Merryn knew that she'd have to find a place to sleep and to think. Seeing a couple of rowdy townsfolk in front of a rickety, two-story tavern, she went over to them.

"Yer a bloody liar, Tom!" one man cried out, shoving the other.

"And yer a dead man," Tom flared, pulling out a dagger.

Merryn hurried into the tavern behind the man who was about to be stabbed, not wanting any of their trouble. She'd have her own trouble to deal with soon enough.

The tavern was dingy and dirty. There were only a few scattered lanterns and a fire in the wall pit illuminating the plank walls. A few tables lined the outer walls; three more dotted the center.

Merryn made her way to the rough wooden bar that lined the left wall. Behind it were clay jugs filled with rough wine and water.

"What currency ya take here?" she asked, her voice low and ambiguous.

"What kind ye got?" the tavern keeper asked, his thick arms spread out across the splintered surface of the bar.

Tugging on the string of her pouch, Merryn's dirt encrusted fingers dug through the treasures within. Her heart stopped when she saw the third gold piece she'd taken off the boy named David.

Gently laying the coin aside, she found a small flask of pepper. *Very valuable to a cook.* Sighing heavily, she pulled the flask out and pulled out the stopper. The barkeep took it and ran it under his bulbous nose. Nodding in agreement, he put the stopper back in and tucked the flask into a pocket of his apron.

"What can I get for ye, boy?"

"Wine and a room for two nights."

"Aye." The large man turned his back, filling a wooden mug with the odorous wine, a bit of the dark liquid sloshing over the rim as it was set down on the bar, along with a long, narrow key. "Last room at the top of the stairs. Ye got a horse, boy?" he asked. At Merryn's nod and description, he told a young boy to take care of it for her, before turning to another customer.

"Ye got a," Merryn looked around, clearing her throat, "bath?"

The tavern keeper stopped pouring a mug of wine, looking at the dark figure at the end of his bar. His heavy beard nearly hid his grin. "Bath, lad?"

"Never mind that," she rolled her eyes, taking her mug off the bar and moving toward her room. As she was about to climb the stairs, she was stopped by the soft voice of a man leaning against the wall next to the staircase.

"There's a lake out the back," the cloaked figure said, indicating the direction with his thumb. Merryn nodded acknowledgment at the information then quickly made her way up the stairs.

The room was tiny, just large enough to fit in a small bed with a chamber pot under it and a tall, square table with a clay pitcher and receiving bowl on it. There was a handy window above the table to empty the wash bowl or the chamber pot out of.

"Well," she muttered, turning in a slow circle. "Here we are, then. Here we are." Reaching up, she unfastened her cloak, tossing the heavy garment across the narrow bed. About to pour some water from a clay pot into the receiving bowl beneath, she paused as there was a knock at the door.

The knock sounded again.

With her hand immediately moving to the grip of her sword, she walked over to the door.

"Who goes there?" she called out, trying to peek through the cracks in the plank door.

"'Tis a maid, sir," a quiet woman's voice said.

Merryn raised the wooden bar that served as a lock, pulling the door open with it. There in the hall stood a young woman, her dirty brown hair half covering her face. She held a bucket filled with water in each hand. She took a stunned step backward, eyes widening as she looked into Merryn's face.

"Oh," the barmaid said, mouth moving but nothing further coming out.

"What ya want, lass? I haven't got all night." Merryn was feeling irritated, her patience low.

"'M sorry, miss. Angus asked me to bring these up fer ya, miss." She glanced down at the buckets she carried.

"Angus?"

"Aye, miss. He wants to speak with ye."

Merryn studied the young girl for a moment, trying to size her up. There seemed to be no malicious intent in her brown eyes, so she nodded.

"He's downstairs, miss. By the stairs." With that, the young girl raised the buckets in question, Merryn nodding as she stepped aside, allowing her to pass. She put her cloak back on, bringing the hood up to cover her face. The women left together and went back down into the tavern.

Merryn felt ill at ease, her eyes constantly darting back and forth, surveying her surroundings.

Just as the maid had said, Angus still leaned against the wall, one booted foot on the table top. When he heard the footfalls upon the wooden steps, Angus turned his dark eyes to the pair.

The maid gave him a small nod and curtsey, then scurried off to do her duties. Merryn pulled out the chair across from the man, a Black Irish with his black hair, beard, and eyes, his pale skin a stark contrast. The often seen Celtic combination of red hair and blue eyes was missing from this lad, as it was from Merryn, which gave Celts of their coloring the name of Black Irish.

Merryn looked out from underneath her hood, boring into the intense dark eyes.

"We have sumethin' common, besides the fire in our blood," he said at length, his accent thick, rich in the strength of the Celts. Merryn said nothing. "Ye're not here by accident, lad." This was a statement.

"We need ta get one thing straight," Merryn said, her voice soft. She pulled the hood back just enough to show her face. To his credit, Angus showed no surprise. "Merryn," she said.

Angus finally nodded, though there seemed to be a slight gleam of admiration in his dark eyes. "Answer me now."

"'M here on business."

"As I thought. As am I, lass." Angus' foot hit the floor with a heavy thud. He leaned forward, a bracer-clad arm coming to rest on the table as a large hand wrapped around his mug of wine. He looked deeply into Merryn's eyes, almost making the girl nervous. It seemed he was looking into her very soul, reading her mind.

Finally tired of fidgeting under the scrutiny, Merryn leaned forward in her own chair, bringing but a few inches between their faces. "If ya plan to stare at me, make it worth my while, lad."

Angus grinned then a soft chuckle began deep in his throat, slowly billowing its way out of his mouth. He nodded with obvious approval.

"I have business with the king," he said simply. At the look in Merryn's eyes, Angus nodded, standing. He nodded for Merryn to follow.

Merryn looked around, seeing the three others in the stable, including the serving wench.

"All of us have lost 'cause of the evil that is King Edward the third," Angus explained, his arm sweeping over the small group, his eyes on the newcomer. "His soldiers be gatherin' folk. The black sickness has killed so many," he paused, lowering his head for a moment. Clearing his throat, Angus brought a hand up, fingers absently stroking his black goatee. "Servants are leavin' their posts, takin' up their own land, the land of the dead. Fer the first time, they be havin' their own place on this land."

"He's gatherin' slaves, then?" Merryn asked, her world beginning to come into focus.

"They'll be his bloody servants now," said a clean faced young man standing in the corner. An axe rested across his lap, and his black-nailed fingers flexed on the handle. "Or dead."

"They killed me sister and nephew!" the third man said, pushing to his feet from his seat on a bale of hay. His fiery red hair hung in his eyes, which blazed green fire.

"They took my friend," Merryn added quietly, her own fury building inside.

"We're tryin' to gather numbers, lass," Angus said, moving to stand between Merryn and the others, blocking her view so she only saw him. His dark eyes shone with determination. "We've got ta fight back. Raise some men," he smiled apologetically at her, "and women. Are ye with us, lass?"

Merryn looked around the big man at the four sets of eyes that were locked on her.

"Are ye with us?" Angus asked again. Merryn met his eyes and finally nodded. "Good." Angus smiled his approval. "We'll make plans from here, mount an army..."

"That'll take time," Merryn said, shaking her head. "I must get her out now."

"Lass, it's far too dangerous..."

"Then I'll go alone!" she growled. Something inside impelled her to act now, not to wait. With quiet determination, she turned to leave, her cloak floating in her wake. She stopped at the stable door as a heavy hand was laid on her shoulder.

"Wait, lass," a deep soft voice said. "I know how you feel. My wife is behind those walls," Angus explained. "But if we don't think this through, 'twe'll all die, surely."

Merryn turned slowly, her eyes blue fire. "Then I die."

It was a battle of wills. Merryn would not back down. She knew as well as she knew her own name that she must act quickly. As Angus looked into her beautiful blue eyes, he saw that truth. Nodding, he broke the gaze, bowing to her stronger will.

"We will help ye, lass."

Merryn looked at the others, all nodding. "Thank ya, then."

Angus sighed, crossing his arms over his chest. "I still think 'tis too soon." He studied the girl for a moment. "Ye should wait, lass. There's not a thing I can say to change yer mind, then?"

Merryn shook her head, her will strong and sure.

"Jest as I thought," Angus grinned. "Stubborn Irish." With a wink, he put an arm around her shoulder, pulled her back into the group. Merryn took a seat on a barrel.

Reaching inside his tunic, Angus pulled out some rolled parchment. Kneeling on the hay-strewn dirt floor, he wiped a clean spot and spread out the parchment, using four rocks to hold the corners. The group gathered around him as he explained.

"We have spies in the castle," he began, tapping the paper on which was the rough plan of a building.

Merryn studied the sketched lines of Middleham castle. She listened as Angus explained that the castle had an unusually long keep, of over one hundred feet, which dominated the structure.

"'Tis divided by a cross wall, length-ways," he ran the tip of a dirk along the sketch of the wall he spoke of. "This curtain wall here, around the keep, 'twill make it a bit harder to get past."

"We can't get over that," Merryn said, brows drawn. Angus nodded.

"I agree. And we can't just walk in. So," he moved his dirk tip, making a circular motion on a spot to the south west of the castle. "William's

Hill," he said, making eye contact with everyone kneeling around the map. "'Tis said tunnels run from this place right into the belly of Middleham."

"We must move by dark," Merryn said, glancing up at Angus. "Go early, before the sun awakens."

"Hold our position till day," Angus grinned. Merryn grinned back, nodding.

"Aye. At dark, bring too much attention ta the lot of us." Merryn met the looks sent her way.

"By the light o' day, we c'n slip through, be anyone." Angus nodded.

"Aye, that." Merryn glanced over at the bale of hay the redheaded young man had been sitting on. There lay a lute. "Ya play that, lad?" she asked, nodding toward it. The boy glanced back to see what she spoke of, then grinned proudly with a nod. Merryn grinned in her turn, mischief in her eyes. "Take it with ya. Travelin' minstrel, ya're."

"All be here two hours before sun up." Angus stood, rolling his parchment.

"Merryn. Merryn, awaken."

Merryn's eyes opened slowly; a gasp escaped her as she saw Cara kneeling by her bed. Cara smiled, reaching out a hand to rest against Merryn's cheek.

"Cara?" Merryn raised herself to her elbows. "What are you doing here? I'm so sorry I lost you..."

"Shhh," Cara whispered, two fingers covering Merryn's lips. "That matters not." Merryn stared at her friend, her mind fuzzy, not able to reconcile the situation, yet not wanting to think too hard for fear Cara would disappear. The hand that rested upon Merryn's cheek moved slowly down to cup her jaw. Cara stared deep into her eyes with utter faith and trust. "Save me."

Merryn's breath caught as she watched Cara's eyes close, her beautiful face, tinted blue in the moonlight, coming closer, closer. Merryn's own eyes slid shut.

"Save me, Merryn. Save me..."

"Merryn?" There was pounding at the door.

Merryn sat up and grabbed her sword, her heart racing. Desperately she looked around the room, still wrapped in moonlight-tinged night. Cara was nowhere to be seen. Merryn almost cried at the pang of disappointment that stung her like the cut of a blade.

The door opened and Angus entered.

"Ye carry a blade, lass," he said, nodding toward the weapon that Merryn held in her hand. "Do ye know how ta use it?"

Indignant, she raised her chin. "Yes."

"Do ye now? Then let us practice."

Not knowing if it were late night or early morning, Merryn followed the dark man out of the tavern, two ghostly figures slipping through the night. She was led far from the tavern into the woods, away from prying, curious eyes and ears.

Angus stopped, pulling his sword with a satisfying hiss. "Show me, lass."

Nodding and swallowing her nerves, Merryn drew her own blade. She'd never really had to fight anyone more than a farmer with a pitchfork. Most of the folk she dealt with were already dead.

Swallowing again, she spread her feet wide, her fingers flexing on the grip of her sword. As Angus raised his blade, she followed the attack, meeting it with an echoing clang.

"Good lass," Angus encouraged. Light on his feet, he made her work for his compliments. Merryn grunted with every parry, every thrust, every block. The Black Irishman nearly had her. Merryn bared her teeth and, with her back to her opponent and her sword held up over her head, blocked what could have been a debilitating blow to the shoulders. She eventually pushed him away, moved out of his reach, and faced him.

"Ye will kill me yet," she panted. Angus grinned, sticking his blade into the forest floor.

"Or try 'n save yer life," he chuckled. "Ye're a natural with a blade, lass. Most impressive." He plucked his sword from the earth. "Come, Merryn. We must get food." Slapping his arm around the girl's shoulder, they went back to the tavern.

The group gathered in the stable once more. This time there were two more women.

"This is Sarah and Fanny," Angus explained. "They've both run from their duties at Middleham Castle 'n have agreed ta help." They both nodded. "We go in, we get out." He met every eye, then turned to Sarah and Fanny. "Where are the captives bein' kept?"

"The tower, my lord," the one named Fanny said quietly, her head bowed.

Angus turned his eyes to Merryn. For long moments they shared a look, each building their own courage.

"Let it begin."

They rode hard and fast in pairs, far from their fellow riders. They were set to meet at William's Hill. It wouldn't do for suspicion to stop their mission before it began.

Merryn rode with Fanny. Both women were strong riders; both were lost in their own thoughts. Merryn was filled with fear and doubt. Angus had shown her just how very little she knew of being a fighter. She could protect herself from highwaymen and thieves, no doubt. But what of a trained, professional soldier protecting his king?

And what of the dream just before she woke? Cara's eyes were so filled with love and trust. It was as if the girl had absolutely no doubt that Merryn would swoop in and ... *"Save me"* ...

Oh, Cara. Don't have more faith in me than I have skill, lass.

When Cara had first been taken, pure rage had driven Merryn on, almost making her foolish enough to attack the soldiers' camp that same night. She would have been ripped to pieces, no doubt. By grace of the gods above she'd kept her head, in spite of her wet clothes and tired muscles.

Now, as she glanced over at her companion who was riding as hard as she, a certain sense of pride filled her body and a smile played across her lips. Since the moment she and Cara met, it had been Merryn's duty, grudgingly at first, to protect Cara. Then as time had passed, Merryn took her job seriously and derived great joy from doing so.

This was no different.

Now it wasn't just about keeping Cara safe from the cold or getting her away from some wayward drunkard. Now it was about saving the girl's life and hopefully her virtue.

"Ya!" she cried, kicking her dark horse onward, speeding through the valleys at breakneck speed, her companion keeping her paces.

"Caaaa! Caaaa!"

Merryn looked around, trying to find the source of the sound.

"Caaaa! Caaaa!"

"Come, Merryn!" Fanny yelled. Merryn followed her into the trees. When Fanny stopped her mount in a thicket, Merryn pulled her horse up beside her.

"What's this?" she asked as she dismounted.

"Angus' signal fer trouble, miss," Fanny whispered. They listened. Merryn's heart beat in her ears. It wasn't long before a small company of soldiers rode past, their cuirasses gleaming in the failing moonlight.

"They travel in lots of two, miss," Fanny whispered, clutching Merryn's sleeve. Merryn nodded, as they both shrank closer to the tree. Within a few moments a second troop of soldiers rode past.

"Let us go," Merryn whispered, keeping an eye on the soldiers until they were out of sight.

Re-mounting their steeds, the women rode on.

The early morning air was crisp, seizing the lungs and making them burn. But, oh, how it made Merryn feel alive! She inhaled deeply, her eyes closing for a moment as her resolve clinched with her focus. Her blue eyes nearly glowed in the early dawn, the earth painted blue.

After meeting up and gathering as a group again, they were but shadows within deeper shadows of early morn, making their way around William's Hill. Fanny and Sarah led the way in complete silence as they used hand gestures to show the other five where the hidden entrance was.

Angus drew his sword, using it as a pick as he began to dig through the thick wall of rock. Merryn quickly joined him. Soon, all the members were working at the entrance, until a small space was revealed. It would be a tight fit for the larger members of the group, but all would be able to pass.

"I go no further," Fanny said, backing away, head shaking. "I'm sorry, my lord."

"'Tis alright, lass. Thank ye."

The woman nodded, looking to her friend. Sarah said nothing, but turned her face away. Fanny gathered her skirts, quickly heading for her mount.

"I'm sorry, my lord," Sarah said, disgust edging her voice. "We, she wanted to help..."

"I'd rather she back out now than get herself killed, lass," Angus said softly.

"Angus," said the redheaded man, whom Merryn had found was named Aaron, "there's a door."

Merryn said nothing as she pushed between the two men, into the cave beyond the barrier they'd dug through. She took the torch that George, the third man, had struck inside the earthen cave.

She fell to her knees at the arched wooden door, the torchlight reflecting dully against the iron ribbing. The lock was large and secure, and rust made the metal orange and dull.

"Hold this, lad," she told George, who stood beside her. She reached into the pouch hanging at her waist, feeling for the two small, thin pieces of iron.

"God's breath," she heard George whisper in excitement.

"Hold the light here," she said, ignoring his whistle of approval. The light showed her work clear and bright. Merryn quickly slid the thin metal into the large key hole. She leaned in, looking as far into the lock as she could as her fingers gingerly moving the picks around in subtle exploration until she felt a catch, then a loud, scraping click.

Holding the picks with one hand, she grabbed the lock in the other, the mechanism filling her entire palm. She tugged gently until it gave way, slipping it from its holdings. Standing, Merryn removed her picks, tossed the lock aside, and waved the others onward.

She felt a secret pride as she heard the whisperings of surprise and elation behind her but it was short lived as she focused back on the mission. She turned when she was tapped on the shoulder. Angus was behind her, handing her a torch, which she happily took. The dark man moved up to walk beside her in silence.

Beyond the gated door, the cave had turned into the expected set of tunnels. They were wide enough for two men to walk fairly comfortably side by side.

Mice and any other manner of tiny beasts scurried to get out of their way as the torch light melted the darkness. Around the bend the group was surprised to find a line of bones, some with remnants of tattered clothing still clinging to them. One set lay on the ground, the grinning skull half buried. Others were pinned to the walls of the tunnel either by shackled wrists and chained necks, or by nails driven through the wrists.

Everyone looked at the bones, and complete silence filled the space. Those poor, lost souls served to remind the group of what could still happen to them.

Torchlight brought to light another door. Once again Merryn fell to her knees, working the ancient, rusted lock. It took several moments, but the lock gave with a scratchy moan. Tossing it aside, she stood, turning to face her new friends.

"Beyond this door, not a sound from any of us," she warned, instinct telling her they were now entering more populated parts of the castle.

"Feel as though I've stepped into a nightmare," Aaron whispered. The group around him received his words in silence, none wanting to admit that they probably had the same feeling.

With a little persuasion, the door creaked open. Merryn listened. The darkness was nearly complete on the other side. The air was foul, the smell of raw sewage floating upon it.

Closing the door, she turned to the five expectant faces before her.

"'Twill be headin' to the bowels o' Middleham," she explained. "Foul stench. Be wary."

Turning to the door once more, she pushed through a second time. Angus hurried to take the lead; he was better and more experienced with a blade if they were they to be surprised.

The hiss of steel being pulled from its sheath was the only sound. A slight glint showed in the light of the one torch, which Sarah held, sandwiched between Angus, Merryn, and Aaron. George and the serving wench, Anna, brought up the rear.

Angus gave the signal to douse the flame as they stopped. The faintest echo of voices filtered through the tunnel. Maybe two hundred paces from them, the barest hint of light could be seen interrupting the darkness. Angus began to move again, followed by the others.

Merryn tightened her grip on her sword, her heart beginning to race and her brow dotting with sweat. Her lips were suddenly dry, and she ran her tongue over them. Soon the faint echoes turned into discernable words.

"O'er here, boy, and be quick about it."

Angus again motioned for silence. They could now see that at the end of the tunnel was iron grating. As they got closer to the grate, the tunnel walls narrowed and the floor sloped down. The ceiling got lower until the group found themselves on their knees.

Angus carefully made his way to the grate. Torchlight illuminated the space beyond. It was a large, stone square room. Inside was an elaborate pipe system being fed by enormous cauldrons of water, which were brought to a boil by stoked fires.

"What 'tis this place?" Merryn whispered in Sarah's ear.

"'Tis the boilers, miss," the woman whispered back. "Gives the king's baths heat."

Sure they were alone in their little corner, Angus carefully removed the grate, wincing as a sharp whine rent the air as the stubborn metal was forced to budge. Holding her breath, Merryn waited for the worst. When nothing happened, she released her breath.

Quickly standing after crawling into the unbearably hot room, Angus held his sword at the ready, scanning the large room to try and find the source of the voices they had heard. The others followed with the exception of Sarah who still crouched in the grate opening.

"North tower, my lord," she whispered to Angus then pulled the grate back into place. The girl set off back down the tunnel and was soon consumed by the deep shadows around her.

Merryn raised her own weapon; her eyes searched every shadow that danced from the flames. There was no one in the room, and the group moved out toward the much cooler hallway beyond.

It seemed the castle was made up of an endless maze of passages and small antechambers that spilled into glorious halls with stone walls and vaulted ceilings. The rooms were dark, lit by sporadic torches, candelabras, and a few massive fireplaces that showed the length of the great halls.

Shadows danced everywhere, often catching Merryn's eye, making her jump. She'd feel a calming hand on her shoulder, then would meet dark, understanding eyes. Thus far they'd run into no soldiers, and it had everyone on edge.

Merryn mentally calculated what she could get for just one of the tapestries that lined the great walls. She smirked, thinking Cara probably wouldn't mind too much if she stole from this bastard.

Easing her way up a long set of stone stairs that wrapped around a huge torch-laden column, Merryn found herself at the top, met by two surprised soldiers. Her heart stopped; then as the two men saw her blade, instinct took over. Her dark brows drew and her white teeth bared.

The guards, dressed in cuir boulli leather breast plates and simple hose, were taken off guard as Merryn struck. She raised the sword high above her head, bringing it down to crash the pommel into the skull of the guard closest to her. The man grunted, folding quickly as the bones of his forehead smashed. His body slipped down the stairs behind Merryn, who stepped neatly out of the way.

Surprise passing quickly, the second guard drew his own blade, releasing a battle cry as he attacked. It took all of Merryn's strength to take his blow against her own sword. Gritting her teeth, she pushed him off, lunging after. She could hear the hurried footfalls of her companions coming up behind her in the stairwell.

Within moments two more guards found their way to the melee. Soon Merryn was at the center of the deafening clank of steel against steel, cries of pain and death, and the almost overwhelming stench of fresh blood.

Anna stood to the side, smacking falling soldiers on the head with a heavy tree branch, making sure they stayed down.

"Anna!" Merryn cried, turning to the girl. Blue eyes met her own, then widened as the serving wench realized something was being tossed her way. She caught the large ring of iron keys Merryn had taken off a fallen soldier, then nodded in understanding.

Merryn cried out as she was hit from behind and knocked to one knee. Quickly turning at the waist, she saw a soldier behind her, his sword raised to make the final blow. Suddenly the man's eyes bulged, and Merryn saw a stream of red blood racing down his body, the tip of a blade barely sticking out of the leather of his armor. Scrambling out of the way, she watched as the soldier's body was kicked off Angus' blade, the dead body falling where she had knelt moments before. Breathing hard with exertion and fear of what could have been, Merryn looked up at her savior.

"Many thanks," she breathed. Angus nodded, then turned as footsteps were heard running toward them. Wincing slightly as she got to her feet, she brought a hand up to her head. Her fingers came away covered in blood. She knew she'd have a *big* headache the next morning, but at least she was alive.

"Merryn!"

She looked up to see a blurred figure running at her. She was nearly knocked to the floor by the force with which Cara threw herself into her arms.

"Cara," she breathed, dropping her blade as she wrapped her arms around her sobbing friend. "I've got ya, lass. I've got ya," she whispered, eyes squeezing shut as she crushed the smaller body to her, one hand behind the girl's head.

"I knew ye'd come," Cara cried, her words barely understandable.

"Shhh, I'm here now."

"Merryn!" Angus hissed. She looked over Cara's head. "Get her out, lass. We'll follow behind."

Nodding, Merryn gently pushed Cara away so she could look in her face. Her heart broke at the sight. The color of Cara's right eye jumped out from the blackened skin around it. Dried blood was caked around her mouth and in her hair.

Knowing there was nothing she could do about it at the moment, Merryn swallowed her grief and anger. Taking Cara by the hand, Merryn picked up her sword, and they were off.

"Move fast, lass," Merryn exclaimed. Cara nodded as she followed closely behind. They quickly made their way down the stairs, Merryn on alert with her blood-covered blade at the ready. Her instincts were piqued as she felt the heat from Cara's body behind her, making this escape the most important thing in the world.

Heading down a passageway, which Merryn knew would lead to the great hall, she placed a hand on Cara's arm, bringing them to a halt. Listening, she heard the unmistakable thud of boots pounding stone. She turned, pushing Cara away from the torch they had stopped by. They slunk away into the shadows of a deep, stone entryway. Placing her body in front of Cara's, Merryn hid her sword behind her leg so no gleam would be seen.

Merryn tried to hold her breath as the soldiers ran by, heading toward the stairs to the north tower.

"Let's go," she hissed, once they'd passed. They moved quickly through the passages, hiding several more times before reaching the chamber containing the boiler. There was a soldier inside, and he turned as they entered.

"Bugger," Merryn hissed, pushing Cara against the wall as she raised her sword to meet the attack. The man was strong and determined. When his blow didn't meet its mark, he swung his fist at her head, hitting her square in the ear with his gauntlet.

Merryn staggered backward, her world ringing and slowing to a crawl. She looked up, her eyes filled with surprise and pain. The man pulled a dagger out of his belt, the blade narrowing into a nasty "v".

From somewhere behind her, Merryn heard a voice, sounding like the warbles of a drunkard. Through a fog, she realized the voice was Cara's and that she was screaming her name.

Blinking rapidly to bring her world back into focus, Merryn felt a force take her over. Something seemed to push her out of the way, moving her beating heart out of death's grip. The soldier lunged again, this time missing his mark so completely that he nearly stumbled into the wall behind Cara.

With her head still ringing, Merryn brought out her blade, blindly trying to find her foe. She didn't have to search for long. With a roar, the soldier ran toward her, the dagger raised over his head, the blade gleaming with the firelight under the cauldrons.

Merryn moved toward him, her eyes mere slits. There was a resounding crunch as the slickness of steel split flesh, slipping through all that made a man stand and breathe. He gasped as his air was stolen from him, and his eyes opened wide with tortured pain and sorrow. The soldier fell into Merryn, his hand grasping her shoulder as his dagger clanged to the stone floor.

Merryn watched in a sort of dazed wonder as his mouth opened and a gurgle of blood sprouted to leak down his chin. Slowly, oh so slowly, he slid down her body, his eyes never leaving hers, until he hit the floor.

Numb and astonished, Merryn tugged at her sword — the dead soldier's body wriggling with the motion. Finally she had to press a booted foot to his shoulder to pull the blade free. With a sickening slurp, the man's blood and fluids slid down the blade's fullered center.

Merryn looked up to see Cara pressed against the wall, her face ashen, making the bruises littering her fine skin stand out all the more. Feeling her resolve double, Merryn reached for Cara's hand, taking it gently in hers as she led her to the grating, which Sarah had already pushed open.

Without a word, Merryn tugged Cara through into the tunnels with a nod of thanks to the castle servant, who scraped the grate back into place until the others would pass.

Placing her sword back into her belt, Merryn grabbed the torch that Sarah had lit for her to guide them back through the black tunnels. The only thing louder than their frantic steps on the stone floor was the sound of Merryn's own heart in her ears. She felt no pain, and her emotions were numb. She had but one focus and that was to get Cara out alive.

Cara's screams startled her, and she stopped to see what had frightened the girl. Seeing the remains of the long dead prisoners, Merryn tugged the girl forward. With one last look and a trembling hand to her mouth, Cara moved on, her torn, dirty skirts causing insects and rodents to scurry and squeal into crevices in the tunnel walls and floors.

Merryn kicked the final door open, tugging Cara through as she saw the light of day at the other end. With her heart still pounding and her lungs breathing heavily, she dropped the torch in the dirt passage and drew her sword again, in case they ran into visitors on the way out.

Gulping in lungfuls of the fresh, morning air, Merryn's eyes were everywhere at once, taking in the dark forest, where her horse awaited them.

The castle had yet to come alive and realize where Merryn and her companions had entered.

"We are clear, but we must hurry," she panted, tugging Cara behind her as she bolted from the entrance of William's Hill, until they were sheltered by the thick trees. Once there, Merryn stopped, dropping her sword and pulling Cara to her.

"I dreamed you'd come for me," Cara whispered, eyes tightly closed as she inhaled all that was Merryn — sweat, leather, dirt mixed with rain, and all that made up her distinctive personal smell. Cara's fingers dug into her rescuer's shoulders, terrified that she'd be ripped away again.

"'M so sorry, Cara," Merryn whispered, her face buried in golden hair. "I'll not leave you again. I swear it. Never!" Her promise was so passionate, that it would have frightened Cara if she hadn't been so relieved by it.

Cara nodded, the terror of the past days were released in a long, shaky sigh.

Part 4

Merryn kicked the great black beast into a fierce gallop. Cara sat before her, with Merryn's protective arm wrapped tightly around her waist. Cara leaned back, her head resting against her friend's cloaked shoulder.

As they rode on, leaving the tiny village of Middleham far behind, Merryn looked out over the land. A numbness began to fill her head, spreading into her eyes. Her vision was becoming fuzzy, her mind throwing evil spells onto her reasoning.

She blinked several times, trying to clear the clouds from her eyes and to still her head. But the numbness spread down into her neck, and darkness began closing in around her world.

Cara was jostled from her restless slumber. She looked around, noting that the horse beneath her was slowing and beginning to wander off course.

"Merryn!" she cried when the arm fell away from her waist and, with a loud thud, Merryn fell to the dirt at the horse's feet.

Wincing, Merryn squeezed her eyes shut, deciding that letting the world in was a bad idea.

"Anu, help me," she muttered with a soft moan.

"Shhh," a soft voice murmured. Merryn sighed when she felt gentle fingers on her face. Keeping her eyes closed, she listened to the soft voice as Cara hummed to help soothe her pain. "I know it hurts," Cara said after a moment. "'Twill pass. I think yer noggin' took a few too many blows today."

"I'd have ta agree, lass." Merryn smiled at the soft chuckle she heard.

"This will soothe the ache," Cara said. Her touch was gentle, like her voice, as she laid a cool, foul-smelling rag to Merryn's head. "I know it smells bad. Trust in me."

Merryn nodded, groaning as that had hurt as well. A cold, soothing touch seemed to seep into her skin, covering the ache until she could barely feel it. Her heart no longer beat within her temples or her throat.

After a moment, she opened her eyes. The sun shone through the leaves of the tree she lay beneath. Cara sat by her side, her fingers gently caressing the side of Merryn's face.

"Look into my eyes," Cara softly requested. Merryn turned her head ever so slightly, watching Cara's concerned face peering closely at her. "The swelling's gone down," Cara whispered, as if to herself.

"I need ta look after ya, Cara," Merryn murmured, seeing the bruises and dried blood that still painted her face. Cara shook her head.

"No. You need to rest."

Merryn didn't argue, knowing she'd not win this battle. Instead, she allowed her eyes to travel around Cara's face, taking in the soft features and the slightly curled corners of the mouth. Those eyes were so deep. Sometimes Merryn felt she could see entirely new worlds in those eyes.

"What?" Cara asked, taking the cloth from Merryn's head and dunking it in a small bowl. She wrung out the excess then replaced the rag. Merryn shook her head slightly at the question, unable to tell Cara just how worried she'd been. Cara smiled, seeming to understand. "Who were your friends?"

"Angus, Anna, George, Sarah and Aaron."

"Oh? Ye've been busy." Cara smiled.

Merryn returned the smile. "A bit of luck, really. They helped me," she quietly explained. She reached her hand up, brows knitting as she gently touched the incredible bruise around Cara's eye. "Does it hurt, lass?" she whispered. Cara nodded, looking down.

"'Twere so many, Merryn," she said, her voice so quiet that she almost missed it. "I was shackled to the wall in that God forsaken room." She swallowed hard. "It was dark and smelled of death. So many had died. Thought I was dying when that girl came runnin' in; an angel come to take me to Heaven."

"Hey." Forgetting about her aching head, Merryn pushed herself up to a sitting position and pulled Cara to her. Cara clung to her as she wept, her body trembling. Merryn rested her cheek against the girl's blonde head, stroking her back.

After some minutes, Cara pulled back and looked at Merryn. "Why did this happen? For what purpose?"

Merryn sighed, running her thumb under the girl's undamaged eye to wipe away her tears. "The king's own selfish reasons," she said softly. "Servants 're runnin', taking as their own lands from those of the dead," she explained, bringing her other hand up to brush Cara's hair from her face. "Edward is capturin' the healthy to replace his servants."

"That is all? He is capturing and murdering to have someone to serve him?" Merryn nodded at the angry question. Cara was stunned, having no idea how to respond to such selfishness or such a vile lack of caring for those Edward ruled.

"Angus wants to build an army, lass." Merryn now had both hands placed on Cara's face, gently caressing the skin with her thumbs, mindful of the girl's bruises. "He wants to storm the daft bastard down."

"And he should."

"Be that as it may." Merryn groaned as she stood up, closing her eyes and resting her hand on the trunk of the tree as a wave of nausea washed through her. Taking several deep breaths, she steadied herself. "I know what 'twill make ye feel better, lass." She grinned.

Cara winced slightly as the cool water washed over the bruises and cuts on her skin. All too happily she dunked her head beneath the surface of the water, slicking her hair back from her face. Wiping the water out of her eyes, Cara looked at her friend, who had joined her in the lake.

"Come here, lass," Merryn said softly, reaching a hand out to her friend to lead her to deeper water. Cara quickly took it, slowly picking her way across the rocky bottom with her friend. When the water was sufficiently deep, Merryn stopped and held up the pouch containing the paste of herbs Cara had mixed for them to cleanse the hair and skin. The pouch immediately released the smell of the rose petals included in the mix.

Grinning, Cara eagerly turned around, giving her back to Merryn.

"Kneel down a bit," Merryn instructed softly. She rinsed the girl's hair, knowing she'd have to be mindful of scalp wounds and the knots made from dried blood. She felt around Cara's head, her fingers brushing against sensitive areas that made the girl gasp or outright hiss. "Sorry, lass," she whispered.

Deciding none of the wounds needed immediate attention, Merryn scooped some of the paste into her hand, rubbing the grainy mixture between her palms before rubbing it into the long, blonde hair.

Cara's eyes closed as her neck relaxed, trusting Merryn's hands on her. She sighed as strong fingers worked the mixture in, massaging and tugging on the hair gently, but just to the point of pleasure, before pain. She loved for Merryn to wash her hair; the stoic girl had a way that was so gentle, that it always amazed and amused Cara.

As Merryn massaged Cara's scalp, somehow the cleansing caresses moved to the back of the neck, feeling the soft skin, the corded veins, and the tendons as her fingers moved slowly around toward Cara's throat. She watched with curious amazement as her fingers trailed up the side of Cara's neck, feeling the proud jaw line there before moving up to feel a soft earlobe.

Cara was surprised at first, feeling Merryn's fingers wandering over her skin, but she found herself leaning back into the taller girl, Merryn's naked breasts against her back. Cara felt her breathing change slightly, and wondered if it was from nerves. If so, that surprised her; she'd never been nervous around Merryn before. She had nothing to be nervous about. But still, as she felt warm breath brushing against her left ear, she felt a strange wave of heat flow through her, almost like nausea, but not unpleasant.

Closing her eyes, she decided to rest fully against Merryn, relaxing and enjoying being with her again, being touched by her.

Merryn watched as her fingers traced a delicate line behind Cara's ears, smiling slightly when she felt a little shiver pass through the girl. Her fingers trailed down her neck once more, finding their way across the smooth, creamy skin of well-defined shoulders. Her fingertips ran lazily down over the rounded shoulders to glide along Cara's arms, meeting her hands beneath the water's surface. Cara's fingers interlaced with her own, bringing their joined hands above the water's surface. She folded her arms across her own breasts, taking Merryn's hands and arms with her, until the taller girl had her wrapped up in a tight embrace.

Merryn's eyes closed as she felt their bodies press together, her lips grazing across Cara's temple. She had no idea what was happening, but her body felt — how could she describe it? — *alive*. Her skin felt as though it were an entity all its own, tiny fingers reaching out to feel and grasp.

For the first time, she was aware of every single curve of her own body, as well as all those of Cara's. She felt the swells of Cara's breasts against the tender skin of the insides of her wrists, and her wrists tingled. She did not understand, but she could not move away. She craved contact with this girl who had grown to become the center of her world, even if Merryn refused to say it aloud.

How could it be that over the past couple of days, when Cara had been away, that Merryn had felt hollow and utterly alone? And now, standing in the lake, holding her so close, she felt complete and whole?

Cara shivered as the early evening breeze blew across her skin, and she felt her body shiver again as the cool water rippled around her.

Merryn felt the goosebumps rise on Cara's skin and knew she had to get her out of the water soon. Giving her one final squeeze, she released the girl, softly telling her to bend down so that her hair could be rinsed. When she finished, Cara turned to face her, smiling softly before returning the favor. They each washed their own bodies, hurrying as the air continued to get colder.

Wordlessly, Cara helped her friend, still somewhat unsteady on her feet, to the shore, where they fought over who would gather the wood, each wanting the other to rest.

"Please, Merryn? For now, for me, please rest," Cara pleaded. She grinned when Merryn finally nodded with a sigh.

Cara was grateful for the bread and dried meat that Merryn had brought from the tavern. Neither of them was in any shape to hunt or fish.

After Cara got a healthy fire burning, she walked over to Merryn, who leaned up against the trunk of a tree. They shared the food, then they sat shoulder to shoulder, heads leaning together as they stared into the flames.

"How is yer head?" Cara asked quietly

"Still feels a wee bit fuzzy," Merryn answered after a moment of mental inventory.

Cara nodded. "And probably will for a few days. Quite a bump you got."

"Aye." Merryn sighed, her eyes beginning to droop further and further. "'M so tired."

"As am I."

Merryn roused slightly and heard only deep, even breathing. Merryn sighed, letting the darkness take her deeper into its embrace.

There it was again.

Suddenly aware, Merryn's eyes snapped open and she grabbed for her sword, thoughts of soldiers finding them in the forest filling her head. It was still very dark; the fire had long ago burned to embers. Stopping all movement she listened intently. The night was quiet; there was nothing out of the ordinary.

Glancing to her right, Merryn saw the figure of Cara asleep no more than an arm's length away. She lay on her side with her back towards Merryn. A small whimper came from Cara's throat.

"No," Cara begged quietly, still in the clutches of sleep. Her body jerked, and she rolled to her back. Merryn was able to make out the tortured look on her friend's beautiful face, and her heart broke. "Please, no."

Once Merryn realized that Cara was crying, she could take no more. Scooting over to her friend, she gently grasped her shoulder.

"Lass," she said softly, "'tis a dream. Wake up, Cara."

"No!" Cara's eyes opened wide in terror before she realized who sat before her looking very concerned. "Merryn?"

"Aye, lass. 'Tis me." She reached out, brushing blonde strands from a pale, shaken face. "Yer safe now, Cara."

"I'm sorry I woke you..."

"Shhh." Merryn moved to lie on her back, pulling Cara to her. "'Tis alright."

Cara moved over to lie next to Merryn, resting her head upon her shoulder and curling her body as close as she possibly could, her heart still racing. The images and terrors of the past few days were still so fresh in her mind. Immediately she felt better as Merryn tightened her grip and Merryn's arms closed around Cara, making her feel as though the world could just slip away.

Merryn's soft voice washed over her again.

"Would ya like ta talk about it?" Merryn felt Cara shake her head slightly. She knew what demons had been chasing her friend through her nightmares, and only wished there was something, *anything*, she could do to take it all away. So she just held her close, trying in the only way she knew how to let the girl know she had somewhere safe to go.

Guilt was eating at Merryn. She felt completely responsible for what had happened to Cara, for her getting caught. Never, *ever* should she have left her for the wolves to devour.

"Merryn?"

She realized that Cara had raised herself to her elbow and was looking down at her. She saw the concern in her eyes; the usual green became a deep gray in the near darkness. Merryn closed her eyes as she felt soft fingertips on her face. It was only then, when she felt the tickle of a tear rolling into her ear that she realized she was crying.

"Why do ye cry?" Cara whispered. Merryn, stubborn, shook her head. "Tell me. Please?"

Finally sighing after getting her emotions under control, Merryn looked up at her concerned friend. "I never should've left ya," she answered softly. "I should've gone back fer ya, or somethin'."

"Shhh," Cara cooed, covering Merryn's lips with two of her fingers. "'Twas a bad thing, Merryn. There was nothing you could have done." She shook her head. "Not one thing."

"I could've tried," Merryn insisted, her voice stronger, yet still filled with so much regret.

Cara sighed softly, knowing there'd be no way to convince the bull-headed woman of anything else. She smiled softly. "Well, I'm here now, aren't I?"

Merryn nodded. "Suppose so."

"Come." Cara laid herself down, snuggling against the strong shoulder beneath her head. "Sleep now."

The warm sun beat down onto Merryn's upraised face. Standing by the lake, she reached up and unclasped her cloak, letting the garment fall to the shore at her feet. Her bare arms opened wide, absorbing the much-needed warmth to melt the ice around her heart.

She kept seeing his eyes — brown, with a ring of gold lining the irises. His face was so close to hers that she could see the tiny hairs on his recently shaved face or the small group of eyelashes that were clumped together. She could see the sweat oozing from his pores from both the heat of the boiler room and his fear.

She closed her eyes as she remembered the feeling of warm, sticky fluids covering her hand, the way that they dried into the cracks of her skin and dried into brown specks on her sword's cross guard and stained the blade. She drew her sword, holding it across her hand, brows drawn as she looked at it.

Suddenly a shiver ran down her spine and, with a growl, she bared her teeth and splashed into the water until it reached the tops of her ankles. Kneeling down, she frantically began to wash the blade, using her fingernails to scrub the dried blood off the metal. A cry of frustration escaped her, as the blood didn't wash away fast enough. She could still see it, vibrant and red.

"Come on," she hissed, the cold water splashing into her face, her bangs hanging limply in her eyes as she desperately tried to cleanse herself. "Get off, ya daft bastard!" She didn't even feel her own blood join that of the soldier as the blade sliced into the palm of her hand.

"Merryn! Merryn, stop!" Cara grabbed at the frantic woman.

"Leave me be!" Merryn roared, pushing the girl from her before turning back to her blade, scrubbing with her fingernails. "Got to get it off."

"Merryn," Cara whispered, slowly taking a step closer to her friend. "Merryn, there's not a thing there." She looked into the panicked eyes of her friend, which were red and swollen. Cara reached a hand out, tentatively cupping her face. "Not a thing there."

Merryn, breathing hard, looked down at her sword, still clutched in a devil's grip in her hand. The blade was clean, reflecting the overhead sun. Hissing, she felt the sting in her palm. Embarrassed and unsteady, she got to her feet, shrugging off Cara's touch.

"Go find yer herbs, lass," she said quietly, knowing Cara needed to replenish her medicines. Much had been left behind in the cave or taken by the soldiers.

Cara stared at her for a moment, not sure what to think. She had been startled awake when she'd heard the thrashing in the lake, thinking that Merryn was being attacked. She worried the girl had been hit on the head harder than first thought.

Gathering her wits about her, Cara walked out of the water, lifting her skirts and wringing out the water. She looked back at her friend. Merryn was standing in the water, her head hanging. Cara knew there was nothing she could do to ease the girl's conscience. What was done was done and, though it had been horrible to watch, Cara knew what soldiers were capable of and felt no regret for the man's death.

As she scanned the nearby woods for the roots she needed, her mind flashed back to the terror of the past few days.

Cara ran from the cave, then from behind the tree, doing her best each time to keep up with Merryn. She tried so hard to keep up but after the continued running, she tired and fell behind Merryn's long strides. After she told Merryn to continue on without her, the soldiers' hounds caught up to her quickly, their hot breath snapping against her legs until one of them finally lunged at her, knocking her to the ground and causing her to scream in fear.

"Cara!!"

She heard Merryn holler in response to her scream, but she was unable to catch her breath after hitting the cold, hard ground. She kicked at the hounds hoping to keep their attention and prevent them from chasing after Merryn. Suddenly, Cara saw four heavily armed men standing above her, one with a sword to her gullet.

"Don't you move, lassie," one of them hissed. Cara swallowed back the tears that threatened. She was terrified for Merryn as she was forced to her feet. Looking over her shoulder in the direction she heard the dogs barking, she silently prayed for Merryn's safety. Shoved from behind, she was forced back through the woods. Three soldiers lifted her onto a horse, tied her hands to the saddle, then led her off into the night.

They arrived at the soldiers' camp, filled with tents, soldiers, knights, and the many squires running around desperately trying to please their masters.

After removing her from the horse, a young soldier growled, "Get in there, filth!" as he shoved Cara into a tent. The interior was nearly black, save for a small lamp at the center near the main wooden pole that held the structure up.

Cara gasped when she realized that the tent was filled with young women, all tied to each other. Dirty, exhausted faces looked up at Cara as she looked from side to side. She was pushed deeper into the tent, then shoved to the ground.

A small cry of surprise left her throat when large hands tugged roughly at her clothing, stripping her of her cloak and the pouch around her waist. "Be nice, wench, and I'll let ye keep those good boots ye got," foul breath muttered into her ear. Her eyes opened wide as she felt that same large hand cover her breast. Squeezing her eyes shut, Cara prayed that the soldier would go away and leave her alone. "Ye feel nice, little one, ye do," he said, his grip rough and painful.

"Rutger!" a voice growled from the mouth of the tent. "Leave her be. You know what the king said."

Cara held her breath, terror filling her. The soldier sighed heavily, almost making her choke on his breath. "We're not done, ye 'n me," he whispered, then was gone.

Two young boys came in and tied Cara where she lay. Strong, prickly rope laced her hands together and connected her to the sturdy log pole at the center of the tent.

Cara tried desperately to blink the tears away, but they refused to go. She blinked rapidly, trying to take in her surroundings better and the faces of those who filled the tent. It was hard to breathe, as the smell of unwashed bodies assaulting her nose. These were simple, frightened village girls.

Cara's biggest fear, other than what the soldiers might have planned, was if someone in the tent were infected with the black sickness. There would be no escape.

Cara leaned her head against the tree, lifting one hand to wipe gently at the moisture on her face. She could never tell Merryn what happened to her; she knew her friend was already reproaching herself for what she saw as her fault.

Cara would pray for the gift of forgiveness. And may God help them get through this and give her the wisdom to heal Merryn's wounds.

Merryn wandered through the woods, her sword bouncing lightly against her hip. She glanced down at her hand, wrapped with a thin piece of cloth ripped from her tunic. A small patch of blood soaked through the material, but she didn't care. The sting kept her mind sharp and her focus clear.

Images of the last few days flashed before her eyes, her mind filled with smells, sounds, and especially the taste of victory as she led Cara out of the tunnels. Merryn had been filled with such pride, a feeling of doing a great thing, the greatest thing she'd ever done. It had been the first time in her life that she'd put someone else's life before her own.

She found a stump to sit upon, resting her elbows on her thighs.

It should have been so easy to let it go, to just keep on her endless travels, leaving Cara to whatever fate might be hers. It certainly wasn't up to Merryn to decide that. Yet she had. Or perhaps it was Cara's fate to survive, to become something far greater than her captors. Could this be true?

Merryn thought of her young friend. Why did she allow Cara to stay? Why did she care about Cara at all? There was just something about Cara that was very difficult to describe — untouchable, yet so very potent and profound. Her eyes — within those eyes was the soul of a wise woman, someone capable of great things. No simple villager was she.

"Greater than all," Merryn whispered. This startled Merryn, having no idea where the words had come from. She was confused and frightened. She had taken a man's life, all for the rescue of one girl.

Merryn glanced to the east, seeing the clouds begin to roll in. The sky was gray and pregnant, with shattering bolts of lightning. She slowly stood up, her mouth open as she watched the unnaturally fast storm approach; it seemed to stop overhead.

Gasping, Merryn took a step back after feeling a cold raindrop splatter against her forehead, followed by another, then another.

Merryn turned, intent on quickly finding shelter before the downpour when she felt something stop her, a force. It felt like the same force that had pushed her out of the way when the soldier had come after her with his dagger.

Squinting against the onslaught, she stared up into the angry skies. It was almost as if time stood still, the day waiting, holding its breath.

"What?" she yelled to the Heavens. "What do ya want from me?"

Merryn's eyes closed, and a series of images flashed through her mind, quick and powerful:

"Hold on, lass. Just hold on," Merryn whispered, cradling Cara's head in her arms, the girl's eyes closed, her face pale ...

... moonlight illuminated the night, Merryn hiding behind a tree. Her intended targets just moving shadows ...

... underneath her eyes, the flames close by. Merryn cupped Cara's face, green eyes sliding closed, leaning into the larger hand. "Merryn, yes," she whispers, the sweet voice echoing inside her head ...

... bashed again into the stone wall. "Tell me," Merryn hisses, pulling the man up by his hair to look at her. "Tell me where he hides, or die now, lad." Merryn brought his face up closer to ...

... her body, being dragged from the battlefield by the arm. The soldier grunts loudly, desperate to get her to safety. "Hold on, Donal. Almost there." Merryn is dragged to safety, behind ...

... those eyes. She knows those eyes. "I know you," she whispers.

Merryn staggered back; the rain brought her back from her own mind. Her heart beat wildly within her chest, almost making her feel weak and faint.

"I don't understand," Merryn gasped, as she looked up into the sky once more. "I don't understand! I'm jest a drifter!" Her cry echoed through the rain, seeming to reverberate off each individual drop. Falling to her knees, her head fell. "What do ya want from me?" Looking at her hands, she was stunned to see them covered in blood. The rain bounced uselessly off the life that she held within her hands. "No," she whispered, tears filling her eyes, head shaking slowly back and forth. "No."

With a cry to the Heavens above, she pulled her sword from its holding and hurled it into the air. Merryn watched, breathless, as the sword flipped head over end several times, arching back to the land. Slicing into the earth with a loud hiss, the blade vibrated back and forth from the impact.

Looking back at her hands, the blood began to run, the rain clearing the flesh of the crimson stain. Merryn felt cold, bitterly cold. After a few moments, she glanced at her blade once more and saw the steel gleaming. Looking up, she saw the clouds beginning to clear, the sun slipping back out.

Slowly, Merryn made her way over to her sword. With a trembling hand, she reached down, carefully gripping the leather-wrapped handle, and flexed her fingers around it. The sun's warmth filled her hand as she pulled up the sword and brought it back to her body.

With a gasp, her blue eyes opened wide, taking in everything around her. Her head was pounding and her hand stung in pulse with her racing blood. Without thought or grace, she sat down on the ground.

Birds sang nearby; the tree she sat under shielded her from the warmth of the day.

"Losin' my bloody mind," she muttered, slowly getting to her feet. She still felt shaky and unsteady, and she braced her hand against the thick trunk of the tree.

Taking a deep breath, Merryn pushed off and started back to camp.

In the distance, thunder rolled.

Merryn sat on the bank with her back against a tree. The pommel of her sword rested on the ground between her legs, the blade lying against her chest and shoulder. She watched, amused, as Cara frolicked in the stream.

"What're ya tryin' at, lass?"

Cara glanced at her over her shoulder before turning back to the water. Holding her skirts up above the water, she looked into the shallow depths.

"Lookin' for a good rock," Cara said, bending to grab at a colorful one that caught her eye.

"What for?"

"Crushin' herbs." Cara brought the rock to the surface, bringing it up to her eyes to examine it. Grinning, she tossed it into the air, quickly snatching it in her fist. She walked over to Merryn, plopping down next to the moody girl. It had been nearly a full month since their adventure at Middleham. Since that time, Merryn had been so hard to reach.

Cara turned to her friend. She noticed yet again the wrinkle of concentration that had formed between Merryn's beautiful eyes so quickly. She seemed to have aged, her face changing from that of a young girl to that of a person of wisdom and responsibility.

Cara raised her hand and ran her thumb along the crease between Merryn's eyes, smoothing her brow.

"What weight of the world you carry, my friend," she whispered, her own brows drawn in concern. Merryn said nothing, her head leaning into Cara's touch. "Please let me not be a burden to ye."

Merryn smiled, soft and filled with affection. "Ya're no burden, lass. None 'tall."

"But I am." Cara caressed the soft skin of Merryn's cheek, turning her hand so the back of her fingers traced her jaw. Merryn closed her eyes, sighing softly at the comforting touch. She could not tell her friend just how right she was. She knew not why, but Merryn was aware that she carried a great responsibility, a destiny yet unfulfilled. She could do it, she could. With Cara by her side, she could do it.

Her dreams were getting worse; they were coming closer together and were more vivid with their warnings and prophetic images.

Stubbornly, Merryn shook her head. She reached up, tucking her hand into Cara's.

"My dearest friend," Cara whispered, moving to her knees to keep her balance. She leaned into Merryn, watching her eyes, compelled to be as close as possible. "My Merryn." Two sets of eyes closed as Cara brushed her lips against Merryn's. It was such a beautiful touch. She leaned back, watching as Merryn's eyes slowly opened, and she smiled, the biggest smile Cara had seen in days.

"I know not, lass!" Merryn growled, glaring Cara who walked by her side.

"Someone poked you with a rock, did they?" Cara tried not to laugh at Merryn's foul mood, knowing it would only make it worse. The dark girl had woken up like this yesterday and again today. By the slight grimace of pain on her face, and as often as they'd needed to stop so she could visit the bushes, Cara knew exactly what the problem was.

"Rest, now, Merryn," she said softly, resting her hand on her friend's shoulder. She was slightly hurt as Merryn pulled away from her touch, but she tried not to heed the feeling, knowing it would do them no good.

"Nay. We must..."

"Rest." Cara's voice was firm, leaving no room for argument. Merryn sighed heavily and nodded in acceptance.

Cara turned to the heavily wooded area around them. She chewed on her lip as she tried to decide which direction to go. Plunging into the undergrowth, her hands brushed over various plants and bushes as her sharp eyes scanned the vegetation.

"Were I monk's pepper, where would I be?" she muttered, kneeling as she saw a small bush growing next to a tree. The plant had the familiar violet flowers but lacked the reddish-black berries she sought. "Bugger." Scanning further around her, she looked for another bush. A wide grin spread quickly across her lips when she found it.

Pushing her cloak over her shoulder, Cara hurried to a small clearing. A clump of the bushes grew together, bearing berries aplenty.

"Thank ye, Lord," she whispered, quickly picking the small berries, making a pocket with her upturned tunic. She hurried back to where she heard the black horse whinnying softly.

"Can we go, then?" Merryn asked, glancing at her from where she was seated under a tree.

Cara nodded with a smile. "Aye."

Cara glanced at her friend from time to time, amused as she saw Merryn's scowl deepen. Her bloated irritation was no secret.

As they traveled, Cara fashioned a drying rack across the back of her cloak, on which she strung the berries with a piece of thin rope. She knew there was no way that she was going to get Merryn to stop for the day to dry the berries out on rocks. So, Cara had to be creative.

Merryn tried to smooth out her forehead, raising her brows, but as soon as she lowered her brows, the skin of her forehead wrinkled up again. She was so tense. And the pulsing clinch of her insides didn't make things any better.

Glancing over at her friend, Merryn glared, seeing the happy-go-lucky smile on Cara's face. Mumbling to herself, Merryn quickened her pace, wanting nothing to do with the happy girl. She felt miserable and, by damn, so should the rest of the world.

Cara felt Merryn's intense gaze on her but didn't dare meet those blue eyes. She kept an eye on her out of the corner of her eye, leaving the irritable girl alone but making sure she was alright at the same time. She smirked slightly when Merryn tripped over a root in the path, nearly falling to her face. Merryn grumbled curses to the Heavens as she moved on.

"Feeling better?" Cara asked, resting against a felled log. She chewed contentedly on the meat she'd dried at their last campsite. Merryn sat across the fire from her, still scowling, and shrugged noncommittally.

Cara got up from her place by the fire, crawling to her cloak. She tested the texture of the berries which had been drying all day.

"Aye," she whispered to herself, "should work." Gathering what she needed, she took the water bladder and a wooden mug, then crawled around the fire to Merryn. Pouring some water into the mug, she crushed the berries between her fingers, sprinkling the dust into the water. Glancing up, she saw Merryn watching her every move, though the blue eyes stubbornly looked away when she saw she was being observed.

"What craziness 're ya makin' now?" she mumbled.

"Somethin' to make ye feel better." Cara swirled the water and berry dust around, then held it out for Merryn. "Drink."

Merryn looked at her as though she'd lost her mind. Cara hardened her eyes.

"Drink, Merryn."

Merryn growled but took the mug. One last petulant look and she drank the peppery mixture in one gulp. Her face scrunched up, and she stuck out her tongue. Cara chuckled quietly, taking the cup from her friend before she threw it into the fire.

"Ya poisoned me!"

"I did no such thing." She took hold of Merryn's cloak, tugging. "Come here," she said softly, pulling the girl's head into her lap. Grudgingly Merryn went. But as soon as she lay down, she turned onto her side, her arm wrapping around the thigh she rested her head on. Closing her eyes, she felt fingers running through her hair, carefully unknotting wind-blown strands. "Yer pain will be soon gone," Cara said.

Merryn could still taste the slightly bitter, peppery taste on her tongue, but she had no idea what Cara had given her. She did know that soon she'd have to go find some privacy and take a clean scrap of cloth with her. But not yet.

Cara stared down at the long, thick tresses that her fingers swam through the firelight making the locks shine. Though Merryn's hair was dark, the flames brought out the red and gold highlights. She could see Merryn's profile, the strong features and proud jaw.

Merryn's eyes were barely open as she studied the tattered material of Cara's dress. "Ya need new clothes, lass," Merryn said quietly, poking her finger through a hole.

Cara smiled, nodding. "Aye. Ye going to steal some fer me?" Cara grinned, teasing in her voice.

Merryn said nothing, only snuggling closer into Cara's lap. She stared into the flames for a moment before her brow wrinkled.

"Cara? Why're ya not married?"

Cara chuckled softly. "I was. I think."

Merryn's brow drew further. She turned so she could look up at her friend. "Aye 'r nay, lass. No thinkin' 'bout it."

"Well," Cara sighed, looking down at her friend and wiping at a small smudge on the girl's cheek. "Will had claimed me as such, to be his wife."

"Claimed ya, did he?" Merryn asked, dark brow rising. Cara blushed deeply, hiding her face.

"Not like that. What do ye take me for? Do not answer that," she hissed at Merryn's further raised brow. "Will was a fool," she continued, chuckling lightly as she played with a bit of the dark hair in her lap. "I had no desire to marry him, but mother felt otherwise. Thought it'd be a good match, she did. The day I was to move into his home, Will got himself killed while hunting."

"Killed on his weddin' day?" Merryn asked, incredulously. She saw Cara's grinning nod. "Daft bugger." Again Cara nodded.

"That he was. Without a heart, I am not. I did not wish Will killed, but I did not want to marry him. I had my head turned to the blacksmith's son."

"Did'ja now?"

Cara nodded. "Aye. I wanted a family." She slowly ran her fingers the entire length of Merryn's thick, beautiful hair, rubbing the ends between her fingers before making another pass.

Merryn closed her eyes and sighed in pleasure. She so loved her hair played with. Eyes still closed she spoke, "Ya still can, lass."

"Nay."

Blue eyes opened, taking in the stubborn set of Cara's jaw. "Nay?"

"Nay. I can't imagine ye'd be willin' to settle down in some village somewhere, livin' next to my husband and me." Cara knew there was no way she could leave her behind. Merryn had become part of her over the months. She'd be lost without her.

Merryn chuckled slightly at the mental image and fought down the ugly pang of sudden jealousy. She shook her head.

"Nay 'tis. Ya don't need me, lass. Ya're fine on ya own."

"What 'bout you, Merryn?" Cara asked, her voice soft.

"A master? Me?" Merryn looked up at Cara as though she'd lost her mind. Cara laughed; the sound was like crystal on the still night air.

"'Tis not a master, Merryn. A husband."

"Not a difference there is, lass. I canna be ruled."

Cara leaned down, hugging Merryn's head to her chest, giving her a soft kiss on top of her head.

Merryn was about to speak, but stopped, nearly knocking Cara over with the speed with which she stood. Her hand flew to the grip of her sword as her eyes scanned the dark night around them.

"What 'tis it?" Cara asked in a whisper, her eyes wide, trying to find what her friend must have heard or seen.

Merryn said nothing, as she stood stock still and tried to comb through all that she saw, trying to find something out of place that would account for what she'd heard. Head snapping to her left, she heard it again. Footsteps, definitely footsteps.

It didn't take long for the noise maker to enter the ring of firelight. Merryn drew her blade, eyeing the dirty, scraggly man. He looked just as surprised as the two women did.

His surprise passed quickly, and he raised his hands in abdication. Merryn kept her eyes on him, noticing that his eyes were sharp, taking in everything around him. She saw that his palms were covered with small scars, much like her own. Such is the fate of flesh dipping into unseen pockets. Many things poked and cut. She knew a kindred spirit when she saw one.

"What of ya, old man?" she asked, her voice low and filled with warning. He gave her a near toothless smile, raising his hands higher.

"I mean ye no harm, lassie," he said, his voice whispery between his rotten and missing teeth. "Have ye no water ta spare?" His beady eyes looked from the point of Merryn's sword up to her face, then moved to Cara. Merryn didn't miss his looking around, trying to see if anyone else was at this camp.

"Be on yer way, lad." Merryn was surprised by the growl in her voice. She had a bad feeling about this drifter.

"Merryn," Cara said from behind her, voice soft and surprised. "We can share."

The man's watery blue eyes latched onto Cara, an ally. He bowed deep, eyes never leaving Cara. "Me thanks, lassie."

Cara handed him the water bladder, then turned hard eyes onto her friend. Merryn avoided the questioning green eyes, instead keeping her own eyes on the stranger.

"Warm yerself." Cara indicated the fire, and the man eagerly lowered himself to the ground, soaking in the warmth. He whistled his thanks once again as he found himself with a bit of meat and dried fruit in his hand.

Merryn grabbed Cara, leading her away from the camp but positioning herself so she could keep the old man in her sights at all times.

"What're ya doing, lass?" she hissed. Cara was shocked, her mouth opening slightly.

"Showing kindness. He has nothin'."

"Ya let 'im stay, and neither will we!" She looked into Cara's eyes, wanting her to know just how serious she was. She knew his kind.

Cara refused to hear it. She shook her head sadly. "How can ye be so cruel, Merryn? 'Tis a cool night, and food is scarce in these times. We have it ta spare. He stays, were he ta wish it." With that, Cara turned, heading back to the camp.

"Cara! Cara!" Merryn hissed, but Cara didn't turn back. "Bugger ta hell," she muttered, heading back to the camp as well.

Merryn sat moodily against a tree, watching as the drifter, Daniel, and Cara talked quietly. The man was telling the young girl of the towns he'd been through, and of how they were faring with the sickness. Some towns were so bad off as to be forced to pull wagons through the streets, calling for the dead to be brought out, loaded onto the wagon, and burned outside of town.

Merryn leaned her head back, her eyes hooded as she watched, trying to keep her sense of doom and jealousy in check. Why was she jealous? Merryn had never been jealous in her life. But then, she'd never exactly had something or someone in her life to be jealous over. She wasn't entirely sure what she thought of this revelation.

Shaking the thought out of her head, Merryn pushed herself to her feet, brushing her hands off on her thighs. She muttered a good night and unrolled her bedroll, ignoring the questioning look Cara sent her way.

Cara was trying to listen to what Daniel was saying but her mind was on her friend. What was wrong with her? Why was she being so rude and inhospitable? And now she was going to bed, not even waiting for Cara to join her?

"M'lady." Daniel stood, bowing deep at the waist. "I bid ye and yer companion a safe travel."

"Wait." Completely charmed, Cara looked at him, then glanced over at Merryn, who lay with her back to them. Turning back to the traveler, she smiled. "Stay the night, Daniel. Be warm 'n safe."

"Well..." he glanced over at Merryn, giving Cara an unsure look.

"Be a guest of mine, sir. Sleep."

The most earnest and beautiful green eyes Daniel had ever seen were looking up at him, beseeching him to accept her gracious nature. He grinned, making sure it was a smile worthy of her trust. With another bow, he accepted.

The night was quiet; there was no noise save the leaves swaying lightly in the breeze and the occasional popping of the dying embers. The sweet smell of the oncoming spring mixed with the acrid smell of wood ash wafted to Merryn's nose.

She started, falling heavily into reality. She could feel the slight weight of Cara's arm across her back and the hard ground beneath her breasts. Not even her bedding could keep out the chill from the cold soil beneath her.

Raising her head slightly, Merryn looked around. She saw something, movement, on the other side of the dying fire.

There it was again.

Easing out from under Cara, Merryn moved as slowly and steadily as she could before she got to her feet and lunged at the dirty bastard who was now rifling through Cara's pouch. Merryn saw the glint of the steel from her own blade lying on the ground next to him.

Without a sound, the two tumbled to the ground, Merryn on top of the drifter, whose eyes only registered his shock for a moment before they turned hard; the eyes of a survivor. Merryn knew that look well, and she knew how dangerous this man really was. He had nothing to lose, save for what he was about to steal from them.

Merryn felt a rage overtake her, boiling up from the pit of her belly until it finally fired out of her fingers. She wrapped her hands around his scrawny neck and squeezed.

"Ya think ya c'n steal from me, ya daft bastard," she hissed, teeth glinting white in the moonlight. "Know yer kind, I do." She raised his head, only to slam it back into the leaf-strewn ground beneath them.

Cara heard a sharp thud, and her eyes flew open. Looking around desperately for Merryn, she saw her straddling Daniel. Her back was to Cara, but she could see the man's legs flailing frantically, his body bucking, trying to get the girl off him.

As Cara watched, Merryn's fist came away, only to slam down into his face, a wet crunch following the impact, then a hoarse, whispery scream.

Merryn watched in satisfaction as she saw what was left of the man's teeth disappear into the dark cavern that was his putrid mouth. Inky blood splattered out, dribbling down the side of his chin.

"Bastard," she hissed again, squeezing harder, using both hands now.

As Daniel began to gasp, his eyes huge and bloodshot, Merryn ceased to see his face. His wide blue eyes were now brown; Daniel's stringy mop of brown hair was now red. He reached for her, the steel of his gauntlet glimmering in the fires beneath the cauldrons.

Behind her, Merryn could hear her name whispered on the wind, floating to her ears before brushing by. She squeezed tighter, feeling the soldier's frantic hand on her triceps, though the grip was weakening significantly.

"Merryn! Stop it! Let go!"

Merryn gasped, as though taking a breath for the first time. The night closed in around her. The rough, hair-covered skin beneath her hands trickled into her conscious mind.

"Yer killing him," was sobbed quietly next to her.

Merryn's hands released their purchase as though they'd been burned. She looked down at the drifter. His eyes were closed, his face twisted in pain and fear, his chest heaving.

She climbed off him, looking around, feeling lost and confused. She heard Cara crawl over to the man, talking to him quietly. She also heard her searching through her pouch until she found the medicines she needed to help with the pain of his destroyed mouth.

Looking down at her hands, Merryn felt her blood go cold and her fingers tingled, so firm had been her hold on him. She grunted as her body fell to the ground, her knees meeting the chilled soil. She couldn't take her eyes off her hands, stunned that she had nearly taken a man's life with them, with just her own touch.

"What evil has me?" she whispered, stunned and feeling shame spread through her like wildfire. She'd lost control. Only the sound of Cara's voice had saved the drifter's life.

Glancing over at her friend who tended to his wounds, she could not meet the watery blue eyes that met her own. Standing, she walked off into the darkness.

Part 5

Cara stayed on her knees, looking at the spot where Daniel had just been. His frantic footprints were still visible in the soil.

"She is a demon!" Daniel gasped as he got to his feet, mouth covered by a foul-tasting paste, its grainy texture making his skin itch.
"Nay, Daniel. She got angry..."
"Demon!" he wheezed, turning and fleeing.

Cara took several deep breaths, looking out in the direction Merryn had gone. Her heart was still beating almost painfully in her chest. Putting her hand over it, she slowly got to her feet, surprised to note she was trembling.

She felt uncertain and scared. Looking around the campsite, she saw what was left of the fire, the disrupted bedding, and their scattered belongings.

She walked over to her own pack, most of the contents of which lay on the ground. Kneeling, she began to put her assortment of herbs and medicines back into the pouch. Her comb had been flung an arms-length away. She quickly grabbed it, tucking it back inside. Cara was about to close the pouch when something occurred to her. Wrenching the bag open once more, she quickly searched through it, pushing some things aside and taking others out.

The pouch hit the dirt as Cara covered her face with her hands. She began to tremble harder, though not from fear this time. The last link to home had been taken from her, by a man she had tried to help.

Getting to her feet once more, she wiped her eyes with a sniffle, then grabbed one of Merryn's daggers, and her sword. Wrapping her hand around the wood grip, she tucked the dagger into her dress. The sword was heavy in her hands, but it gave her a feeling of security as she walked into the dark wood.

Merryn could feel the rough bark against her cheek. She reached down, pushing with her hand as she readjusted her body in the fork of the massive branches that supported her weight. The night around her was cool, the sky filled with twinkling lights, winking at her.

"Merryn?" a distant voice called out. Merryn glanced in that direction, knowing it was Cara. The girl was to the west. She stayed quiet. She wasn't entirely sure she wished to be found. "Merryn!"

Merryn sighed, hearing the beginnings of panic in the voice, which was coming closer.

"O'er here, lass." The rustle of foliage increased as Cara approached. Merryn looked down at the confused girl. "Up."

Cara's head snapped at the voice, barely able to make out a dark figure nestled in the large tree before her.

"What are you doin' up there?"

Merryn didn't answer but, instead, quickly climbed down. Her talent and ability to make herself disappear after a life of stealing had been shaped from a very young age.

Cara stepped back as Merryn's boots hit the ground. She hadn't even realized she'd done it until she saw Merryn's eyes fall. She thought about this for a moment, stunned to realize that, yes, she was slightly frightened by Merryn who was obviously capable of much.

"Won't hurt ya, Cara." Merryn's voice was soft, almost a shameful whisper. She could not meet her friend's eyes.

Cara took several deep breaths, then she put a smile on her face, trying to reassure Merryn as much as herself. She stepped forward again, coming to stand just in front of her friend.

Merryn felt her heart break when she saw the way her friend trembled. Cara had never been frightened of her before, yet here it was. She wanted to climb back up into that tree and never come down again.

Cara took that last step toward Merryn, tucking her head just below her chin, arms snaking around her waist.

Merryn's eyes squeezed shut in bittersweet contentment. She could still feel Cara trembling against her. She knew it was the girl's brave soul and unending trust and faith in people that kept her in their embrace.

She wrapped her arms around the smaller body, holding her close, resting her cheek against the soft blonde hair that smelled of rose petals and the spice of herbs.

"He took my coins," Cara said, her voice soft and filled with hurt.

Merryn's eyes squeezed shut, the quenched anger beginning to boil once more. She swallowed heavily to keep it at bay. Cara needed a friend, not an uncontrolled heathen.

"'M sorry, lass."

"I should have listened te ye." Cara snuggled in closer, the tears stinging behind her closed lids.

"Shhh," Merryn soothed, kissing the top of the girl's head. "'M sorry, Cara."

Merryn didn't feel comfortable at their campsite, afraid the drifter may come back or, out of vengeance, he may have alerted the local magistrate. Even so, it wasn't safe to travel at night. She told Cara none of her fears, wishing for her friend to find peace in sleep. What Cara did not know was that Merryn's eyes never closed that night. She kept vigilant guard.

Merryn looked down at the prize in her hand that she'd taken from her own bag. Glancing up, she saw Cara holding her skirts as she walked through the shallow waters of the natural rain pond at the center of the wood. Looking back to her palm, Merryn gathered spit in her mouth, let it dribble onto the coin in her palm, then cleaned it with the edge of her cloak. She held the coin up to the light, marveling at how it shone.

"Cara?" she stepped closer to the girl. "C'mere, lass."

Cara raised her skirts further as she made her way out of the cool waters. She kicked the excess off her feet as she stepped on a flat rock, so as not to get her feet dirty.

"We need to find a lake or river, Merryn. We have not bathed in many days."

Merryn grinned, rolling her eyes. "Hold out yer hand, Cara."

Cara cocked her head to the side in question. She could see from Merryn's face that the dark girl did not jest. She lifted her arm and held her hand out with an open palm. The single gold coin was dropped onto it.

Cara looked down at the gold piece, immediately recognizing it. She looked up into Merryn's smiling blue face in fear and wonder.

"Daniel..."

"Took yers, lass. This," Merryn folded Cara's fingers over the last remaining physical memory of her village and family, "'tis the last o' the three, Cara."

Cara was stunned, her eyes widening. "Ye've had it all this time?" At Merryn's nod, Cara felt anger and betrayal fill her quickly, but it was just as quickly replaced by relieved gratitude. If Merryn had given her all the gold pieces that first night, she would have none left now.

Merryn smiled as Cara threw herself into her arms.

"Thank ye, Merryn. Thank ye, so much," Cara whispered. Merryn nodded against her. After a moment and a quick kiss to Cara's temple, Merryn pulled back.

"Come, lass. We best be movin'." She looked up into the early afternoon sky. "Storm brewin' out ta east." She pulled back from the girl and went back to their gear to pack.

Merryn looked around, keeping low so as not to crack her head on the sharp rock above. She felt around the floor, feeling only cool, dusty stone.

"Hand me that torch, lass," she called down to Cara, who looked up at her as she leaned out of the cave opening, high in the rock wall. Cara quickly handed her friend the torch she was holding then looked around the darkening day, the comforting light of the sun was gone. Waiting, she kept a tight hold on the horse's rope.

Merryn waved the light around, making sure they hadn't stumbled upon an animal's den. There were a few bones scattered at the back of the pocket in the rock face, but it was obvious they'd been there for many a year. There are no signs that the cave had been used recently.

Mounting the torch in a crag in the wall, she turned back to the mouth, calling for Cara to lift their equipment and supplies to her. Once in hand, she shoved it further back into the cave pocket. Merryn turned back to the mouth, anchoring herself as best she could. "Give me yer hand, Cara."

Having already secured the horse to a nearby tree, Cara took one last look behind her, then raised her hands to Merryn.

"Climb as I pull ya," Merryn grunted, pulling with all her body weight. She could hear a few rocks being displaced as Cara desperately pushed her booted feet against the wall of the rock face. "I've got'cha," Merryn gasped, moving further back into the space as Cara reached the mouth of the cave.

Glad to be in the chilled confines of the small cave, Cara slid down the inside wall, sighing as she sat. "I do not like this climbing," she panted, hearing the soft chuckle of her friend.

"'Tis better than bein' down there this night, lass." Merryn gathered the wood they'd brought up with them, creating a fire ring of rock before piling kindling for the burn.

Off in the not-so-far distance, thunder rumbled through the lightning brilliant skies.

"'T belly o' the beast is hungry tonight," Merryn said absently, tossing a few more sticks onto the fledgling fire, which she'd lit with their torch.

Cara set about camp duties, bringing out the skinned rabbit, caught earlier, as well as their pot and cooking utensils. Merryn set about finding a way to block the small entrance to their shelter with her cloak, as she could feel this was a bad storm coming. They needed more protection from it.

It wasn't long before they were settled. Merryn's cloak bowed by the incoming wind. She crawled across the floor, setting a few more rocks on the garment to keep it in place. Moving back to the fire, Merryn took a bit of hot rabbit in her mouth. She sucked in air to cool the morsel of meat. Finally she had to pinch it between her fingertips and pull it out into the air.

Cara laughed. "Silly girl."

Merryn glared before blowing on it and tossing it back into her mouth, chewing happily.

"'Tis good, lass. A witch with spices, ya're."

Cara shook her head, blowing on her own bit of meat. "Nay. No magic, Merryn. I am just skilled." She grinned.

Cara chewed happily, glad to be under shelter and safe. Then her thoughts began to turn towards dark areas, drifting among all the questions she had. Glancing up, she watched Merryn across the fire, drinking water from the bladder. Blue eyes locked on her from over the drinking bag. Slowly lowering it, Merryn swallowed and wiped her mouth.

"What?"

Cara chewed thoughtfully, trying to think of the best way to phrase her question. Finally she decided on honesty. "Why did ye try to kill Daniel?"

Merryn wasn't surprised by the question and had, in fact, been expecting it. With a sigh, she handed the water bladder over to Cara, who took it with a grateful smile. Merryn studied the fire for a moment as her mind raced back to the events of two nights ago.

"When he came to the camp, I knew he was trouble. I saw meself in 'im." Her voice softened, ashamed to tell Cara the next part, seeing her confusion. "I did the same, lass. Lyin', thievin'." She threw a bit of gristle into the fire, angry with herself. "When I saw 'im goin' through yer pouch and tryin' to steal me blade, I became lost in my own anger and shame." Her head dropped, but she held up her hand to halt Cara's crawl around the fire. "I lost control, Cara." *I saw that bloody soldier. I wanted ta kill 'im all over again.*

"Nay, Merryn," Cara said, brushing the stalling hand aside. "Yer strong. Ye grow stronger with the passage of each day." She looked deep into troubled blue eyes. "Embrace it, Merryn. Learn te use it."

They both turned as the wind and rain outside increased. The lightning was almost continuous, the thunder deafening. Cara trembled at the fierce sound. She had always hated thunder and lightning at night.

"Come, lass." Merryn took the Cara's bowl from her, stacking it inside hers, and placed them against the wall. Enough talk for tonight. She crawled over to the bedrolls, patting the spot next to her.

Cara scurried over, anxious to lie down, and hopefully fall asleep so she couldn't hear the storm anymore. She curled up next to Merryn, sighing in contentment as she felt the warmth of her friend begin to wrap itself around her like a blanket.

Merryn wove her arm around her, pulling her close. She felt Cara take her normal position — face buried in her neck with half of the girl's upper body on top of hers, a breast pressed against one of her own.

During the past few weeks, Merryn had begun to realize that the feel of the girl's body against her own caused a warmth to pass through her, resting in her stomach and between her legs. Her skin would become particularly sensitive, especially where their breasts touched. And when she had received a small kiss from her...Merryn rolled her eyes in pleasure at the thought.

Spending the first part of her childhood with the nuns, Merryn had been taught that carnal pleasure was a sin. She had taken these teachings to heart, though her natural curiosity had taken its course. She'd never experienced it first hand, but had seen carnality — in the wild, in the various taverns, and couples in dark alleys. She'd seen it all.

Merryn knew that what Cara made her feel were feelings of a carnal nature. Since she no longer believed in the God of her youth, she had also thrown out the doctrine damning the practice. But even so, what was right? Yes, coupling between a man and a woman was necessary to birth children. But was there more to it than that? If birthing children was all it was used for, why should Merryn bring herself pleasure of a carnal nature? The heat that coursed through her body when her own fingers explored, was the same sensation that Cara caused. Should she feel guilty? Was it wrong?

Cara raised her head, resting her cheek in her palm. Looking down at Merryn, she could tell she was deep in thought.

"Give ye two pence for yer thoughts," she said with a smile.

"Ya donna have two pence, lass." Merryn chuckled at the look that received. She shook her head, knowing there was no way she could tell Cara what she'd been thinking about. "Nothin'."

It was obvious Cara didn't believe her, but she said nothing, just stared down at the other girl. She studied the blue irises in Merryn's eyes.

"Ye have the most beautiful eyes," she said absently, brushing a few wild strands of dark hair from Merryn's face. "Like the sky of a summer solstice."

"Aye. And yers the grass below."

Cara smiled at that, feeling herself being drawn to the girl. She felt almost as comfortable with Merryn as she had with her own family. But in a different way. Merryn was so strong and beautiful. It was as if Cara couldn't get enough of her beauty, wanting to touch it, commit it to memory.

Tracing a finger along the bridge of Merryn's nose, as she had done so many times before, Cara leaned down a bit, brushing her lips across the girl's cheek. Merryn closed her eyes at the soft contact, her stomach doing a flip flop. She had to fight the shiver that threatened to rush through her body.

A bolt of lightning lanced through the night sky, flashing the cave for a moment before another crash of thunder ripped the night apart. Cara gasped.

"Shhh," Merryn cooed, turning her head so their lips were a fingernails width apart. She looked into Cara's frightened eyes. "'Tis alright, lass."

"I know I act foolish."

"Nay," Merryn whispered, shaking her head slightly. She felt Cara lean forward again, hesitating a small moment before bringing their lips together.

Cara's body was trembling, though only partially from the storm. She had lain next to Merryn for months, but never had they kissed while in their bedrolls. It didn't feel wrong to her, it just felt...intimate. She felt a vulnerability that she was unsure about, not even knowing if she really wanted it to go away.

Merryn sighed as she felt a gentle pressing against her lips instead of the usual brushing. She pressed her mouth against Cara's, her body becoming acutely aware of where her body touched Cara's. Cara brought one of her hands to Merryn's face, caressing her cheek and rubbing her thumb over the soft skin.

Cara kept her eyes closed, allowing her sense of touch to do the seeing for her. She could feel the softness of Merryn's skin, the fine bone structure beneath it. She could feel the heat of Merryn's body underneath her own.

Her eyes flew open when she felt herself being pulled fully on top of Merryn. She looked down into twinkling blue eyes, unsure of how to react to the warmth that began to suffuse her.

Merryn wrapped her arms around her, desperately wanting to feel the girl's weight on her. She looked up into Cara's beautiful, trusting face, the golden hair falling and acting as a curtain around them. Reaching up, she tucked one side of the girl's hair behind her back, where it fell around the other side of her face. In the light of the fire, not two arms lengths away, Cara's hair truly did look like spun gold.

Cara watched the way the light danced in Merryn's eyes, which were fixed so intently on her. She marveled at how beautiful the girl was. She looked like a goddess from ancient times. Closing her eyes, she brought their lips together once more, feeling the softness. Her body seemed to sink into Merryn's, feeling all of her soft places against her own.

Merryn ran her hands down the girl's back, feeling the strong plane and dip of her lower back, then slid them to Cara's sides on the return trip. It amazed her to feel the differences in their bodies, how much smaller Cara was than herself. Even so, she could feel the power locked within that small body.

Cara felt as though she'd been struck by one of the bolts of lightning raging outside. Merryn's hands left a crackle along their wake. She was buzzing, her body tingling everywhere she was touched.

Merryn moved her lips, opening them just enough to bring Cara's lower lip in between her own. She heard a slight gasp at that, but Cara quickly understood and suddenly the kiss had taken a turn from innocent exploration to sensual expression.

Cara and Merryn sighed into the kiss, one of Merryn's hands returning to the girl's hair, cupping the back of Cara's head to bring her even closer.

Outside the storm picked up even more, the rain and wind threatening to blow the cloak out of the cave opening, almost simultaneous lightning and thunder rocking the night.

Cara jumped off Merryn's body at the intense noise and sudden light. Merryn scurried over to the cave mouth, securing the makeshift door, shivering at the cold that she could feel just on the other side. As she crawled back over to the bedrolls, her heart swelled at the sight of Cara curled up, leaning against the cave wall. The poor girl was terrified.

Tending to the fire quickly, Merryn hurried back to their beds, wrapping Cara in protective arms.

"Try 'n get some sleep, lass," she whispered in the girl's ear. "Let yer dreams take ya from the storm."

Soon, both managed to fall asleep.

"Looks as though yer god has quite the temper," Merryn commented, looking at all the destruction around them. The storm from the night before had pulled trees up by their roots; branches and leaves lay in heaps where they'd been blown by the fierce winds, then pelted into mulch by the harsh deluge.

"Bloody right," Cara murmured, climbing over a felled tree. She was amazed to see how very different the forest looked after the storm. She couldn't imagine what it must have been like to be out in the storm. Their horse had been so badly frightened that she'd bolted, leaving but a piece of her tethering still tied to the tree next to the cave wall.

The sound of the ocean could be heard, not too far off to the north, the waves crashing against a cliff face. Another sound was heard, that of boots being suctioned into the mud. Curses were muttered as Merryn had either to get herself unstuck, or to help Cara.

"Wait, Merryn," Cara growled, leaning a hand against the trunk of a tree. Her boots were becoming so caked with mud that they were getting too heavy to lift. She looked at the sole of the boot, grimacing as she used her fingers to clean it, leaving four narrow trails through the goo. "Give me a dagger."

Merryn pulled one out of her baldric, balancing on one of her own feet as she too tried to clean her boot. She tossed the dagger into the mud at Cara's feet. Quickly the weapon sank to half the handle. Merryn grinned mischievously at the glare she got.

Muttering to herself, Cara tried to balance against the tree as she leaned over to pick up the dagger. The cold mud instantly chilled her fingers as she grabbed the handle and pulled the dagger out with a loud slurp.

"Bugger," Merryn muttered, nearly dropping her own dagger as she grabbed onto a tree with both hands. She looked down, trying to figure out what made her lose her balance. Glancing over at Cara, she saw that it hadn't just been her. Wide green eyes looked back at her briefly before looking to the ground at their feet.

Feeling steady, Merryn released her hold on the tree, carefully running her fingers down the blade of her dagger, sliding the mud down. The brown, gooey mess fell to the ground with a plop. She tucked the dagger back into her belt.

Feeling her irritation grow, Cara returned to her boot. She had removed most of the mud from the sole of her right boot. Putting her foot down, she lifted her other one, grunting slightly at the task. The mud was thick, heavy clay.

Suddenly there was a roaring sound and, with a yelp, Cara found herself lying on her back, mud oozing into every crevice. She lay still, trying to understand how she ended up looking into the blue skies above. Getting her breath back, she tried to find some purchase to push herself up. Suddenly she was back in the mud and moving.

Merryn shook mud-coated strands of her hair from her face, eyes huge as she tried to work out what had happened. She was no longer standing next to the tree but lying flat on her back. She also realized that her leg was beating to the rhythm of her heart, a shot of pain with every thump. Looking down the length of her body, she saw that her leg had been caught up in a small outcropping of rocks that surged above the surface of the mud. Luckily the mud that encased the leg was so cold, it was keeping her numb. She had a bad feeling about her injury.

Clearing her mind of this, she looked around, expecting to see a frightened Cara. She was nowhere to be seen.

"Cara?" Only silence answered. Even the echo of the forest was sucked up in the thick mud, which had shifted mightily in the landslide. With a small cry, Merryn managed to get herself free from the rocks. A white hot, shooting pain threw her back into the mud as she tried to bend her injured leg. Panting heavily as she tried to clear the blackness from the edges of her vision, Merryn tried a new tactic. With a heave, she managed to unbury her sword. Sitting up she thrust it into the mud, trying to bury it far enough down to get some stability. Taking several deep breaths, she prepared herself for the fresh pain.

Getting to her feet, Merryn tried to see what had happened and, more importantly, where Cara was. Her face was a mask of clenched pain as she turned in a slow circle, seeing nothing but a sea of thick mud, pushing against the standing trees in thick waves.

Realizing what had thrown her to the ground, Merryn felt the waves of panic crash against her heart. The mud had swept down the sloping forest floor, toward the cliffs that dropped to the ocean below.

"No," she breathed, balancing on her sword as she made her way as quickly as possible to the edge. "Cara!"

Teeth bared as she tried to ignore the pain of her injured leg, she went on. She had to be careful; the mud was slick and still unstable. Random branches, roots and rock outcroppings littered the area. She scanned each of them for any sign of Cara. She prayed that sign wouldn't be blood.

The forest floor suddenly sloped at a dangerous angle, the crashing waves of the ocean getting louder as the cliff edge came into sight.

Merryn felt her heart stop. She didn't realized her legs had given out from under her until she felt the sharp pain in her injured leg and the cold of the mud making solid contact with her backside. A cold numbness spread through her, making her start to tremble.

She felt a strange sensation behind her eyes, a sting. Something Merryn hadn't felt in many years. Lowering her head, Merryn let out a shaky breath.

"Ung."

Hearing the sound, Merryn lifted her head slowly, her eyes nearly glowing as the tears threatened to spill over. She listened, her entire body tuned to the world around her. Even the birds and animals of the forest hadn't recovered yet from the storm and the mudslide.

She heard grunting, gasping and the sound of rocks becoming loose, sliding down more rock.

Without thought, Merryn dragged herself through the mud, toward the cliff edge. The noises, though still faint, were getting louder.

Reaching the edge, Merryn squeezed her eyes shut, afraid of what she might see. After several deep breaths, she looked over the side. What she saw stunned her. Far below, huddled on a rock ledge, Cara looked back up at her. The only thing recognizable of the girl was her green eyes. The rest of her was completely covered with mud.

"Cara!" Merryn cried, her relief palpable. "Hold on, lass!" she called down. She could see the relieved smile on the girl's face, her teeth blindingly white against her mud-covered skin.

Her mind flipped over how to get Cara back up the cliff. The ledge she had landed on was too far above the sea for her to jump, yet too far below the cliff for her to climb back. Not to mention that the rocks were slimy and covered in slick mud. Untying her rope from around her waist, Merryn peeled it from the thick mud and dirt layers that had glued it to her tunic. She was doubtful it would be long enough but they had to try.

She looked around quickly, trying to find something to tie one end of the rope to. She spotted a thick trunk, the rest of the tree having broken off during the storm. She hissed as the jagged edges of the wood scraped against her skin as she tied the rope to the stump.

"Grab this, lass!" she called, tossing the rope down to the girl. Looking over the edge, she saw Cara trying to jump for the rope. Merryn cried out when the girl nearly fell off the ledge. Her heart pounding, making her leg hurt worse, she looked into the eyes that looked back up at her.

"'Tis not long enough! I cannot reach!" Cara yelled back.

Merryn growled deep in her throat, looking around frantically for an idea to strike her. Like a Phoenix in the ashes, she saw a slim column of rock sprouting up through the mud near the edge of the cliff. Scrambling over to it, she wrapped her hands around it, tugging with all her weight. The column didn't budge.

"Hold on, Cara!" she called down, letting the girl know she was still trying to rescue her. She untied the rope from the tree stump and wrapped the end of it around her own waist, tugging hard, making sure the knot would hold.

"Condatis, do not take us now," she whispered her prayer, then grabbed hold of the column of stone and swung around. Her body hung down the cliff face, the rope falling closer to Cara.

Cara gasped, seeing Merryn hurl herself over the edge, dangling. The rope swung gently just next to the ledge. With her heart pounding in her ears, Cara grabbed it, tugging slightly to let Merryn know she had it.

"Climb, lass!" Merryn called, desperation in her voice. "Be quick 'bout it!"

Cara heaved herself up, trying to get a good grip on the rope, which was just as muddy as she was. After a few slips, she got a good grip and began to scale the cliff wall.

Merryn could feel the strain in her arms, even as she did her best to hug the column close to her chest. The tug on her body, with each pull from Cara, was in turn reassuring and frightening. Merryn was terrified she'd lose her grip and they'd both fall to their deaths, yet each tug brought Cara closer to solid ground.

Cara's boot slipped from a medium-sized jutting rock. Her heart stopped for a moment, breath stolen from her lungs. Squeezing her eyes shut for only a moment to get her courage back, Cara began to climb again. She was now within reach of Merryn's boot.

Merryn felt a brief touch on her right boot. She sucked a breath in, about to open her mouth in warning about her left leg.

Cara had grabbed on to Merryn's left leg and almost let go of the rope when a shrill scream tore through the air. Cara was so shocked that she almost let go of the rope altogether. She had no idea what had happened but managed to get her grip back on the rope, having slid down slightly at the sudden chaos and was not touching Merryn.

Merryn could not breathe; her face was white and clammy as pain such as she'd never known vibrated through her. It took all she had to keep her arms wrapped around the stone column. She could no longer feel anything in her lower body, save for the pulsing of white pain which threatened to take her consciousness.

Sensing something was very wrong, Cara quickly scrambled back up to Merryn's body, tentatively touching the right leg. Merryn was trembling dangerously, but touching the leg didn't seem to make it worse.

Merryn could not speak, could not utter a sound, so lost was she in a sea of pain. Somewhere in the back of her head she heard Cara murmuring to her. Then she was aware of the discomfort of her chin skimming the rock beneath her as Cara climbed completely up her body, bumping the back of Merryn's head with her boot as she passed.

Her hold was getting weak.

Cara, on hands and knees as she reached the cliff top, turned to see Merryn, head down and arms shaking as she held onto the column of stone.

"Merryn," she breathed. She could tell the girl was about to let go. She grabbed her by her tunic and cloak, tugging. "Pull yerself up, Merryn," she grunted, her heels digging into the mud. "Help me, Merryn!" she cried, hearing the telltale ripping of fabric.

Merryn blinked rapidly, shaking her head to clear the fogginess from her eyes. She heard Cara's voice then saw her, pulling with all her might, trying to bring Merryn back from the edge.

Swallowing down her haze of pain, Merryn used her good leg to push herself back up. Once she felt her hands and knees come into contact with the slick rock of the cliff top, she leaned over. The remains of her breakfast were pushed out by the nausea caused by the intense pain.

When Merryn had finished vomiting, she looked over at Cara and relief flooded her. She grabbed Cara to her, and they both fell into the mud as they clung to each other.

Cara, still unsure about what happened, felt Merryn bury her face in her neck, Merryn's strong grip on her almost painful. No doubt Cara's hold was just as intense.

Merryn pulled away, bringing her finger to Cara's face, tracing a channel through the mud. She gave a weak smile. "Are ya alright, lass?" she asked, her voice weak from the pain.

Cara nodded, bringing their foreheads together. She absorbed the presence of her friend. She was still in awe that she was alive, convinced that she'd never survive when the mud completely covered her, followed by the push over the cliff, and then having no idea how she was to get back up the cliff.

Finally coming around, she pulled back, looking down the length of Merryn's sprawled body. Immediately she went to work, trying to find out what had happened.

"Yaaaaaa!" Merryn's head hit the mud with a wet squish. Cara quickly took off the boot on Merryn's left leg, then grabbed a dagger from Merryn's belt, slicing the leg of her britches open. The bone had not broken through the skin, but it was deathly pale with the bruising around the break a sickening dark color in contrast.

"I think I set yer bone when I hung onto it," she said. Merryn said nothing, just nodded slightly, trying to keep her breathing under control. "I need a brace." Cara grabbed for the blade that had been tossed near the edge of the cliff during the chaos.

"Nay," Merryn said, her voice quiet and breathy. She put a hand to the girl's. "Not that."

"Then what..." Cara stopped for a moment, closing her eyes. She slowed her own breathing as she concentrated on the vision that began to appear before her mind's eye.

Merryn watched in fascination as Cara, eyes still closed, took one of the daggers, and began to slice into the material of her own dress, shredding the skirt.

"Forgive me, Merryn," she whispered, and began to tear the pant leg to shreds. Eyes opening, Cara moved to her knees, using her hands to gather great amounts of mud around Merryn's leg, scooping it up to cover it, packing it in tightly. Merryn bared her teeth, but said nothing, taking her pain in shallow breaths.

Cara smoothed her hand over her creation, streamlining it down either side of Merryn's leg. With a gentle command for her patient to hold still, she wrapped the shreds of cloth from her dress around it. When the mud-packed leg was completely covered and tied tight, though loose enough to not cause pain, Cara looked at her friend.

"This must dry, Merryn," she explained softly. Cara stood, looking around. She noticed that not too far away the mud wasn't very deep. Getting to her knees, she quickly began to push the mud aside, making a dry spot where Merryn could lie down.

"Come, Merryn," she whispered as she lifted Merryn behind her shoulders and grabbing hold of her under her arms. "'Twill hurt, but you must not allow your leg to drag the ground."

Merryn nodded, not fully understanding, but trusting her friend. A cry ripped from her throat as she held the leg aloft, her body being jarred as it was dragged toward the cleared area.

Getting her settled as comfortably as possible, Cara set out with a quick kiss to Merryn's cheek and a whispered, "I will return."

Merryn sucked in lungfuls of fresh, clean air. Cara had left her with Merryn's own cloak rolled up under her head, the warm sun shining down on her face, warming her still pain-chilled body. Cara had tried to get her some herbs for pain, but her pouch was filled with mud, and all medicines inside were ruined.

She could feel an ache in her leg, which had turned into a dull, yet powerful rhythm, still beating with each pump of her heart.

Merryn tried to relax, consciously easing her breathing into a steady rhythm. She was trying to calm her heartbeat; the slower her heart beat, the less it pounded through her leg. She could feel the mud drying, tightening around her leg, becoming stiff. She was amazed at the way it helped with the pain.

"How are you?" Cara asked, kneeling next to her friend.

Merryn looked at her. She hadn't even heard her come back. "I'll live."

"Indeed." Cara sat, the sun shining down on her legs, the skirt being torn nearly to mid-thigh. She set down the handful of roots and weeds she'd found. Taking a pinch of damlon weed, she tore the stocks in half, tossing the scaly side to the ground, the leafy side going into her mouth. She winced at the bitter taste but chewed quickly. Taking the tiny ball of mush out of her mouth, she grabbed the hard, scaly part of the weed she'd discarded and wrapped the mush inside. Packing it all into a small, hard wad, she grabbed the water bladder. "Lift yer head."

Merryn did as she was told, opening her mouth so Cara could place the small bit on her tongue. She dutifully drank from the bladder, swallowing it down.

"Should start working soon, Merryn." Cara leaned over, giving her a small kiss on the temple. "There is a swollen stream just over that way," she pointed back toward the west. "I'm going te wash then come back te wash ye." She stood up, smoothing muddy strands of hair out of her face. She smiled down at Merryn. "If yer still awake."

Cara hurried back into the forest, a dagger at the ready. She couldn't imagine anyone out in this miserable mud, but anything was possible.

Cara was just now getting her breath back after what had happened. She had been so frightened and, when she'd hurt Merryn, she'd felt awful. True, she'd had no idea that the girl was injured, but still. Although, she would have had to set Merryn's leg anyway, her hanging on the broken limb did get that over with.

Setting all their mud-covered and -filled belongings at the side of the small body of water, she took one more look around before removing what was left of her dress. She'd be better to tear it all up for scrap. She would have to have a new outfit now. This one had become indecent. She would like to get some britches; they seemed far more practical for life on the road.

The water was freezing, most of it rain water from the night before. It stole Cara's breath away. She shivered as she carefully made her way in. She made quick work of dunking her entire body, crying out from the shock. Her skin exploded in goosebumps, and her nipples were like tiny rocks.

Teeth chattering, she did the best she could to rinse the mud from her skin and hair, as all her cleaning herbs and mixtures had been destroyed in the mudslide. Her hair was sticky, making her grimace involuntarily. Her village had never understood her need for cleanliness, and she knew Merryn thought she was crazy as a loon.

Merryn.

Cara couldn't keep the smile from her face, the thought of her friend more powerful than the cold, which was slowly turning her lips blue. She thought of the night before in the cave. She had always loved Merryn's kisses, but last night...

Cara's eyes closed, and she wrapped her arms around her own body. A wave of heat burned hot in her in spite of the frigid temperature of the water in which she stood waist deep.

Once Cara had accidentally seen Mark and Muriel in his cooper shop. He had her against a table, her skirts up around her waist. Cara had been so embarrassed, that she quickly turned away. But the noises they made...there was no way to run from those. Red from head to toe, Cara had wandered into the woods, thinking about what she'd seen and heard. She remembered Mark's big, calloused hands on Muriel's breasts; the farmer's daughter's dress was open, the top laces undone.

She had never been able to forget those images. When she'd heard stories of how awful the act between men and women was, and how much it hurt, Cara had brought those images to mind. Muriel hadn't looked as though she were in pain. She had looked as though she were enjoying what Mark was doing to her.

Cara looked down at her own breasts, the nipples still hard and a deep rose color. She brought her hands up, cupping the breasts. Her palms were painful against her cold nipples. Soon the warmth from her hands eased the rigid peaks, making the skin soft and pliant.

Afraid of catching a chill, Cara quickly finished washing the mud from her body and hurried from the cold depths of the water. The sun of high day felt glorious on her cold skin. She wished for a warm rock to lie upon and dry. Alas, with the mud, it was not to be.

Merryn awoke to a crackling fire and a gentle touch. Opening her eyes, she was surprised to see that the sun had set, leaving the night with all its twinkling lights above. Her eyes moved to the left where she saw just the edge of cloth, and could feel the cool dampness of moisture.

"Ye really shouldn't play in mud puddles, Merryn," Cara said, her voice soft and soothing near her head. Merryn smiled.

"Do me best." She looked up at Cara, seeing the twinkle in her eyes and the color of her skin. "Bathe, did ya?"

"I did. We need more cleansing herbs." Cara wrung out the rag she was using to clean the mud from Merryn's face. She washed her patient's neck, gently wiping away the dirt and grime from the day. "My dress is ruined. We'll have to make our way te town soon."

Merryn nodded, sighing in pleasure at Cara's gentle touch.

Cara continued to bathe the girl with her rag and clean water, fingers lightly caressing where she had recently cleaned. Merryn's skin was so soft under her fingers. She smiled as Merryn sighed, her head falling to the side, giving her more access.

The need was too great to resist. Cara bent her head and placed gentle lips against the side of Merryn's neck. Heat radiated from the flesh, nearly burning Cara's lips. She lifted her head slightly, glancing into Merryn's face. There was a slight smile curving those full lips.

Lowering her head once more, Cara's eyes closed, and she brushed her lips over Merryn's ear, then back to her neck. She pressed them to the warm skin once more, a lingering caress.

Merryn sighed, tingles flowing all through her body. She forgot all about the pain in her leg as wonderful sensations awakened within her. As her body began to respond, she reached a hand up, caressing Cara's newly bared leg. The skin of her thigh was soft, yet prickly with tiny blonde hairs. Their months of walking had hardened the muscles, making her legs shapely and beautiful.

Cara moved her body so she lay alongside Merryn. She rested on her elbow, looking down upon her friend. "How is yer leg?" she asked, running lazy fingers back and forth over Merryn's arm, making the girl tingle even more. Her eyes closed as warmth flooded her.

"I'd feel better if ya'd kiss me, lass," she breathed, her heart pounding. She didn't see Cara's smile at her words.

Though they'd just kissed the night before, Cara had almost forgotten how soft Merryn's lips were. She gently moved her body so their breasts were touching, though was mindful of Merryn's lower body, staying clear of her leg still wrapped in hardened mud and cloth.

Merryn sighed into Cara's mouth, sensations exploding as she felt soft breasts upon her own. She brought her hands up, burying them in Cara's hair. The strands were stiff and clumped. She knew it must be maddening to Cara to be so dirty. Pushing the thought away, she deepened the kiss, bringing Cara's bottom lip inside her mouth. She wanted to feel it, taste it.

Cara gasped slightly as she felt the warm softness of Merryn's tongue gloss over her lip. It felt wonderful and sent the most surprising sensations through her body. She opened her mouth a little, feeling Merryn slide her tongue just to the very edge of the inside of Cara's lips.

Cara felt an ache between her legs, a pulsing that was pleasurable yet painful at the same time. She didn't understand it, but knew that Merryn was both the cause and cure. Moving her body, she lay carefully on top of her, feeling the cold smoothness of the mud pack on Merryn's leg. For a moment she almost pulled away, worried she'd cause pain. Merryn stopped her with a firm hand to her hip, bringing Cara's mouth back to her own.

Merryn was becoming lost in the feel of Cara's mouth and body on her own. She was slowly, tentatively exploring the inside of Cara's mouth with her tongue — feeling her teeth, the insides of both lips, her tongue.

A shiver ran through her, landing squarely between her legs as Cara shifted, her leg falling slightly between Merryn's thighs. The slight pressure between her legs nearly made her jump out of her skin. Her mouth opened with a soft gasp, and her hands flew to the girl's hips. Cara wasn't sure what she'd done, but she liked Merryn's reaction. She left Merryn's mouth to kiss her neck again. Taking what she'd just learned, she placed gentle kisses along Merryn's jaw then lightly touched her tongue to the side of her warm neck.

Merryn gasped loudly, taking in a mouthful of air at the contact. Her hands pressed into the soft flesh of Cara's hips. Cara's mouth continued, her tongue taking in the taste of Merryn's skin, sweat, and the earthiness of left over mud that had yet to be wiped away. Her body began to respond, communicating with Merryn's.

Suddenly feeling Merryn's body stiffen, Cara stopped. She knew that either the injured leg had been bumped, or that Merryn was in pain. Lifting her head, she looked into the beautiful face of the one person who was her world. Merryn's eyes were squeezed shut, her face ashen.

Carefully climbing off her, Cara quickly grabbed another of the medicine bundles she'd made while Merryn had slept on. Grabbing the water bladder, she gently held up her head.

"Swallow this, my love," she whispered. Merryn did as she was told. She had been rocked to the core as the healing effects of the herbs had suddenly vanished, making her realize with painful clarity that her leg was indeed broken. The pain wasn't as intense as it had been before, but she felt chilled and hot at the same time, her skin crawly and clammy.

Cara set the bladder aside after Merryn had swallowed her medicine. She scooted over to her, gently laying Merryn's head in her lap, cradling her and running her fingers through the long, dark strands, until finally Merryn's lids fell heavy and she fell asleep.

Part 6

"What?" Cara asked, starting to feel slightly irritated as she looked up at her friend.

"Healing herbs?" Merryn asked yet again. She reached down to balance herself, her palm placed against the warm, scratchy hair of the ass she sat upon.

"Ye do not believe me?" Cara asked, brows raised. Merryn said nothing, muttering to herself. Cara turned back to the road ahead, relishing the sun which warmed her face. She had made her way to a small town that morning, using what little they had left to trade for some things they needed. Including a way for Merryn to travel and stay off her leg.

The gentle breeze blew through Cara's new dress, weaving the material around her legs. It felt wonderful. It also felt wonderful to be clean, with her long hair falling down her back in golden waves. She had been able to restock her medicines, which she then traded for a donkey.

"Did'ja get more o' this, lass?" Merryn asked, holding up the last little bit of smoked meat she was eating. Cara chuckled, nodding.

"Though no more fer ye today," she said, waggling a warning finger at her friend. Merryn rolled her eyes. She had hated to stay back at camp, feeling useless. Not for the first time, she cursed that bloody mudslide and storm.

Cara walked contentedly next to the lumbering animal, now understanding why the owner had been so willing to part with the beast. Simon walked slowly, stopping to sniff and taste everything he came upon in the road. Cara could tell Merryn was getting frustrated, too.

Merryn had become practiced at ignoring the constant ache in her leg, yet still every step the animal took jarred it again. She could only do so much to keep the mud encrusted leg from banging against the donkey's barrel rib cage.

"Are ye not going to answer me, then?" Cara asked, glancing up at her friend again.

"Aye, where would I go... Let me think," Merryn said, chewing on the inside of her cheek. "I want to see my homeland, lass. Go ta my people, I would."

"Te Ireland?"

"Aye." Merryn smiled at the thought. She'd dreamt of her homeland, her people, and their ways. "And ya, lass?"

Cara looked up at her, using a hand to shield her eyes from the sun. She smiled wide. "Ireland sounds beautiful."

Merryn smiled back, but the smile slowly began to slide from her face. Looking around, a wrinkle of concentration gathered between her eyes.

"Merryn..."

Merryn held up a hand, sniffing the air.

"Arawn," she whispered, tugging on the donkey's reins, trying to lead the stubborn animal to the east.

Cara brought her hand to her nose to try and block out the sweet stench that was getting stronger the further they went into the woods.

"The sweet smell of death," Cara whispered, a small cabin coming into view. Merryn nodded.

"Aye, lass. Arawn has been here."

The cabin was dark, a bag lying upon the ground outside the door, crops rolled out to dry on the ground. They were half eaten by insects and rats.

Cara helped Merryn dismount the animal and let her lean on her as they made their way toward the closed plank door. The sweet smell of rot was getting stronger, burning their lungs and making Cara's eyes water.

"Stay here, Merryn," she said, helping her to sit on a barrel. Merryn tried to protest, but Cara stopped her with a soft kiss. "Return, I will."

Cara did not want to see what she knew she'd see, but she also knew they had to find a safe place to stay while Merryn's leg mended. It would take a great deal of reasoning to get her to agree, but Cara knew it was the best thing to do. Merryn's leg would never heal if she was forever on it, climbing, running, and hunting.

The silence of the dead was an eerie thing to feel. The sound of their lifeless bodies could be deafening. Glancing over her shoulder, she saw Merryn still seated on the barrel, looking as though she'd jump off any moment. Cara held up a hand, silently telling her to stay where she sat. She could tell that Merryn didn't like it, but she did stay seated.

Cara rested her hand on the frame of the door, the other on the door itself, and gently pushed on the door. When it didn't budge, she pushed harder. With a loud creak, the door swung open, releasing such a pungent odor of death, Cara almost fell to her knees. She held her breath and bravely made her way into the darkened cabin.

Sunlight sliced through the cracks and slats in the walls, crisscross beams tracing patterns on the dirt floor. A table could be seen against the far left wall. Various objects were silhouetted on the table's surface; she thought she could make out a lantern and a jug with a rounded handle.

Cara's gaze traveled down a shaft of sunlight to see the blackened fingers of a hand hanging off the edge of a pallet. The thumb had been partially eaten by some sort of rodent. Cara brought her hand to her mouth as she quickly tore her eyes from the sight. She saw a wooden plate with rotten fruit lying on the floor, worm holes blackened and shriveled.

Cara nearly jumped out of her skin when she felt a touch on her shoulder. Whirling round, she saw Merryn leaning against the doorframe, using her sword as a walking stick.

"Dead," Cara said simply, turning to walk out. Merryn nodded, knowing as much. "Black sickness." Again, Merryn nodded.

"Should go, lass." She looked up at the skies. Blasted spring rain.

"Nay." Cara looked at her friend, eyes serious and stubborn. "Ye need to rest, Merryn." She nodded toward the cabin behind her. "Take care of that poor soul, I will, then ye shall rest."

Merryn studied the girl. Surely she wasn't serious? She shook her head.

"Nay, Cara. 'Tis cursed."

Cara rolled her eyes, walking to the donkey. She grabbed their flint stones from the saddle bag and walked back toward the cabin. Merryn stopped her with a touch to her shoulder. She gazed intently at her.

"Nay," she hissed. Cara held her gaze.

"Merryn, we cannot go on with yer leg such as 'tis. 'Twill never heal. We must get ye settled, and I know ye saw that stormin' sky," she said, pointing to the sky. Merryn sighed, shaking her head.

"Nay," she said stubbornly.

"Ye've no choice. Simon is bein' as stubborn as ye. I am not goin' te be stuck out in the rain cause of yer stubborn arse." With that she took another deep breath, then stepped inside the cabin. Walking over to the table, she used what little light there was to see the lantern. It took a few licks of the flint, but she got her spark, setting the wick aflame.

She kept her eyes closed, not wanting to see what lay to her right, what was left of the previous tenant. Instead, she grabbed a rat-eaten blanket she saw in the corner of the room and threw it over the body.

"Merryn?" she called, setting the flint stones down. She left the lantern burning as she left the cabin, taking several deep breaths as she walked into the fresh air of the day. "We must burn this poor soul."

"Aye."

Night was beginning to fall as Cara laid the last piece of wood on the wrapped body, still on its sleeping pallet. It had taken some effort to get it out of the cabin, as she had to work alone. Once clear of the narrow door, she had tied the pallet to Simon, finally getting the beast to pull it free as dusk fell upon the land.

Cara stood before the fire, the flames painting her features golden orange. Head bowed, she raised her hands, a rosary wrapped around her clasped palms. Her lips moved in silent prayer over the lost soul of the one who had died alone. A single tear escaped a closed lid, sliding lazily over her cheek and off the side of her chin, landing on her left thumb.

Her heart filled with grief and sorrow, Cara set the soul free.

She could see the man in his cabin, the sickness coming on over the span of three days. Alone, scared, and huddled up on the simple bed roll, he lay down on his side, his breath coming in short spasms, his eyes open wide as he looked to the Heavens. A hand came into Cara's view, reaching for his hand, which hung off the pallet. She realized it was her own hand, taking the trembling hand of the man. He looked at her, a smile of thanks on his features, darkened by the black sickness. Lesions dotted his features, his skin looked bruised and beaten.

She could feel the coolness of his fingers as the life began to bleed from him with each labored breath.

Sleep now. Sleep.

With a final, wheezing breath, his fingers relaxed in Cara's, his head falling back, eyes forever frozen to the skies.

"Cara?" Merryn said, her voice soft. Cara's eyes opened, filled with tears. With a cry of grief, she turned to Merryn, burying herself in her arms.

Merryn held the girl as she cried for long moments, stroking her back and hair. Finally Cara sniffled out the rest of her pain, then raised her head with a grateful smile. Merryn returned that smile with a small nod.

"T' benzoin 'n amber is burnin', lass."

"Thank ye, Merryn." She turned to the pyre once more, then turned to head back toward the cabin, whose lantern light could be seen through the dark. Merryn walked alongside her friend, using a tall branch she'd found as a walking stick.

To Merryn's consternation, Cara had insisted that everything in the cabin be burned along with its owner. All that remained in the near empty cabin was the table and the man's lantern.

Exhausted, both laid out their bedrolls on the dirt floor and fell fast asleep.

Merryn woke up, looking around, disoriented. The log walls that surrounded her allowed shafts of morning sunshine in, blazing bright streaks across the floor. Cara was nowhere to be seen.

With a grunt from exertion, Merryn got herself to her feet, holding onto the edge of the heavy table while she grabbed her walking stick. She stood there for a moment, gathering the energy to walk. The mud that tightly held her leg together was heavy and took much time to maneuver.

"Cara?" she called, limping out of the cabin. The sun hit her face with welcoming warmth. Shielding her eyes, she looked around the small property. Simon was tethered to a wooden water bin, with wild grass piled near him. The donkey drank noisily, glancing up at Merryn before turning back to his breakfast.

"Good morn." Cara stepped out of the woods with a bright smile on her face and a small cloth pouch in her hand. She walked over to Merryn, laying a gentle kiss to her lips. She raised her pouch. "Mornin' meal." She hurried past her, into the cabin, where she set her bundle down, then reached up and tore the heavy cloth from the window. The small structure was filled with bright sunshine, making Cara's smile broaden even more.

Merryn made her way back into the cabin, watching Cara, who was actually humming. She couldn't help her own smile as she leaned against the frame of the door, walking stick resting inside her bent arm.

Cara grabbed the saddle bag from the floor, taking out wrapped dry strips of meat. Placing them on the table, she set them aside, focusing her attention on the pouch. Quickly opening it, she took out some shiny, red berries, plump and filled with sweet juices.

Merryn's nose was taking over for her, making her take wobbly steps toward the table. She stopped when Cara glanced back at her.

"Somethin' ye want?" she asked, her voice low and teasing. Merryn blushed, turning away. She heard the soft chuckle of her friend then felt a hand on her arm. Cara helped her sit back down on their bedrolls, promising breakfast with a kiss.

Cara cut the meat up into bite-sized cubes, put them into a wooden bowl, and the berries in a second bowl. Tucking the water bladder, freshly filled, under her arm, she knelt beside Merryn.

"I have brought to you all that is good 'n sweet." Cara gently took Merryn's walking stick, setting it aside. Putting her hands on her shoulders, she nudged her friend to sit back against the wall, making sure the girl's injured leg was properly raised and padded.

Merryn watched all of this, loving to watch every move Cara made. She was fascinated with every movement, every word, every thought Cara made, said, or had. She watched the way the girl's hands moved so graceful and tender. Even the way her fingers wrapped around the walking stick was graceful, treating a piece of wild wood with the gentle touch of pure gold.

Cara turned twinkling eyes to her friend, now that she was sure she was comfortable. Taking the bowl of meat, she raised it, snatching a small piece between her fingers, and brought it to Merryn's lips.

"Open," she said, a gentle command.

Merryn opened her lips, watching Cara as she gently tucked the meat inside her mouth. She could taste just the barest hint of Cara's skin on her tongue as fingers were drawn away, and she began to chew.

Cara felt a slight shiver down her spine at the soft, brief touch of Merryn's tongue against the tip of her finger. She plucked a piece of meat for herself, quickly chewing as she selected another for Merryn. The very tip of Merryn's tongue glistened in the sunlight as she awaited her next bite. Cara smiled at this, then placed a second piece of meat in her mouth.

Merryn watched as Cara looked at her mouth and lips as she chewed. She was amused to see those green eyes follow her tongue as it swiped across her bottom lip, catching a bit of spice from the piece of meat.

Cara felt her breath hitch, watching that tongue. Suddenly she wanted that tongue badly. Setting the bowl aside, she raised a hand, cupping Merryn's cheek and bringing her face up, as Cara rose on her knees.

Merryn closed her eyes as she felt Cara's breath upon her brow. Soft lips touched that same brow, moments later, followed by kisses to her forehead and both cheeks. She waited, heart pounding, until finally she felt the lips on her own.

With a sigh, Cara leaned into Merryn, the hand upon her cheek sliding around to the back of her head, soft hair brushing against her fingers.

She tilted her head allowing Merryn's lips to mold to her own before opening them, allowing her tongue to enter.

Merryn's hunger for food was quickly overtaken by a hunger of another kind. She brought both her hands up, cupping Cara's head, kissing her deeply, with a great passion she found within.

Cara felt herself being pulled into Merryn's lap. She rested her knees on either side of Merryn's outer thighs.

"I thinks t' mornin' meal c'n wait, lass," Merryn whispered. "I wish," she looked into Cara's flushed face. "I know not what I wish," she said, not sure how to put her body's wants into words. She didn't understand what she needed, only that she *needed*.

Cara saw something in Merryn's eyes that called to her, and her body wanted badly to respond. Thinking back to Muriel and Mark, she did the only thing she could think of, her instinct speaking for desires she did not understand.

Taking Merryn's hand in amazingly calm, trusting fingers, Cara rested it on her own breast.

Merryn's breath hitched and a jolt of sensation shot between her legs, almost making her cry out with its intensity. With her other hand, Merryn cupped Cara's face.

"Merryn, yes," Cara whispered, her sweet voice breathy at the unexpected pleasure of Merryn's touch upon her breast.

Merryn looked at her hand, marveling at the gift she held. She was surprised to feel the flesh beneath her palm respond to her touch as Cara's nipple grew rigid and hard. She had seen those nipples many, many times while they bathed, and could picture the dark color so clearly in her mind.

At Cara's soft whimper, Merryn looked into her face, seeing Cara's eyes closed and her lips slightly parted as her head fell back. Merryn brought her lips to the girl's throat, tasting her skin, hearing more of the soft sounds Cara made deep in her throat. She brought her free hand to Cara's other breast, where the nipple was already hard in anticipation.

Cara felt lost in a sea of sensation — pleasure seeped through her from the points of her breasts to between her legs, where she was damp with what she had come to realize was her wanting for Merryn. She needed...she needed so much, such pressure and pulsing.

Merryn's mouth slid down Cara's throat, teeth nipping at the skin she found at the hollow. Cara moaned, her head falling further back. Hands leaving Cara's breasts, Merryn used nimble fingers to gently tug at the laces of the new dress' bodice. She wanted more skin to taste.

Cara felt Merryn's arms wrap around her back and clutch the back of her shoulders, allowing Cara to lean back into Merryn's embrace. As she did, she felt Merryn's mouth on her upper chest, licking along the bones of her shoulders as one side of the dress slipped from it. The top of her cleavage was exposed, to Merryn's hungry eyes.

"So lovely, lass," she whispered, her voice reverent.

Cara gasped as a wet tongue teased the top of her right breast. Her eyes opened, and she looked down at Merryn, seeing her eyes closed and her face flushed with passionate discovery. She wished to feel Merryn's body upon her own.

Gently, she pulled away, stopping any protest with two fingers to Merryn's lips. She climbed off Merryn's lap, and laid herself back on the blankets. She reached for Merryn, gently tugging on her hand. Merryn carefully got herself turned around, mindful of her leg.

Cara moaned at the feel of Merryn's body pressing into her own. Merryn held herself still, absorbing the feel of Cara beneath her. Finally she raised her head, looking deep into the most beautiful green eyes, seeing the love and want reflected in them.

Cara brought Merryn down to her, bringing their lips together. She had no idea what she needed or wanted Merryn to do, but she knew that she needed to ease the pressure that was building between her legs. Her hips were moving of their own accord, Merryn's meeting them with her own rhythm.

Merryn brought a hand down to Cara's hip, her fingers sliding between the girl and the bedding, feeling Cara's backside fill her hand. She pressed against it, bringing the girl's body even closer to her own. Cara gasped, her own hand running down Merryn's back, squeezing the flesh, arching up into her.

The ache between Merryn's legs was almost painful, pounding throughout her entire body. She needed to ease that ache. Using her knee, she pushed into Cara's legs until they opened, allowing Merryn to slip between. Her head shot up as Cara's thigh made contact between her legs. A wave of sensation shot through her body, and by the way Cara cried out and clung to her, she was experiencing the same sensation.

It took a moment for Cara to catch her breath as she pressed herself against Merryn.

Holding still for a moment, Merryn clung to Cara, holding herself tightly to the girl's thigh, pleasure echoing through her. It wasn't until she felt Cara began to move her hips against her that she took a breath, moving her own hips.

A bud of sensation was planted in Cara's lower belly, and it was quickly beginning to bloom into a flower of pure pleasure, its petals reaching all throughout her body. She cried out, her arms wrapping tightly around Merryn's body as she convulsed. It wasn't long before she felt Merryn's own body still, as a gurgled cry erupting from her throat.

It took Merryn a moment for reality to come back to her in the form of a small cabin with a warm body beneath her own. Raising herself on her hands, she looked down into Cara's flushed face.

"What've we done?" she asked, her body still pulsing. Cara smiled, shaking her head.

"I know not. 'Twas beautiful."

"Aye." Merryn lowered herself, taking Cara's lips in a soft kiss. She pressed her forehead to that of the girl. "'M hungry."

Hearing Cara singing to herself as she gathered branches in the woods around the cabin, Merryn pressed two branches together as she sat outside the cabin on the ground. She held the branches firmly, ticking fingers off silently in her head. She looked at her handy work, examining the hold and strength of the wood as well as the glue that had been made when they boiled the swim bladder from their dinner the previous night.

"It'll work," she muttered to herself, banging the wood against the ground, pleased when the wood did not slip or falter. She heard the soft, sweet voice of Cara entering into the clearing of the cabin. Looking up, she saw Cara carrying large branches tucked under her arm. "Bring 'em 'ere, lass."

Cara dropped the branches and squatted beside her. She looked over what had already been done. The frame was sturdy and solid.

"Merryn?" she asked, her voice soft, filled with question.

"Aye?" she said absently, setting the frame aside and beginning to free the new branches of twigs and offshoots.

"Do ye like it here?"

"Aye."

Cara smiled, falling back to sit on her bottom, ankles crossed, and leaning back on her hands. "As do I."

Merryn glanced up, seeing the look of contented happiness on Cara's face. She rubbed her thumb over the handle of her dagger for a moment, contemplating the girl before her.

"Ya wish ta stay." It was a statement, not a question. Cara met her eyes and, with a smile, nodded.

"Aye, that. 'M happy." Cara studied Merryn's eyes, thoughts hidden behind them. "Are ye not?"

As Merryn studied the other girl, almost missing her question, she felt a sense of peace steal over her, a sense of belonging that she had never known. Family.

After a moment, during which Cara had started to squirm, Merryn nodded.

"Aye. That I am."

Cara's smile was blinding. Merryn couldn't help but return it. A quick kiss, and the girl was up on her feet once more.

"'M goin' ta burn more benzoin and amber," she announced, disappearing inside the cabin. Soon Merryn could smell the fragrant crystals wafting out into the late afternoon. They'd burnt some every day over the two weeks they'd been at the cabin to help with the smell. Death almost seemed never to have lived there at all.

As night fell, Merryn brought in the newly made bed pallet, laying it against the wall. Cara stood back, watching in amazement at what had been created. Merryn quickly covered the pallet with their layers of bedding.

"'Twill be nice ta be off the floor," Cara said quietly, leaning against the wall to stay out of the way. The cabin was small, and only one person could really be active at once.

Stepping back, Merryn admired her handy work. She'd never been much of a builder but had done a good job. She knew their sleep tonight would be much better than it had been over the span of the past months. She blushed lightly at the thought of what else would be better.

Turning her face away from Cara's very keen eyes, Merryn finished getting their sleeping area ready then turned to her friend.

"Ye ready, then?" Cara asked, pushing over a barrel for Merryn to sit upon. She nodded, sitting. Cara sat on a second barrel, bringing the girl's injured left leg up and resting the foot in her own lap. "Yell if I go too deep."

Merryn nodded, handing over the small mallet she'd made to use on the pallet. Cara took it, setting it in her lap. She used what was left of a fingernail to pick the edge of the fabric dressing away from the light brown, dried mud underneath. Finally peeling it all off, she took the mallet, pressing the point of a particularly dull dagger against the side of the leg, and tapped the metal tip lightly against the hard packed mud.

Merryn watched with curious eyes as Cara tapped an even line down the length of the encasement. Small cracks began to spread through the mud, and small chunks of it fell to the dirt floor.

"Here we are," Cara whispered, setting aside her tools, and gently tugging at the ends of the mud sleeve. Merryn winced slightly, a sharp pain shooting briefly through her leg before the cool, night air hit the pale, shriveled skin that had been hidden away for weeks.

One side of the mud cast completely fell free, cracking into several large pieces and dusty chunks. Merryn's eyes closed at how good it felt to be rid of that heavy monstrosity. That relief was quickly taken over as Cara carefully pulled the other half off. When the mud had been wet, it had suctioned to all the tiny black hairs on her leg, and they ripped out of her flesh as the mud came off.

Cara dropped the tools and took the small vile of Carmelite water from the table. Uncorking the bottle, she poured some of the scented oil into her palm, warming it in-between her hands before rubbing it into the tender flesh of Merryn's calf.

She glanced up at her patient. "How does it feel?" she asked softly. Merryn sighed in contentment.

"'Tis good, lass."

"Can ye walk?" Cara sat back, giving her room to stand. Merryn winced slightly as she lowered her leg to the floor. It felt no more than a feather. She gave Cara an encouraging smile, then slowly raised herself to her feet. She was shaky, having to grab the hand that Cara offered, but once steady, she let go and stood on her own.

"Hurts a bit," Merryn said, tentatively taking a step, then another, then a third. She reached the far wall, slowly turning and walking back to a smiling Cara.

Spitting out the mouthful of cold water, Merryn glanced up as she heard footsteps. Tucking a couple of lovage leaves into her mouth, she began to chew, the spicy taste replacing that of the morning.

She could hear three steps in all — two feet and a walking stick. Merryn limped slightly as she walked over to the cabin, her sword in view. She could still hear Cara inside the cabin, chopping the meat Merryn had just brought back from her morning hunt.

He came around the bend in the path, breath coming in bursts from his tired body. Merryn stepped away from the cabin with her blade, spitting out some of the chewed lovage.

"God's blessings to ye, lassie," the good friar gasped as he entered the yard. He stopped, leaning on his stick as he looked around the sun-filled day.

Merryn took a step toward him, never taking her eyes off his stick. She said nothing.

The man with the thin, graying hair smiled at her, his grizzled face creasing. "'Tis a fine morn', God gave us."

"Aye. What say ya, ol' man?"

"Where be Ben?" The old friar finally reached Merryn, his breath rank and smelling of wine.

"Dead. Taken by t' black sickness, he was." Merryn cocked her head slightly, squinting in the early morning sun.

"Mm," the friar nodded. "Thought he may. Odd lad, that one. Lived all 'lone." The friar tucked his tall walking stick into the crook of his arm as he pulled out a copper opium pipe from the folds of his robes. Merryn watched him load the pipe as he chattered on about the previous tenant, and how Ben used to bring the thatched baskets he made to town to sell. Then one day he stopped coming.

"Merryn?" Cara came out of the cabin, a friendly smile on her face. "Father," she said, bowing her head slightly, voice filled with respect.

"Good morn', me young lass." The friar gave a toothy grin, raising his pipe in greeting.

"Join us fer morn' meal, Father?"

The friar stayed until late in the day. He and Cara were walking through the woods, talking of things Merryn could never understand. They spoke of a spiritual power larger than anything on the land and bigger than the world.

Merryn heard their voices come in and out between the thickets of trees they passed through. She leaned her head back against the tree she sat under, watching the sky. The clouds floated by, the sun darting in and out. Merryn sighed, content and happy.

She brought the small pipe up, taking in another lungful, exhaling with slow ease. As she looked out over the yard, the small cabin tucked near a thicket of green growth, she felt at peace. Yes, she could stay here with Cara. They could be happy together. A slow smile spread over her features as she watched the smoke lazily float through the air.

The voices got closer, then Cara and the friar emerged from the trees to Merryn's right. She smiled at Cara, who smiled back before turning to the friar.

Merryn watched as she gave the old man a hug. The friar turned to Merryn with a smile.

"Until the morrow, lassie." Wrapping fingers around his walking stick, the good man headed back the way he'd come.

As the friar tapped his way down around the bend, Merryn stood, walking over to Cara, who looked at her with questioning eyes.

She extended the pipe to Cara, eyes never leaving the curious green. Cara took it, slowly bringing it to her lips. She inhaled deeply, feeling the smoke invade her body, burning, choking, until she had to cough it out. Merryn smiled, taking the pipe from the coughing girl.

"Ya all right, lass?" she asked. Cara nodded, reaching for the pipe again. Merryn watched her carefully, making sure she was all right as she inhaled once more.

Cara felt a sense of ease fall over her, like a veil of peace. Her body relaxed, eyes falling closed as she let the day absorb into her very soul. She felt soft fingers brushing against her cheek. She saw Merryn looking into her face, taking in every detail, every curve, nuance, and shadow.

Cara's eyes closed again, her head falling back. Merryn's fingers followed, running down her throat, then sweeping around, under the heavy blonde hair, until finally her hand cupped the back of Cara's neck.

Merryn leaned in, brushing her cheek against Cara's, inhaling her scent mixed with the nutty smell of the opium smoke. Cara shivered, feeling the hot breath on the side of her face and neck. A small whimper escaped her when that hot breath turned to a kiss, then to a lick.

"Come inside with me, lass," Merryn breathed into Cara's warm skin. At the nod she felt, Merryn took her by the hand, leading her toward the cabin.

Cara felt as though the world around her had disappeared, leaving only sensation in its wake. She was laid down on the bed pallet, her eyes closing as Merryn settled on top of her and pressed their mouths together. She met her lips with a passion she'd never felt before. She gave into the pressure of Merryn's lips, quickly opening her mouth to draw her in.

Cara broke the kiss in surprise when she felt her dress being removed. This had never happened before. She watched Merryn, a determination on the girl's face, her eyes widening at the sight before them.

Merryn ran her hands down the sides of Cara's soft thighs, the gold patch of hair between them glistening in the sunlight streaming in through the window. Her hands slid up, over softly rounded hips, over the goosebump-covered flesh of her stomach and ribs. Merryn's hands glanced the sides of Cara's breasts, making them both sigh with pleasure. Keeping control, Merryn ran her hands up across strong shoulders.

Cara felt as though her skin were on fire, alive and breathing. She sighed, closing her eyes again. Never had her bare skin been touched before, except in washing. The feeling was exquisite and amplified by the humming throughout her body.

She gasped, when she felt bare skin touching her own. Looking up into Merryn's eyes, she saw love reflected there.

"Mo Shearc," Merryn whispered, brushing her lips against Cara's, then kissing a trail down her jaw to her neck. The words she'd whispered echoed through her head, words she should have said long ago — *My Love*.

She sighed as their naked breasts pressed together, making her body shiver against Cara's warmth. Never had she lain naked with the girl before, but she felt the need to be as close as possible. She knew not if it was right or not. It didn't matter.

She wanted to touch every part of Cara's body, and be touched by every part of Cara. She used her mouth and hands, bringing her love inside.

The cabin was filled with the sounds of soft sighs and whispered words of love, and the sound of skin on skin, as the day slipped away.

Later, Cara lay on Merryn, her head resting upon Merryn's heart. She smiled.

"C'n hear yer heart."

Merryn smiled, gently running her fingers through the soft, blonde hair, splayed out across her naked chest. "'N what 'tis it sayin' to ya, lass?"

Cara placed a soft kiss to the skin above the sacred organ. "Says yer my Merryn."

"Aye."

Cara sighed, her eyes heavy from an afternoon spent seeking the pleasures of the body. As she drifted off to sleep, she was still amazed at all that was possible, her body pulsing and alive.

Cara finished rinsing her hair, running her hands down the thick rope of wet hair, squeezing the water out. She felt the warm sun overhead as she made her way out of the stream, her thickly calloused feet barely noticing the scattered rocks as she walked over to her dress, which hung on a low branch.

Using a scrap of material she kept for when she bathes, she dried her face then ran the material over her arms and body. She hung the saturated cloth on a branch and grabbed her dress.

A little breathless, she leaned against the tree, resting. She'd woken up the morning before feeling a bit achy, her head pulsing with a dull pain.

After a moment, she finished putting on her dress, laced up the front, and gathered her things.

"Ya alright, lass?" Merryn asked, glancing over at her. Cara nodded, still leaning against the table, her head bowed. The herbs, berries, and roots lay before her untouched. She had been making a new batch of monk's pepper and cleaning paste when a wave of heat had settled over her.

Swiping her hand across her forehead, she was surprised to feel moisture. Looking at her fingers, she could see sweat glistening on her fingertips. She had no idea why she'd be sweating when she was chilled.

Remembering Merryn had asked her a question, she nodded again. "Aye."

Merryn's eyes opened, her conscious mind bringing the sounds of heavy breathing and moaning to her ears.

Coming fully awake, she felt Cara struggling with their blankets, legs kicking to free herself from her nocturnal demons.

"Please, no," Cara said, her voice a pleading whisper. "No!" she thrust her hips, neck arching.

"Cara!" Merryn grabbed the girl, her hand coming to settle on cold, clammy flesh.

"No! Please, Lord, save me! Merryn!" Her eyes opened, wide and unfocused.

"Cara, 'm here, lass. Cara!" Merryn cried when the girl tried to push her away, still trapped in her nightmare. "'Tis me. Merryn."

"Merryn?" Cara asked, her eyes resting on Merryn for a moment, before becoming unfocused and clouded again.

"Yer burnin' up, lass," Merryn whispered, resting her hand against the girl's forehead, sliding down her cheek to her neck. The skin was hot to the touch.

"Merryn," Cara whispered, falling back to the bed, her hair plastered to her face and forehead.

"'M here, lass." Merryn placed a soft kiss on her forehead, then climbed off the bed pallet. She grabbed a rag, running out to dip it in the closest water barrel. "C'mere, Cara." Merryn sat next to the girl, bringing Cara's head to her lap. Dark brows were drawn in concern. Her mind raced, trying to think of what Cara had given her when she'd been ill last winter.

She pressed the cool rag to the girl's face. Cara hissing at the chill that ran from her forehead through her body.

"Merryn," she whispered, her voice weak. "'Tis cold." She tried to push away from Merryn's lap, but she was held fast.

"I know, lass. I know. Ya've got a fever, Cara."

Cara mumbled something unintelligible before her eyes slipping closed. She seemed to fall asleep again. Merryn studied her, fingers brushing away long, sweat-slick strands of hair. She leaned down, brushing her lips where the cool rag had just been. She ran the rag all along Cara's face and neck, pushing the blankets down, exposing the tops of her naked breasts. Cara gasped and shivered as the rag was run along her upper chest.

Even in the moonlight, Merryn could see beads of sweat shimmering as Cara shivered. Gently placing Cara's head back to the cloak rolled beneath it, Merryn slipped from the bedroll once more. Lighting the lantern, she raised it to the shelf she'd built for Cara's medicines and healing herbs.

Studying each container, each root and flower, she tried to remember, tried to think like Cara.

"Hydromel," she whispered, seeing the small jar of the honey mixture. Removing the stopper, she sniffed. The strong, potent mixture burned the inside of her nose. She glanced back at Cara, who was beginning to murmur in her sleep, as she tossed restlessly.

Merryn felt helpless, not sure what to do, and whether the thick potion would even do anything.

"Cara," she whispered, falling to her knees beside the bed pallet. "Lass." Cupping the back of her head, she gently raised Cara. Her eyes barely opened, looking up at Merryn.

"Merryn," she said, a smile gracing her lips, a look of relief on her pale features.

"Take this, lass." Merryn dipped her finger into the mixture, bringing it to Cara's lips. She snaked her tongue out, lapping weakly at the medicine. Her nose wrinkled as the taste made her taste buds explode. "More, lass. Come, Cara."

Cara took some more of the healing mixture in, recognizing it, but unable to find the name for it in her jumbled head. She smacked her lips, trying to get all of it off her tongue. This would have been an adorable gesture if Merryn had not been so worried about the girl.

As Merryn climbed back into the bed pallet, Cara snuggled up closer, shivering dangerously. She wrapped her naked body around that of Cara, trying to use her natural body heat to keep the girl warm. This seemed to work until moments later, Cara was kicking off the blankets.

Merryn awoke before sunrise. Cara was finally sleeping soundly, curled up in a ball. Merryn made sure Cara was covered, then she felt her forehead. The fever seemed to have gone down somewhat, making Merryn sigh in relief. Maybe the hydromel had done the job after all.

Heading out into the early morning, she pulled her cloak closer around herself, glancing at Simon, who snorted at her.

Walking further out into the yard, she looked up into the sky, seeing all the twinkles beginning to disappear. The creatures of the night were still awake and chattering amongst themselves in the woods all around;

something scampered by, trying to get away from the much larger animal that was pursuing it.

Sighing deeply, Merryn began her morning duties, feeding the donkey, fetching fresh water for the day, setting the water bladders and a basket filled with wild roots and potatoes on the table, Merryn looked to her friend. The rays of sunlight were streaming in, brushing new life upon Cara's flushed face. The girl was still, lying on her back, head resting on its right side.

Merryn walked over to the pallet and knelt down. Reaching out a hand, she felt Cara's neck. The skin was hot to the touch. Merryn frowned slightly as she swept strands of golden hair aside; it had turned the color of spring wheat from sweat.

"Mo Shearc," she whispered, leaning carefully forward, brushing Cara's cheek with her lips, resting her forehead against hers. Cara didn't move, her breathing even and calm. Another soft kiss and Merryn stood.

Cara's eyes opened, squeezing shut quickly as the bright light of high day streamed in. She took mental stock of where she was and what she was doing there. Still in the bedroll, a heavy layer of blankets covered her naked body. She could feel slickness between her legs and under her arms. It was making her shiver.

As she pushed the blankets aside, the warm air in the cabin began to dry the sweat from her body, making her sigh in relief. She sat up, shaky and woozy, holding on to the wall close to the pallet for balance.

Assured she wouldn't fall over, Cara released the wall and took several deep breaths. She looked around the small cabin, seeing the stoppered jar of hydromel. Tasting the remnants on her tongue, she swung her legs around and put her feet to the ground.

Standing on shaky legs, she brought one of the blankets up with her, tucking it under her arms and clasping it closed at her chest. Stepping through the open doorway, she felt the sun's rays beat down on her, warming her chilled skin. Simon glanced briefly at her from across the yard, where he was munching on wild grass. Off in the distance she could hear the soft notes of her flute.

Cara walked slowly towards the music, her head feeling as though it wasn't attached to her body, feeling hollow and achy.

Merryn sat against a tree by the stream, the water glittering like precious gems. Her head rested against the bark, the flute to her lips. The song she played was soft and sad. One leg was bent, while the other lay casually on the ground.

Cara watched her for a moment, letting the melancholy music float over her, eyes closing, fingers clutching the blanket tighter as the music sailed to her soul, making her chest swell, and eyes sting.

Merryn covered and uncovered the holes of the small instrument in time to make the notes that told the day of her worry for her friend. Her fear was palpable. She'd hung around the cabin for the majority of the morning, but eventually had needed to get away, to clear her head and think.

While Cara had slept, she had dreamt and had spoken of those who chased her through her nightmares. Merryn had heard of the torments she had faced while imprisoned by Edward's men.

"Please, no, no," Cara whimpered, bringing her hands to her chest, tucking them in the safety of the ball her body made. "'T fire, burns," she gasped, thrashing to her back, neck arching as her face crumbled. "I know naught. I beg of ye! No more."

When Merryn had tried to waken her, the girl had simply gone quiet, falling into a peaceful sleep but it hadn't been long before she was dogged yet again by another nocturnal assailant.

Merryn's tune came to an end. She lowered the flute and stared out into the day, wondering how such beauty could surround her when her heart was filled with black ugliness.

"Merryn?" Cara's voice was soft.

Merryn's head shot up, surprised that she wasn't alone. She quickly got to her feet.

"Cara." Relief washed over her in harsh waves, nearly knocking her to her knees. She reached for the girl, then quickly snatched her hand back. Cara smiled softly, closing the distance between them. She tucked herself against Merryn, sighing when she felt strong arms wrap around her.

Merryn inhaled the scent of the small body against her; though it was the smell of sweat and a body not washed, it was Cara. She allowed it to fill her, ease her tension and fear.

"Ye've become good on the flute," Cara murmured, eyes closed as she relished the feel of Merryn's warmth against her. She felt Merryn's chuckle against her ear.

"Had a good teacher."

Cara hummed into Merryn's chest, a smile cracking her pale, dry lips.

"Come, lass," Merryn whispered into her ear. "Let us get ya washed."

Cara moved slowly; the water cascaded down her body like a blade slicing all the way down. She brought her hand to her stomach, as she fought nausea.

Getting to the shore, she fell to her knees. Her body convulsed as her stomach rebelled, the small bit of dried meat she'd eaten before her bath spilled out to the rocky shore. Weak and panting, Cara fell to the shore, the cool water lapping at her feet.

"Cara?" Merryn ran to her, dropping the dress she'd run back to the cabin to fetch. She fell to her knees, mindful of Cara's vomit to her left. "I've got'cha, lass."

Cara clung to Merryn as she was pulled to her feet. Another wave of nausea rushed through her. Pushing Merryn away, she fell to her knees again, another spasm rocking her body. She felt a hand on her back, and her hair being held in a gentle hand.

Weak and dehydrated, Cara pushed herself to her feet; Merryn supported her.

"We've got ta get ya well, Cara," Merryn exclaimed. Her heart was pounding and her skin was prickly with sweat as fear gripped her.

Cara tried to think of what would help. Her mind was fuzzy; very few thoughts were making sense. Everything jumbled into a mix of thoughts and images, none staying long enough for her to make sense of them.

"We're almost there, Cara. Almost there," Merryn whispered, feeling Cara leaning on her more and more. By the time they reached the cabin, Merryn was almost carrying her. She butted the door open and was panting by the time she got Cara to the bedroll.

Cara began to shiver as her body curled in on itself. She heard Merryn speaking to her, but the words were lost as her mind shut down, lost in a maze of sound and delirium.

"Me 'n ya, lass," Merryn whispered, pulling the blankets from under the girl's body from where Cara had collapsed. "We'll fight this." Tossing the covering aside, she gently turned Cara to her side. "No," she breathed. White pustules and lesions littered Cara's upper back, near her left shoulder.

Merryn sat back on her haunches, stunned and unable to look away. She felt her heart seize in her chest. What was she to do about this? She knew nothing to cure it.

Knowing nothing else to do, Merryn climbed in behind Cara, pulling her close. They'd see their fate through together.

Cara saw lights, so many colorful lights. She looked toward them. She did not feel the ground; her feet were far above the land. A smile spread across her face as her hands reached for the beauty before her.

"Mother?"

Merryn's eyes opened, feeling heavy and filled with sand. She tried to discover what had awoken her.

"Mother, 'tis Cara." Cara's voice was so soft, so filled with awe and longing.

Merryn pushed herself up to her elbow. Cara lay on her back, eyes open and unfocused.

Cara reached a hand out, fingers spread. "Mother."

Merryn gathered Cara, so hot, skin slick with sweat. "Hold on, lass. Just hold on," Merryn whispered, cradling Cara's head in her arms. Cara's eyes closed, and her face was pale. Her breathing was becoming labored. "Please, Cara. Please," Merryn begged, a tear slipping down her cheek. She felt Cara's body go limp in her arms. "Mo Shearc, please, please dona leave me. Please." Her words were cut off as a sob escaped her throat, her face buried in Cara's hair. She couldn't breathe; her body shook as the strength of her sobs grew, finally shaking them both. Raising her face to the Heavens, Merryn squeezed her eyes shut. "No!"

The sun rose, its brilliant light spreading over the land like a golden plague. Merryn stared straight ahead, unblinking, unfeeling, cold and empty.

The sound of Simon snorting outside made her blink for the first time in many moments; her eyes were dry and stinging. Looking down at the bundle in her arms, she brought up a hand, caressing Cara's cheek. It was cold and clammy. Leaning down, she placed a soft kiss upon her dry lips, lingering for a moment, running her fingers through the cool strands of gold. She had no idea how long she stayed like that, hugging Cara to her, cheek pressed to the top of her head.

Squeezing her eyes shut, Merryn let the girl go. She carefully laid her down in the bedding, tucking her in for her long sleep.

Getting to her feet, she looked around the small cabin. Dressing, she pulled on her boots, leaving Cara's neatly lined up against the wall. She took her pouch from its hook on the wall, loading it with food, some healing herbs, and medicines.

Merryn took down the small jar of rose water. After inhaling its scent, Merryn's head bowed. She felt her shoulders begin to shake as new tears came, making her eyes sting all the more. Carefully replacing the stopper in the small bottle, she tucked it into her pouch. Something glittering caught her eye. Cara's coin lay on the table, next to her pouch. Merryn took it between trembling fingers, holding it up and examining the detail of their ruler, King Edward III, and his son, the Dark Prince.

Kissing the small token, she tucked it into her pouch, cinching the bag then stringing the rope through it. As she tied the rope around her waist, she glanced again at Cara, so peaceful. So beautiful.

Tearing her eyes away, she quickly tethered her baldric in place and slid her sword home. For a moment she thought about pulling the blade free and ramming it into her own gullet. The only thing that stopped her was knowing that Cara would never forgive her on the other side.

Merryn felt numb as she took one last look around, carefully avoiding the bed pallet. Heading out into the warm day, she saw Simon looking at her, his dark eyes expressionless.

Slicing through the tether, Merryn walked past the animal and disappeared into the trees.

Part 7

Her smile was wide and her eyes twinkled. Merryn watched the golden hair blowing in the unfelt breeze, her fingers reaching out to touch it.

"Merryn," she heard whispered. "Merryn." A warm hand was touching the side of her cheek. Her eyes closed and she leaned into the touch, her cheek twitching with the tickle of a single tear.

"Cara," she breathed, reaching up to hold the hand cupping her face. "My Cara."

"Aye. Always. Forever."

Her eyes flew open, and she looked around frantically. Merryn jumped to one knee, her breathing already heavy in desperation. As reality set in, her heart felt as it was breaking. She fell back and hung her head in sorrow.

Lifting her face to the moonless sky, she let out a cry like a wounded animal. Getting to her feet, she grabbed her blade and walked over to a hapless tree. With a cry of rage, she hacked into the tree causing pieces of bark to fly up and hit her, a large piece cutting her cheek as it whizzed by. She didn't feel it. She didn't feel anything but loss.

Haunted by visions of Cara for the last month, Merryn was being slowly driven mad with grief.

Falling to her knees exhausted and emotionally broken, Merryn released the grip of her blade. It clanged uselessly against a tree.

Merryn looked to the skies once more. The line of tears chilled the skin of her neck; tears trailed down, tickling her upper chest before her tunic absorbed them. Leaning her head against the tree, she sighed. How was it possible for someone who'd never had anything to feel like she'd lost everything?

Her face slowly crumbled, her chin falling to her chest. How did a body have so many tears in it? Doesn't it run out? Oh, how Merryn wished hers would. She had nothing left to give.

Getting to shaky legs, she picked up her sword. She examined the blade, looking for chinks and scratches. Then she ran her fingers down the length, feeling the cold steel against her flesh. Tapping her fingertip against the sharpened tip, she felt the slight sting, followed by warmth as a small bead of blood trickled around to her fingernail. Bringing her hand closer to her face, she watched the thin red line run slowly down her finger. Her eyes slowly trailed back to the blade in her other hand.

Absently sucking her wounded finger into her mouth, she kept her eyes on the blade. The coppery taste of her own blood glazed her tongue. Bowing her head and closing her eyes, she offered a small prayer for forgiveness. Her strength waning, she took her blade in both hands, closing her eyes as she looked to the Heavens. Bringing her arms up, she touched the point to her tunic-clad stomach. She could feel the slight indent on her flesh as she used a bit more pressure.

Taking a deep breath, she flexed the muscles in her arms, preparing to push.

"Please, no! Timothy!"

Merryn's eyes snapped open, releasing the pressure on her blade. Listening, she heard nothing but the early morning chatter of waking birds. Taking a deep breath, she flexed her fingers around the grip, again readying herself. Holding her breath, she was about to plunge when she heard yelling, then the telltale sound of a scuffle.

Lowering her sword completely, Merryn tried to see through the pre-dawn blackness. A gurgle, a grunt. Then the morning was split open by the screech of a terrified woman.

Running blindly, Merryn plowed through the foliage, hissing as branches scraped across her face and arms. She nearly tripped over a body lying on the ground before instinct made her jump over it and into the fray.

Without thought, she grabbed the soldier from behind, grabbing hold of his head and twisting viciously. Soundlessly, he fell heavily to the ground. With wild eyes, she saw two other soldiers, one attacking a woman, the other heading straight for her.

With her heart pounding and her breathing rapid, Merryn bared her teeth, her face twisting in violent rage, and met the soldier halfway. A violent kick to his gut had him on his knees, allowing her to give her attention to the man attacking the woman. He heard her coming, having seen his comrade fall. With a roar, he turned on her, raising his blade.

Merryn tried to move out of the way of his blow, but he managed to nick her in the arm. Ignoring the sting, she raised her blade, blocking his follow-up blow. She grunted under the strength of his attack. Using all her own strength, she managed to push him off. With a violent shove, Merryn sent the woman flying out of the way.

Merryn snagged the downed soldier's blade, trying to adjust to the weight of the foreign sword. She slashed at the oncoming soldier's face with her left hand while thrusting with her right. He yelped in surprise at the double attack. He jumped behind a tree in time so that Merryn sliced the bark where his face had been.

Following him behind the tree, Merryn growled as she parried his thrust, using the advantage to slash again with her left hand. The blade hit its mark, and the man cried out as a chunk of skin and muscle was removed from his shoulder with a zing of steel.

"Pay fer that, ye will," he growled, coming at her with full force. Merryn's eyes grew huge as she tried to follow everything he did. She backed up further and further until she hit a tree; the collision knocked the wind out of her.

She saw him coming at her, his mouth open in a scream that she could no longer hear. Time slowed down as her eyes settled on his sword, newborn sun glinting off its steel.

"Move, Merryn! Move!"

Cara's voice echoed in her head as her mind stopped and pure instinct made her roll her body around the trunk of the tree. She heard the sound of the blade connecting and piercing the bark, the soldier grunting at the resulting vibration that ran through him. The blade was mere inches from her face.

Seeing his blade stuck to the tree, Merryn raised her own blade high over head, bringing it down to the back of his unprotected neck. She felt the blade grind into the vertebrae, neatly severing his brain stem from his spine. A soft hiss escaped his ruined throat as the head fell to the ground with a thud, and the soldier's body fell to the ground with a metallic plop as the mail that covered his chest and legs hit the dirt.

Looking up, Merryn saw the horrified face of the woman who had backed up against a tree, a small boy hidden within her skirts.

"Wakin' up, he is," she whispered, pointing to the other soldier. There was a groan as the man brought a hand to his head. He'd hit a rock as he hit the ground, and there was blood on his palm.

Merryn looked at the woman. "Get outta 'ere," she hissed.

"Can't leave me husband," the woman said, her voice shaky with unshed tears. It was only then that Merryn saw a man lying not far from the soldier that still lived. He was obviously dead, his gut slashed open.

"He's dead."

Merryn walked over to the soldier who was trying to get to his feet. With eyes filled with anger, she kicked him in the gut a second time, knocking him back to the ground. He looked up at her with questioning, pain-filled eyes.

"Why're ya here, ya daft bastard?" she hissed. He said nothing, clutching his stomach as he began to roll to his knees. "I asked, why?"

The soldier cried out, falling to his back, as Merryn's boot made contact with his ribs.

"Get the lad out of here," Merryn said to the woman. The woman, her face ashen, nodded, grabbing her young son and hurrying into the shadows of the trees.

Merryn turned back to the soldier and fell to one knee. She grabbed him by his mail shirt. His coif fell from his head, revealing the face of a youth, barely a man. He cried out in pain; no doubt his ribs were broken. She didn't care. She doubted his fellow soldiers cared about that when they were torturing their captives.

He looked up at her, fear in his eyes.

"Yer hunt is over," she hissed. He tried to speak, but Merryn silenced him, slamming him in the mouth with her fist. A sick, crunching sound rent the air, followed by gurgling as the soldier began to choke on his own teeth and blood.

Without another word, she stood, looking down at the soldier who gasped for breath. His eyes were wide as the final panic settled in, his hands reaching blindly for Merryn. She stepped away and watched — jaw set, eyes cold. He choked, trying to suck in air, instead sucking his teeth further down his throat. His mouth open in a silent gasp, the soldier's body convulsed, desperately trying to draw breath.

Merryn felt her stomach churn at her own actions and turned away. She walked to the other soldier who lay dead at the foot of the tree. She eyed him, looking at his boots. Mentally sizing them, she squatted next to him and tugged at them with a grunt. Pulling off her own boots, worn from more than a year's travel, she tossed them aside. Pulling on the soldier's boots, she sighed in contentment at their comfort. Quickly turning him over, she looked at the mail he wore. It was too heavy and cumbersome to meet her requirements.

Deciding to only take the boots and a bladder filled with wine, Merryn went back toward her own camp, wiping her blade on the jerkin of one of the dead soldiers as she passed.

She felt numb, her fingers cold where they wrapped around the grip of her sword. The sun's rays lit her path, warming her skin, which was pale and splattered with blood. Just off the side of the camp sat the woman, leaning against the tree she'd attacked earlier, her son curled up in her lap. Merryn saw the boy's eyes peeking out from under long bangs. His mother eyed her, nervous relief shining in the dark eyes.

Merryn ignored them, grabbed her baldric, and slipped it over her head. Belting it into place, she slid her sword home.

Glancing over her shoulder, Merryn saw the woman had risen and stood holding her son.

"Mightn't we travel with ye, m'lady?" she asked, her voice quiet and laced with fear. She knew not what to think of this strange girl who dressed like a man and fought better than most. Merryn looked at her for a moment then turned back to her gear. She flipped her cloak across her shoulders, quickly clipping it in place.

"Why were ya attacked, lass?" she asked, flipping one side of the cloak over her back so she could tie her rope around her waist, tucking her daggers inside.

"I know naught." The woman ducked her head, shielding her eyes from Merryn's piercing gaze. Merryn turned to face her full on.

"Lie not, lass." Her voice was stern and irritated. She wanted to be alone, wallowing in her own self-pity, not dealing with these two. It was only the murmurings of Cara's goodness that kept her from leaving them at the roadside.

The woman nodded, looking up at her with heavy eyes. "Me husband and li'l boy was leavin' London. Death everywhere." The woman shivered at the memory of bodies piled in the streets, the stench of death thick and heavy, and rats crawling all over the corpses. She shivered again. "Soldiers says the rebels must die."

"Rebels?"

"Aye." The dark haired woman nodded, wisps of hair falling into her eyes.

"Soldiers thought ya were a rebel?"

"Aye."

Merryn studied the woman's eyes, seeing nothing but truth. She could also tell she was barely holding together. Soon, the shock would wear off, and the hysteria of grief would set in. Merryn knew much about that.

"What rebels 're these?"

The woman shook her head. "I know naught."

Merryn nodded, turning away, kneeling by the rest of her meager possessions. "Get yer belongings, lass. I leave now."

It had been a long day traveling, and Merryn was resentful of the duo who sat on the opposite side of the fire. She glanced at them through the flames — a young mother with a son no more than five years of age. Her husband was killed by the soldiers; his body was left to rot in the forest with that of his murderers. And for what? To stop *possible* rebels? And what of these rebels? Rebelling against what? Whom? The king, for certain.

Merryn tossed it out of her mind. It did not concern her, nor did she care for it to. At the moment, she needed to tend to her arm where the soldier had managed to slice her.

She could feel the boy's eyes on her every move as she searched through the medicines she'd taken from the cabin, trying to decide which would work best for her wound.

Grabbing a small pinch of crushed arnica root, she mixed it with a bit of water until a thick soup was made. Letting that sit, she cleaned out the wound, already scabbed over with crusted blood. Merryn winced as she gently scrubbed the dried blood away, revealing an ugly slash.

Looking up, she saw the small boy standing not a full arm's length away, watching her, dark eyes wide with fascination.

"C'n I help ya, lad?" she asked, trying to hide her irritation. He said nothing, glancing up into her eyes before his gaze trailed back down to the wound on her arm. Deciding to ignore the boy, Merryn continued to clean the wound, tossing the soiled cloth aside. She applied the arnica mixture, hissing as the mixture stung. Clinching her teeth together, she rubbed the mixture inside the wound, making sure it was liberally coated.

The boy took in every movement, his lower lip tucking into his mouth before being released. His eyes flickered up to the Merryn's face as she began to clean out the scratches made by the tree branches as she'd raced to get to the screaming woman.

As she finished cleaning herself up, she noticed some bruised swelling on the boy's forehead.

"Have ya got a name, lad?" Merryn asked, grabbing a clean scrap of material from her pack. She held out a hand to the boy, but he stood where he was, staring down at the hand, then bringing a finger to his mouth, chewing nervously. He glanced over his shoulder to his mother, who had moved closer, watching the exchange. The woman nodded. The boy turned back to Merryn, finger still hooked onto his lower teeth, he stepped forward.

Merryn rose up to her knees so she could reach the boy's face.

"Me boy be mute, m'lady."

Merryn glanced at the boy's mother before looking back to him where she began to clean the dirt carefully from his face.

"What 'tis his name?" she asked, grabbing the remaining arnica mixture.

"Paul, m'lady."

"Ya were brave, Paul," Merryn said, her voice soft as she applied the healing herb. "Protected yer mother, ya did." She smiled, getting a small, weak one from the boy in return. She patted his shoulder, standing. "All better, lad."

The small boy raised a hand to his face, fingers tentatively touching the drying paste, big eyes still latched on the tall woman.

Turning away from the two, Merryn picked up her sword. "Sleep, now," she instructed. "More soldiers'll be on t' lookout." With that, she made her way into the forest.

The night was filled with life, the warm summer moon lighting Merryn's way. She watched as a fox chased a small rodent. The fox stopped and sniffed in the hole the small mouse had crawled into for safety. Sticking a paw in the hole sent the rodent running again, the fox took chase and, finally, caught its dinner.

She was mindful to make sure that the sounds around her were night creatures and not night stalkers by way of royal soldiers.

"Bugger," she muttered, looking up into the clear, night sky. Who was she trying to fool? She was no hero, no rescuer of the downtrodden. Truth be told, Paul and his mother would be better off staying at the next town they came to.

Finding a large rock, Merryn sat, poking at the dirt at her feet with her sword, hands clasped around the grip. With a sigh, she flipped her hair over a shoulder. A smile spread across her lips as she thought of Cara.

She could see her, imagine what her eyes would look like under the bright moonlight. She could see the girl looking up into the sky, up at Heaven's bright spots.

"Merryn?"

"Hmm?"

"Do ye ever wonder what else might be out there?" Cara asked, her voice soft. She lay on her bedroll, hands tucked under her head. She

stared up into the night sky, a sliver of a moon winking at them through the trees.

Merryn glanced over at her friend from her perch on a log.

"'Aven't thought much 'bou't, lass." She returned her attention to her bracer. The leather was wearing badly, the thin, leather laces break-ing more and more. Soon there'd be none left on the right bracer she held in her hand.

"I have." Cara's eyes took in the sky in its entirety. "What lies beyond the darkness?" she whispered.

Merryn tossed her bracer to her pile of belongings, shoving off the log and scooting to her bedroll next to Cara's. Without a word, Cara rolled over, resting her head on Merryn's shoulder.

Affection between the two was new, and Merryn sighed, rolling her eyes. It was a part she had to play, never letting Cara know how much she loved the little one to cuddle up to her. Cara reached behind her, grabbing Merryn's arm and placing it across her own waist. Merryn smiled, tightening her hold.

"Do ye wonder what's beyond the Heavens? God? Nothin' at all. More land?"

Merryn's brows drew as she contemplated what her friend was say-ing. These were things she'd never thought about before. She'd looked up into the sky, saw all that glittered, and thought it was beautiful, but she never wondered what, if anything, lay beyond.

"Could be angels," she said, her voice as soft as her friend's, "winkin' their wings at ya." She smiled at Cara's laugh.

"Aye. Golden haloes in the night, they are."

Merryn smiled, snuggling in closer to her friend. Her eyelids heavy, she yawned.

"'Night, lass," Merryn whispered, and they slept.

The smile was still on Merryn's face as she opened her eyes, though it quickly disappeared as she felt the cold rock under her and the fireless night. Her arms were empty, save for the cold, comfortless steel of her blade.

Bringing a hand up, she swiped a single finger under her left eye, rubbing the wetness she found there.

Merryn tried not to smile at the big, fat tears that were threatening to dive off those dark lashes.

Paul looked up at his mother, begging her with his expressive eyes. His mother — Tamara, she had told Merryn — knelt down before her son, held him by narrow shoulders, and smiled.

"Best listen to Merryn, me boy." Her words were soft and filled with loving understanding. "Ye don't wanna get sick like Nanna, do ye?" The boy shook his head vigorously. "Alright then." Getting to her feet, Tamara turned trusting eyes to Merryn. The mother took the pouch of strange, gray paste from their rescuer, then hiked her skirts up. Her son's hand in her own, she led the boy into the water.

Merryn did stifle a chuckle as the boy's tears finally fell as he was made to take a bath. His mother removed his small tunic, tossing it to a rock on shore, and then took off her own skirt, the heavy material flopping atop her son's clothing. Kneeling down in the knee-high water, she began to scrub the lad clean.

Merryn watched as she ran her fingers through her own hair, wondering how she'd ever lived as filthy as most the people of the land did. She smiled at her own stubbornness when Cara had insisted she bathe. She had acted not much better than the boy who silently cried, bottom lip sticking out in silent testament to his unhappiness.

Finishing her own washing, Merryn lay on a long, flat rock, allowing the sun to shine down upon her glistening skin. She felt good for the first time in many, many weeks. One eye peeked open at the sound of splashing water. This time she wasn't able to hide her smile as she watched a pouting boy drench his mother with a tantrum.

Tamara gasped at the cool water, her dark hair hanging in her face in dripping ropes.

"Paul! Skin ye, I will!" She grabbed the lad by the arm. Merryn closed her eyes again as the mother punished her child. She had no desire to see the boy whipped.

The air was much fresher as the trio traveled on. They were a quiet trio as Paul made not one sound and Merryn was the only other person for Tamara to carry a conversation with. She made it clear, by walking a few paces ahead, that she had no interest in conversation.

She had spoken with the woman earlier in the morning, trying to find out just exactly how long she would be stuck with them. Tamara was headed north, to Scotland. Her family was up that way, and she'd heard the black sickness was not as bad. She wanted her son to have a chance to survive. Merryn had agreed to get them as far as Hexham. They now traveled toward Lancaster and further north.

Weary travelers they passed had tales of local magistrates and the King's own men attacking, either themselves or other travelers, as tales passed from one set of ears to another.

"Be on yer guard, lassie," one such traveler had warned Merryn. "Vicious killers, they are! Me own son died!"

"Merryn?" Tamara began, her voice quiet, unsure. Her dark eyes, so much like her son's, never left the dagger in her right hand and the half cleaned fish in her left. Merryn glanced over at the young mother. "Will we get there?" She was barely able to spare a glance at the younger girl before her eyes dropped back to her task.

Merryn looked at her, meeting the fleeting gaze. She sighed quietly. "Hope so, lass."

Merryn and Cara had traveled the woods, living on the edge of civilization, only venturing into towns when they needed supplies. As she led Tamara and Paul through Lancaster, Merryn kept a careful eye on those around her, though few. The streets were eerily quiet, many homes deathly so. The telltale stench met their noses immediately, making Merryn's stomach curdle. She could feel Tamara stepping a little closer to her as those in the town eyed them suspiciously, wondering if the three strangers were bringing them more death.

The streets were filthy and rats climbed all over piles of dumped waste, both human and animal. Bodies littered alleys between the houses, some barely on carts where they'd been stacked waiting to be taken by those from the highlands. There were groups of rustic men who charged high fees to come down from the hills and take the bodies out to deep pits, their curse buried for all time.

Merryn's gaze ran up the length of the road to what sounded like — she listened, straining to hear — chanting? Shouting?

"Stay close," she muttered to Tamara as her hand hovered near the handle of her sword.

Around the bend, the chanting got louder, followed by a thunderous *Thwap! Thwap! Thwap!* Soon a large group of men came into focus, wearing only britches, their bare chests covered with splatters, which Merryn quickly realized were specks of blood. The men carried cat-o-nine-tails in their hands, the strands of leather covered in their blood.

Stunned, Merryn took an unwitting step backward, her eyes glued to the group coming up the road toward them. A crowd followed the men, who continued to flagellate themselves. The men cried out with every stroke of their leather whips — blood and bits of flesh clinging to the ends. The crowd behind them chanted with every lashing. Some women were crying, some praying. One woman was walking behind a man using a scrap of cloth to catch his blood. She lifted the cloth up in her hands, screamed in a foreign tongue, then rubbed the blood on her face.

"They've all gone bloody mad," Merryn whispered, stepping further back from the road as the crowd got closer. The crowd's voices filled the late morning with cries of pain and joy.

"Nay."

Merryn turned to the voice behind her. A man stood, arms crossed over his tunic-clad chest. The scrap of turban on his head hid dark hair while his darker beard covered his face.

"Called the Flagellants, they are." He grinned at her look of confusion, exposing his rotten teeth and expelling rancid breath. "Mad men from Germany, they are. Thinks they're riddin' themselves of God's curse, they do." He sighed, shaking his head. He raised a hand, wiping the turban from his head; long, dirty strands of hair fell into his eyes. His other hand scratched a spot to the left of his part. Smoothing it all back, he replaced the turban, his eyes never leaving the passing chaos.

Merryn's eyes also returned to the spectacle. Once the Flagellants had passed, she grabbed for Tamara and the frightened boy being held in his mother's arms.

The man gazed at them with dark, steady eyes. "Travelin' through, are ye?" he asked. At Merryn's nod, he indicated the passing crowd with the tip of his head. "Best be mindful. They'll stone ye as surely as wish ye mornin' greetin'." At Merryn's look of confusion, he explained. "Lookin' fer ta blame," he said as he gestured toward a pile of rotting bodies. Looking back to the small group, he added, "Come, sup with me wife 'n me." He looked between Merryn and Tamara. "What say ye?"

Merryn looked at her two charges, seeing the fear and hunger in two sets of eyes. Turning back to their benefactor, she nodded. "Aye."

Merryn carried their belongings while Tamara carried her son. His big, brown eyes darted all around, frightened. His finger had never left his mouth.

The man led back through dark alleys of small shacks and businesses which formed a tunnel of shadow. Finally they were ushered into a modest timber frame house. The panels were filled with wattle, made by weaving hazel twigs with the upright panels. The wattle had been daubed with a mixture of clay, straw, cow dung, and mutton fat, and the surface had been sealed with a mixture of lime plaster and cow hair.

"Evela?" the man called as they entered the two-room structure. A woman with black hair, a stripe of silver running the length of it, stepped out from the sleeping chamber. Merryn was surprised to see the sign of old age, when the woman was obviously young like herself. Shy blue eyes looked up at her before flicking to her husband. "We've guests."

The girl nodded, rushing out of the narrow door to the town beyond. Merryn looked around the home, amazed to see some sort of thatch covering on the floor, protecting the occupants from the dirt below. The room was scantily appointed — a plank table with four chairs, and a plank work surface on which stood small spools of threads and cow gut, which caught incoming sunlight from the stone-framed window above. Cupboards stacked with wooden plates and mugs lined three walls. The corners of the room were stacked with burlap sacks of grain, flour, and some spices.

"Me name is Ezra," the man said, tugging Merryn from her inspection of the room. She looked at him, seeing a smile almost hidden behind his thick beard. "I'm the local blacksmith here."

"Merryn." She looked to the frightened woman who stood behind her, still clutching her son. "'Tis Tamara, 'n ta lad is Paul."

Ezra nodded at Tamara's shy smile. He signaled for them to sit at the table and mugs of water were placed before them. Merryn drank, grateful for the refreshment and to be sitting. They'd been walking since sun up.

Evela came back in, carrying a large, freshly plucked chicken. Immediately Tamara was on her feet, helping the young woman who offered a shy word of gratitude.

Without word, Tamara had deposited Paul in Merryn's lap. Surprised, she looked down at him as if she'd just been given a rabid dog. Ezra, seeing the surprised look, chuckled as he sat at the table. He eyed this girl sitting across from him, wondering what a young thing like her was doing wandering through Lancaster, unescorted, and dressed like a lad. And who was the mother and child? He decided to continue their conversation from the street.

"Not safe fer ya here, lassie," he said, drinking from his mug, eyeing the girl over the rim. "Word has it the Pope, hisself, leaves Avignon in terror."

"Clement t' sixth 'tis a rat bastard," Merryn muttered, readjusting the boy on her lap. His eyelids were growing heavy, as his head rested against her chest.

"Aye," Ezra nodded. "Fear grips this land." He leaned in, lowering his voice. With eyes wide and filled with fire, he continued, "They've begun murderin' those they suspect." He pointed to the wall of the house. "Draggin' 'em outta their homes, kickin' 'n screamin', they are."

Merryn stared at him, surprised by his words. "What of the soldiers' attacks?" she asked, her voice quiet, her head spinning from everything she was hearing. If not for the bloody woman and her son, she'd be safe in the woods or dead by now.

"Bah," Ezra waved her words away, sipping more water. He glanced over at the women who were working efficiently to make supper. "Edward 'tis weak. Lost his daughter, Joan, to the black sickness, he did." He grinned. "He's run tail to the countryside, along with all the nobles. Bastards leave us here to die in their stead." He shared a quick glance with his wife, then continued, voice changing, becoming strong and sure. "People 're fightin' back, Merryn."

She looked at him, seeing the light in his eyes. She was unsure what he was leading to, but she had an idea.

"People 're takin' back the land stolen from them by the royalty 'n their Godless line."

"T' rebels," Merryn said, a statement. Ezra sat back, though his surprise was short lived.

"Ye's seen 'em, then?"

Merryn shook her head. "King's men, attackin' travelers, killed the lad's father." She flicked her eyes down to a sleeping Paul. Ezra followed her gaze, then met her own. She shook her head. "Want no part o' this, Ezra."

Merryn grinned, hearing laughter just past the small stand of trees. She redoubled her efforts, putting her long legs to use. A scream of surprise, and Cara went speeding away from her hiding place.

Merryn took a sharp turn to the left, trying to head Cara off before she was able to reach the lake, which was the ending point of their race.

There was no way she could allow her to win! The loser was pledged to do the cooking for an entire week.

She stopped, listening, holding her breath. The corner of her mouth quirked up when she heard a nervous giggle coming from her right. Peering through the leaves of the bush she hid behind, she tried to pick out gold amongst the green.

"Got'cha, lass," she whispered, her target in her sites as she silently moved around the bush, fingers flexing at her sides. She made her move, quick as the hawk swooping down on its prey.

Cara squealed in surprise as she heard the attack and tried to rush from her hiding place, but instead found herself tumbling down to the forest floor in a mess of arms and legs. She was laughing so hard that she hardly noticed the rock that jammed into her left hip.

Merryn pinned her down, an evil smile spreading over her lips. She looked down into Cara's face, flushed from exertion and merriment. Placing a small kiss on the girl's lips, she helped her to her feet. However, unsteadiness brought Cara into her arms.

"Steady, there, lass," she chuckled. Cara glared up at her.

"Ye fall on me like the Devil chasin' yer arse, and ye tell me ta be steady?"

Merryn chuckled again, putting her arm around Cara's slight shoulders. "Come, lass. My mouth is waterin' jus' thinkin' of what ye'll make ta sup on."

Grumbling, Cara walked along side her. The overhead sun was pleasant, warm without being hot. They walked on in silence, both absorbing the day and each other. Finally at the lake, Merryn released the girl and turned to her water bladder. Merryn guzzled half of it in one go before tossing it to Cara, who took it with a grateful smile.

A rare treat of duck was eaten and the bones buried by the time the sun began to slide from the sky. Merryn felt eyes on her as she sat leaning against the foot of a large rock, her legs stretched out and crossed at the ankles. She glanced to her friend, who sat in a similar position against the tree across from the fire of their small camp. Cara studied her, head slightly cocked.

"Ye doubt yerself," she said, as though she were reading her mind. Getting no response, nor needing one, she continued. "Ye c'n do this, Merryn. Ye've the strength of mind and heart." She met the intense blue eyes of her friend, who smiled softly. "Biggest heart of anyone, ye have."

"Nay," Merryn murmured, her gaze drifting off toward the dying rays sparkling on the water.

"Aye." Cara crawled over to her, rising to her knees before her friend. Her hands came up and cupped Merryn's face. She was but a breath away, her eyes looking into Merryn's with poignant intent. "Ye c'n do this, Merryn. Ye must."

Merryn started, eyes popping open. She didn't have time to think of what had awoken her as she looked around the home of Ezra and Evela. Tamara was also roused from her place on the floor, Paul tucked against her. Their eyes met briefly before another crashing sound got Merryn to her feet.

She looked in horror as the night glowed with fiery intensity, and the smell of burning wood and grass filtering in through the window. The yelling voices of a frantic crowd shattered the stillness of the night. Loud cries of "*Demon Jew*" rushed into the home.

Merryn saw movement at the window, then something was thrown in.

"Blasted!" she yelled, realizing it was a torch. The fire took a heartbeat before igniting the grass mat spread across the floor. The flames began to lick at the leg of the table.

"We must go!" Ezra yelled above the hysteria outside. He was tugging his tunic over his head as he spoke, his long hair hiding half his face.

Merryn followed him, grabbing what she could. He yelled out instructions to the household, yelling for Tamara to get the boy out. Ezra herded them all into the sleeping chamber and down through an open cellar door, where Evela had already disappeared.

Another crash, then an immense rush of heat as the walls caught fire, and the main room was engulfed in flames and victorious cries from the townspeople.

Breathing hard, Merryn tried to get her bearings, her eyes as wide open as possible to try and see into the earthen tunnel. She heard a loud pounding and Ezra grunting as he tried to kick through a wooden door. Finally getting the wood to buckle, then splinter, he pushed his way through, tearing his hands and bare feet open in the process. On the other side of the door, there was a set of dirt stairs that lead up and into the night. He shoved his wife through the broken door, followed by Tamara and Paul, and finally he reached for Merryn. Before pushing her through, he hissed in her ear, "Run for the woods!"

Merryn looked at the other two women and held a finger before her mouth. They both nodded; Evela's eyes were clear and focused, while Tamara looked as though she would fall apart at any moment. Paul sagged in Tamara's arms, so Merryn ripped the boy away, gesturing wildly for her to run.

Frozen in fear, Tamara didn't move. Merryn was grateful when Evela grabbed her hand and pulled her along as they disappeared into the dark of night. Merryn glanced over her shoulder once, hearing Ezra coming up the steps as he, too, emerged into the night. She rushed toward the blackness of the trees, Paul bouncing in her arms.

She heard a whispered "over here" and hurried in the direction of Evela's voice. The two women were pressed inside a shallow cave, just barely able to hold their slight bulk. Merryn handed Paul off to his mother and turned to see if Ezra had escaped.

The crowd's frightened and misplaced vengeance could still be heard. Lancaster was on fire making the night glow.

Merryn was stunned, frightened, and out of breath. She looked to Evela for answers. The small woman looked at her, just as frightened.

"Jews," she whispered. "They blame Jews."

Merryn nodded, looking back toward the town in the distance.

Soon a figure appeared out of the darkness. Evela threw herself into her husband's arms in relief. "All right," he said, gulping in lungfuls of air, trying to calm himself. "We go." Evela hugged him tighter.

Merryn didn't think anyone from the town was following them, but the possibility was still there. They forged on through the night, knowing they could very well run into a worse enemy — the king's soldiers. The four of them took turns carrying Paul and trying to keep the boy quiet.

Merryn felt a hand on her arm. Turning, she saw Ezra's face close to her own. He sent her attention to the west with his eyes. Seeing what had caught his eye, she turned back to him.

"C'n ye use that, Merryn?" he whispered, tapping the pommel of her sword. She nodded, though she felt her stomach turning. Her use, thus far, had been born of luck, not skill.

Ezra grabbed a fist-sized rock in his left hand, his thumb rubbing over the rough surface. He was relieved when he heard his wife pulling Tamara back into the thick of the woods, out of danger. Hopefully, she'll be able to keep her and the boy quiet. He motioned for Merryn to flank right while he took the left; she nodded her understanding and left. Her silent movement impressed him, making the dark man wonder about her lot in life.

Pale moonlight illuminated the night. Merryn hid behind a tree; her intended targets were just moving shadows. With the silent grace and focus of the mythical tiger, she moved toward the two of them. She noticed that they crouched as they moved, making no more noise than herself. They stopped and whispered, just a slight disturbance of he night air. Merryn couldn't hear what was being said, but she decided that it would be the right time to strike, while they were in discussion.

Catching Ezra's gaze, she indicated her intent with the flick of her head. He nodded.

The two shadows gasped in surprise as they both found themselves splayed out on the ground. One looked up with wide eyes, as he saw a heavy rock coming down at his head and hollered, "Wait!"

Ezra stopped, mid-strike, his heart pounding in his neck. The man beneath him was whimpering, trembling at what could have been and what could still be.

Merryn felt the adrenaline and blood pounding through her as she looked down at the wide-eyed man she straddled, her fingers wrapped tightly around the grip of her blade. She tried to control her heartbeat as she looked into his face, a face she thought she knew...

"George?"

Part 8

Merryn's eyes closed in pleasure, as the ale burned a trail down her throat and warmed her stomach. She sat back against the fire-warmed wall of the cave and felt the soft touch of Evela's fingers graze her own as the woman took the bladder from her.

Ezra and Frederick, the man who had been with George, began to talk again.

"T' time is now, lad."

Merryn turned away from the men. With a grunt of exhaustion, she pushed herself to her feet and made her way to the mouth of the cave.

She leaned against the cool, stone wall and let the soft breeze of the late night wash over her. The strong ale along with the fire-warmed inner cave had warmed her to an uncomfortable level. Needing to cool off and find some solitude, she pushed off the wall and found a dark area near the cave to sit.

Wishing she had a bladder of ale to herself, she sighed, wallowing in the sounds of night around her. Blindly reaching to the ground, she felt a small assortment of twigs and leaves. Grabbing one of the larger of the twigs, she held it in her hand, her fingers feeling the shape and size. With her hands busy, it left her mind free to wander.

Now that they'd met up with George and Frederick, she could leave Tamara and Paul in their care. Merryn had a clear conscience about her actions, knowing they'd be safe. So what lay ahead for her?

Before meeting Cara, she'd been wandering aimlessly, surviving on scrounging from the dead and pick-pocketing the living. She had no direction, just lived by the adventure of each day. Either the local magistrate on her tail or the need to find solitude or supplies had guided her movements.

Then there was Cara. She had given Merryn what she'd never had before, nor even knew she wanted or needed — a sense of belonging — a family, even if it had only been the two of them. Now she felt lost and lonelier than she could have ever imagined. How could she go back to living a life with only herself and creatures of the forest to talk to, when she'd had such a wonderful person to share thoughts and dreams with? Someone who made her laugh, even when she didn't want to. She had tried so hard to keep her true thoughts and feelings hidden from Cara, even though somehow the girl had always seen through the façade, seeming to know within moments what was really going on in Merryn's head.

Merryn raised a hand, gently wiping at a single tear that had begun to slide from her left eye. No one had made her laugh, or cry, as much as Cara had.

"What makes ye so sad, Merryn?" asked a voice, no louder than the softest breeze. Merryn glanced to her right, barely able to see Evela standing near a tree.

Seeing that she neither scared nor angered Merryn, Evela made her way over to her. Lowering herself gracefully to the ground, she studied her.

"Who do ye think of?"

Merryn shook her head, wiping her wet fingertip on her tunic. She blinked rapidly, trying to get her emotions under control. She wasn't sure why, but she began to speak. "Her name was Cara." Her voice was soft, eyes focused on the leaves of a tree, the moonlight making them glow.

Evela waited. When Merryn said no more, she cleared her throat softly. "Who was this Cara?"

Merryn glanced over at her, a smile curling her lips. "She was my best friend, my family." She sighed, eyes finding the glowing leaves again. "She was my friend."

"'M sorry, Merryn. What happened ta her?"

"Sickness."

Evela nodded, not surprised. They were quiet for a while, both watching as the moon began to slowly fade from the sky. The darkest part of night was upon them.

"Will ye travel with us?" Evela asked at length. Merryn sighed, shaking her head. "'N why not?"

"I dona belong," she said simply.

Evela smiled gently, laying a warm hand on her arm. When she saw she had the girl's attention, she spoke. "We all find 'r way, Merryn, 'n cannot do it alone."

Merryn stared into caring, dark eyes. She saw truth and acceptance.

Evela stood about to return to the cave. She looked at Merryn with kindness in her dark eyes. "A family c'n come at any time." With those soft words, she was gone.

Merryn sat in the back of the wagon, her body swaying with the movement of the horses' steps over the rough terrain. She looked at Paul. When he saw he had her attention, he smiled, big and bright. She smiled back.

Looking over her right shoulder, she saw the movement of the brown and tan horses' rumps, muscles flexing in their flanks as they did their master's bidding. She sighed, wondering not for the first time what she was doing there.

Paul may say nothing with his mouth, but he spoke much with his eyes. She thought about the night before.

Everyone had found a place to sleep in the warm cave, as the fire began to burn down. Merryn surveyed them all; everyone was exhausted from a long night filled with fear and running. Slowly getting to her feet, she gathered what few of her belongings she'd managed to grab from Ezra's house, and tucked them in her belt as she picked her way over the bodies toward the mouth of the cave.

Nearly stumbling over Frederick, she caught herself with a hand to the stone to steady herself. Once she had her footing again, she moved out into the pre-dawn. There was a chill in the air, and she pulled her cloak around her body. Taking a deep breath, she was about to start out when she felt a tug on her cloak.

She was surprised to see Paul looking up at her. Frowning slightly, she knelt down in front of him. "What's t' matter, lad?" she asked, her voice soft. He stared into her eyes, blindly grabbing for her large hand and holding it in both his warm, little ones.

She raised a brow at this, but waited to see what he was going to do. She felt a slight tug, the little boy grunting slightly as he used a good amount of his body weight. Not understanding, Merryn cocked her head to the side. Standing, she mussed his hair, trying to take her hand from his. He refused to let it go.

"I've ta go, Paul," she said, her voice a bit more stern. The boy held her hand in one of his now. Turning his little body toward the cave, he tried his best to tug her with him.

Curious, she followed the boy. Paul nearly stumbled since he no longer had resistance. She caught him by tugging on his hand. Getting his footing, he lead her back into the cave. He looked up at her, tucked in his lower lip, and yanked down on her hand. She bent down and was lightly pushed to her butt by the little boy. About to protest, her words died in her mouth as Paul crawled into her lap, curled up against her, and fell asleep.

Sighing, and resting her hand protectively upon his shoulder, Merryn's head fell back against the stone wall behind her. She glanced to her right, seeing everyone still asleep — almost everyone. Evela's eyes were open, a smile on her lips.

With a sigh, she relaxed during the rest of the ride.

Cayshire Castle. It stood on its own island, on top of a rocky hill, attached to the land by a stone bridge which spanned the raging sea. The winding road leading up to its ruined keep was treacherous, and the horses whinnied at the path they were forced to travel. Merryn could hear Frederick yelling at the poor beasts, trying to get them to keep their paces.

After entering the property, the wagon was met by a young boy, perhaps ten years of age, who unhooked the horses from the wagon then led them through an archway.

Merryn looked around the large, courtyard of the castle. The walls were crumbling with age and the marks of battle. She pushed herself up from where she had been earlier dozing, the sway of the wagon almost as good as a lullaby Cara might have offered.

They were led around toward a set of stone steps, the top one split in half. The heavy wooden door was braced with iron. Standing in the doorway was a man; his blond and wild hair reached the middle of his wide back. His feet were set wide apart. Thick, leather lacings wrapped around his calves to just under his knee to secure the high top turn shoe. His hand rested on the pommel of a large sword. Piercing, suspicious gray eyes watched the approach of the strangers.

"Gerik, we've guests," George called out, seeing the look in his eyes. The blond man's eyes did not leave the five strangers.

"Me eyes do not deceive, George," he muttered, bringing his arms up to cross over his chest.

George ignored him, helping Tamara and Evela up the steps. Merryn looked up to see Gerik staring at her, roaming up and down her body, distaste pulling up his lip. She ignored him, too.

"Come!" George said, waving everyone else up the steps, his voice filled with pride. He looked up at Gerik, who had yet to move to allow the women entrance. George stood his ground, his jaw clenched, and his gaze never flickering. Without a sound, the giant of a man finally stepped aside, continuing to scrutinize all who passed before him.

Merryn was uncomfortable as she walked through the short passageway until the sun shone down on her once more as she stepped out into the main courtyard. Turning in a small circle, she took in the walls, which were cracked and filled with hundreds of arrow slits. It didn't surprise her when she saw faces appear in those windows as George called out the arrival of the strangers.

Another door opened, the left side of a pair. The person standing there was lost in deep shadow. Merryn knew she was being stared at. She swallowed, trying to keep her anger in check. She hated the feeling of not being in control of a situation.

"Returned, have ye?" came from the shadows of the open door. She stopped, knowing that voice — deep, a full rumble from the chest. A smile began with the twitch of the corner of her mouth before spreading across her lips. The owner of the voice stepped out of the shadows, the sun shining down on him.

"Angus," she said, walking over to him. The Irishman smiled, his mouth visible, as the heavy beard of a year ago was gone.

"Dia duit," he said, meeting her half way.

She smiled. "God 'n Mary ta ya, as well."

"Who're yer friends?" he asked, looking past her at the small group, who were looking around the courtyard.

"Ezra, his wife, Evela, Tamara, 'n the lad is Paul." She pointed to each person named. Angus nodded, looking back at her.

"'N yer friend?" He saw the sadness fill the girl's eyes before she looked down. He nodded, needing to hear no more. "Come," he said, voice soft. "Let us feed ye."

Merryn was amazed at Angus' old castle. She and the others were led into the dark and chilled confines of great halls — wood and stone ceilings so high that they defied sight. They passed many people, most smiling or nodding a welcome, but all bustling around to perform a given duty. Inside the castle was a town, self-sufficient and alive.

They were taken up a long, winding staircase to a second floor. This floor was very dark, only lit by the torch of the nameless woman who was their guide. Golden waves of light illuminated the stone walls as they walked past. Merryn felt a gentle touch and looked down. Paul grinned up at her, both his hands wrapped around her larger one. She smiled and reached down to grab the boy, pulling him up to rest on her hip. He happily draped an arm around her shoulders as he enjoyed the new perspective.

A large, iron-ribbed door squeaked open, the torch throwing light into the deeply shadowed room.

"Lot o' us sleep 'ere." The guide tilted the torch toward the wall, lighting a second torch in a sconce. Without another word, the heavy-set woman waddled out of the room, leaving the five of them to their own devices. Tamara jumped as the woman called over her shoulder, halfway down the hall, "Suppa 'n an hour!"

Ezra took the torch from the wall, waving it around the large, cold room. Scattered all over the straw-covered stone floor were bedrolls, pallets, blankets, and various personal belongings. He walked further into the room, chasing the shadows away, revealing a huge fireplace stretching along one wall, tall enough for a grown man to stand inside. There was one window, tall and narrow, with wooden shutters keeping the night air from seeping through the unglazed gap. Along that stretch, near the window, was the only bare space on the floor.

Merryn removed her cloak, balling it up and tossing it to the floor. She heard the others begin to organize their supplies as well. Some things she kept on her person, not trusting anyone around her to not rob her. She smirked at that thought, considering that at one time that's exactly what she would have done to every person in the castle.

A fire roared and smoked in the massive fireplace in the Great Hall. Torches lined the walls and lamps stood on the long, scarred tabletops. Merryn was surprised to see people at every table, several dozen all told.

Angus stood with a small group of men, talking and laughing, sipping from a wooden mug. His dark eyes caught Merryn's. Turning from his friends, he grinned, walking over to her.

"Welcome!" he boomed, arms spread wide. Walking up to Merryn, he placed a hand on her shoulder.

Merryn smiled at her old acquaintance. She wasn't sure how to feel about such attention but tried to accept it with grace. She respected the man; after all, if not for him, she would never have had more time with Cara.

"Come," he said, leading her toward the longest of the tables. "May ye and yer friends be guests o' honor!" He indicated five chairs near the empty one at the end. "Bring out t' feast!" he called out, clapping large hands.

The huge room was filled with murmurs as some scattered to fetch and serve supper while others milled around, finding their seats. Merryn gathered Ezra, Evela, Tamara, and Paul, showing them to their seats.

They were all amazed at the feeling of family and camaraderie that surrounded them. There was much laughter and loud voices, much teasing and a few tossed morsels of bread.

Merryn was astonished at what she was witnessing, having never experienced anything like it. Other than a couple of sets of watchful eyes, everyone enfolded Merryn and her friends with open arms and happy hearts.

Evela watched quietly, as seemed to be her way, taking in everything she saw with a smile curling her lips. Her husband, meanwhile, talked and laughed, sharing his own stories to make his listeners roar with laughter. Tamara seemed most comfortable helping the serving party, and Paul took little time in finding other children his age to run around the seemingly endless space of the Great Hall.

Merryn had to restrain herself from using two hands as she ate her fill. The food was some of the best she'd ever had, and it was certainly more bountiful than she ever believed possible. She glanced over at their host, who had a bemused look on his face.

"Wha'?" she asked, brows drawn. Angus rested his chin on his fist.

"Ye starvin', lass?"

"No. 'N dona call me lass!" She pointed the dagger she'd been using to spear her food, at his throat. He chuckled, turning back to his own food.

The food was wonderful, the company entertaining, but Merryn needed some time alone. She left the Great Hall after dipping her hands in the waiting bowls of water, to rinse the juices from the meat off her fingertips. Her boot heels made hollow thuds on the stone as she walked down the long, cold, corridors. She felt naked dressed only in her tunic, breeches, and boots without all her equipment hanging from her. She stepped out onto the turret, placing her hands along its cut stone edges. It was cold up there; the ocean brought in ripples of chill with every break of its waves.

Looking out over the island, she could see random bits of light coming from fires burning in windows or through doors, in the castle. The outer apron lined the rocky edge of the island, leaving little room for anything else.

Walking to the other side of the tower, away from the ocean, her eyes ran along the stone bridge leading back to land. It was dark, but she remembered the farms and small, well-kept houses that dotted the landscape.

Glancing up to the sky, she saw the moon had finally decided to grow and would be full in a few nights time.

Merryn sighed, running her hands through thick hair. The weight of the past few days was bearing on her. Coupled with the fact she hadn't had a good night's sleep since the night before Cara...well, she hadn't slept.

After a huge yawn nearly split her face in two, she decided it was time to turn in.

"Angus?" Merryn looked around the large room, gray light painted in long rectangles from the windows making a patchwork for her to walk through.

"Aye. Over here, Merryn."

Hearing the man's voice in the far corner of the huge Great Hall, Merryn headed that way, her boots making hollow thuds on the stone. She started as the corner of the room was suddenly ablaze with golden firelight. Angus was a simple silhouette before the massive fireplace.

"T' difference fire c'n make," he said quietly, eyes burning orange. Merryn nodded, but said nothing. She had been summoned there, so she waited for Angus to tell her why. Having his fill of the fire, he turned to her with a smile. "Merryn, let us talk."

Merryn watched him, arms crossing over her chest. She had a slight feeling of unease.

"Ye've been here fer three days," he began, sipping from a wooden mug. Merryn said nothing. He eyed her, sizing her up. Merryn didn't like the scrutiny, but she kept her silence. "Have ye enjoyed yer time?"

"Aye," Merryn said slowly, carefully.

"I am glad." He put his mug down, clasping his hands behind his back. "I'd like ye ta stay on, Merryn. Ye have good instincts. Yer strong, good on yer feet..."

"I'm not here ta fight, Angus."

"Wha'?" he looked at her, surprised. "'N why not?"

"'M done. I'm not a fighter. What I had ta fight fer," she looked away then lowered her eyes, "well, 'tis gone."

Merryn flinched slightly when she heard his swift footsteps walking over to her. She felt Angus' presence in front of her. Finally, she lifted challenging eyes.

"We went in there, Merryn, 'n we got Cara out." His voice was carefully controlled, though his anger was boiling just under the surface. "She was alive. Frightened, a wee worse fer wear, but alive." He was beginning to breathe through his nose now, keeping the calm. "My wife, Teresa, was not so lucky."

Merryn looked at him, stunned. She could see the pain in his eyes, slowly overcoming the anger. The dark man turned away, shoulders slumped as he was overcome with the memory of seeing his beloved wife beaten and tortured. Taking a deep breath, he turned back to Merryn.

"Merryn, my people, *our* people, deserve ta be free. These bloody tyrants ran to the hills!" his booming voice echoed off the stone walls around them. "They ran, leaving us ta die 'n be ravaged by this, this, madness! Some call it God's wrath, others t' work o' witches. Dona matter. 'Tis here, 'n I'm gonna take back what's ours."

"Ta what end, Angus?" Merryn asked, her own anger building. "Ta get yer people slaughtered by trained, hired killers?"

"Hired," he said, holding up a finger. "Hired soldiers dona care, but fer their pence. We fight fer our lives, our freedom. 'N as Teresa looks down from Heaven, I want her ta know she'll be avenged."

"Cara didna die from soldiers, Angus," Merryn said, her voice soft, feeling the man's pain.

"Nay. She is gone. What have ye got now?" He looked deeply into her eyes, not allowing her gaze to falter. "What have ye got ta go back ta, Merryn?"

"I've got me," she said, her anger returning as Angus pointed out truth she didn't want to face.

"Then why're ye here, lass?" he asked, eyes wide, voice quiet with accusation. She had no answer.

"Cara..."

"Cara is dead!" he boomed, brows drawing and creating dark shadows which hid his eyes. "'N she's lookin' down at ye, and she sees a coward!"

Merryn held her ground, her hands closing into tight fists as her short, jagged nails bit into the palms of her hands. She didn't want to admit he was right.

Angus ran his hands through his hair, trying to get himself under control. Taking several deep breaths, he gave her a smile.

"If ye dona want te fight, you dona want te fight. But, Merryn, stay. Have a family again."

She looked into his dark eyes, seeing the genuine care for her in them. After a moment, she nodded. His smile grew. Without another word, Merryn hurried from the Great Hall.

Merryn raised the bow, testing the tension. Satisfied, she shouldered the weapon, a quiver filled with well-made arrows already attached to her back.

Stepping out of the armory, Merryn set off for the keep and then the stables. She planned to take a horse and ride out into the woods on the mainland. The sun was just moments away from chasing the dreariness of the castle away, when she noticed big, brown eyes watching her.

"Wha'?" she asked. Paul, looking up at her, began to chew on his lower lip, his hands fidgeting with the hem of his tunic. His big eyes trailed from hers to the bow over her shoulder, back to her eyes. Merryn followed his gaze. Smiling, she reached out a hand. With a huge grin, the boy took it, happily joining her.

Some time later, Merryn brought the horse to a stop, dismounted, then reached up to lift the boy off, his small feet touched the ground with uncertainty. She smiled and wondered if that had been his first time on a horse.

Hand in hand, they walked into the dense forest. Stopping, she sat on a rock, pulling the boy to stand before her.

"Alright, lad," she began, pulling an arrow from her quiver. "When I was a small lass, livin' in that church, Father Joseph would take me ta hunt with 'im. Blind as a bat, was he." She smiled at the memory, which made the boy smile, his eyes still riveted to the arrow. "This, lad, is called an arrow," she began to explain. "This," she said, brushing gray feathers against the boy's nose, making him sneeze, "is the fletching. Goose feathers, these." Next she ran her fingers down the long, wooden shaft. "This, lad, is the stele. 'N this, the arrow. Sharp." She grabbed his small hand, bringing a single finger to push gently against the tip. Paul snatched his hand away, holding it in the other, surprised at the little tingle the point sent through his finger and up his small arm.

Setting the arrow aside, Merryn swung the bow off her shoulder, spreading her knees to place the bow between, one end resting in the rich soil at their feet.

"Tug on this, lad," she nodded toward the string of the bow. The boy grabbed it in his fist, grunting slightly as he tried to pull against the great tension. Merryn chuckled. Getting to her feet, she took her bow, holding a finger to her lips. Paul nodded.

As they got deeper into the forest, Merryn moved with cat-like stealth and silence, eyes turned to her surroundings, allowing her body to call out to the life around her, feeling the pulse of the rapid heartbeat of her quarry. Suddenly she stopped, falling to her knees. Peeking through the thick foliage, she saw the flicker of a white tail, then the brown body, hidden well by the forest.

"Nock yer arrow, lad," she whispered, doing as she said. Paul watched with large eyes. Bringing the bow up, Merryn closed her right eye, focusing with her left, then let her arrow fly. The deer cried out in surprise before it collapsed. Paul looked on with huge eyes. He quickly followed Merryn as she hurried over to the felled animal.

"This, lad, is how to butcher."

Europe 1351

Merryn whipped around, her left hand already slicing through the air before she'd completed her turn, her right arm immediately rising to ward off the blow she sensed was coming. Her right leg swung out, making solid contact with the side of her opponent's thigh. The blade in her left hand slashed through the neck region, her right coming down to pound the top of the head.

"I'm down! I'm down!" Erik exclaimed, covering his face with his arms. Merryn swung one final time, the blade in her left hand coming within a hair's breadth of his nose. He looked up at her with wide, frightened eyes.

Grinning, Merryn collected both blades in her left hand, using her right to reach down and help the man to his feet.

"Second blade's a killer, it is," he panted, gaining his breath.

"Aye." She looked at the blade in question, happy with the sword Ezra had created especially for her in his blacksmith's shop. It was much like a Roman gladius, short, light and deadly sharp. Merryn had always been able to use her left hand as easily as her right and she found fighting was no different. Over the six months she'd been at Cayshire Castle, she'd worked to make each arm as strong as the other, both functioning equally, with equal speed and skill. She came at her opponents like a storm, all steel and intensity. She had become feared and respected, even among those who still refused to see her as nothing more than a woman invading their world.

Since she refused to fight herself, Angus had asked her to train others to fight. She had a natural skill and instinct that many of the growing army lacked. Angus had been lovingly crafting his forces; Ezra and the other blacksmiths worked feverishly to create enough armor and arms for the men.

The castle had become a fortress to be reckoned with. Merryn had convinced Angus to talk to the men and make them bathe at least three times a week. Merryn worked on the women, the elderly, and the lame. If an outbreak of the black sickness erupted, it would be disastrous. They grew all of their own food, made their own supplies and weapons, and had very little contact with the outside world. The thought was in everyone's mind every day, but they lived as though they'd never get sick, continuing with the plan.

Merryn sheathed her blades in the double baldric, running a hand through her sticky, sweaty hair.

"That, lads, 'tis what ye *dona* want te do." There was a round of chuckles as Erik brushed himself off, a slight limp as he walked back to his place in line. "Watch their feet. Weapons, too." She looked at each and every expectant face, many meeting her gaze with obvious respect and admiration. These men were farmers and peasants. Merryn almost laughed. They knew no better. "Off with ya!" she waved them all off. The large, wooden tubs were already set out in the yard, and the men disrobed as they walked over to them.

Walking back toward the keep, she noticed someone standing in the shadows. The sheer size of the hidden figure told her who it was.

"Ya need ta call yer dog off, Angus," she muttered, storming into the Great Hall. The Great Hall had been turned into the gathering place for Angus' army and officers. Angus, going over a map with two other men, stood, surprised by the outburst. She walked over to him, eyes burning. "If ya do not, I'll do it myself."

"Are ye outta yer mind?" Angus asked, anger burning in his dark eyes. Merryn met his gaze straight on. She pointed a warning finger at him and left, leaving Angus and the rest to look after her.

Merryn was furious. Gerik had made known his thoughts about a woman being anywhere but in the kitchen or chasing after the numerous children. Merryn had heard rumors that he was talking to other soldiers of a like mind. She worried that the giant and his followers would cause discord in the smooth running operation that was Cayshire.

Merryn went up the circular staircase that led to the living space that she and Ezra had built for the five of them. The large room had been walled off into three separate spaces — one for Evela and Ezra, one for Merryn alone, and one for Tamara and Paul, though Paul stayed with Merryn most the time.

She stripped out of her mail, the metal falling to the stone in a loud clump. She was angry, her breathing uneven. She had worked so hard at the castle, deciding that Angus was right — she had no one and nothing beyond the walls of Cayshire. So she had embraced it, helping to rebuild the crumbling walls. A smile spread across her lips as she remembered the birth of the now two month old Isaak.

"Merryn! Merryn, please help me," Jane begged, crouched over, arms crossed over her protruding stomach. Merryn, who had been going down an adjoining hall, turned, her eyes growing wide at the puddle of water at the young woman's feet.

Hurrying over to the young woman, she helped her to the floor, murmuring words of encouragement.

"Hang on, lass. I'll get help—"

"No! It's comin'!" Jane cried, her voice hoarse and her fingers claw-like as they dug desperately into Merryn's arm.

"All right." Merryn could feel her heart pounding in her temples. She helped the mother-to-be to a squatting position, her back leaning against the cold stone wall. Merryn reached up, grabbed the torch from its sconce, and brought it down, chasing the shadows away from between Jane's spread knees. Her breath caught; she had never witnessed anything like it before. The baby's head had already crowned, and Jane screamed as her flesh ripped. The insides of her thighs were streaked with red. Unsure what to do, Merryn reached in, feeling the hot, slimy flesh of the baby. Jane's chest heaved with every breath and every cry.

"It's comin', lass," Merryn breathed, exhilarated and frightened at the same time. "Push, lass. Push!"

Jane's head fell back against the wall, her hair hanging in sweaty strands. Squeezing her eyes shut, she gave one final scream, and Merryn screamed along with her as the baby slid out with a liquid gush.

"Ya've gotta son, Jane!" *Merryn looked up at the exhausted mother with tear-filled eyes. The baby began to whine as he was getting used to filling his lungs with cold air instead of warm liquid. It didn't take him long to push out his first cry. To Merryn's surprise, a round of applause erupted in the hallway. She looked up over her shoulder, seeing smiling members of the household, some of the women hurrying over to the new mother. Jolene, a midwife, immediately set about checking Jane's health and state of her sex.*

Merryn turned to some of the men and boys hanging around. "Well now, stand around like a bunch of oxes," *she chastised. Getting the point, the men jumped into action, lifting the poor girl to a comfortable bed.*

The baby had been taken from Merryn's arms, but she still stood in the corridor, tears in her eyes and a lightness in her heart. Looking down at her hands, she saw they were covered with the blood and juices of new life. She felt someone was still with her in the hall and glanced up.

Evela was watching her, a smile on her face. "Ye did good, Merryn," *she said softly.*

Merryn grinned. "Thank ya." *She had never been so proud of anything else she'd ever done in her life.*

"Cara smiles down upon ye, now."

"Ye think?" *Merryn asked. She'd eventually told Ezra's wife of her life, though short, with Cara. It was wonderful to have the memory live inside of another besides herself.*

Evela nodded. "Aye." *She walked over to the still stunned woman.* "Come. Let us clean you up."

Merryn rested her head back against the wall, a smile curving her lips. The business of Gerik constantly watching and stalking her had been temporarily forgotten. She saw that baby in her arms again; how tiny he was, yet how big his cry.

She felt a special bond with the child, which his mother recognized. Jane tried to give Merryn as much time with Isaak as possible. At first, it scared her. She had not one clue how to handle babies, how to hold them or change them. Her smile grew at the memory of the first time she'd tried to clean the lad after changing his soiled cloth. The fresh one she'd put on him had slid right down his legs. His tiny bladder had been unable to hold in his need any longer, and the next thing Merryn knew the front of her tunic was being sprayed and marked.

She chuckled lightly at the memory.

"I wish ya could see 'im, lass," she whispered.

Merryn looked down and smiled at the little sounds Isaak made, his tiny fingers wrapped around one of hers. Her eyes scanned his pinched face, looking at his tiny nose, nostrils flared as the baby instinctually took in everything around him.

"'Tis a beautiful child, Merryn."

She turned to her right. She instantly smiled, matching that of Cara's. Merryn nodded, turning back to the child in her arms.

"Aye." She looked again at Cara. "Would ya like ta hold 'im?" Cara's smile at the offer warmed Merryn's entire being.

"Very much so."

"Support his head, lass," Merryn whispered as she handed the tiny body into Cara's tender embrace. The girl looked down into the child's face, her smile soft and wistful.

"Hello, little Isaak," she cooed, bringing a hand up to touch the soft skin of the baby's face, lightly tapping his pert nose with a fingertip. Merryn moved behind Cara, resting her chin on her shoulder, seeing what she was seeing. For a moment, it seemed as if the impossible had happened, and the child in Cara's arms was their child, born of the love Merryn shared with Cara.

"He's got yer eyes, Merryn," Cara said, glancing at her.

"Aye. Yer hair."

Cara smiled, nodding. Merryn leaned into her, inhaling the smell of the golden hair, her eyes closing in bliss. She felt Cara lean back into her. Merryn wrapped her arms around Cara's waist, both looking into the child's face.

"Ye must head the family, Merryn," Cara said softly, leaning down to place a light kiss on Isaak's forehead. "With yer guidance, the family will grow 'n be grand." Cara stepped away from Merryn, turning to face her. Cara looked up at her with the softest green eyes, head slightly cocked to the side. Cradling the baby in the crook of one arm, she raised her other. Gently resting her hand on Merryn's cheek, she used her thumb to wipe away a single tear. Merryn leaned into the touch, eyes closing for a moment. She knew their time was coming to an end. "Lead yer family, Merryn," Cara whispered. She placed a gentle kiss to Merryn's lips. As she pulled away, she smiled. "Now wake."

As Merryn's eyes blinked open, she was surprised to feel the tickle of her dream tear really making its way to the corner of her mouth. Sniffling and wiping it away, she sighed.

Suddenly the hair on the back of her neck stood on end. Instinctively, she threw herself to the side. Sparks from steel against stone flew, with a deafening clang. Rolling to her feet, Merryn immediately grabbed for her blades, speedily unsheathing them.

Gerik turned to her, teeth bared as anger coursed through him. He'd thought he would certainly have the element of surprise with the slumbering *woman.*

Breathing hard, Merryn's eyes were fixed on the huge man, his blond hair half covering his face. He looked like the wild ones of the Highlands.

Legs spread wide for balance, Merryn flexed her fingers on the grips of her blades, her palms becoming sweaty. Gerik mirrored her stance; one large hand flexing, the other wrapped around the hand-and-a-half grip of his long blade, the tip gleaming menacingly in the sparse early-morning sunlight.

Merryn could feel sweat dribbling down her back and between her breasts. Keeping calm, she brought in air through her nose, exhaling between slightly parted lips.

With the cry of the beast, Gerik lunged, bringing his blade down. Merryn met his thrust, using her body strength to push him back. With a growl, he came back for another blow, Merryn blocking it with her left blade, bringing her right blade up under his to push it away. Gerik nearly lost his sword altogether. This angered him even more, and his face was red as he began to swing blindly, pushing Merryn further and further across the small room. His fist balling, he lashed out, catching her across the jaw. Blood flew from her mouth as she bit her tongue. Pain seared throughout Merryn's head, but she couldn't get lost in the pain or she was dead.

Merryn knew she would be trapped soon between the wall and Gerik's massive body. Ducking his blow, she used as much force as she could in a kick, which hit him square in the gut. Coughing as he stumbled backward, he raised his blade as Merryn came at him with dizzying speed and ferocity, both blades catching the sun to look like slashes of light coming at him. One caught him on the arm, the other sliced his cheek. She kicked at him again, this time catching him between the legs.

Gerik's eyes flew wide open as pain spread throughout his body. Even still, he threw himself to the ground, rolling out of the way of the wicked blades.

Getting to his feet behind her, he raised his blade high overhead, bringing it down toward her shoulder. Merryn brought both her blades up, catching and dislodging Gerik's blow. The sword flew out of his large hands, leaving him defenseless as Merryn whirled to face him. Another kick caught him in the chest, then one across the jaw, whipping his head to the side. Yet another kick landed on his knee, bringing him to the ground.

Merryn stood over him, her nostrils flaring with murderous intent. She looked into his terrified gray eyes, then saw him reaching for a dagger in his boot. She kicked him once more, and Gerik abandoned his dagger. But with the rage of near defeat, he lunged at her legs, bringing her to the ground and sending her blades flying off into the shadows.

Merryn cried out as pain licked up her spine, her head bouncing off the floor, nearly knocking her out. She blinked rapidly, biting her tongue again to make the pain wake her up.

Gerik was on top of her in a heartbeat, his snarling face in hers as one huge fist found its way to her jaw, making her head bounce again. Her vision began to grow dark around the edges, as her eyes rolled in their sockets. Bringing her hands up, she began to pound uselessly against his shoulders and sides. She was stunned once more as a fist was slammed into her ribs. She knew immediately that the fragile bones were broken.

Bringing her hand up once more in one last desperate attempt to save her life, she reached for his eyes, her fingers turning into claws.

Gerik screamed, trying to get away. Pain shot through his head and down into his neck as his world went black.

Merryn cried out in pain as she moved with him, not daring to let him go. Her fingers were firmly latched onto the man's eye sockets. Blood flowed down his face and over her hand. Gerik's shrill screams made her blood run cold.

Finally pushing away from him, she watched in horror as the huge man convulsed on the floor in agony his hands covering his face.

Gasping for breath and clutching her side, Merryn saw his blade. She went over and picked it up in her blood-covered hand.

Angus laughed with Lukas and John, two of his most trusted officers, in the yard. The army was drilling, their grunts and the clank of steel disturbing the morning air.

Suddenly all noise stopped and the day became deathly silent. Wondering what was wrong, Angus turned from his officers and was stunned by what he saw.

Merryn limped into the yard. She was half hunched over, her mouth a bloody mess, and her tunic covered in gore. She looked at everyone present, eyes wild and filled with rage. Wincing as she raised Gerik's blade, she shouted into the still day.

"Any o' ya wish ta fight me, do it now." No one moved or even breathed. With that, she threw the blade to the ground, slowly walking away, barely making it to a doorway before sliding down to her knees.

Angus ran over to her, falling beside her. "Merryn," he breathed, stunned and worried. He brought her hanging head up, looking into the broken face. "By God, Merryn, who did this?"

"Yer pup was spanked," she whispered. With that, she passed out.

Merryn had to cough, really needed to cough, and was about to choke on her cough — but didn't dare to cough. Squeezing her eyes shut, she tried to swallow it down, but began to choke. Finally giving in, she coughed then cried out in pain, her midsection making its injuries known with a howling scream.

"'Tis all right," Evela cooed, helping her back to the bed, her eyes squeezed shut in intense pain. Evela brushed dark strands away from the beautiful, angular face, so filled with pain. "'Tis all right, dear Merryn."

Merryn tried to relax, to even out her breathing, which was already shallow. The more she breathed, the more it tore at her midsection. Her face was beginning to hurt too, now the adrenaline had gone. Her skin was stiff and sticky from healing pastes. Evela had already gently washed away the blood and gore from Merryn's face, neck, and hands. She was bruised badly, her pupils dilated.

Merryn could hear soft murmurings from another part of the room, someone saying that Gerik was alive but blinded. She couldn't feel pleasure from this news. It had been unnecessary, and she resented Gerik forcing her hand.

"How is she?" Angus asked, his deep voice hushed.

"Alive," Evela said, her touch felt cool on Merryn's forehead.

"Shall we call fer t' Healer, Angus?" someone else asked. There was silence, and Merryn could feel eyes on her. She didn't have the strength to open her eyes or wave off such a crazy notion.

Finally Angus spoke for her. "Nay. Merryn's a fighter."

"Aye," Evela agreed. "She'll be back on her feet shortly." Merryn felt that hand gently caress the side of her head. "Won't ye, Merryn?"

"Aye," she whispered, moving her face as little as possible.

"Out with ye." Evela shooed the gathered crowed. Everyone filed out obediently, some giving one last mournful look to one of their own. Soon it was just Evela and Merryn.

Merryn winced as shooting pain ripped through her middle, stealing her breath along the way. After a moment, it passed, leaving her weak and gasping.

"Merryn, take this."

Merryn felt her head being carefully lifted and something being placed against her lips, making her wince yet again. She opened her mouth with soft encouragement, tasting the bitter herb.

"Coriander te help ye sleep, Merryn."

Merryn nodded, taking a sip from the mug at her lips. She swallowed the herb, then lay back down, praying for a quick effect. The last thing she remembered before drifting off was the feel of a small body climbing onto the bed and curling up next to her.

Part 9

Holding her breath slightly and leaning on the walking stick Ezra had fashioned for her, Merryn walked to the Great Hall. During her fight with Gerik, she'd re-injured the leg that had been broken. The pain had become less and less, but she still didn't trust the strength of her leg to walk on unassisted.

Resting in bed had been driving her close to madness. She was restless, fidgety, and irritating Evela terribly with her whining. To her credit, Evela had held her tongue. Even so, she had very expressive eyes and Merryn was in no doubt of her feelings. She had been acting like a petulant child, and the quiet women could let her know it with a single look.

Paul walked with her, his short steps echoing alongside her own, his little fist clasped around an end of her tunic, as was his habit. She glanced down at the boy, who immediately looked up at her. He stood to her waist, and she ran her free hand gently through his soft, brown hair before turning her focus back to her walking. It was a slow process, but Paul was a patient boy.

Voices could be heard in the Great Hall, men laughing and talking. Excitement was high, as the plan would be enacted within the month. Merryn was on her way to ask if she could join. She had made a decision the day Gerik attacked her. No man, no *one*, would ever steer her destiny, nor attempt to, again. She would no longer hide behind her own fears or selfishness, wrapped up in a transparent bundle of anger and apathy.

As she entered the Hall, voices slowly hushed. Hundreds of men turned to stare at the two silhouettes in the grand archway. Merryn's proud features slowly came into view as torchlight forced her into dancing shadow and light. She looked around in confusion as one by one, the men began to fall to one knee, heads bowing. The room was filled with the sounds of mail hitting stone, leather rubbing steel, and steel scraping against steel.

Looking across the sea of bowed heads, Merryn found twinkling dark eyes. Angus smiled, then he, too, fell to one knee. Finding Paul's curious eyes looking back up at her, the boy shrugged. Merryn looked over the room again. She walked further in, not a man meeting her eye as she passed. A myriad of emotions flowed through her as she made her way along the path made for her by the crowd. She reached Angus and turned to the army.

"Rise!" she called, wincing slightly at the pain speaking loudly caused in her ribs. Just as noisily as they had knelt, the men regained their feet. She turned to Angus, confusion in her eyes. He smiled, giving her a slight bow, his eyes never leaving her own. "What 'tis this?" she asked, incredulous.

"They honor 'n respect ye, Merryn," he explained softly, ruffling Paul's hair. "They know ye c'n kick their arses now."

"Madness," she hissed, though in a secret place that she'd never admit to anyone, she was greatly pleased. She turned to the men, bowing slightly to them, letting them know she respected every man in the room in return. She also felt her chest fill a little more, her spine straighten a little. "I come ta tell ya I wish ta join ya, Angus."

He studied her, looking deeply into her eyes. She could see how he'd aged since she'd first seen him nearly two years ago — there were additional lines around his mouth and between his eyes. His forehead was criss-crossed with them. He nodded his approval.

"I'd love to have ye fight by my side, Merryn," he said quietly. She nodded. It was set. Looking out over the army once more, her gaze twitched, suddenly nervous.

"As ya were," she muttered, then grabbed Paul's hand, hurrying from the room as quickly as her leg and healing body would allow.

The cold, winter night found Merryn in her favorite place of isolation — at the top of the turret. She leaned against the stone, a mug of hot cider cradled between her palms. Her cloak was tightly wrapped around her shoulders, the hood barely over her head. A few long strands of dark hair whipped around her face. With a sigh that crystallized just outside of her lips, she took a sip of her steaming drink.

She looked out over Cayshire below her, and at the mainland. Many fires dotted the darkness. A small smile curled her lips as she thought of all the people down there — families and, amazingly enough, friends. She could call each by name and knew things about each one. Was this what it felt like to be happy? Surely that wasn't a possibility for her, was it?

Happiness. And without Cara. Merryn thought that was an impossibility. Somehow — and it had crept up on her — light had once again dawned in her life, chasing away the darkness to clear a lit path.

"Who do you think of?"

Merryn glanced over her shoulder, seeing Evela standing just outside the narrow stone doorway, leading back into the tower. The young woman, with the wisp of white hair, was a steadfast friend and silent protector.

Merryn turned back to gaze out over the moonlit sea below. She heard Evela walk over to her and lean against the stones.

"How did ye meet her?"

Merryn smiled. Evela always seemed to know what was on her mind. She reached up, absently taking the coin she'd had a hole drilled through and strung on a leather thong around her neck. She rubbed her thumb over the rough gold, a gesture she'd done thousands of times.

"She was bein' attacked by a bandit," Merryn explained, her voice soft and wistful. She thought back to that night. Oh, how differently she would behave now. She would be kind, willing to lend a helping hand and hold the frightened girl.

"Saved her, did ye?" Evela smiled, seeing her friend nod her dark head, though her features were barely visible under the shadow of the hood.

"Aye," Merryn said unnecessarily.

"How long did ye travel together?" Evela moved a bit closer, hoping to share a bit of body heat in the cold night. Merryn's mood of late was dark and morose. Evela knew it had to do with the girl's injuries and, perhaps, the upcoming plan. She also knew that if she wanted to talk to her, or spend time with her, it had to be on Merryn's terms.

"Not long enough." Merryn was surprised she had spoken aloud. She cleared her throat, trying to cover her embarrassment. "A year 'n a bit."

"'M sorry, Merryn," Evela said, her voice soft, filled with genuine sorrow. She could feel the pain, deep and profound. She wished there was something she could do to ease it. These were hard times, and death was all around them, waiting his turn to gallop in on his black horse and trample the spirits of the living. "Ezra and I lost our child to the sickness."

Merryn turned to her, only seeing her in profile, her face pale against the darkness. The streak of white seemed to glow.

"Sarah weren't but three." Evela took a deep breath, trying to keep the pain of her own loss at bay, squashed where it had remained all these long, two years.

"'Tis a pain that does not leave," Merryn whispered, turning back to the night. She felt Evela's nod.

"Aye."

Merryn took several deep breaths then allowed young Alex to help her don her mail, full shirt, and sleeves. The heavy metal fell to her upper thighs. She took the belt offered by the boy, cinching it around her waist. The mail bagged over it slightly, bringing its length to crotch level. The quilted surcoat was placed over the top, with another belt lying above that.

Merryn moved her arms and twisted at the waist, making sure her movement was fluid, already feeling the weight and heat of the armor. Taking the coif from the lad, she carefully tugged it over her closely pinned hair. Alex straightened the mail around her shoulders and neck and then efficiently got her baldric in place, fastening it while Merryn pulled on her gauntlets. Flexing her fingers, she was ready.

Merryn joined the small army that would be used this night. The majority of the men were being held back. Tonight was about surprise and attack.

Mounting her horse, she watched with pride as man after man did the same. Every window and door of Cayshire was filled with well-wishers as the double row of warriors passed through the lanes, the light of torches glinting off wickedly sharp steel until the light of the moon led the group.

The ride was silent, each lost in his own head, knowing full well how things could turn out. Not a man there was without a cross, band of garlic, or some sort of token of faith in something larger and more powerful than himself. Merryn could feel the warm gold against her upper chest.

The party decided to make camp by a lake as morning approached. They'd travel the rest of the way when night fell.

Merryn rolled over, readjusting her blankets, the fire crackling close by. She heard movement and opened her eyes. Angus stood up from his place across the fire and walked toward the lake. Merryn quietly followed him.

The dark man glanced over his shoulder before tossing a pebble in the water, breaking the mirror-perfect surface. "Canna sleep?" he asked, looking back to the water.

Merryn smirked. "Was gonna ask ya the same." She picked up her own stone and tossed it.

Angus looked down at his boots for a moment. Merryn waited him out, knowing he would speak when he was ready.

"Merryn," he began, clearing his throat and keeping his voice low so as not to be overheard, "do ye think I'm leadin' these lads to their deaths?" he glanced at the small army camped behind them, then looked deeply into Merryn's eyes.

She studied him for a long moment, trying to give him as true an answer as possible. Finally she smiled, gently and fondly. "Angus, they follow ya o' their own will. The risks 're high, 'tis true," she nodded. "They know this." She could still see the concern on his face and the dregs of doubt. Placing a hand on his shoulder, she turned him to look at her. "Angus, they look ta ya. If ya doubt now, they're dead." She paused, waiting for her words to sink in. "Turn back now, if ya dona believe in what ya do. Teresa would understand."

Angus sighed, looking back out over the water. Shaking his head, he turned back to her. "Nay. We do this."

Merryn smiled, giving a sharp nod. "Aye. We do this." She raised her hand; he clasped his around it with the strength of the warrior.

"Together."

"Together."

Using birdcalls as signals, Merryn directed her archers to the hills near Middleham. The rest of the men were placed in strategic locations near the bridge and drawbridge.

She glanced at Angus, who nodded to her. With cat-like grace and silence, they made their way toward the mouth of William's Hill, where two guards were standing sentinel. Merryn smirked; apparently they'd become wiser after Cara's rescue.

Without a sound, she moved up behind the closest guard, seeing Angus out of the corner of her eye creeping toward the other one.

A short grunt split the night, then all was silent.

Merryn reached into the small pouch at her hip, bringing out the small picklocks, and made short work of the new locks that had been put on the doors inside the tunnel. The new locks were even easier to pick than the others had been, for they had formed no rust.

The heat could be felt almost as soon as the second door had been opened, closed, and wedged from the inside. The boiler room was working double time, which surprised Merryn, as the king wasn't in the castle. It appeared that his remaining men were enjoying themselves.

Angus followed quickly behind, his blade ready for anything. They tried to be as quiet and swift as possible. The heavy mail made their progress slightly slower than he felt comfortable with. The whole plan was on his shoulders, and that of the young girl just in front of him. If they failed, the plan would fail. Merryn pushed open the iron grate at the end of the tunnel; everything was exactly as it had been when they were last here.

Merryn was amazed at the calm that filled her, her inner peace as she traveled the passageways in the bowels of the castle. It had been decided that she would descend into the pits of Middleham hell to release the captives and the condemned, while Angus made his way through the castle.

The knighted men would be strongly loyal to their King, but the hired soldiers were just that — hired. Angus and Merryn could use that to their advantage.

Merryn moved along the dark halls, creeping along like a thief in the night. She stopped as she heard two men talking just ahead, her fingers flexed on the grip of her blade.

"Now get outta 'ere and feed the bastards!" someone hissed, muttering to himself as the person he was talking to left to carry out his orders. Peeking around the corner, she saw the soldier sitting in a wooden chair, tilted back against the stone wall. His eyes were hooded, boredom clearly written on his face. She scanned his body, seeing only a sword. No keys.

Checking again that they were alone, Merryn scurried over to him, slamming her fist into his jaw and knocking him off his chair. Her hand around his throat kept him quiet.

"Where's t' key holder?" she hissed. He just stared up at her. She pushed his head into the stone wall behind him. "Where?" The stunned soldier's head was bashed against the wall. "Tell me," Merryn hissed, pulling the man up by his hair to look at her. "Tell me where he hides or die now, lad." Merryn brought his face up closer to her own, letting him know she meant every hit upon that stone.

The soldier was trembling, his eyes drifting toward the iron door at the end of the hall. "Feeding them," he gasped, eyes beginning to tear from the raging headache splitting his skull.

Merryn shoved him, and the soldier fell off the chair, landing in a heap on the dirt. Knocking him out with another blow, she grabbed him by the boots and dragged him to a shadow-filled doorway, leaving him there. Running to the iron door, Merryn glanced over her shoulder once more and then slid inside.

She wrinkled her nose immediately as the stench of human bodies, feces, urine, and every other body fluid hit her. The smell was nearly unbearable. The room was dark, filled with dancing shadows from scattered torches. Thick wood doors, ribbed with steel, lined either side of the narrow room. Small, barred squares were cut out of each door at eye level. Fingers could be seen wrapped around some of the bars.

Merryn was surprised at the relative quiet of the dungeon. She glanced into some of the cells. Shackles hung from the stone walls, most hanging open with the cells' occupants lying in their own filth. She wasn't sure if all of them were alive.

Movement caught Merryn's eye, her own presence seeming to catch the guard by surprise. He held a large pail of something, bits of gray slime dripping off one side. Throwing away the pail, his face hardened in resolve as he immediately drew his blade.

Not giving him a chance, Merryn ran at him full speed, barreling him over with a full body tackle and falling in a heap with him onto the straw.

The soldier tried to roll them over, but Merryn kept him on his back. She clamped her thighs into his sides, using the powerful muscles to keep him down. She raised her gauntleted hand, growling. The soldier saw what was coming, the steel-covered hand gleaming in the torchlight. He covered his face with his bracers, and Merryn caught him instead on the side of the head. He grunted in surprised pain.

"Work with me, lad, and I'll spare ya," she panted, bringing the tip of a dagger to his throat. He looked at her with surprised brown eyes, one hand covering his ringing ear. She knew all too well how much what she had done to him hurt.

"Who are ye?" he asked, his voice shaky. He was young and quite unsure of what to make of this seemingly demon woman. New to the King's army, he had been put on dungeon duty.

"Yer worst nightmare if ya refuse," she growled. Teeth clanging together, he nodded vigorously. He was stunned at the beauty of Merryn's smile as she stood, holding a hand down to him. He took it, eyes unable to leave hers. Still holding his hand, she pulled him close, his face a mere breath away. "If ye betray me, lad..." the boy's eyes nearly popped out of his skull at the feel of a dagger against his privates. Understanding her message loud and clear, he nodded again. "I want ya ta take these prisoners out through t' tunnel. Ya know t' tunnel?"

"Aye," he whimpered.

Merryn shoved him away, snatching the keys from his belt. Hurrying over to one of the cell doors, Merryn inserted the large, iron key into the equally large lock. She steadily went through each key until she found the one that unlocked the cell door. She looked through the small, square hole. An old man looked back at her, tired and haggard. His eyes were mere shadows of the man he once was.

"Stay quiet, and ya'll live," she hissed. He nodded. Down the line she went, issuing the same demand at each cell door. When all the prisoners were released, Merryn made sure the young soldier did as he had been told, then moved on into the upper sections of the castle.

Merryn took the stairs two at a time, her heart beating out of control. Angus had managed to lower the gates, letting the rest of the men charge in, roaring loudly with the blades raised high over their heads. The soldiers of the king were fighting back bravely, trying to defend their stronghold.

The king had gone in hiding at his country estate, taking the bulk of his army with him. There was but a skeleton garrison keeping watch over Middleham Castle.

Merryn made her way into the fray, both blades flying through the air, a whirlwind of motion and grace. Had it not been so deadly, it would have been a beautiful sight.

Carnage. That was all Merryn could think of. Panting, bruised, and bleeding, she looked around. The fight had moved out to the keep, and there were bodies littering the ground, some in the colors of the king and some in those of Cayshire.

Suddenly it was over. She fell to her knees, her body about to give out. Glancing to her left, she saw Angus limping over to her. Relieved to see he'd survived, she gave him a weak smile. Collapsing next to her, he sighed deeply, running his right hand through sweat-slicked hair and leaving a thin trail of blood near his temple.

"'Tis such a loss," he said, almost whispering. He was battle fatigued and weary, and the left side of his head was covered with blood. Merryn nodded, falling to a sitting position, her head resting against a nearby door.

"How many dead?"

"Near thirty o' ours. Double that theirn."

"Captives?"

"Safe."

With a groan, Merryn pushed herself to her feet; she knew that if she didn't rise now, she wouldn't be able to. There was still work to be done, and it had to be done now. She helped Angus up. It was time to set about removing bodies, tossing them into the moat.

"Ya men!" she called out to a small group of their men. When she had their collective attention, she continued, "Stephen, get a wagon, get a horse, and begin gettin' them out." She pointed to the bodies around.

"Save weapons," Angus said, his voice very shaky. Merryn turned to look at her friend, just in time to see him collapse.

"Boil more rags, now!" Merryn called out, dabbing arnica paste on her patient. She shot a concerned glance over to her friend. Angus was finally awake and the castle's physician was attending to his wounds, digging through the thick, black hair, looking for the source of the blood that had poured down his face.

Sure that Angus was being cared for, she turned her attention back to the soldier she was looking after.

"Merryn?"

"Aye?" she muttered absently, quickly wrapping her patient's arm with the newly brought cloth. He was losing a lot of blood from the gash.

One of the soldiers came over to her. "Let me have a look at ye, Merryn. Yer bleed—"

"Take care o' these men!" she hissed, turning to the surprised young soldier. Softening her voice, she turned back to her task. "Dona worry 'bout me, Thomas. Help them first." She nodded at the room filled with moaning men. Some were crying. With a quick nod, the soldier hurried to follow her orders.

Merryn's head snapped round at the sound of a loud cry. Angus thrashed on the chair where he sat, his head buried in his hands. She saw the physician, trying to pick his way out of the room.

"Stop 'im!" she yelled, running over to the screaming Angus. Two soldiers tackled the man, all going down in a clang of mail. "Angus, Angus," she breathed, trying to pry his hands away from his head.

"Burns!" he cried, jerking back in the chair so hard he head-butted Merryn. Staggering back, she shook off an echo of pain rattling around in her head, stepping back over to her friend.

"Let me see, Angus," she murmured, using all her force to pull his hands free. The wound at the side of his head was fizzing. His hair clung to his hands, and his skin was peeling back from his skull. "Ah, Lord in Heaven," she gasped. Looking around, she saw the scrap of cloth the physician had been using. Snatching it, she sniffed at it, grimacing at the acidic smell. She turned to the physician who was held between the two soldiers "Bryony?" she asked, waving the cloth around. "Ya bastard!" Throwing the cloth to the floor, she turned back to the whimpering Angus. "Someone bring me some white wine!" she bellowed, "with..." she tried desperately to remember what Cara would have used. "Bugger ta Hell," she muttered. "Anise! White wine and anise!"

"Aye!" someone yelled out.

Within moments, Merryn had what she needed in her hands. "Hang on, Angus," she whispered, tipping the herb into the wineskin and shaking the ingredients together vigorously, before soaking a clean cloth with the mixture. "Take this," she said, tossing the wineskin to a soldier standing close by. Placing her hand on the other side of Angus' head, she pressed the soaked cloth to the angry wound, making him cry out again.

"What are ye doin'?" Thomas asked, his eyes wide as he watched her snatch up the wineskin, and pour small amounts onto the wound. With each washing, Thomas felt his stomach roil. What Merryn had called bryony, had burned through Angus' hair, leaving a bald, bloody spot just above his left ear. The skin was scorched and angry.

Merryn ignored the question, instead concentrating on cleaning off the rest of the poison. Lukas, one of the officers, stood behind her, watching.

"Bryony wouldn't do that alone, would it?" he asked, his voice low. He saw the girl shake her head.

"Nay." She glanced again at the physician, still held by the two soldiers. "Finish this," she tossed over her shoulder, passing the wineskin to Lukas and grabbing a dagger from her belt as she walked over to the captive man. Without a word, she drew her hand back and thrust the blade into his gut. His gray eyes protruded from their sockets. The blade went in easily, the hilt stopping its advance. Merryn felt warm blood cover her hand and grip of the dagger. With a vicious snarl, she shoved the man off her dagger, letting him fall to the floor with a plop.

As she walked away, the men moved out of her way. Silence following her out of the room.

Merryn was glad to feel the chill of fresh air against her heated skin. She was filled with the adrenaline of looking death in the eye, watching it cut down one man after another around her, only to bow out of her shadow. She could still see every face that fell pale before her, still see their blood, as her sword sliced through the armor they prayed would keep them safe.

Walking the cold passageways of the huge castle, Merryn wondered what all this was for. What was the purpose of so many losing their lives this night? Her own hand had taken many.

Running her hands, which were still covered in blood and gore, through her hair, she felt her body begin to tremble, as she let out a shaky breath. She was surprised to feel her eyes stinging. Letting a few tears of relief and release slip out from her lids, she took several more deep breaths. Returning the way she'd come, she heard soft murmurings and the obvious sounds of feasting.

Curiosity drew the exhausted girl to the sounds. She recognized many of the people gathered around a long table, which was strewn with food and drink. Their ragged clothing hung off their terribly thin frames and they were shoving as much food into their mouths as possible.

Merryn wandered through the room, wondering why they were back. She had expected that they would scatter to wherever they had come from. There were a couple dozen people — some men, but mostly women and two children huddled around the skirts of what looked to be their mother.

Merryn smiled at some, nodded at others, and received an overwhelmingly enthusiastic hug from one man who remembered her from the dungeon.

"Thank ye, thank ye!" he cried, fat tears falling down dirt-smudged cheeks.

Merryn smiled. "Yer welcome."

With that, he hurried back to his place at the table, guzzling water from a wooden mug, the liquid flowing down either side of his mouth, leaving clean trails.

For the first time that night, Merryn felt relaxed. She saw the excitement and relief on the faces of these people. These were not hardened criminals, who had deserved to be chained and starved. These were the people of an uncaring ruler who needed to be stopped.

"This must end," she whispered. Turning to leave, she caught a flash of gold out of the corner of her eye She raised to her toes to see above the heads of those at the table. On the other side of the room, near the wall, stood a young girl, her thin body hunched and her dress faded and torn. Her face was covered by long, golden hair.

Merryn made her way around the room, brows drawn. She felt her heartbeat quicken, a softening of her entire being. There was something familiar about this young girl, who was maybe ten years of age. As she neared, the girl lifted her head, her bright green eyes blinking, focusing on the approaching figure. Seeing the blood, the armor and weapons, she shrank back.

Stopping, Merryn raised her hands in supplication. "Fear not, lass," she said, her voice soft. The girl did not relax, but she stopped trying to press into the wall. "How long have ya been here?"

The girl raised her eyes to the ceiling for a moment, thinking, before looking again at Merryn. "Two years, milady." Her voice was soft and a little shaky.

Unable to take her eyes from the girl, Merryn reached behind her, for a chair. She dragged it over to the girl, indicating that she should sit. With a small smile, she did. Merryn fell to her haunches before her, looking up into the gentle face.

"What 'tis yer name, lass?"

"Grace, milady."

Merryn couldn't stop the tears from welling in her eyes, as her heart missed a beat. She swallowed, bringing a hand up to wipe the tears before they fell.

"Where're yer family, Grace?" She felt horrible for asking as the girl's face fell, the golden curtain of her hair hiding her pain.

"Dead, milady."

"Have ya nowhere to go, lass?" She watched the girl shake her head, and her shoulders dipping further. "Grace?" she reached up, gently tipping the little girl's chin up. Watery green eyes met her own. "Would ya like to come with us? Ta a place where there is no cruelty. No shackles." Grace's eyes widened slightly, hope briefly flitting through her eyes before swiftly disappearing.

"Aye, milady," she whispered.

"Call me Merryn, Grace." Merryn gave her the biggest smile she could manage, trying to assuage the girl's fears. She stood, clenching her teeth so she wouldn't wince as pain sliced up her leg. A soldier, who she'd then run through, had kicked her.

"'Tis nice ta meet ye, Merryn."

Merryn looked down at the smiling girl. The sight made her heart clench in profound sorrow once more. So like Cara.

"'Tis so nice ta meet ya, lass," she whispered, walking away.

Part 10

"How do ya feel, Angus?" He turned from the window he stood before. The moonlight shone off the white cloth wrapped around his head.

"Survivin'," he said, turning back to the window, looking out over Cayshire. Merryn walked up to stand next to him. "We did it." He grinned at her, though his smile was broken.

"Aye." Merryn glanced at him as she began to speak her mind. "What 'tis yer plan, Angus?"

He sighed, shaking his head. Angus had been beaten down at Middleham. His wounds had almost killed him, and Merryn sensed a fear that had sprung inside him. A fire had been lit inside her.

Turning fully to him, she looked deeply into his eyes. "Let us finish this thing, Angus," she said, her voice strong and confident. "Let us take t' bastard." Her voice gained strength with every word. "Angus, we could take it all! Dona ya see?" She waved her arm over the shire below. "These people, *our* people, Angus, depend on us."

Angus sighed and looked down. "No. I've done what I came ta do, Merryn." He refused to look at her. She shook her head.

"I dona believe that. Ya started this, yer heart is in this." She smacked the windowsill before them. "Ya got scared, didn'cha?"

He sighed, but said nothing, turning his attention back to the world beyond the window.

"Fine." Merryn pushed away from the window, walking across half the expanse of the room. Jaw clenched, she turned back to him, her voice booming, "But I refuse to end this!"

Merryn heard footfalls behind her as she slammed through the double doors that led to a small garden. Staring up at the moon, she wanted to howl.

"Yer leg still bothering ye, is it?"

Merryn didn't have to turn to know it was Evela who stood not three steps behind her. She didn't answer.

"Perhaps it should be looked at?"

Merryn shook her head. "Nay."

"What troubles ye this night, Merryn?"

"'Re all men so stubborn?" she looked over her shoulder at her friend, blue eyes narrowed. They narrowed further when they saw the emerging smile on Evela's lips.

"Never married, then?"

Merryn chuckled, shaking her head.

"Save fer perhaps…" Evela let her words drop away, no need to finish.

Merryn looked at her, surprise in her eyes. Evela was smiling gently at her. She sighed long and deep, turning from her friend to look out into the night once more. "A miracle has happened, Evela," she said, her voice soft and filled with the wonder she felt.

"And what is that?"

Merryn felt a soft touch on her shoulder, then she was slowly turned to face her friend. Evela's head fell slightly to the side as she saw the glimmer of emotion in Merryn's eyes.

"At t' castle," Merryn began, "I saw someone, a young girl, who," she swallowed, taking a deep breath to keep her emotions in check. It was a losing battle. "She looks just like her, Evela," she whispered. Evela said nothing, her hand dropping from the taller woman's shoulder, caressing her upper arm.

"Grace. Cara's Grace lives."

Evela didn't understand, but she could feel Merryn's tumultuous emotions oozing from every pore.

"Come here, Merryn." She eased her head onto her shoulder, her own dark eyes closing as she rubbed gentle circles over Merryn's back.

Merryn allowed herself to be held, her own arms wrapped around Evela's back.

"Cara spoke so of'en of her," she said absently, a finger absently playing with a loose string on Evela's dress.

"Who is Grace?" Evela asked, her hand rising to gently caress Merryn's dark hair, fingers running through the soft, cool strands. She smiled at the soft sigh that evoked.

"Her younger sister. Cara thought she'd perished with her mother."

"So what has ye so angry?" Evela gently pulled away, just enough to look into Merryn's eyes and caress the soft skin of her face with her thumb.

"Angus." Merryn ran her hands through her hair, wincing slightly as her fingers grazed a bruise.

"What of him? What has he done?" Evela saw Merryn's rueful smile.

"'Tis what he won't do. Evela, he could lead these people." Merryn felt her heart beginning to pound with the passion this subject aroused. "Edward, he's weak! We could bring back the land, free these people." She swung her arm over the expanse of the garden. "This country is bein' ripped apart by sickness 'n fear. Edward has done not a thing, naught but run away. These people 're dyin', Evela."

Evela looked up into the passionate eyes and couldn't help but feel inspired and moved. Something inside told her that if the land was to be saved, it would be Merryn who could do it.

"And Angus?"

"Is afraid." Merryn sighed again, giving her back to the other woman.

"So make him *un*afraid, Merryn. If anyone can, 'tis you."

Merryn looked at her friend once more with brows drawn. She saw nothing but honesty and affection in those dark eyes. Evela smiled at her uncertainty. She reached up and cupped Merryn's cheek, her thumb running along a prominent cheekbone.

"Be the leader ye were born ta be, Merryn."

Merryn closed her eyes, feeling a gentle tug on the back of her neck. Her heart began to pound, blood racing as she felt warm breath on her face. The soft touch of lips on her forehead made her sigh in contentment at the human touch. How she missed being touched!

Opening her eyes, she looked at her friend, sharing a smile.

Merryn walked the long halls of Cayshire castle, her thoughts tumbling over each other, not one staying long enough to reach a conclusion. She did have a destination in mind, however. The smells and sounds would have told her long before she arrived that she was headed for the kitchen.

A swarm of women bounced around the small, stone room. There was hot steam wafting from two huge cauldrons placed over well-built fires. One woman stood near one such cauldron, bringing a wooden spoon to her lips, blowing across the broth she'd scooped from the simmering stew.

"'Tis not ready," she announced, sticking the long-handled spoon back into the pot and using both hands to stir.

Merryn looked around seeing a small group of women standing near the bread ovens, talking and tittering like young girls. She smirked, amused at their giggles. She'd never understood such behavior. One woman in particular caught her eyes.

Tamara quickly excused herself from the others and, wiping her hands on her skirts, walked over to Merryn.

"C'n I ask ye a favor, lass?" Merryn asked, leading her to a small alcove. Tamara nodded, meeting her eyes for just a moment. "The young girl, Grace, brought from Middleham," Tamara nodded in recognition. "I want ya to take 'er under yer wing, lass. Teach her what ya know, let 'er help ya here in the kitchens."

"Aye, Merryn."

Merryn smiled with a nod of thanks. Leaving Tamara to re-join her friends, Merryn went out in search of some solitude.

Dropping her weapons in her room first, Merryn felt light and somewhat naked in her tunic, hose, and boots, with her cloak draped over her arm. She stopped into Tamara's room before heading up to her favorite place. It was late, and she was glad to see Paul had gone to sleep already.

Kneeling next to the large bed the boy shared with his mother, she brought the warm blankets up, tucking them just under the boy's chin. Brushing dark locks back from his face, she leaned up, placing a soft kiss on his forehead.

Satisfied that the lad was warm and comfortable, Merryn headed up to the turret. Wrapping the cloak over her shoulders, she shrugged into it, clasping it at her throat. The night air was cold against her skin, making her feel alive and attentive.

She smiled as she thought of recent events. Never would she have believed she'd find a purpose in life, other than basic survival. And who would have thought it would involve so many other people and have such a wide scope? Sometimes she still thought it madness. Perhaps Angus was right.

Eyes closed, Merryn inhaled the refreshing, smoke-scented air, allowing it to fill her lungs and her entire being with peace. Her body still hurt terribly from the beating she'd taken at Middleham and she wasn't even entirely healed from her fight with Gerik. She smiled, thinking of Paul. He'd sat upon her lap, his big, brown eyes studying her face. He'd reached up a small hand, placing a light touch on every bruise and cut, wanting to know what had caused each one. Merryn had gone into a tale for each, satisfying the boy's unending curiosity.

Cara would have loved the lad, so inquisitive and so quick-witted. He and Merryn had come to some sort of gesture understanding. He would communicate with movements in his hands, his eyes, and the cocking of his head. There wasn't much that she didn't understand from the boy.

Grace. Merryn's mind flew off in an entirely new direction. She had seen the young girl earlier that day. She was so quiet, nothing like her sister. Cara could talk to anyone, putting the angriest of men at ease with just a smile. Grace was shy and soft spoken. Her eyes were guarded. Again, they were nothing like Cara's, always so filled with questions and wonder. The coloring was near to being exactly the same, however.

Merryn thought of no greater gift she could offer to Cara than to care for her beloved sister, making sure the girl was properly treated and happy. She'd do everything in her power to make that happen. Tamara was the right person for the job, that she knew. Their temperament seemed to be somewhat similar, and Tamara didn't have an intimidating bone in her small body.

Confident that all would be well with Grace, Merryn's thoughts turned once again to Angus and his sudden cowardice. She wondered if he still stood at his window, looking out over the same night she herself watched over. What stopped him? They were so close. More than one hundred of the surviving soldiers from Middleham had joined them. For those who did, they were allowed to help plunder Middleham, keeping their prize as their raise in pay.

Those who had refused to join them... Merryn sighed, not wanting to think about that. Their dispatch had been regrettable but necessary in its brutality. Merryn knew that Edward would not allow this to go unpunished. They needed to take this bull by the horns now, turning the people against their king and winning their favor and loyalty. They needed to do the same with the nobles also.

"Blasted, Angus," she hissed, slamming her scarred fist into the stone she rested on. Once again she saw the terrified people running from those open cell doors. Some had been too frightened to leave and had needed to be coaxed to freedom.

When they'd left the castle, a small contingent of soldiers and their officers stayed behind. The captives, who had nothing to lose and everything to gain, had traveled with Merryn and her forces. Most were so grateful, they offered any skill they had and any assistance they could give. Merryn had been deeply touched by their gratitude. Placement within Cayshire had been swift upon arrival.

That was three days ago. Now further action was needed.

Merryn nodded to herself, new determination made her stand a little straighter and hold her head a little higher. She'd talk with Angus again. She had to.

Whistling with new purpose, Merryn tossed her breakfast into the air, snatching the apple as it fell, before taking a healthy bite. Her boots echoed through the stone halls with long, confident strides. The sunlight of the cold, January day shone down upon her as she entered the keep.

At the end of the yard by the stables, she saw who she was looking for. Jogging across the expanse, she caught the reins of the great, black horse. The rider looked down at her. She met his gaze.

"We need ta talk, Angus."

He sighed, looking out over the keep and those who hurried along with their daily duties. Finally meeting her gaze, he sighed again. "Very well."

Merryn stepped back as he climbed down off his horse, his grunt of pain in sharp contrast to his usual, poised grace on dismounting. His black hair flopped over the white bindings around his head.

"Come."

With long, loping strides, Merryn led Angus to the blacksmith's shop. Ezra and his men hadn't started work yet. She wanted somewhere quiet for them to talk.

Merryn was almost giddy with what she had to say. She'd lain in bed the night before, her mind a whirlwind of thought and ideas.

Eyes bright, she began. "We're gonna finish this, Angus. Do it not, 'n we die where we stand."

"Meanin'?" he spread his legs wide, arms crossing his chest.

"Meanin', do ya think Edward is gonna jus' roll over dead when he hears Middleham has been sacked?" Merryn saw Angus' jaw clench briefly before he shook his head. "We've strength in numbers, Angus. Our army has doubled o'er night, the king's own men joinin' our fight."

"Aye." He was listening.

"I've got it all worked out in my head." Merryn took a breath as she got her thoughts in order, wanting to say it all just right. Looking him in the eyes, she spoke in an even, calm voice. "First, we use the nobles against 'im..."

The two horses galloped along the dirt path, dust and debris flying off the beating hooves. Cloaks flew from the riders' shoulders, the winter wind blowing them from hunched backs, as they urging their mounts to go faster, harder.

"... We give them a choice, lettin' them decide their own fate..."

"Lord Robert expects you," the guard said, his face impassive as he led the guests through the halls of the grand estate house, finally opening double doors. Beyond lay an expensively appointed study with roaring fire at its core. A massive oak desk sat near the back wall, the nobleman sitting behind it, head bent as he scribed with his quill. Glancing up, he smiled at his guests.

"Welcome." He sat back in his chair, eyeing the man and woman before him, fingers steepled under a bearded chin. "You sacked Middleham and wish for my cooperation."

"... If they dona cooperate..." Merryn raised a brow.

"Guard!" the young scribe ran from the room, his ashen face a twisted mask of horror and stomach sickness. The household was chaos itself as Lord Robert of Weshire was released from where he'd been pinned to the wall of his study, a bejeweled dagger pulled from his throat.

"... then we convince them."

"You are wanting an army, yes?" the Barron of Middlesex asked, pacing before his guests. He eyed them, knowing he was in the room with Satan, Himself. But then again, he had been promised extensive lands, including that of his idiotic and very dead cousin, Robert, as well as more titles.

John stopped, a smile spreading across his pasty features.

"You have full use and loyalty, of course." Bowing at the waist, the baron glanced at the woman, eyes twinkling as he took in her womanly curves. Ignoring the sneer he got in return, he stood to his full height. "Tell me what you need, and it shall be so."

"... 'n we will grow, Angus."

The sun gleamed off the helms of thousands of soldiers, all bearing the colors of the rebels, the rising power of England. The men stood in lines, row upon row of steel and pure human will.

Merryn flexed her fingers around the grip of her blade. She held only one, the other hand holding her shield against her body, its heavy weight known to her flexed forearm. She felt the comforting hang of her other blade against her hip.

She felt the body heat of the men around her, feeling their anxiety and anticipation. Across the field stood similar lines of soldiers wearing the colors of their king, Edward III, who watched, mounted on a steed.

Merryn could feel the blood pulsing at her temples, heart racing as her body twitched from muscles restless and ready to move. Raising her sword, eyes still glued to the army across from her, she swallowed then shouted.

"Archers!"

The men at the rear were too far away for her to hear their answer to her calling, though she was able to hear the call of her officers as the request was shouted back through the ranks.

Lowering her arm sharply, she shouted again. "Fire!"

Almost holding her breath at the sheer beauty of it all, a blanket of arrows caressed the skies, covering the overhead sun, like a black fog. Her eyes scanned down to the soldiers across the way. The soldiers stared up to the Heavens then brought up their own shields, arrows pounding into them. Cries were barely heard through the thick, spring air.

Merryn raised her sword again, signaling the second wave of arrows. Once again, English soldiers were brought down, others hiding behind their shields.

"... 'n we will fight..."

"Charge!" Merryn led the cry of her men, each surging forward with a blade raised in aggression. The clang of steel meeting steel was nearly deafening as the two sides collided.

"... 'n we will win."

Merryn felt a fresh wave of blood wash over her as she slit the soldier's throat, not bothering to watch him fall before she raised her left blade, blocking a blow from behind, her leg reaching out in a flash to sweep the soldier off his feet. Once he was down, she pounced. Her blade sliced easily across his exposed throat, his mail and plate armor useless.

Crying out in pain and surprise, Merryn turned, feeling the sting in her thigh, knowing the blood was soaking through the material of her pants. She met her attacker head on, nearly frozen when she saw her own colors. Perhaps he'd made a mistake, overtaken by battle lust and attacked blindly?

Merryn quickly threw that idea out of her head when she saw the look in his eyes; murderous intent shone clear. Rotten teeth bared, he struck again, his blow easily blocked by one of Merryn's blades.

"There will be those who fight against us," Angus said, his words slow and thoughtful.

"Aye." Merryn nodded. "'N those who betray."

With a deafening cry of rage, Merryn pressed her blades together, whipping around, the double edge slicing clean. Wide blue eyes watched in horrified fascination as his head toppled to the ground, rolling a few steps before rocking against the body of a fallen English soldier.

"We will overcome," Merryn said, nodding at her own belief. Angus smiled, holding out his hand. She quickly took it, unifying their shared goal and vision.
"Aye. We will overcome."

Eying the figure before her, Merryn grabbed the reins of the horse, used the full force of her body to shove the soldier from the mount, and flung her own body upon its back. The horse whinnied and reared in surprise at its rough handling. Getting the beast under control, Merryn kicked the animal hard in its flanks, urging it to follow upon the heels of the pinto the king raced on.
"Ha! Ha!" Merryn cried, urging her mount on faster and faster. Edward of England looked over his shoulder, eyes opening wide when he saw he was being chased down. Merryn looked like a savage, her face bloody, hair flying behind her as she leaned dangerously over the animal's neck. Reaching out, she managed to take hold of the king's cloak, yanking the man off his mount. Throwing herself from her own horse, she landed with a grunt, rolling away from the galloping hooves.
Shaking herself out of her daze, Merryn saw the English ruler trying to get to his feet, his heavy armor keeping him down. Throwing herself over to him, her leg too badly injured from the stabbing and her fall to get to her feet, she pinned him with her own body.
Edward tried to get to his feet, or at least turn to his back, but the brute upon his back would have none of it. Merryn brought out a dagger from her belt and, with little fanfare, grabbed the ruler by his hair, lifting his head. A quick slice across his throat and the king was gasping, blood gurgling from his fatal wound.
Raising herself from the monarch's prone body, Merryn cried out as pain shot up through her leg and into her hip. The pain was of no matter. Quickly, she was overwhelmed by her soldiers who pulled her to her feet, then she was launched onto their shoulders.
Merryn's smile was huge as the deafening voices of victory filled her ears and heart. A chant began, though was unintelligible for but a moment. The brunette was surprised to hear what was being shouted all around her:
"Donal! Donal! Donal!"
In honor of her Gaelic ancestry, her men placed the title of world ruler upon her shoulders.

Part 11

With a broad grin, Merryn jumped off her mount, her heavy armor clanging as she hit the ground. Falling to her knees, she caught a very enthusiastic little boy as he ran into her arms. Relief washed over her as she held Paul. When she'd said goodbye to him three days before, she had no idea if it was for good.

Giving him one last squeeze, she groaned as she got to her feet, Paul hanging onto her hand. He was growing rapidly, seemingly right before Merryn's observant eyes.

"We are victorious!" Angus called, his voice echoing throughout the day and answered by cheers of the soldiers as well as those who now called Middleham Castle home. Some still stayed on at Cayshire, but Middleham was far more centrally located and much better fortified than the crumbling structure by the sea. The move occurred just before the final surge on the king and his men.

Merryn walked over to Angus, standing with his hand firmly placed on the head of his cane. He looked tired and weary. His health had begun to deteriorate since his wound at Middleham and his nearly incapacitating headaches and dizziness had kept him from the battlefield. He seemed to have aged overnight, and Merryn worried about him greatly.

With a smile, Merryn accepted his hug of congratulations. With a fond slap on the back, Angus presented her to the gathered crowds, nearby villagers filling all the gaps in the ranks of assembled soldiers and household members.

"'T King is dead!" he shouted, as more cheers erupted and swords were thrust into the air with pumping arms of victory.

"Our Donal!" Frederick called, his eyes wide with the excitement and rush of such a victorious campaign.

Angus looked at Merryn, his brows drawing. She met his gaze, her smile faltering at the look in his eyes. She knew he was deeply troubled by the new limitations of his physicality. She felt her heart drop as he swallowed, forcing a smile back to his face.

"Aye." He smiled, though it was tight. Nodding, he turned back to the crowd. "Donal! Leader and conqueror, though not sure if it be fer t' world." A round of amused and polite chuckles followed Angus' announcement. With one final smile, he turned from Merryn and walked away.

She watched him go, sighing heavily. Suddenly her victory didn't seem quite so satisfying.

It was a time to celebrate, a time for new beginnings, and a time of new rule.

After helping her husband ready for the evening celebrations, Evela went down to the kitchens. So much food had been prepared over the past several days. She prayed that it would not all be in vain. It had been quietly agreed that were Merryn to fail, the food would be for a funeral celebration.

The material of her dress billowing around her as she hurried down the stone stairs, Evela spoke quietly with a few household members, giving orders and directions. Guests would be arriving soon — local nobles who had all put their own necks on the chopping block. They hadn't realized they'd put all their faith in a woman, thinking instead that Angus ruled this roost. Evela smiled to herself. This was not the case and most now knew it.

The young girls around the land looked up to Merryn, a woman who had broken through tradition and expectation. The men either refused to see her gender, instead seeing the brave, capable warrior and leader she was, or they hated her. Evela feared this would always be so. Trouble brewed in the castle walls; she just wasn't sure from which direction it would ooze.

Everyone bustled about, wanting to make things perfect for the night's events as well as honor Merryn with the perfection. Because of her bravery, they were free people. The new regime was anxiously awaited.

The important guests of the new kingdom had arrived, dressed in their finest. There was lively music adding to the cheerful festivities. Evela helped to serve the guests, even as Ezra begged her to join him at the table. She knew how important it was to make a good impression this night, so she refused his requests.

As the food was served, the gaiety of the evening continued as a local minstrel entertained the masses. Merryn stood against a wall, watching the officers and men make the rounds — talking, laughing, dancing, and enjoying themselves for the first time in many months. Tensions had been high; no one was sure what to expect of such a battle, nor what Edward would do. His attack could have come at any time, and they had been on tenterhooks for months.

Evela sipped from her mug of wine, finally deciding to enjoy herself. Evela saw that Merryn watched everything with slightly hooded eyes and a smile gracing her lips. Everyone had dined, and it was time for merriment. Evela had even given in to a dance with Ezra, drinking her wine helped cool her body down from the exertions.

Glancing back at Merryn standing by herself, Evela's attention was taken away by movement. She saw a young girl, dressed in a gray robe walking toward the new ruler, a single mug on her tray. Seeing the girl, Merryn set her old mug on the tray and took the new full one. The girl bowed respectfully, but as she walked away, Evela saw her glance over her shoulder, watching Merryn as she brought the mug to her lips.

A sickening chill flowed through Evela and she felt her stomach clench. Nearly throwing her own mug at a very confused Ezra, she ran toward Merryn, trying with all her might to move her legs as quickly as possible.

The mug was nearly to Merryn's lips, the wine inside just about to reach her tongue when the mug was suddenly sent flying, the red liquid splashing all over her and the wall behind her. Her blue eyes rose to meet the panicked face of Evela.

Evela's chest was heaving as she fell to her knees, grabbing the mug in her hands. She sniffed tentatively at the contents that still stained the inside of the cup.

Stunned, but recovering quickly, Merryn fell to her knees beside her friend.

"Poison," Evela said, her voice dark and quiet.

"Ya sure?" Merryn asked, taking the mug. Evela nodded as Merryn brought the mug to her own nose. She smelled the acrid smell right away, then stuck her finger into the mug, bringing up tiny white granules on her fingertip. She studied them closely. She could feel Evela's breath on her cheek as the woman got close, looking at her find.

"Who would do this?" Evela asked, glancing at Merryn, who shook her head.

Suddenly something occurred to Merryn. She raised her hand to her mouth and then began to look around the room. They'd attracted a small crowd, but Ezra was trying to keep it at bay.

"What 'tis it?" Evela asked, her voice dropping further.

"On t' battlefield, I was attacked." She sighed, running a hand through her hair. "By one o' our side."

"Ye believe that is related ta this?" Evela held up the mug.

"Maybe."

"What 'tis this?" Ezra whispered, standing over them. His wife looked up into his eyes.

"Find the serving girl in a gray robe."

Merryn got to her feet as Ezra scurried off. She saw that he grabbed one of his fellow blacksmiths before they left the Great Hall. Turning to her friend, Merryn sighed. "Thank you, lass. How did ya know?"

Evela shook her head. "Had a bad feelin', and when I saw the girl check ta see if you were indeed drinkin' what she brought ye..." she shrugged, "It felt wrong."

"Is there a problem?" John, Baron of Middlesex walked up to them. The smile never left his face, his hands clasped behind his back.

"All is well," Merryn said, her own smile not reaching her eyes.

The man studied her, though said nothing. As Ezra returned with the serving girl, he walked away.

Merryn followed his retreat, her jaw clenching. Once the baron disappeared in the crowd, she turned to the terrified girl. "Come."

Merryn held her emotions in check as she led the small precession out of the Great Hall, away from the noise and celebrating. Pushing through the doors of the kitchen, Merryn turned, pinning the girl with piercing eyes. She decided to let her sweat, her dark eyes moving about, uncomfortable and afraid.

"Leave us," Merryn said finally, her voice quiet and deceptively soft. She heard the footfalls of Evela, Ezra, and the kitchen staff, echoing out of the room. The serving girl's pulse began to race, beads of sweat rolled down her back and slightly developed chest. "Sit, lass," Merryn said.

The girl quickly made her way to a stool, tucking her hands in her lap, her legs pulled tightly together. She looked down, frightened of the anger on the face of the woman she'd grown to admire and respect.

Taking a deep breath and knowing that the girl was not responsible for what could have happened, Merryn tried to calm herself. She stepped towards her, remembering that the girl's name was Ruth. The castle was so large, and its occupants so many, it was often hard to keep track of them.

"How did this happen, lass?" Merryn asked at long last, forcing her breathing to remain calm and even. Instantly tears welled in the girl's eyes.

"'M so sorry, milady." The girl shook her head. "I knew not what 'twas in the cup!"

Merryn studied the girl by reading her eyes; she saw nothing but truth. She paced a few times, staring down at her boots before asking the next question. "Who gave ya t' mug?"

"A dark man, milady." The tears began to flow down her cheeks in earnest now.

"What dark man?" She leaned in, her face close to that of the sobbing girl as her two fingers lifted up Ruth's chin. "What dark man?" she whispered again, feeling her blood begin to boil. How dare he, whoever this *dark man* was, put this girl through this?

"The big man, milady," she whispered, her eyes finally meeting those of her questioner. Her gaze was huge, her fright turning from Merryn to the image in her head. "The big man with the mask!" She brought her hand up, covering the upper part of her face.

Merryn stood, her thoughts racing. "Bastard," she whispered, then turned back to the girl. She forced a smile, bending down again. "Ya've done well, lass." Gently squeezing the girl's shoulder, she left the room, taking the backstairs two at a time.

"What 'tis this all about, Merryn?"

She didn't turn at the sound of Angus' voice. She answered as she slid her swords home, making sure the buckle of her baldric was tight. "Gerik." She turned to look at him over her shoulder before tucking her daggers into her belt. "He ordered two assassins. One here tonight; t'other on t' battlefield."

"What?" Angus moved further into the room, his cane tapping lightly on the stone.

"Aye."

"Then we get 'im."

"Aye," Merryn said again. "He's here, Angus."

"Then we find 'im."

The clatter of armor and boots echoed through the empty halls of Middle-ham. Torchlight bounced off the stone walls, glazing the darkness with gold.

Shouts could be heard as rooms were proclaimed clear. Footsteps were heard running up stairs. Tapestries were moved as curious eyes peered behind.

Merryn ran to the north tower, her boots thudding along the stairs, her hand on the pommel of the blade bouncing against her right hip. From the yard she'd seen a dim glow from the depths of a room in the tower. No one stayed in that room. Until now.

She stopped at the closed door; the crack underneath it was dark. She smelled sulfur, sulfur from a recently blown out candle. Resting her ear to the wood, she listened with closed eyes to allow her sense of hearing to flow out over the expanse beyond the door. There was movement inside, just on the other side of the thick wood.

With a snarl, Merryn pushed the door open, hearing the satisfying grunt of surprise and the thud of a body hitting the stone floor. Crashing into the room, she felt around, her hands "seeing" for her as she tried to orientate herself.

A second before it hit her over the head, Merryn dove out of the way of something that whooshed through the air. She rolled to her feet, widening her eyes as she tried to see through the inky darkness. The air in front of her nose was disturbed, causing her to jump back.

"I c'n hear yer heart poundin', ye Demon of Satan!" hissed a deep voice near the door.

Merryn snarled as hatred boiled through her body. "Could only Satan survive yer cowardice?" she asked, moving silently around the tower room. As her eyes adjusted to the darkness, she could see the outline of the hulking man, his head raised as he tried desperately to hear what his ruined eyes could no longer see. "Havin' trouble seein' me, 're ye?" she asked, brow raised in amusement. "Shall I light a torch far ya, Gerik?" She could also see the crumpled form of Gerik's servant, whom she had crushed against the wall when she stormed into the room. She needn't worry about him at the moment.

With a snarl, the big man lunged at her with the thick stick in his hands. He missed where she'd been standing by just a hair.

"Ye pay, ye bitch of Hell," he hissed, his voice low, guttural.

"Ya send a child ta do a man's job, Gerik. And ya try on t' battlefield, eh?" Clicking her tongue, she shook her head, eyes never leaving his bulk. "Ya dona learn, ya daft bastard."

"I do learn from me mistakes," Gerik growled, his big feet moving him slowly around the room, his back grazing the wall as he went. "Kill ye this time, I will."

Merryn smirked, slowly drawing out her blades, Gerik's head tilting slightly at the sound of steel sliding against leather. His massive hands flexed on the end of the stick he held like a sword. He cursed quietly as he bumped into a small table, nearly sending it falling to the floor. Merryn wanted to laugh at his pathetic stance, but couldn't bring herself to do so. This man, a young, very capable lad, need not be as he was. He could have been a good, valuable member of her army. It was a waste of talent and a life, as Merryn knew one of them would lose their own this night. Gerik would not stop at any cost — this he had shown twice. His hatred and resentment of her femaleness blinded him more than his ruined eyes.

She jumped out of the way as Gerik lunged, his stick swiping through the air with vicious intent, the end making solid contact with her hip, nearly batting her off her feet. The big man grinned, hissing triumphantly through his teeth.

Knowing she needed to end this, Merryn leaned her body back, throwing out a long leg that caught Gerik under the chin. Startled, he was slammed back against the wall.

"Dona do this, Gerik," she panted, standing at the ready for anything he might do. "Ya canna win this."

"I'd rather die than watch ye and that fool ruin this country," he breathed, adjusting his jaw as he gained his feet.

Merryn felt a wave of anger rush through her at his words, which was no doubt his intent. Baring her teeth, she lashed out again with her boot, catching him at the temple. He stumbled back into the wall again but caught her boot before she was able to pull it away. She cried out as her leg was twisted, her old injury yet again inflamed.

Quickly hobbling away before the big man could do any more damage, Merryn regrouped. She watched as Gerik wiped blood from the corner of his mouth, then threw his hair out of his face with the whip of his head. The rag tied around his head, covering his ruined eyes, was knocked slightly askew from her last kick.

Outside the closed door she heard the sound of boots.

"Stay out!" she called and ducked the swinging stick. Gerik used the opportunity of her calling out to find her. "'Tis between me 'n the giant." She ducked another blow and struck out again, using the pommel of her blade to catch him under the chin. She could hear the click of his teeth and then saw blood seeping out the corner of his mouth. She felt as though they were playing with each other, like a cat and mouse at war. She didn't want to admit she was enjoying it.

Gerik's tongue slipped out of his split lips, licking some blood that dribbled to soak into the hair of his goatee.

"Ya coulda been a great warrior," she whispered, a sudden sadness gripping her as he lunged at her with renewed vigor and purpose. She felt that sadness seep out with her sweat. He was obviously not playing anymore. "So be it," she breathed, grunting at the force with which she landed a kick to his knees. The big man cried out, as his legs buckled under him. The stick flew out of his hands as he hit the stone floor, his head bouncing slightly. Merryn was on him instantly, bringing her hand down as the pommel landed a solid blow to his temple. With a final sigh, Gerik's head fell to the side, unmoving.

Panting, Merryn got off him, pulling the door open. Beyond stood a small band of soldiers, their faces glowing from the torches they held. She nodded toward the room behind her.

"Take 'im."

Merryn fingered the soft petals on the new spring flowers. The moonlight made them silver, her fingertips caressing the precious glow. So soft, so gentle and beautiful.

The paths that wound through the gardens were clear and easy to follow. The greenery had been pruned to perfection; the fragrance was an intoxicating mix of God's best perfumes.

"The night makes it magical, does it not?" Evela asked quietly as she walked along the path at Merryn's side. She saw her quiet companion nod in agreement, as she plucked a small, white flower and twisted it in her long, calloused fingers.

"'Re ya gonna attend the festivities tomorrow?" Merryn asked softly, bringing the flower up to her nose, inhaling the sweet fragrance. She heard a soft sigh from her friend.

"I know not. Seems such a waste."

"Aye. That 'tis. He could've been valuable in this."

"What is 'this', Merryn?"

Merryn chuckled at the grin she received after tucking the flower she'd nearly mutilated into Evela's hair. Sobering, she sighed. "'Tis a new beginning," she said, her voice a whisper filled with wistful hope. "'Tis a way to find our way back home."

"Is this yer home, Merryn?" Evela asked, glancing at her friend before returning her attention to the trees that lined the path.

"Aye, Evela, that 'tis." She smiled sadly. "Never thought I'd have it again."

"Have what?"

"A home."

"Will ye tell Grace about Cara and ye?" Evela asked, stopping their stroll to sit upon a carved stone bench. Merryn stood next to it, resting her booted foot on the seat. She shook her head.

"Nay. The child thinks Cara is dead already. I need not give her more pain that her sister lived further."

Evela nodded her understanding. She had got to know the young girl well and liked her quite a bit. She was quiet and thoughtful, a very good worker. Tamara was training the girl well.

"T'morrow should be an interesting day."

"Aye." Merryn nodded, dreading what the morning would bring. Sighing, she removed her foot from the bench. "Sleep well, lass." With that, she turned and headed back toward the castle.

Merryn felt sick as she made her way out to the courtyard. The crowds were already gathered; news had spread quickly through the hamlet of Middleham. No one loved anything more than the spectacle of an execution. The builders had been up early, quickly constructing a gallows.

She saw Angus and he nodded to her, looking every bit as uncomfortable as she was. She stepped up to the dais where two chairs had been set up, front row seats for the event. Walking over to Angus, she grimaced slightly as she took in the side of his head and face, behind his ear. The bandage was off for the first time, and she felt nauseous, knowing the disfiguration would be permanent.

"I canna believe 'tis come te this," he said, shaking his head sadly. Merryn nodded, glancing over at the noose, ready for its victim.

"Aye." Merryn nodded again, sighing. Looking back to her friend, she gave him a rueful smile. "Gerik must be made an example of." Angus nodded in agreement. "Let us get on with it."

Merryn walked to the front of the dais, raising her arms to gain attention. A hush began to spread through the crowd, as all eyes focused on her. When she saw she had everyone's complete attention, she began to speak.

"People of Middleham, hear me." She looked around, making eye contact with as many as she could. Her gaze was firm, yet troubled. "Ya've been under t' thumb of a tyrant far many years." She paused, letting her words sink in. "No longer!" The crowd erupted in shrill cheers of hope and joy. She waited until they died down before she continued. "We've fought far ya, bled far ya, and died far ya. Know this," Merryn held up a finger in warning, "we will *not* tolerate traitors!"

With that, a set of double doors opened and two armed men escorted Gerik into the yard. The crowd grew quiet, and all eyes were on the large man, his head held high and his hands bound in front of him. The cloth around his eyes had been removed, and Merryn winced at the sight of the shriveled sockets. Scar tissue criss-crossed the skin around them.

Booted feet clanked on the wood of the gallows as Gerik was moved into position. Turning back to the crowd, Merryn continued.

"This man would not follow a woman," she could feel fresh rage flowing through her, "yet he was too cowardly to lead himself. If ya have a problem with me, tell me now." Merryn's nostrils flared as she glared out over expectant faces, her hands balling into fists at her sides. No one spoke, nor breathed. They could feel her rage rolling over them in waves. She turned and walked back to her chair. The guards took this as their cue to continue. One man fell to his haunches, quickly wrapping a rope around Gerik's ankles and pulling the knot tight.

Merryn couldn't take her eyes off the proceedings. She didn't feel guilt, but deep regret. Deep down she knew that this was necessary to let the people know she was quite serious, but it still seemed so senseless.

Gerik's head was covered by a sack; the fabric pulsed with his breathing which was quickening as fear gripped him. The noose was put over his head and tightened; the thick knot placed just behind his left ear.

The noise level in the crowd was beginning to rise. One soldier left the platform, hurrying down the stairs, leaving just the executioner to carry out the sentence.

The man with long, dirty gray hair wrapped his hands around the thick lever for the trap door. He looked to the dais, waiting for the signal. Merryn took several deep breaths then met the executioner's eye. With a curt nod of her head, the lever was pulled back, releasing the trap door in the platform. The crowd sent out a collective gasp as the large man fell through the large, square opening, the double doors flinging back and forth on their hinges. Gerik's body began to convulse, his tied legs wiggling, swinging his whole body like a fish out of water. His head was bent at a fatal angle, and slight gurgling sounds came from beneath the hood over his face.

Merryn made herself watch, feeling a punch in the pit of her stomach. The man struggled for what seemed like hours but was actually mere moments. Finally all movement ceased, and Gerik's body swung uselessly. The castle physician made his way up to the gallows, checking for a pulse and any signs of life. Looking up at the dais, he shook his head.

"'T traitor is dead!" Angus exclaimed, the crowd roaring at the declaration. Merryn stood, walking across the dais and into the castle.

Principality of Novgorod 1360

Heavy boots pushed up clouds of dust in the hot, arid day. Such weather was unusual for this part of the world. Merryn ran a cloth across her forehead, mopping at the sweat that threatened to drip into her eyes. Glancing up at the sun, she could see it was late afternoon.

"Donal!"

Turning to the path beyond the camp, she saw a rider approaching. Shielding her eyes from the sun's rays, she smiled and raised a hand in greeting.

"Ho, David." She walked toward the dismounting rider, reaching for the folded parchment he offered. Unwrapping it, she quickly read over the lines, nodding with a sigh. She looked out over the camp, seeing her men taking care of their weapons while some were eating or drinking. None stood around, nor slacked in any way. Her men were well-trained and filled their commander with pride. The pride spread across her face briefly before being replaced by a look of concern at the severity of the situation at hand.

"Troops 're movin' in through t' north." Merryn looked to the direction in question, sighing heavily. "Bastards."

"Do ye think there'll be a sneak attack, Donal?" The Donal's silence lasted so long the soldier thought she hadn't heard his question. He cleared his throat, about to ask again, when she nodded.

"Aye." Her face was lined from many years of sun, harsh weather, and battle scars, all affecting her more than skin deep.

The soldier, a loyal lifer, nodded. He waited just a moment, as her requests usually came within that span of time. When none were forthcoming, he hurried off.

Merryn walked toward the sand dunes, the wind rustling up the dry grains, hitting her in the face and making her squint against the onslaught. Resting her palm against the old friend, her blade, she looked out over the dunes, seeing nothing but an expanse of sand and barren land. She knew her generals thought she was crazy for taking such land, but it meant expansion as well as control of important trading posts. She had been steadily working her way across the map of Europe, claiming as she went. Her campaign in Germany complete, her army had marched south.

A small smile stretched sun-dried lips, white teeth blinding against darkly tanned skin. She had been gone from her seat in London for more than a year. Sometimes she forgot what home looked like. Her home had become a tent and her steed, Wilhelm. She often laughed when Angus called her "Little Lionheart" in teasing from the king of old, Richard. Richard the Lionheart was the French-born king of England, who spent less than a year in his kingdom. The road and battles kept him away. She was the very same.

"At least I speak the language," she muttered. Brushing long strands of dark hair out of her face, it immediately flew back before her eyes. She thought of Angus. He was back at his estates near the castle, ruling in her absence. Many years ago, he'd come to her, worry furrowing his dark brow.

"But 'tis yer people, Angus!" Merryn argued, pacing. He nodded.

"Aye. But they follow ye, Merryn. They look ta ye, not me, Donal." His eyes were twinkling when she glared at him. Seeing his good humor, she smiled then looked down. "Ye've earned such a title, my friend." A large hand on her shoulder had stopped her movement. Meeting his eyes, she saw the affection in them.

"Rule with me, Angus," she said, voice quiet, yet firm. "Ya've got the diplomacy, I have naught." She stared at him for long moments before finally he nodded.

"Alright then. But ye're t' Donal."

Angus had not fought since that last battle against Edward III. He had found his place in the office of politics, which Merryn happily left to him. She cared for her people, kept them fed and happy, but stayed out of the daily diplomacy. She made her kingdom grow, bringing prosperity to all she touched.

She felt a pride spread through her that she had not allowed herself time to feel in many years. She led her men through blood and tears, their victorious cries a balm to her tattered soul. Merryn was happy and felt a contented satisfaction in the life she'd created for so many. Yet she felt great loneliness too, and it was an empty bedfellow.

As she made her way down the hill, she saw the face of the boy she'd adopted so long ago. Paul was a young man now, nearly fifteen years in age with a lifetime of wisdom already. His dark eyes shone with intelligence; his mind was a sponge, never soaking in enough information or knowledge. A fighter, he would never be. Merryn had made sure he had the finest tutors in theology, science, and the world around him. It had been quite the fight, as the Church saw science as heretical. After all, only their God created and molded. Surely there was nothing to the sciences nor to the minds of man.

That was rubbish as far as Merryn was concerned. She wanted Paul to have the right to decide for himself. She missed him dearly when she was away on campaign, but she tried to write to him as often as possible. It wasn't always easy to get a rider out to race back home and deliver her messages.

"Donal, the men are ready." Lukas walked up to her, matching her stride toward the Commander's tent. Merryn nodded in approval.

"I'll be joinin' them."

"Donal," he stopped, placing a hand on her shoulder. She looked down at his hand then looked in his eyes. "Do ye think that is wise?"

Slightly annoyed, Merryn shifted her weight to one hip, hand resting on the other one. "'N why not?"

"Well, ye should rest fer the morrow's battle, is all." Lukas looked remarkably uncomfortable suddenly, and she was suddenly amused.

"I see. Ya're older than I am, Lukas." She smirked as a blush flared across his cheeks.

Clearing his throat, he spoke. "Thus, why I wait here this night, Donal."

Merryn's head fell back, a hearty laugh erupting from her throat. Lukas looked at the Commander, a small smirk teasing the corner of his lips. With a slap to the back, Merryn went back to her tent to prepare for a long night.

Eyes closed, Merryn leaned back in the tub that had been brought to her tent. She had made it a standing rule that all soldiers must bathe at least three times a week. Most grumbled, but all conceded. The punishment for disobedience was not worth the annoyance of taking time to clean themselves.

Long, deeply tanned arms lined the edges of the round tub. The water just barely bobbed above firm, ghostly white breasts; the nipples were the only dark part of her torso. Merryn's body had grown hard and defined from years of handling weapons and opponents sometimes twice her size. She's had a military career for almost a decade.

Bathing was one of the few times she found any peace. No one was allowed in her tent or rooms while she bathed, no matter how urgent the problem. She needed the time to regroup, relax, and regain her sanity and clarity.

As her blue eyes slowly slid open, she thought of what lay ahead. The fighters of Novgorod were known for their sneak attacks, small groups of soldiers were dispatched to infiltrate and assassinate. Not this time.

Water fell in noisy waves from the long, lean body that stood up and stepped out from the tub. A soft robe waited for Merryn, the thick material absorbing the excess water immediately. She grabbed her long hair into a thick rope, squeezing and twisting the water out.

Donning her armor, a look of single-minded determination slid across her features; a mask she knew and wore well. As she prepared herself physically, Merryn's mental state was shutting down to focus on the battle to come. All irrelevant thoughts were locked away until she was alone once more, victory unlocking the gates.

Buckling her baldric into place, her twin blades, razor sharp, were slid home. The comforting weight at her hips helped to ease her into that dark place she had to take herself before every battle. It was a place where no light could enter; where there was no conscience or no care, save for that of her men. This was a place of ultimate sacrifice, where her own body and safety meant nothing next to theirs, and that of her people.

With her hair pulled back into a tight knot on top of her head, her helm was pulled down into place. Tugging on her gauntlets and flexing her fingers, she was ready.

The early morning was blessedly cool, with a slight breeze blowing over the small attack party. The enemy's camp was not far now, just over the dunes. The small camp was dark; the soldiers fast asleep. Intelligence had told Merryn that the pre-attack was to happen the following morning, just before dawn. She could not allow that. She would strike the head of the snake first.

Using hand gestures, she told her small party where they needed to be. Nods from steel-covered heads told her that her commands were being heeded and followed to the very letter.

Merryn's vision through the slits in her helm told her that she was in the clear as she ran across an open valley, and the dark outline of tents came into view. Her blades left their sheaths with a satisfying hiss. She heard similar hisses all around her.

Suddenly she heard a barrage of battle cries coming from the dunes surrounding them. Eyes opening wide, she was horrified to see her men being cut down as the enemy poured in on them from all sides. The clash of steel was instant. She shrugged out of her surprise quickly, running full force into the fray, blades dancing.

The whistling of incoming arrows caused men of both sides to fall around her. Her attention was ripped from the volley of arrows by the sound of an attack coming from behind. She whirled around, her own breathing echoing through her ears inside their cave of steel. She met the blow with her left blade, kicking out with her right leg. Her attacker was quick, whirling out of her way, then knocking her with a kick of his own, catching her in the armpit, and nearly winding her. She ignored the pain that ran through her body, instead slicing with her right blade, hearing the satisfying howl of a target cut. Her attacker wasn't finished with her, however. He swung with his saber, nicking her in the shoulder, the armor neatly absorbing the blow. Angry, she redoubled her efforts, her blades a blur of motion, confusing her opponent until he was trying to parry a thrust that had been there a breath ago. Finally Merryn felt the penetration of her blade making contact with pliant skin.

As soon as she pulled her sword free, she turned to the next man who dare cross her blades. Surprised to see him running, she bared her teeth as she ran after him, not wanting the cowardly bastard to escape.

This thought was no more out of her brain when Merryn was pitched off her feet. Landing on her side, she tried to get up, but cried out as pain lanced through her chest — tentacles of agony raced up into her left shoulder and down her arm. Her hand convulsed and her sword fell to the ground. She tried to raise herself to her knee but she was knocked down again. Breathing was becoming nearly impossible, the coppery taste of blood filling her mouth. Merryn began to choke, desperately grabbing at her helm with her right hand, tugging frantically until she felt the cool, night air run through her hair.

She cried out in agonizing pain now leeching out through her chest and into the rest of her body, which was suddenly being dragged from the battlefield. The soldier dragging her grunted loudly, desperate to get her to safety.

"Hold on, Donal. Almost there," he panted.

Merryn couldn't think, her mind taken over by the intensity of her pain. Her head bounced against a rock as she was dragged, her eyes rolling back into her head as the jolt stole her breath. Wet heat flowed down her chin, gathering in her mouth, making her choke.

"Roll 'er over," someone hissed.

Merryn felt hands on her sides, her shoulder screaming out as she was rolled onto it, the blood in her mouth spilling out the side of her mouth, making her chin and cheek feel sticky.

Voices were heard, mumbled and distant. The smell of earth was under her nose, then a cooling breeze spreading over her suddenly naked skin. Words entered her ears, though made little sense — *arrow...penetrated lung...Healer...ride hard!*

Surrounded by white pain as clawed fingers reached into every fiber of her being, she was aware of a night fire and concerned brown eyes peering down at her. Her lids were opened one at a time, and a worried face peered at her.

Was that a hand on her breast?

"Must eat, Donal."

Merryn groaned as she was lifted from the litter she'd been strapped to. Her head lolled back. Her body was limp and covered in sweat and blood, both dried and fresh. A constant groan oozed from her throat as she was carried inside and gently laid upon softness. Her brain was fuzzy and she could not focus her eyes. She felt so hot, yet she shivered with a chill that made her body scream in agony. Raising a hand, she tried to touch the pain that webbed across her chest, but she was too weak to move her hand more than a small bit.

Merryn's world went black again, the pain slowly easing into the darkness. The next thing she was conscious of was the coolness of a cloth across her forehead. Words were murmured, though she could not make them out. Her lips moved uselessly, her tongue filled the space of her mouth, and no words were able to escape her parched lips.

Hovering. Someone was hovering. She could feel it. She cried out, as there was a touch to her shoulder which stole her breath and the power to think. More hovering, she sensed. Green eyes looked into her own. The eyes were soft, filled with concern and love.

A smile slowly spread across her face, which ended up a bit lopsided. *Those eyes. I know those eyes.* "I know you," she whispered, the smile sliding off her lips as her eyes lost their focus as darkness crept in once more, stealing her pain.

"Sleep, Merryn. Ye must sleep now."

Merryn's brain raced at the voice. She tried to focus as her eyes searched for those green eyes. Her brain wanted to connect the eyes and the voice. She saw golden hair brushing into those green eyes. With eyes wide, she tried to focus. Her arms tried to reach out to grab her, touch her.

"Cara!" she cried out, as tears drained into her ears, her body convulsing with her pain and loss. "Don't leave me, Cara. Not again."

The hovering, cloaked figure was there, always there, offering soft words and a healing touch.

Merryn took a deep breath, grimacing at the pain that movement caused. Easing the breath out, she opened her eyes. Looking around the room, she realized she was in her own bed, recognizing the rich, dark wood posts and embroidered canopy. Glancing to her left, she saw a water basin, with a soaked rag hanging off the rim. Bottles and apothecary bowls of medicines and herbs littered the table. Moving her eyes around the large room, she saw the fire burning brightly in the corner and the tightly closed wooden shutters.

She looked to the other side of her bed. Near the door, Angus stood with George and a few of the house servants, speaking in hushed tones. One saw her opened eyes and cleared his throat. Angus turned to look over his shoulder, a wide smile instantly upon his lips. He left the small group, moving quickly around the bed to her side.

"How do ye feel?" he asked, his voice soft. Merryn took mental stock of her body, locating every single area that hurt or was sore.

"I'll live," she said, her voice broken and raspy.

"Aye. So 'twas said. Gave us a mighty scare, ye did."

Merryn smiled weakly, a light cough escaping her lips. This made her eyes squeeze shut as pain rocked her body again.

"Rest now, Merryn."

Nodding, she closed her eyes. Just before she fell back to sleep, she heard Angus call for the Healer.

Part 12

A deep intake of breath brought Merryn back to the light of day — four days after she'd been brought to her bedchamber. Memories of her time on the battlefield quickly returned to her, and she moved slightly, testing her body. She was sore; sharp pains stabbed at her shoulder and upper chest, but it was not excruciating as it had been.

Eyes slowly opening, she saw the sunlight coming in through the open windows trying to penetrate the darkness of the room but falling short. Lit candles and lamps tried to make up for the dimness. Looking down at herself, she saw that a soft, cotton gown had been placed over her long frame, though buttons down the front could be opened so her wounds could be tended to. She was clean, dry, and tightly bandaged, though she could feel a stiffness on her skin where a healing paste of some sort had been spread.

"Healer, how is she?" Angus asked, his voice hushed. Merryn looked toward the door. She saw Angus walking toward a cloaked figure, whose back was to the bed. Soft voices breezed over Merryn's ears, the words "Donal" and "will survive" uttered time and again. With a nod, Angus turned and left the room. Merryn looked again at the figure who was now turning back toward the large table that had been set up, its surface covered in raw herbs, some bundled together. A pale hand reached out from the oversized sleeve of the cloak, taking a bowl, the other reaching for a neatly folded cloth.

Merryn watched as the figure turned, but the deep shadows of the hood obscured the face. She felt her heartbeat quicken as the bowl and rag were laid back on the table.

"How do ye feel, Yer Highness?" asked a soft voice, the sound melodious on the morning air. Merryn couldn't breathe, nor answer. She waited, praying the Healer would remove the hood that hid her face. The deep shadows under the hood were now facing her. The pale hands reached up and pushed back the hood, revealing short, golden hair, a soft brow, and dark blonde brows slightly knitted with a wrinkle of concentration bunched between them. The nose was small and finely shaped, as were the pale lips.

Merryn's breath and heart caught as the green eyes met her own. She felt the sting of tears as she took in the expanse of the beautiful face. She gasped softly at the slight scarring she saw littering the left side, leading down her neck and disappearing into the dark material of the full cloak she wore.

"'Twasn't a dream," she whispered, her voice hoarse.

"We must clean yer wounds, Sire." The Healer's voice was soft yet stern. The green eyes flickered away, back to the medicines.

"Cara?" The Healer did not respond but gently pushed the blankets aside, revealing Merryn's cotton-clad torso.

"I must unbutton yer gown, Yer Highness." Nimble fingers began to work on the buttons, slowly revealing badly bruised skin which disappeared into white bandages. Though there was pain, Merryn was unable to take her eyes from the woman before her.

The Healer worked with gentle efficiency, her touch warm, her ministrations knowing and restorative. Even so, her manner was aloof and detached. Merryn looked up into eyes which were filled with a calm wisdom that instantly put her at ease. Those eyes were so familiar, yet looked at her with nothing other than the kindness her profession required. The flickering of the candlelight next to the bed drew the scarring into pitted shadows.

The Healer gently removed the bandages, revealing Merryn's creamy white flesh dotted with bruises, cuts, and the two wounds made by the arrows of a good marksman.

The Donal winced slightly as the rag, soaked in a cleaning solution, carefully moved across and inside one of her wounds.

She closed her eyes, no longer able to stare at the woman who hovered over her. She pushed the pain away by thinking, disappearing into her mind and thoughts.

The Healer. Was Merryn losing her mind? Was her feverish state causing her to see something, or some*one*, that was not really there? Was her brush with death making her wish for what could never be? If that were the case, then she'd rather they had let her die. The disappointment alone would kill her.

"This will hurt a bit," the Healer said, her fingers lining Merryn's wound with a thick, grainy paste. Merryn sucked in her breath, almost unable to breathe. The Healer rested a comforting hand on a strong shoulder, also helping to keep the Donal flat on the bed. "'M sorry," she whispered. She took her fingers away, dipped them into the paste again, and sealed the wound with it. She placed a clean bandage on that wound then turned her attention to the other wound. "We'll be turnin' ye over, as well."

Merryn said nothing, just closed her eyes, and allowed the soft touch to sink in to her skin, regardless of the pain the gentle fingers were inflicting. Her mind was foggy; it was almost as though she was watching from outside her body. She opened her eyes and saw the Healer leaning over her; a small figure wrapped in a dark cloak, with golden hair sticking up in various places. The bangs were a bit too long, brushing into beautiful green eyes. The Healer stood, having finished cleaning and packing the second wound.

"Hold on ta me," she said, her hands grabbing Merryn's waist and gently turning her over. Merryn cried out softly as pain shot through her midsection. She felt the gown being taken off her completely, leaving her back exposed, save for the exit wounds that were still packed from earlier. "I know it hurts."

Merryn closed her eyes, trying to catch her breath. The Healer stepped away from the bed for a moment, but she was quickly back. Fingers were suddenly placed at Merryn's mouth.

"Yer Highness, eat this." A sweet paste was put on her tongue. She recognized it as something Cara used to make. She knew she'd be asleep within moments. She also registered the slight salty taste of the Healer's skin. As she drifted off, her pain faded into the darkness and her skin sensitized as she felt soft touches and heard soft words.

"Merryn..."

She opened her eyes, an instant smile gracing her face as she saw Cara looking down at her. Merryn was lying on their soft bed, Cara next to her, holding her head up on her elbow. Cara's fingers were tenderly caressing Merryn's uninjured shoulder.

"Merryn," Cara said again. When she saw she had Merryn's full attention, her smile widened and her eyes twinkled. "Ye once called me Mo Shearc." Merryn smiled at the term of endearment and nodded. "Am I still yer love?"

"Aye, lass." Merryn reached up to touch Cara's soft cheek. "Always," she whispered. Merryn's eyes closed as she felt soft fingers brush the skin of a bared shoulder, breezing up over her cheek then running back down her neck. She moved her head to the side, exposing more of her neck to the soft fingers and gentle touch. A voice whispered in the air and Merryn strained to hear what was said. Her sensitive ears finally picked it up.

"Why did ye leave me?"

Paul stood, stretching his arms far above his head, and squeezed his eyes tightly shut as the stretch flowed through his entire body. Shaking it off, he walked over to the massive fireplace that spanned one entire wall of the sleeping chamber. Poking at the hearth, he caused the embers to burst into flames again, the heat nearly searing his face as he stepped away. Like Merryn who he'd come to see as his guide in all things, he preferred to do things himself. The young man never felt right about having a servant called to do what he was more than capable of doing himself. There was no need to call a servant who was needed elsewhere. He understood that a castle, the size of this one, needed much help to run it.

Glancing toward the huge bed, he saw Merryn still deeply asleep. Needing to be close to her since she'd been so gravely wounded more than a week ago, Paul had brought his studies into her bedchamber. All his books and writings were set out over the huge desk that his adopted mother used to work at when she was home.

Merryn, the name which nobody used anymore, had claimed the heart of the young boy many, many years ago. His own mother, Tamara, had died nearly five years ago now, bearing the child of a soldier she had fallen in love with. Both mother and child had been lost, regardless of anything the castle physician did to save them.

Distraught, Paul had turned to the fiercely protective Merryn. The boy had really been raised by the entire household, but no one could soothe him like she could.

Walking over to the desk, the handsome boy looked down at his books.

The castle had been in absolute chaos when they'd received word that the Donal had been so seriously wounded. It was true that she had been wounded many times over the years, but she was always able to be treated either on the battlefield or at camp with the camp physician. This time, all knew was it could be a mortal wound. There was only one person that might be able to help her, and that was the Healer.

The Healer was known throughout Europe. It was said that she had the touch of the divine, that her skills were as if Jesus had come back from the cross. No one knew who she was or where she came from, just that she could work magic with her herbs and potions. Her quiet, soothing demeanor was almost as legendary as her healing skills. It was even said she had studied with famed French physician to Pope Clement VI, Guy de Chauliac. Working within a religious setting was unusual. Considering the Church often saw healers as charlatans, since only God could truly heal, it wasn't uncommon for healers and physicians to be found guilty of witchery.

Paul glanced over his shoulder at the table loaded with her potions and bundles of herbs. Some he recognized from the teachings of his adoptive mother over the years. He'd not spent much time with the Healer, but when he had watched her on first arrival, he had been amazed. Her touch was amazingly gentle and sure. Though she said little, she had a core of calm within her that seeped into her patient, putting them at ease and staunching their fears. When she had spoken to his adoptive mother, the voice had been soft, almost reminding the boy of the running water in a stream — clear and calm, and highly refreshing to the wounded soul.

He could learn much from her. The Healer had been very patient with him, softly explaining what she was doing. Paul had been allowed to stay as he helped to calm his mother, holding her cold, pale hand in his own.

The young man looked over his shoulder as one side of the double doors was pushed open. Wearing her familiar dark cloak, the Healer entered the room. Her hood was pushed back slightly from her face, leaving her features partially in shadow.

"Good afternoon," she said softly to the boy as she walked over to the bed. Paul hurried over to her, smiling his greeting. He thought the Healer understood his inability to speak, but she said nothing of it. If she did speak with him, she either asked no questions he'd have to answer, or simply asked him to do tasks that he could respond to without speech. Such as now. She turned to the lad. "Mightn't ye fill this?" she handed him a water bladder. With a big smile, he nodded and took the container from her, hurrying from the room.

The Healer turned back to Merryn, still asleep in the large bed. Her facial features were at peace, forehead free of lines of pain or worry. Dark brows, finely arched, rested over pale lids, which fluttered slightly. The Donal must be dreaming.

She pulled back the blankets, revealing a new, dry gown on her patient. The wound had created fever, which in turn caused the garments to be soaked through with sweat often. When the Healer had checked her patient earlier in the morning, she had changed the gown, bundling the old to be washed.

Nimble fingers made quick work of the buttons on the simple cotton, deftly pulling the ends apart to reveal skin that was quickly becoming more of a natural color. The deep bruising had come out over many days, turning every color of the bruise spectrum; it was now urine yellow.

The Donal's head began to turn restlessly. She opened her eyes. Unobserved, Merryn was able to study the face of her healer. Slight lines spread from the corners of her eyes, and there was a wrinkle that gathered between her brows with her concern. The skin of the Healer's face was tanned, which Merryn reasoned was from scouring the forests or private gardens for just the right herbs — growing them, nurturing them to healing perfection.

"Might I get up 'n about today?" Merryn asked. After a moment, the Healer nodded.

"For a bit."

Merryn was eternally grateful. She was becoming restless, as the pain had subsided substantially. Now she felt sore, as though she'd been dragged behind a horse for a couple of days.

The door opened, and an instant smile spread across the Donal's face as Paul entered the room, a fat water bladder in his hands. The Healer quickly covered Merryn's breasts as the boy stepped over to the bed. She smiled a thank you to the lad, taking the water and creating her mixture in the apothecary bowl with the marble grinder.

Merryn held out a hand to her son. It was quickly taken. She watched carefully as Paul told her all about his day, what he'd been doing, and about his studies of the ancient Egyptians and their marvelous structures. His hands were a blur in his excitement.

The Healer glanced over at the boy from time to time, trying to understand what he was explaining. She was at a loss, though the Donal seemed enthralled. Soon she turned her full attention back to her patient, grateful that the young man was keeping her attention. She did her best to keep her patient's dignity, but when she tended to the wound near her lung, she had no choice but to expose the Donal's right breast.

The wounds were healing nicely from the inside. Also, the skin was knitting together. The Healer knew it was painful for her patient, sharp pains shooting through the wounds, as the flesh came back together, blood vessels healed themselves, and she became whole once more.

Soon her job would be complete, and she could leave.

The Donal held her breath as she buckled her baldric into place. Whimpering, she quickly tore the thing from her body. Even without the weight of her blades, the leather strap was too much across her shoulder and chest.

Taking several deep breaths, she ran her hands through her hair, attempting to regain her composure.

"Ye do too much, Merryn."

She glanced into the mirror, seeing Evela's reflection walking up behind her while frowning. Her friend and confidante was the only one in the entire kingdom who still called her by her given name. Everyone else, including her chief officers and Angus, had become so used to "Donal" that it had stuck.

She grunted her response, impatient and irritated at her body's limitations. She hated limitations and refused to allow her men, or her people, to live by them, so why should she?

With a knowing smile, Evela helped her to finish dressing. The household had prepared a dinner in her honor, and the entire castle, and all those living at court, was buzzing with excitement and relief.

"Ye look troubled," Evela said, her voice quiet.

"'Tis nothing." The Donal walked away, grabbing a thick, leather belt that she belted over her jerkin, tucking her dress dagger inside. She felt naked without a weapon, even in her own home. Many years ago Gerik had taught her that she was never truly safe.

"Ye lie."

Merryn caught the dark, amused gaze. With a sigh, she turned her back to her friend, unable to look at her for what she needed to say. She felt she'd lost her own mind as it was and didn't need to see the pity on Evela's face.

"'T Healer."

"What of her?"

The Donal grinned ruefully. "Ye'll think I've gone mad." When she got no response, she continued. "My heart tells me 'tis Cara, yet," she sat heavily on a large, high-backed chair, "she seems ta not know me." Burying her face in her hands, her head fell. She felt even more upset for saying it aloud. It was not possible!

Evela knelt next to the chair, gently pulling her friend's hands from her face.

"Merryn," she said, her voice a near whisper. "What tells ye this? Is this how Cara looked?"

"Aye. But," Merryn frowned, "different." She shook her head, trying to understand just exactly what she meant. "She has changed, aye," she nodded, "yet I feel it. I canna explain it."

Evela studied her for long moments, then smiled. "Yer soul feels this, Merryn. But was she not dead?"

Merryn sighed, her shoulders sagging. She looked at Evela, shaking her head. "I know not. I thought so. Lord knows I've been grievin' fer the past ten years." With that, she stood, mentally readying herself for what she knew would be an exhausting night.

Evela walked beside the Donal as she entered the Great Hall. As soon as she was spotted, thunderous applause rocked the great room. Surprised, the ruler tried to receive it with as much grace and aplomb as she could. She stopped, holding her arms out at her sides, and looked at everyone, letting them know she was alive and well. As the cheers and applause died down, Merryn moved to speak.

"'Tis nice ta be up 'n about." She smiled, getting nods and applause of approval. "I have so many ta thank who are not here, but fight for our kingdom. Thank ya all fer bein' patient with me. I know 'm not t' best patient in t' world." This got a full out grin from her and boisterous laughter from the court. "However," she paused, looking for the one person she wished to personally thank. As though she was understood by all present, the crowd began to part, slowly revealing a lone figure dressed in a gown of emerald green, made from the finest materials the kingdom of England had to offer.

The Donal was taken off guard, so beautiful was her healer. She took a step down from the dais, her boots echoing on the stone floor. All eyes followed her progress as she made her way through the parted sea of well wishers, stopping before the Healer.

The Healer's hair was freshly washed and glowed in the light of the hundreds of lit torches and the fireplaces throughout the hall. Jewels dangled from her ears and winked from a perfect throat. Gone was the heavy, dark cloak.

Looking into her eyes, the color stunned Merryn anew. The eyes were so different, not the open, loving eyes Merryn had once known. These eyes were guarded, allowing no feeling to show. They were alive, yet dead — belonging to a woman who was very much alive, yet whose soul had floundered.

It took all Merryn had to not grab her and hold her close, to see if her heart could puzzle out this mystery for her. She felt so confused, and deeply sad. Pushing all these thoughts from her mind, she lowered her head, grunting slightly as she fell to one knee.

"My deepest gratitude, great Healer."

As one, the entire room followed suit, every person bowing before the Healer, who looked on with wide eyes, at a loss of what to do. Glancing up, Merryn found herself looking into two glistening green eyes. The emotion was quickly gone, replaced by the habitual wall that lay beyond the brilliant color.

"Please arise, Yer Highness," she whispered, looking slightly embarrassed. The Donal found her feet, reaching out to take a small, pale hand between her two larger, deeply tanned and calloused ones.

"Thank ya," she whispered back, trying so desperately to grab the Healer's full attention. The green eyes would only look into her own for a breath before they were looking elsewhere. The Healer nodded but said nothing.

Dinner was served, the Great Hall filled with echoes of laughter and conversation. The music was quickly overshadowed by the gaiety. For the entire night, Merryn was surrounded by swarms of people, not getting a moment to herself. Even still, her eyes tried to follow the Healer around. Her heart ached as she wanted so badly to run over to her and take her into her arms, never letting her go. Even if it wasn't her Cara but fate's cruel joke, the small woman brought her love back, if only just for a while.

"Has been quite t' day, eh?"

Merryn looked to see Angus standing next to her, his hands tucked behind his back. He gave her a sideways glance, dark eyes sparkling. She nodded with a smile.

"Aye. Glad ta be up." She rolled her eyes, making Angus chuckle.

"Aye. 'Tis 'bout time ye did yer job." They both laughed, mostly out of final relief. Angus soon grew sober, and he frowned. "We thought we'd lost ye, Donal. Ye'd lost so much blood." He shook his head at the memory. Paul himself had ridden out at breakneck speed despite his lack of equine grace, desperate to get to the hospice run by the Healer in Kendal. He'd nearly collapsed in her arms as he handed her the frantic message.

"What of this Healer?" Merryn asked, catching a brief sight of her, a gracious smile upon her lips as she spoke with a member of court.

"She's known throughout t' land. It's been said she was touched by God Himself, His healing grace in her fingertips." The dark man glanced at his long-time friend. "So it shows."

Merryn nodded. "Aye. Indeed it does." It didn't seem Angus recognized the woman, which set even more doubt in the Donal's mind. Maybe she was mistaken. Perhaps it was trick of the light, coincidence, and purity of hope and desire unfulfilled. With a sigh, she realized just how exhausted she really was. It had, indeed, been a long night.

The announcement of her departure was made, wishes for a good night's rest exchanged, and soon Merryn was back in her rooms. She was sore and out of breath. It hurt like hell to bend over and remove her boots. Finally getting one off, she tossed it to the floor before lying back against the bed. She panted and her eyes squeezed shut at the pain that threaded its way through her insides. Taking several deep breaths, she was about to pull herself back up to sit at the edge of the bed, ready to tug off the other boot.

"Allow me, Yer Highness."

Her eyes popped open, and she was surprised to see the Healer kneeling before her, taking the heavy boot between pale hands.

"Ye mustn't pull yer wounds open once again," she said softly tugging at the boot, which slid off and hit the floor with a thud. Merryn could not speak. She felt as weak as the kittens that ran free throughout the castle. She felt herself being gently pulled up off the bed, only to be guided back down, her head coming to rest on the soft pillows. Her nose took in the smell of fresh linens.

She looked at the Healer in her beautiful dress, her hair slightly mussed from the exertion of pulling her boot off then supporting Merryn's precarious steps further up the massive bed. It seemed as though the Healer was avoiding eye contact.

As she was efficiently being disrobed, Merryn spoke, her voice soft, nearly a whisper. Her tongue felt thickened from the large quantity of ale she'd drunk. "Where've ya been?" Green eyes glanced up, meeting hers for but a moment.

"With yer guests, Yer Highness."

"Nay," the Donal whispered, her voice vulnerable with emotion. "I thought ya were..." she swallowed, unable to say the words. "Where've ya been?"

"I've been healin'," she whispered back, refusing to look at Merryn. "I am t' Healer, after all." Her smile was sardonic.

Her fingers made quick work of the Donal's clothing, though Merryn was surprised when she heard a soft gasp. Looking into the Healer's face, she glanced down at herself, feeling the cool metal of the gold coin around her neck. She had put it back on while getting ready for the festivities. It had been removed when she'd arrived back at the castle, and she never went without it.

The Healer quickly turned to Merryn's belt, removing the dagger and setting it aside, then working on the tight breeches.

"'Tis fer luck," Merryn said quietly, her fingers reaching up to touch the coin. This bout with death had been the only time it had left her neck since she'd put it on so many years before. The Healer said nothing, instead helping the Donal into another gown, her fingers trembling as she buttoned the garment. Merryn continued. "I never take it off."

"Take this," the Healer ordered, her voice cold and harsh. Surprised, Merryn took the white, compacted powder from the Healer's fingers, swallowing with the water given her. "Ye need ta rest now." The Healer turned away, though her voice had cracked. Gathering her skirts she hurried from the chamber.

Merryn smiled, a soft sigh escaping through closed lips as her head rolled to the side. Soft lips brushed her throat, moving to the side of her neck, by her ear. She could feel warm breath against her ear, then a wet tongue lapping at the lobe.

Sighing again, hands moved to rest on the warm skin of the naked back of the body that lay upon her. Her fingers could feel the movement of muscle and spine as her love pushed herself up further, dragging her body more fully upon her. Merryn's head turned, blindly seeking the mouth of her lover, which she quickly found. Her lips were as soft as Merryn remembered, her taste all her own. A soft tongue brushed against her own, the warmth of the body on top of her making her own flare to life.

She heard a soft voice murmur against her mouth, a soft pleading to be loved and touched. Merryn felt her gown being slowly unbuttoned, soft, warm fingers exploring the exposed skin as they went. She gasped loudly as a palm found her breast, her nipple immediately growing into the touch.

Soft lips and tongue moved down over her neck, a burning trail left in their wake until finally they wrapped around the nipple, sucking it into the warmth. Merryn felt her entire body erupt in flames, a pulsing beginning in her lower belly, spreading throughout her body.

Her eyes flew open as a gasp left her mouth. Merryn's body convulsed then continued to pulse as small aftershocks hit her repeatedly. For a moment she was baffled, but then a memory, long dead, grew new life as her body began to calm. Slowly pushing herself to a sitting position, only wincing slightly, Merryn's hand made its way to her chest to feel her heart, which was pounding rapidly. The pleasures of the body had been something she had thrown from her mind. After Cara, there was no one else — there could not be.

Pulling herself out of the bed, she shivered again as the movement caused a tightening in her sex. Somewhat confused, and even more amused, she peeled her completely saturated undergarments down her long legs, picking them up and tossing them into the fire. It wouldn't do to have the household know the Donal was having nocturnal adventures. And a castle was the best place for gossip of any kind.

She padded over to the window and opened one side of the shutters, the light of early dawn greeting her. The frigid air coming in kissed the skin of her still heated face. Her eyes closed as she reveled in the feel.

Knowing that the Healer would soon be with her to change her bandages, Merryn walked over to her wardrobe, opening the massive doors. Tugging on a fresh pair of undergarments, she moved over to the fire and stoked it.

She had no idea how she could face the Healer. After her reaction to seeing the coin that had been fashioned into a necklace, Merryn was positive it was Cara. Someone once said the heart doesn't lie, and hers was screaming for what was lost. The recognition had been instant and fierce. Why doesn't Cara see it? She had to *make* her see it, *make* her remember.

Merryn's heart was heavy as she walked to the table where Cara worked, where she kept her herbs and medicines. Starting, Merryn realized the table was now empty. Gone were the apothecary bowls and grinders, bundles of herbs, fresh and dried. Gone was the flask of white wine used as a mixer. Gone was any trace of the Healer.

A sick feeling in her gut, Merryn quickly found clothing to pull on. Pants tugged on, she didn't bother to lace them as she pulled on one boot then hopped toward the door to her chambers as she pulled on the second.

The servant in the passage outside the bed chamber nearly dropped her tray when the double doors slammed open and the frantic ruler rushed out.

"Donal!" she gasped, heart jumping to her throat.

"Thea!" Merryn breathed, taking the young girl by the shoulders. "Where's t' Healer?"

"Sh...she left, Donal."

"What? Where? When?"

The girl tried to draw back from the intense gaze and harsh touch. She was held fast. "I know naught, Donal. Lady Evela asked me ta bring ye this and tell ye she'd be up ta tend ta ye." The girl almost dropped the tray of breakfast in her agitation.

Without another word, Merryn ran past the trembling girl, calling out Evela's name.

The Donal ignored everyone she passed, save for a quick glance to see if any were her friend. Her heavy boots thudded against the stone, her fingers reaching down to tie the laces of her breeches as she ran, her tunic flapping against the backs of her upper thighs in the commotion of movement.

Nearly skidding to a stop, she caught a glimpse of white hair and pushed through the door that led to the kitchens. There she found Evela who turned to look at her with wide eyes. Merryn was nearly out of breath, her still-healing lungs screaming at her. Holding up a finger, she caught her breath, then spoke.

"Where is she?"

"Who?"

"The Healer!" Merryn was about to continue when she saw green eyes studying her. Grace stood there, the heavy jug of cream held steadily in her hand. Still taking deep breaths to get herself under control, Merryn walked over to the beautiful young woman. Her long, golden hair was piled up on her head to keep it out of her eyes. With a kind and tender smile, she caressed the girl's cheek.

Grace smiled with utter trust. "'Tis so good ye are alright," she said, her voice so soft, much like her sister's.

"Aye. 'N how is t' little one?" Merryn asked, placing her hand over the bulging stomach beneath the girl's dress. Smiling wide, the kitchen girl covered the larger hand with her own.

"Should be arrivin' soon, Donal."

"Aye. I will make sure David is home in time."

"Thank ye, Donal."

Turning back to Evela, completely calm now, she asked again. "Where is the Healer, Evela? I must know."

"She's gone, Merryn," Evela said, her voice soft, filled with sorrow.

"But why?" Merryn was surprised to feel a lump forming in her throat as she asked the question. Her heart was shattering all over again.

Evela shook her head. "I know naught, Merryn."

The Donal's head fell. Glancing over at a very concerned looking Grace, the girl's hand instinctively resting upon her protruding belly in protection, she shook her head.

"Nay. I canna let her go again." Storming from the kitchen, she headed toward the keep. "Saddle my horse!" she called out. Turning to head back inside, she hurried to return to her bedchambers to grab her cloak and weapons.

"Donal!" George ran up behind her, trying to catch her before she disappeared inside. The ruler turned, boring fierce blue eyes into her long-time friend.

"Not now, George," she hissed, about to turn away again. He caught her arm.

"What are ye doin', Donal? Ye can't be off ridin' in yer condition."

"I have to, George. I canna let her get away again."

"Who?"

"Cara!"

"What?" Confused, the man shook his head. "I thought…"

"Cara is the Healer! She's *alive!*" she exclaimed, taking the man by the arms. "I have ta find her."

Expecting the girl had left on foot, she could not have gotten very far. Certainly not so far that a small army on horseback couldn't find her.

There was no way Merryn was going to sit back and wait for Cara to be found, but it had been a fight to get her way. She did promise to take it easy and search the closer villages and towns while the rest of the men traveled further. Each small group carried a horn and was to alert the others when something had been found. One such horn was sounded, its deep resonating sound rocking the day.

Merryn pulled the reins of her mount, clicking her tongue against her teeth as she got the beast turned toward the sound. Townspeople were coming out of their homes, unaccustomed to seeing their ruler in their town, especially with the Donal looking less than regal as she searched frantically for the Healer.

Her body was screaming every time the horse's hooves pounded the ground beneath her, but she shut it out of her mind. Nothing mattered except that she race toward the small village where the horn had sounded.

As she got closer, she heard much commotion and yelling. Riding in to town, she saw men of her search party were in a fray, pushing and shoving through a chaotic crowd trying to get to the core of the trouble. Seeing the glint of golden hair, she pulled her mount to a stop and, without thought, jumped down, jarring her entire frame. She shoved her way through the crowds, which parted like Moses' sea as realization dawned on the villagers. The noise died down to a deathly silence. At the center of the violent chaos was a huddled figure, dressed in a black cloak.

"Cara," she breathed as she ran over to her. Merryn knelt down next to the trembling woman. Cara's face was buried in her arms, in an attempt to protect herself from the incensed townspeople. The stones that had been thrown at her still littered the ground around their feet. Using two fingers, Merryn lifted the Healer's face. The Donal nearly cried out when she saw the blood seeping from a gash on the side of her face where bruises were already appearing.

Taking several deep breaths, she pulled the Healer into her arms. Cara went willingly, her forehead resting against Merryn's shoulder.

"Can ya stand?" she asked softly. At the nod she received, she got them both to their feet. Her wild, fierce eyes looked out at the crowd. "What 'tis t' matter with you?" she growled, daring anyone to look her in the eye.

"She's a witch!" someone yelled out, too cowardly to show his face.

"A witch, ya say?" she bellowed, holding the Healer close. "She saved my life!" She looked around, as heads bowed in shame, eyes looking anywhere but at her. The Donal began to lead Cara toward her horse, her men standing sentinel to make sure no one attempted further harm. More of her troops were arriving. "Up ya go."

With gentle hands, Merryn got Cara settled on the horse. Before climbing up behind, she turned back to her people. "Ya should be ashamed. Each one o' ya!" Once sitting behind Cara, a protective arm wrapped around her, she had one last exclamation for them. "Since when does God tell ya ta hate?"

The Donal got the party turned around, holding Cara close to her, and headed for home. She could feel the slight body against her own, and she inhaled the scent of the short, blonde hair, so close to her face.

A wave of sensation crashed over Merryn, so strong that it nearly knocked her backward. She felt a click as all the broken pieces of who she had become fell into place, and the parts of her soul slid together, bonding and knitting. There would forever be scars at the joinings but, by God, she was home!

Merryn felt Cara relax against her and felt the softest touch of a hand over one of hers resting against Cara's stomach. The touch was brief, then it was gone.

"Ye shouldn't be ridin'," the Healer said, her voice quiet, but still able to rise above the noise of pounding hooves below them.

"I had ta find ya," the Donal said in her ear, closing her eyes as her cheek brushed briefly against soft hair. Cara said nothing, just rested her head back against a sturdy shoulder.

The Donal breathed out in relief as she gently placed her bundle down upon the soft bed, careful not to jar her too much. Cara looked up at her, but said nothing.

Straightening, Merryn moved out of the way as Evela leaned in, adjusting the pillows behind Cara's head. She gave the Healer the softest, most genuine smile she had. Cara returned it, then looked away overwhelmed by the intense kindness.

"We must check ye," Evela said, her voice as soft as her smile. Cara nodded.

"I do not think anythin's broken," Cara said, but allowed her cloak to be removed. Beneath it she wore a very simple dress, light blue, the material thin and worn.

Evela was about to remove the dress when Merryn stopped her movements. "Evela, please let me do this." Evela noticed Cara's small hand resting on Merryn's and, after a moment, Evela smiled sweetly and backed away.

"I'll just get some things ta wash her."

"Get her a gown, Evela!" Merryn called after the retreating figure. Turning back to Cara, she brushed a couple blonde strands out of her eyes. Cara looked into her eyes, then looked away. "Sit up, lass," Merryn whispered. She gathered up the material of the light blue dress, tugging it over Cara's head. Merryn gave Cara her dignity, concentrating fully on what she was doing, trying to support the Healer and helping her lay back down.

She removed the girl's turnshoes, laying them gently on the floor near the bed. Turning back toward the bed, she saw the Healer's back; there were bruises littered up and down it. About to ask if they hurt, her question froze in her throat.

Merryn sat on the edge of the bed, slowly, as though in a daze. Her eyes were riveted to the skin of Cara's upper back, to the left of her shoulder blade...

Her eyes opened wide, hands freezing as she lifted the blanket. Tossing the covering aside, she gently turned Cara to her side. "No," she breathed. White pustules and lesions littered Cara's upper back, near her left shoulder.

Merryn sat back on her haunches, stunned and unable to look away. She felt her heart seize in her chest. What was she to do about this? She knew nothing to cure it.

Swallowing, she felt her eyes sting as her fingers reached out, touching the scarred skin with the barest touch. At the first touch, Cara stiffened and quickly moved away, turning angry green eyes on her. Shocked by the sudden move, Merryn looked into her eyes, as she dropped her hand. She was about to speak when she heard Evela enter the room. Turning she saw a gown slung over her arm and supplies in her hands.

Evela looked from one to the other, saying nothing as she set everything down on a small table that she dragged over to the bed. Soon after, two young men entered with extra kindling and wood, making short work of creating a roaring fire in the fireplace, then quickly leaving, only to be replaced by three more young men carrying in a large, wooden tub. Setting it down, they then brought bucket upon bucket of steaming water to fill it.

Evela turned to Cara, gently pushing Merryn away. She had the feeling that perhaps Merryn's touch wasn't quite appreciated at the moment.

Checking the Healer over, she was relieved to see that all the wounds were superficial and, though Cara would be very sore and slow moving for the next week, no permanent damage had been done. She noticed the scarring on the girl's back immediately and felt her stomach fall. She knew that kind of scarring — just maybe Merryn was right. Could this be Cara?

"Let me help ye, child," she said, her voice soft as she helped the Healer to her feet and over to the steaming tub. Merryn stood aside, her hands trembling as she tried to wrap her mind around all of this. She had no idea how to handle all the emotions streaming through her — from intense and profound grief, to intense and profound relief.

"Merryn," she heard Evela's soft voice. "Come." Cara was soaking in the warm waters. Evela led Merryn from the room.

Once the doors were closed tightly behind them, Evela turned to Merryn, taking her in a soft, soothing embrace. She felt the pain of her friend coming off her in waves, seeping into Evela's own soul. She said nothing; no words were necessary. She knew Merryn wasn't crying, but she was trying to silently give her permission to do so if she wished. Merryn had been through so much over the weeks.

Merryn allowed herself to be held and felt comforted by the gentle circles being drawn upon her back. The soft warmth of her friend helped her to relax, her head resting against Evela's shoulder, arms hanging limply at her side.

"Come, Merryn. Let us get ye warm ale and some of those pastries ye love so much."

Merryn raised her head, a smile across her lips. She felt like a child as she was led toward the kitchens by a warm hand in her own.

A cry echoed in the stone block cavern. Sitting up, Merryn sighed, running shaky hands through her hair, the strands sticking to her fingers with sweat. The nightmare had been horribly realistic; her heart was still pounding in her throat.

Looking around the huge bedchamber, she saw that the fire had burned down nearly to embers, as she'd asked not to be disturbed throughout the night. Gaining shaky legs, she slid her feet into her boots; the cold of the stone floor sent a shock throughout her whole body.

She glanced over at the chair in front of the large window. It was there she'd sat for long hours before finally giving in to sleep. She contemplated sitting once again to overlook the grounds of her beloved Castle Saoirse. Deciding against it, she pulled on a cloak and left her rooms.

The castle was quiet; the moon still high in the sky. Merryn smiled during this peaceful time, remembering when she had renamed the castle after the Irish word for freedom. Passing the occasional patrol, the Donal stopped to speak with each man for a few moments before moving on.

It was bitter cold in the castle, despite the approach of summer. In some less-inhabited parts of the castle, she saw her breath puffing before her. She felt like a ghost as she walked through the shadows, many soldiers walking right by her with no idea of her presence.

Slowly she made her way back to the residential apartments. Before climbing the steps to her own suite, she glanced to her left, seeing the double doors that led to Cara's rooms. As if on cue, she heard steps behind her. Turning, she saw Raymond with an armload of wood. Bringing a finger to her lips, she stopped the young man, taking his load from him.

"Go rest, lad. I'll take this," she whispered. Confused, but bowing, the boy scurried off.

Pushing one side of the massive doors open, Merryn glanced around the large room. The fire was beginning to burn down.

Walking over to the massive fireplace, she placed her wood in the holder next to it, squatting as she prodded the burning log with an iron poker. Loading more wood in, her face glowed orange as the flames rose and danced.

Glancing over to the bed, she saw Cara's face, shadows dancing across her sleep-softened features. Rising, she walked over to the Healer, noting how she shivered in her sleep. Grabbing an extra quilt from the wardrobe, Merryn spread it across the large bed, gently tucking it around the small body. Making sure she didn't disturb Cara, Merryn sat upon the side of the bed, her face softening at the sight before her.

She reached out to touch the softest hair she's ever known, longing to run her fingers through the locks and feeling them swim over her skin.

She examined Cara's face. The brow was relaxed, though a slight wrinkle of concentration still lingered between the dark blonde brows. The lines around her eyes were relaxed in sleep as well. Soft, full lips were slightly parted, warm breath easing out between them and the slightest glistening of saliva leaking out one corner. Merryn smiled at this, wanting to brush it away, but worried she'd awaken her.

Cara.

Merryn's eyes closed at the thought of the name, so long banned to her lips. Never had she believed in Cara's god, but now she raised her face to the Heavens, her heart opening in eternal gratitude. Peace washing over her, she opened her eyes, looking back into the peaceful face. Leaning down, she placed the softest of kisses to Cara's forehead then raised herself from the bed.

"Mo Shearc."

Green eyes watched her leave the room.

Part 13

There was a smile on her lips as the Donal saw to the morning's activities in the castle. The kitchen fires were burning bright and the smells of fresh bread and roasting meats wafting seductively under her nose. For the first time in nearly two weeks she had an appetite and couldn't wait for the first meal, which would be served at around ten that morning. Though she'd had little sleep, she felt lighter and more alive than she ever had before.

She had checked on her most welcome guest first thing and saw the Healer sleeping peacefully. Her bruises stood out darkly this day, as the wounds settled in. She knew the Healer would be hurting badly and ordered a fresh bushel of arnica to be brought in, along with white wine. She knew that was what Cara would prefer for her wounds. She also knew better than to presume she could attend to the wounds better than the great Healer herself, so just had the ingredients brought up to Cara's room, along with breakfast and fresh clothes.

It had been a busy morning. The Donal had already met with the builders, and a separate, private bathing chamber was being planned for Cara's bathing pleasure. No doubt she was still as adamant as ever about her daily baths. Merryn grinned as her thoughts turned to so long ago and how she had objected to having to take so many baths.

Spying Grace, she grinned and winked. She'd told the girl earlier that she had a surprise for her, and the young woman seemed beside herself at the prospect, though Merryn had made sure no one who knew the Healer's true identity told her. She was almost beside herself to reunite the sisters. Merryn could never remember feeling so giddy as she made her way up the stairs to Cara's rooms, taking two at a time. Each jolt made her shoulder ache slightly, but she didn't care. There was nothing that could spoil her good mood that day.

One of the double doors was open, and Evela was already with Cara, helping her dress. Merryn noted the arnica already had been pulverized to make the healing paste. The two women stood by the window, the fresh air coming in to gently blow Cara's hair from her face. Evela was speaking to her in soft tones as she brushed the short strands into place.

Merryn stood back from them, hands clasped. Evela glanced over her shoulder, smiling when she saw the unsure look on Merryn's face. She called her in with the hook of her finger then put a finger to her lips. Merryn moved silently to the pair. Mid-stroke, she found the brush in her hand, Evela moving back, silently making her way out of the room. Cara's soft voice continued.

"...Germany from France." She stopped, a smile brushing her lips, eyes half-hooded as she enjoyed the feel of her hair being gently brushed. The strands had long become knot-free, but she was enjoying it so much, she said nothing. "'Twas then I learned many, many healing herbs." She sighed, her hands gently playing with the flowing material of her yellow dress. "Ta answer yer earlier question, I came back to England four years ago. I've been in Kendal ever since."

Merryn said nothing, but took in the feel of the golden hair against her hand as she ran the brush over the nearly glowing strands. Her eyes studied them up close, seeing each individual strand, some fluttering from her own breath. Her eyes ran down to Cara's ears, the very tips slightly flushed, her own natural coloring, and her slender neck where wisps of gold hair brushed it before it disappeared into the dress.

Merryn's closed as her nose to inhaled deeply, immediately recognizing the freshness of cleaning herbs, as well as fresh air, and, most importantly, the smell of Cara.

"Evela?" Cara's voice was soft, wistful, almost a whisper. Merryn's eyes opened at the sound. She waited for her to turn around and discover the ploy, but, to her surprise, Cara continued. Merryn changed the brush to her left hand, raising her right again, gently touching the golden hair, sighing softly as her fingers ran through it. She was surprised to see a resulting shiver run briefly through Cara. Smiling, she waited, loving the coolness of the hair, the softness so wonderful. "Has," Cara paused, "the *Donal*, taken care of herself?"

Merryn was surprised as her title and adopted name sounded so foreign on Cara's tongue, as though she wasn't comfortable with it. She swallowed, nodding, though she knew Cara couldn't see it.

"Aye." Her voice was just as soft as her companion's. She wasn't surprised to see Cara whirl around, wide green eyes taking her in. Smiling sheepishly, she raised the brush, wiggling it before handing it back to the Healer. "The Donal did t' best she could, filling her emptiness with t' love o' her people, tryin' ta find what she lost."

Cara stared at her for long moments, her eyes filled with a myriad of emotions and glistening unnaturally in the morning light.

"Yer Highness," she said, her voice shaky, and her eyes turning angry.

"Please dona call me that, Cara," Merryn begged in a whisper. She tried to plead with her eyes.

Without a word, Cara pushed past her and hurried from the room. Head falling, Merryn studied her hands, the feel of golden hair still like a ghostly touch against her skin.

Blindly, she found her way to a large chair and sat down heavily. She wasn't sure how long she had been there when she heard footsteps walking across the room. She felt a soft touch on her hand then she saw Evela fall to her knees next to the chair, her dress gathering around her on the floor like a small ocean.

"Merryn?" she asked, concern knitting her brows. Tortured blue eyes looked at her.

"She hates me."

"No," Evela shook her head. "I think she's angry with ye. She had t' pox, Merryn. She was saved by a friar."

The Donal's eyes widened at the news. "Pox? Friar?" She saw her friend nod. "Father Michael," she whispered, remembering the friar well. Her head fell. "She was dead."

"Nay, Merryn. She was not."

A stab ripped through Merryn's heart at this. She had left her? No! About to open her mouth again, an out of breath Caleb ran into the room.

"Donal!" he screeched, his changing voice shattering on the word. "'Tis Paul."

The Donal and Evela burst out into the keep, noticing a group huddle near the gate. A horse was being led away. Seeing a flash of dark hair on the ground, Merryn ran over to him, pushing people aside as she fell to her knees.

"Get outta my way!" she snarled, scaring the daylights out of a cobbler. He quickly jumped from the fray, watching from the hushed sidelines. Frantically, she took in the boy's pale face and his splayed body. She barely registered someone explaining how Paul had mounted the horse, but the beast had reared, sending him to the ground. His eyes were closed, and blood was pooling under his head on the dirt. "Paul?" she said, her hands cupping the boy's face. "Paul?" she asked again, her voice becoming higher, tingeing on hysterical. Terror making her act irrationally, she began to shake him, becoming more and more frantic as he didn't respond.

"Yer Highness, stop."

Ignoring the soft request, she shook him again. "Paul! Wake up, lad! Wake up, son." She tried to push away the cool hands she suddenly felt on either side of her face. The touch refused to fall away and, in fact, she was almost painfully grasped.

"Merryn!"

Looking up, she saw Cara looking intently at her. Cara refused to lose her gaze. "Stop. Let me do me job."

Nodding slowly, Merryn sat back on her haunches, watching the Healer and praying for a miracle. It was deathly quiet as everyone watched Cara. She checked the boy's pulse, then leaned over him, carefully opening first one eyelid then the other. She called for a litter.

Getting to her feet, Merryn watched numbly as her son was loaded onto the litter then carried inside the castle and up to his rooms. She followed, doing her best to stay out of the way. She could see that the lad was breathing, his chest rising and falling, relieving some of her fear with every breath. She knew that if anyone could help him, it would be Cara.

She sat in the corner of Paul's chamber, listening as the Healer called out orders, asking for various herbs and flowers, for wine, water, and privacy. No one dared ask the Donal to leave.

With a brief, comforting hug, Evela was the last to go, closing the doors behind her. Merryn's gaze never left the boy or the woman hovering over him, talking to him in a soft and soothing voice. To Merryn's immense relief, Paul was able to answer her questions, his responses slow, fingers slightly uncoordinated, but correct.

"Very good, Paul," Cara said with a smile after the boy had wiggled the fingers of his right hand. "'N t' other? Nicely done." Sitting on the side of the bed, she raised three fingers. "How many fingers do I hold, Paul?"

He studied her for a moment, squinting, then raised a weak hand, holding up three fingers.

"Very good, aye." Cara turned to the anxiously watching Donal. "Would ye help me, Yer Highness?"

Swallowing with a nod, Merryn got to her feet and made her way to the large bed. Together she and Cara rolled the young man over. The pillow beneath his head already had a large patch of blood on it. Seeing that, Merryn turned to the Healer.

"He'll need stitches," Cara explained, her fingers coming to rest at the wound, feeling around in the dark hair to see if it was just one wound or several. She nodded to herself. "Aye, a dozen should do it."

"Why does he bleed so?" Donal asked, surprised that only a dozen stitches were needed. Cara squinted slightly as a small smile spreading across angelic features.

"Come now, warrior. Ye should know how badly head wounds bleed."

Feeling stupid and chastised, Merryn nodded, lowering her eyes. She watched Cara work her magic, holding her son's hand as she knew how painful stitches could be. He did well and was brave, like his mother.

Cara began to clear up her medicines, as Paul slept comfortably. He would be fine, and the relief on his mother's face had made it all worth it. Cara started slightly at the light touch to her shoulder.

"Thank ya, Cara. I canna show ma gratitude enough." Merryn's voice was soft and filled with relief. Her heart warmed slightly at the small smile and nod she received. Swallowing, Merryn decided to take a chance. "Would ya come wit' me?"

"Where?" the Healer asked.

"Just come." Merryn held out her hand, which Cara looked at for a brief moment before, hesitantly, putting her own small, pale hand in it. Feeling the soft flesh within her own, Merryn closed her fingers over Cara's and, with one last look at her son, led the Healer from the room.

They walked the long halls of Saoirse, the Donal smiling at those they passed, many of whom thanked and congratulated Cara in her achievements. One servant even gave her a crown of fresh flowers she'd made in thanks for all of Cara's healing powers. She smiled graciously, accepting the gift with a small hug.

"Ye know, Yer Highness," she began softly, a slight smile edging her voice. "I believe ye keep making these things happen ta keep me here."

Merryn glanced over at her companion, a smile of her own on her lips. "Ye do, do ye?"

"Aye." Cara sobered slightly. "I was gonna leave."

Merryn felt her heart fall. She said nothing, praying that maybe she had one last card up her sleeve to keep the Healer with her.

They turned down one last passage, with a closed door at the end. Smells of fresh baked goods already filled the air. The kitchen door opened and a figure stepped out into the hall. The girl was wiping her hands on the white cloth wrapped around her waist, her protruding belly making it difficult to keep her apron in place.

Merryn heard a gasp beside her when the girl at the end of the hall looked up. Watching Cara's face carefully, she saw the look of shock as Cara's hand flew to her mouth. Glancing down the corridor, she saw the young kitchen wench standing there, head slightly cocked to the side, her brows knit in perplexity.

Turning back to Cara, Merryn saw Cara's face crumple and heard a small cry released from her throat. Shaking her head in disbelief, Cara took a careful step forward then stopped. Tear-filled eyes looked up to Merryn, who nodded slightly. Turning back to the young women, who had begun to take careful steps toward them, Cara took off at a dead run.

"Grace!"

Merryn watched in wonder as the two sisters met halfway, nearly knocking each other over. Cara was crying heavily, holding the younger girl to her so tightly that it looked painful. Pulling away slightly, hands buried in the long, blonde hair, just a little lighter than her own, Cara saw Grace's red, tear-streaked face. Unable to believe her eyes, she pulled the girl to her again, gently rocking her back and forth, her younger sister sobbing into her neck.

"Oh, Grace," Cara whispered, a sense of peace flowing over her face in waves. Merryn could see the need that Cara had to love and protect this girl. Pulling away again, Cara wiped tears away from her sister's face. "Oh, my Grace," she said again, wonder in her voice. "How is this possible?" Her voice broke again, fresh tears running down her cheeks.

Merryn watched from her place at the end of the hall, her face about to break open with her smile. She crossed her arms over her chest, feeling her eyes grow heavy with tears of her own. Holding them back, she decided the sisters needed some privacy for their long overdue reunion. Pushing off the wall she'd been leaning against, she quietly made her way back down the long, cold corridors to her son.

Paul lay still in his bed, his breathing calm and even. The bandage Cara had wrapped around his head was still clean; there was no new bleeding. She sat on the side of his bed, careful not to jog him. Reaching out a hand, she felt the cool skin of his cheek. He wasn't clammy, which meant he had no fever.

She smiled, with love and pride, and brushed some hair back from the top of the bandage, her long fingers caressing his cheek lightly before taking his hand in both of hers. His dark hair stood out in stark contrast to the paleness of his features. He was a handsome boy. His features were proud and strong, as was his young body.

She had prayed a long time ago that the boy wouldn't want to be a fighter like her. Her prayer had been answered many years ago when the boy's interests, even as a small child, leaned far more toward the curiosities of life. His brain was like a sponge, absorbing everything and wanting more. He was incredibly bright and followed around any scholar he could, picking their brains with his thirst for knowledge. Merryn had seen the way he'd followed Cara around already, eager to learn this new sort of knowledge — the ability to heal.

Someday the lad would make a wonderful ruler. His mind was sharp, his temperament even and fair. Pride glowed anew within Merryn as she leaned up and kissed his forehead.

Grace closed her eyes as the soft cloth was run over her face, gathering her tears, which she couldn't seem to stop flowing down her cheeks. Her beloved older sister smiled at this, catching all her new ones, too.

"Is this t' surprise the Donal spoke of?" the girl asked, Cara's free hand wrapped possessively in her own. She refused to let go. The Healer smiled, brushing back more hair.

"I know not, my sister." Cara smiled as her own tears began again. "My sister," she whispered, taking the young girl in her arms again, pulled Grace from the stool in the kitchen where she was seated, and held her tight.

Sighing deeply, she felt her heart beginning to slow, the cadence returning to normal. Pulling away again, she helped the younger girl sit once more, mindful of the girl's swollen belly. She'd ask about that later, but first she had to know how this had happened.

"Ye did not die with our mother?" she asked, wiping at her own tears. Grace shook her head.

"Taken, I was. Brought ta Middleham."

"Ye were in Middleham?" Cara whispered, thinking of her own captivity. "Fer how long?"

"Two long years." Taking a deep breath, Grace ran trembling fingers through her long hair at the memories that admission brought forth. Sensing this, Cara took her sister's hand. She remembered her own brief time in the clutches of Edward III.

"How did ye get out?"

Instantly Grace's face brightened, and a smile spread across her features as the sunlight blesses the land. "The Donal. Rescued me, she did! She brought me ta live with her." She squeezed her sister's hand, completely unaware of the Healer's relationship with the ruler. "She's so kind, Cara! She's brought in t' orphans from t' black sickness and had them schooled! She has saved this land, she has. 'N everyone in it."

Cara listened, frowning slightly as she heard the obvious love and appreciation in the girl's voice. She listened as Grace spoke of how Merryn stood up for her, and even fought a fellow soldier once who was trying to take advantage of the then fifteen-year-old girl.

"Sister, please stay," Grace finished, her voice falling in profound pleading. "Please, please don't leave me again. Mother..." her eyes began to fill again, "when ye didn't come back on the second day, as ye promised, she thought ye were dead." She brought a hand up, swiping at a tear that was squeezing out from the corner of her eye. "She had already come down with t' sickness. Dyin', she was. I waited, prayin' ye'd come back fer me." The girl lost control and cried feely once more. She had no idea she could cry so much! And two very different types of tears within moments. Feeling the warm, strong embrace of a sister long missed, she allowed the tattered remains of her shattered childhood to heal.

"'M so sorry, Grace," Cara whispered, kissing the top of the girl's head. "Please forgive me fer not bein' there fer ye. I thought ye were dead, too." She stroked her sister's back, warm circles over the taut dress the girl wore.

Merryn watched the sun setting from the chair in her son's rooms. Rising, she gave him one last kiss and tucked him in further, then returned to her own rooms. The hours she'd spent with Paul had given her torturous thoughts. She'd done it again. She'd failed Cara in the worst way possible.

Closing the large double doors behind her, she looked at the roaring fire that had been prepared for her then turned away. There was no heat that could melt through her frozen soul. Walking over to the massive desk tucked in the corner, she dragged the huge chair over to the window. Pulling open the shutters, she felt the cool breeze of night wash in, gently pushing at a few strands of her hair. The night air was actually warmer than the castle around her. Sitting heavily in the chair, she stared up at the moon, whose light shone down, painting her face in shades of silver and blue.

For not the first time that night, she thought back to that cabin she and Cara had called home for the happiest times of her life. The way they had cleaned it, made repairs, and then made it their own. The walls of the small structure had seen so much laughter and love. Merryn smiled at the memory. Such bitter, bittersweet memories they were. It didn't take long for the memories to turn dark. Cara had started to get sick so soon, within days. There had been no warning, no inkling of what was to come, nothing.

Merryn felt the tickle of a tear at the corner of her eye as she remembered holding the delirious blonde in her arms.

Merryn's eyes opened, feeling heavy and filled with sand. She tried to discover what had awakened her.

"Mother, 'tis Cara." Cara's voice was so soft, so filled with awe and longing. Merryn pushed herself up to her elbow. Cara lay on her back, eyes opened and unfocused. She reached a hand out, fingers spread. "Mother."

Merryn gathered Cara, so hot, her skin slick with sweat. "Hold on, lass. Just hold on," Merryn whispered, cradling her head in her arms. Cara's eyes closed, and her face was pale. Her breathing was becoming labored. "Please, Cara. Please," Merryn begged, a tear slipping down her cheek. She felt Cara's body go limp in her arms. "Mo Shearc, please, please dona leave me. Please." Her words were cut off as a sob escaped her throat, her face buried in Cara's hair. She couldn't breathe, her body shaking as the strength of her sobs grew, finally shaking them both. Raising her face to the Heavens, Merryn squeezed her eyes shut. "No!"

Merryn had been unable to burn the body of her love, could not watch Cara go up in flames. No matter how much sickness spread, it didn't matter. A stream of tears was flowing from her eyes, her heart shattering all over again. How could she have been so wrong? Cara was dead! She slammed her fist into the hard, wooden arm of the chair she sat in, her anger at herself beginning to rear its very ugly head. She had promised.

"I dreamed you'd come for me," Cara whispered, eyes tightly closed as she inhaled all that was Merryn — sweat, leather, dirt mixed with rain, and all that made up the distinctive smell. Her fingers dug into her rescuer's shoulders, terrified that she'd be ripped away again.

"'M so sorry, Cara," Merryn whispered, her face buried in golden hair. "I'll not leave you again. I swear it. Never!"

Burying her face in her hands, she felt the tears coming in earnest, though she tried to hold them back. There was no use anymore. Part of her wished she still thought Cara dead. At least that way she wouldn't be hated, and she'd already dealt with the pain. This pain was nearly worse than any other she'd ever known. Was this to be her Hell?

Merryn was startled when she felt a hand come to rest on her shoulder. Expecting to see the gentle concern of Evela, she was stunned to see Cara standing next to her chair. Green eyes were filled with overwhelming understanding and...love?

Raw sobs pulled from Merryn's throat. "'M so sorry, Cara!" she sobbed. "So sorry."

Cara moved around to stand before the woman who was falling apart before her very eyes. With gentle fingers, she brought the dark head to rest against her chest, hugging her arms around Merryn's head. She leaned down, resting her own cheek against the top of her head. She felt her own tears sting behind her eyelids.

Merryn's arms wrapped tightly around Cara's waist, hugging her so close, her sorrow and grief finally able to let go. She needed Cara to know just how sorry she truly was, how deeply, profoundly she hurt.

She felt gentle fingers running through her hair, heard the soothing heartbeat of her Healer, could smell the fresh scent of herbs and flowers on her dress and against her cheek.

"I love ya so much, Cara," she whispered, her tears still flowing, but the sobs gradually calming.

"I love ye, too, Merryn," came the whispered reply.

Relief flooded Merryn's body, her soul filling to the point of bursting with gratitude and love for the woman she held. She refused to release her hold, instead snuggling deeper into the warm embrace, feeling the warm breath of the Healer on the top of her head, ruffling the dark strands of her hair.

"Thank ye fer caring fer Grace." Cara kept her eyes closed, allowing herself to feel safe for the first time in more than ten years. The heat that radiated from Merryn's body filled her with peace, the devastation that had lasted for so long finally finding a balm. She could feel the edges of her heart starting to mend, though she knew it would be a very slow process.

"'Twas t' only gift I could give ya. I knew how much ya loved her," Merryn explained softly. She felt Cara pull back slightly, just enough so she could look down into the wounded face before her.

Reaching down, Cara used her thumbs to wipe away the tears which were quickly replaced by more. She stared into the tortured eyes, which at one time used to be her home. Merryn had always been the most beautiful woman she'd ever seen, and that had not changed. All around Europe, she'd been meeting royals and peasants alike. None could ever offer the pure, radiant beauty of Merryn.

Looking into Merryn's eyes, Cara saw the exhaustion and knew it was probably both physical and of the heart — like her own. She knew it was time they both got some rest, but somehow she was afraid if she let Merryn go, she'd awaken to find that it had all been a dream and that she was still wandering, heavy heart and pain restored.

Making a decision, she stepped back taking Merryn's hand in her own and tugging gently until she stood. "Come," she said. Moving away from the chair, the Healer led Merryn to the huge bed, pulling the blankets down. Using gentle pressure, she pushed her to sit on the edge, grabbing her boots and pulling them off. With careful fingers, she removed Merryn's tunic, tossing it and her weapons belt to a nearby chair.

"I'd like ta check yer wounds," Cara said, her voice hushed in the large expanse of the room.

Merryn nodded. Her heart was thumping in her chest, a tempest of emotions flowing through her. The feel of Cara so close to her was bliss, but she was terrified what the morrow would bring. Never would she want the Healer to know just how much she truly hurt, but seeing Cara by her chair, Merryn had lost control. She had wept out the fears and pain that she had kept locked up for so long. And to hear that Cara loved her still... Merryn took a deep breath, swallowing back fresh tears of joy and relief.

Looking up at Cara, who was so skillfully checking her healing wounds, made Merryn's heart beat all the more. Tender, warm fingers, fingertips slightly shriveled from wiping away endless tears, both of Merryn and Grace, touched the bruised skin. Cara was amazed at how quickly Merryn healed. Some things never changed.

Satisfied that all was well, she walked over to the wardrobe, taking out a thick, comfortable gown. Helping her patient into it, she smiled, tucking a few wild strands of dark hair back into place.

"Time fer ye ta get some rest, Donal." She grinned. "Healer's orders."

Merryn smiled, though it was a sad smile. She hated that their night had to end. Standing, she wiggled the gown down the length of her body. Cara held the covers back for her to slide in between. Dutifully she did so, looking up at the beautiful woman standing next to the bed.

"Cara?" she said, her voice a whisper.

"Aye?" the Healer whispered back.

"Promise me ya'll be here t'morrow."

Cara smiled wide. "Move over."

Stunned, and almost giddy, Merryn slid over in the expansive bed. She watched as Cara removed her shoes, then her dress, leaving her underdress on. She slid into the bed beside Merryn and was immediately pulled into a warm, protective embrace. A golden head lay on Merryn's shoulder, an arm resting over her midriff. Cara quietly asked if she was hurting Merryn by lying on her shoulder. Though it did make it ache a little, Merryn kept her there. There was no way she was going to push Cara away now.

Merryn felt Cara settle against her. With a smile, Merryn fell asleep.

She woke to green eyes looking at her, no more than a half an arm away. Cara was lying on her side, facing her, studying her features, following the curve of her nose and brow.

Merryn wanted to tell Cara just how beautiful she was, but something stopped her. Instead she tentatively reached for her, a fingertip brushing along her cheek, down to her jaw line, over her chin, then finally her hand cupped the side of her face. Merryn smiled slightly when Cara didn't pull away, but instead seemed to lean into her touch. She was in awe of the sight before her.

Tenderly her fingers began to move again, feeling the smoothness of Cara's skin until she reached the scarring at the left side of her face, back by her ear. Cara's eyes closed, her head shrinking away from the touch.

"Shhh," Merryn cooed. Cara opened her guarded eyes. Merryn traced over the slightly pitted skin, deciding it must have been caused by more of the pustules during her pox outbreak.

One of the doors to the bedchamber opened. A servant tip-toed in, his eyes focused on the fire, which was beginning to burn out. Quickly stoking it, he turned to leave when he spotted the two women. His eyes grew wide, and his mouth fell open. Merryn chuckled.

"Thank ya, Matthew," she said softly. Cara glanced over her shoulder, suddenly feeling shy. She turned back to Merryn, burying her face in the woman's upper chest.

"G'night, Donal." The lad scurried out of the room. Merryn knew that what he had seen would spread through the castle like wildfire, no matter how innocent it was.

Turning back to the Healer, Merryn smiled, running her fingers through the blonde hair on the head that was still buried at her upper chest.

"He's gone," she chuckled. Cara pulled back, giving her a sheepish grin, which quickly disappeared. She had something on her mind.

"Why do ye wish me ta stay, Merryn?"

Merryn looked deeply into her eyes, and without a second's hesitation, she spoke her heart. "If 'tweren't for my fear 'n grief, we'd still be in t' cabin, by t' woods."

"Do ye mean it?" Cara whispered. At the nod she received, she swallowed. "And what of yer people? Ye're the leader of this land."

"I'd give it all up in a moment." Merryn smiled at the memory she was about to impart. "When on t' battlefield when things seemed they could get no worse, I used ta dream of ya, lass. Ya'd smile at me, 'n give me t' courage ta go on. Somehow I knew ya'd want me ta do whatever it be I was doin'."

Cara looked at her for a moment, stunned. "I used ta dream of ye, too, Merryn. Though I didn't want ta." Her smile was sheepish again. "Ye would come ta me, comfort me. 'Tis madness, I know." She sighed.

"Cara, I dona want ya ta leave. I..." she swallowed, then tried again. "I understand ya have yer own life, now, in Kendal. But..." she cut herself off when the most beautiful green eyes looked at her. Swallowing yet again, she finished, "please allow me ta be in yer life. Somewhere."

"I won't go anywhere, Merryn." She shook her head. "There're too many reasons fer me ta stay."

"Oh, thank t' Heavens!" From the smirk she got, Merryn realized the extent of her enthusiasm and relief, and blushed. She was relieved for the reprieve when she felt Cara turn to her other side, reaching back to grab Merryn's arm. Cara began to relax back to sleep after tugging Merryn's arm around her waist and clasping her hand in her own. Merryn saw Cara smile as she spooned up behind her.

Merryn walked to the Great Hall, feeling relaxed and comfortable. Her wounds had all but healed, and she felt relieved to have her blades back in place. It felt as though life was returning to normal, with a bonus. But as much as she didn't want to allow Cara out of her sight, she had to return to the business of ruling. Besides, it gave Cara and her sister a chance to spend the day together.

"Donal!" Angus grinned, long strides eating up the distance between him and the ruler. Merryn grinned, taking the brief embrace from her comrade.

"How goes it, Angus?"

"Good, good. Though I'd say not as good as ye, eh?" He raised a brow. At the smile he got from his long-time friend and respected leader, Angus put a hand to her uninjured shoulder. "Cara's back with ye, eh?"

"Aye. She's come back ta me, Angus." Her voice was a whisper of awe. Angus was thrilled for his friend.

"Well, take some o' that good luck with ye fer this meetin'."

The long table had already been set; jugs of wine and plates of meats and cheeses were set out for the honored guests. Torches and lamps lit the large space, and a roaring fire glowed in the hearth.

"Yer Grace," Merryn bowed, her eyes never leaving the face of the man dressed in a white robe with a red satin shoulder cape. A large, golden cross hung from a gold chain around his neck.

"Your Highness," the Bishop of Rutherford nodded acknowledgement. He held out his left hand, where shone a large gold ring with a dark ruby caped with a golden crown with a cross through it. Merryn all but clenched her jaw as she placed her lips to the cool stone. The man's finery almost matched her own.

"Please, enjoy t' bounty we have brought fer ya." She smiled, sitting down at the head of the large table, Angus sitting to her right. The Bishop's large entourage sat on his side of the table, at the other end. The elderly cleric looked at the ruler, disdain and disapproval clear on his wrinkled face.

"I've not come to *enjoy* anything, *Donal*." He shoved at the servant who had brought him a tray of food. Merryn felt her anger begin to build, the muscles in her arms and thighs already beginning to tense getting ready to push herself up from the chair where she sat. She felt a hand on her arm. Glancing at Angus, she tried to relax.

It was well known throughout the English empire that the Donal and the Church did not see eye to eye. Unlike those before her, Merryn refused to give the Church the power they craved through their hypocrisy and the domination they exercised through fear. Though she didn't believe in the Christian God, she felt it was wrong to use His name and Word as a weapon of rule. The people were not allowed to pray of their own volition, nor were they able to read the Bible as it was written in Latin. The average villager could barely read English, let alone a different language, if they could read at all.

Looking across the expanse of the table, seeing the bishop in his fine robes and glittering gold, Merryn suddenly felt her anger building again, but keeping her mouth shut, she waited.

"His Holiness, the Pope, wishes for more influence with your righteous people. And," he raised a heavily jeweled hand, "with you, Your Highness."

"I see," Merryn said, sipping from a goblet of wine. She remained quiet as the pompous man continued.

"His Holiness does not feel he has your support, Donal. He feels, as do I, that you, in fact, appear to be working *against* the Church." He laughed politely. "Surely this is not so."

"T' Pope is yer superior, Yer Grace, not mine." Merryn kept her voice low, not allowing her anger to take over. Though she may not agree with the Church, or its ideals and doctrines, she had to maintain relations with it. "My people find peace and solace 'n their god. Not 'n ye."

The bishop looked on, his small eyes widening. "Careful, Donal," he warned. "Some might mistake ye for a heretic. His Holiness, Innocent VI can offer guidance to ye and your people, Donal. He is the only one who can save them..."

"Wrong!" Merryn shot to her feet, slamming a fist to the table. "If my people need protecting, they turn ta me. What is Urban gonna do? *Pray?*"

"Donal," Angus hissed under his breath. She ignored him.

"My people turn ta me, Yer Grace. *I* rule, *I* decide," she pounded her own chest. She was tired of the harassment by the Church, clerks and priests being sent to ensure support from the ruler. "Ye sit there in yer finest robes. More went inta that outfit than a man in London could spend in a year! 'N ye do it by takin' coins from t' trusting," she hissed, her long-held disgust seething. She had a deep-seated hatred for the Church and those who ran it from her days as an orphan.

Incensed, the Bishop got to his feet, followed by his entourage. His nostrils were flaring, and his eyes never left the Donal. "Ye'll burn in Hell, Donal," he growled. "Unnatural as ye are. Burn in Hell!"

"I'll see ya there."

With a huff, the bishop stormed out of the room, shouting at a castle servant who got in his way. Merryn felt her body vibrating with rage. She had lost control, and it would mean trouble.

"What have ye done?!" Angus yelled, once the Bishop was gone. He was near trembling with rage.

"I lost control," Merryn meekly explained, a hand running through her hair.

"Ye've done more than that, lass." He glared at her, daring her to correct the title he knew she hated. He knew she was in no place to make any sort of demands at that moment. "T' Pope already resents a woman tellin' him what he can and canna do." He stared her down, seeing recognition of the truth in her eyes. "Now ye go 'n insult him? And his Bishop?" Angus was furious with her, and he shoved her, watching her stagger back a few steps.

"My people deserve ta make their own choices, Angus," she stated.

"Aye, that they do," he conceded, "but a good ruler is diplomatic, Donal! Today ye were a beast! Retribution will be swift." He was beginning to calm, but his mind was racing.

Merryn sighed, again running her hands through her hair. She had to put this right; Angus was right. Despite its teaching, the Church was *not* forgiving.

Sighing again, she turned to Angus. She stood tall and unflinching. Making a decision that could change much, she spoke her mind.

"Angus, I canna fall to the Church. I have not these past years, and I will not now. They will *not* rule me, or this realm. Do ya understand me?"

Angus also stood tall, breathing in through his nose. He heard what his Donal had said, and although he agreed, he was also a practical man, knowing when it was time to agree just to keep peace. Alas, it was not his decision. He nodded.

"Aye, Donal."

"Good. Now come," she slapped the man on his back. "We've a festival to arrange."

Cara listened willingly to her sister prattle on and on about her life in the castle, and how awed and overwhelmed she'd been at first. She told Cara all about Cayshire, and how the Donal and Angus had brought in anyone who needed a place to stay, or who wanted a better life.

Cara watched Grace, unable to take the smile from her face, so proud was she at the beautiful, intelligent, responsible young adult the girl had become. And she knew that their mother would have been so happy to know she would have been a grandmother.

"What?" Grace asked, noticing that she was being stared at. Her sister smiled, shaking her head before putting an arm around her shoulders. They continued through the gardens, gathering fresh herbs and plants for Cara's collection.

"I am just tryin' to absorb the fact that ye're here," Cara said, gently squeezing the narrow shoulders in her grasp. Grace smiled.

"Aye. T' same fer me." Slinging her arm across her big sister's back, she pressed their sides together. "Canna wait fer David to come home ta meet ye." The girl's grin was infectious.

"When do I meet the boy?"

Grace sighed heavily, her free hand resting upon her belly. "When the wars in Novgorod end."

"I see."

"'Tis where the Donal was wounded. So scared, I was," she whispered.

"Scared for the Donal?"

"Aye. More so that it was me David brought back."

Cara nodded in understanding. Releasing the younger girl, she squatted next to a patch of parsley, arranging her cloak around her body. Glancing up to the skies, she could see rain was near. She could smell it.

"Hold this, Grace." Once the girl had taken the small basket from the Healer's hand, Cara turned back to the small patch. Digging through it, she bent down until her face was mere finger-lengths from the wild herb.

Using her nose, she separated the spongy green plant until she found what she was looking for. With a triumphant grin, she found a sprig that was about to turn bad.

Pulling a small dagger from her belt, she cut the plant and examined it from every angle. Satisfied, she handed it back to her sister to place in the basket.

Grace grinned, helping her sister to her feet. She arranged a few of the herbs in the basket.

"What?" Cara asked, noting the big smile.

"Makes me think of when we were children, back home. Mother yellin' fer us ta hurry up fer supper."

Cara sighed at the happy thoughts. "Aye." She hugged her sister. "Come. Let's go back fer the buckbean I saw before."

They began to make their way back into the trees when Grace stopped, her eyes opening wide. Cara glanced over at her when she felt a stopping hand on her arm. The girl's mouth opened, but nothing came out. Not until a scream was ripped from her throat.

Merryn waited for the town crier to finish writing what she'd said. His wife stood nearby, shyly smiling at the ruler. The Donal smiled back at her, trying to put the fidgeting woman at ease. Finally her husband finished scratching the announcements on his parchment. He handed it to Merryn to read over and make sure it was correct. As she opened her mouth to ask for a change, a piercing cry echoed off the stone walls.

Throwing the parchment at the stunned crier, she ran toward the noise. She saw a couple of servants running toward the physician's room. Following them down the dark hall, she stopped just short of bowling over a group of curious onlookers.

She pushed her way through into the room.

"Stop, Grace! Do not push." Cara's brows were knit as she placed her hands upon her sister's swollen stomach. Closing her eyes, she allowed her sense of touch to take over. Her hands smoothed over the heated skin of Grace's belly, her head rising as she concentrated on what she felt. "Yer child is breach, my sister," she whispered. Cara's eyes opened as she felt a presence beside her. Seeing Merryn, she smiled at her then turned back to her patient. "I need ye ta hold still fer me, Grace. Can ye do that?"

"Aye," Grace whimpered, head lolling from side to side as pain ripped through her insides.

"Good girl."

Cara quickly untied her cloak, tossing it to the floor in her haste to get to her task. Arms and hands bared, she glanced down between her sister's spread legs. The girl's sex was swollen and moist from her water breaking. The girl was dilated and seeping, as her body readied itself for the miracle of birth.

Cara's brows knit once more as she pressed her hand against the incredibly hot opening of the birth canal. Her fingers slid easily inside, followed by her thumb. Inside the girl to her wrist, she glanced at her sister, gauging the girl's condition. She was relieved to see Merryn standing at Grace's head, leaning over her, whispering soft words of encouragement into the girl's ear, as well as gently stroking her hair and side of her face.

Turning back to her hand, Cara concentrated on what she felt. Soft warmth and liquids surrounded her flesh, softening the skin as it wrinkled. She tried to ignore the murmurs and whimpers of pain from Grace. She had to do this. Both mother and child were at risk if she couldn't get the baby turned around to come out properly.

Her reaching fingers came into contact with the soft skin of what felt like a foot. Knowing she was where she needed to be, she grunted slightly, biting her lower lip as she reached for the baby's head. She felt the umbilical cord floating around, brushing against her wrist. It was thankfully not wrapped around the baby's neck. Feeling the side of her hand brush against a tiny cleft, Cara smiled.

"I believe ye have a girl, Grace," she said softly, meeting her sister's eyes for a brief moment before returning her attention to her niece. Gently urging the tiny body inside her sister's womb, Cara got her turned around so that her head was directed downward. The baby immediately began to slide through the birth canal. Cara also felt the inner muscles of Grace's cervix pushing on her hand. Quickly removing it, she watched as her hand, covered in blood and a dark liquid, emerged.

"Push now, Grace!" she urged. The girl cried out, her eyes squeezing shut as she pushed with all her might.

"That's it, lass!" Merryn cried, standing, taking hold of one of Grace's hands, the smaller fingers squeezing tightly, painfully, around her own.

"Almost there, Grace, come on." Cara was panting with exhilaration as the baby's head crowned. Grace screamed out her agony when the child managed to push through, her tiny, sickly white shoulders squeezing out of the tiny opening.

The angry cry of a brand new babe filled the air as she took her first breaths. Immediately Cara had her fingers in the child's mouth, clearing the airway of any left over mucus or liquids. Coughing, the baby resumed her crying, her tiny body shaking with every strong pull of her lungs.

"It's a girl," Cara breathed, tears running from her eyes as she looked down at her niece. She quickly wrapped her up in a cloth handed to her. Grace watched, half exhausted and half beside herself with happiness. The baby was given to Grace as Cara still helped to support the baby, afraid that in her weakened state, Grace wouldn't be as careful as she normally would be.

Grace smiled through her tears. "Chloe 'tis," she murmured.

Merryn stood off to the side, arms crossed over her chest as she watched the beautiful scene unfolding before her. As Cara handed the child off to a mid-wife, she turned to Merryn, her face split with a smile. Merryn opened her arms, and Cara flew into them.

"Good on ye, lass," Merryn whispered. "'M happy fer ya 'n yer sister."

"Thank ye."

Grace was sound asleep, her head turned to the side as her body found some peace after nine months of strain and exhaustion.

Cara stood at Chloe's crib, the baby in her arms. She looked down and smiled at the little sounds her niece made, tiny fingers wrapped around one of hers. Her eyes scanned Chloe's pinched face, taking in the tiny nose. Nostrils flared as the baby instinctively took in everything around her, the smells in the air would remind her of her mother.

"'Tis a beautiful child, Cara."

The Healer turned to Merryn and nodded.

"Aye. Would ye like ta hold her?" Merryn's smile at the offer warmed Cara's entire being.

"Very much so."

"Support her head," Cara whispered as she handed the tiny body into Merryn's tender embrace. Merryn looked down into the child's face, her smile growing soft and wistful.

"Hello, little Chloe," she cooed, bringing a hand up to touch the soft skin of the baby's face, lightly tapping her pert nose with a fingertip. Cara moved behind Merryn, resting her chin on her shoulder, seeing what Merryn was seeing. For a moment, it seemed as if the impossible had happened, and the child in Merryn's arms was their child, borne of the love they had shared. "A miracle, 'tis."

"Aye." Cara sighed with contentment, bringing her own hand up, tracing a light track down the babe's cheek. She smiled as the newborn's tongue instinctively moved to that side of her tiny mouth.

"She hungry?" Merryn asked, never taking her eyes off the bundle in her arms.

"Nay. Grace fed her before I gave her an herb ta sleep."

Merryn nodded her approval. "Let us let ya sleep, little Chloe," she whispered in a sing-songy voice, turning toward the crib. Gently laying her down, she watched as Cara tucked the baby in, her tiny swaddled body barely squirming.

"G'night ta ye, my love," Cara whispered, placing a gentle kiss on the baby's forehead. Standing once again, she turned to Merryn. She felt uncertainty grip her. A feeling she did not like.

Merryn looked into her exhausted green eyes. She knew Cara needed sleep badly, and she also knew she wanted Cara to join her again in her bedchambers. The thought of sleeping soundly, knowing Cara was somewhere nearby, was unthinkable.

Cara felt her body beginning to sway as the need for sleep became a demand instead of a wish. Merryn had said nothing, had not suggested she join her. She would not press an issue that she, herself, was uncertain of. Eyes faltering for a moment, she ran an unsteady hand through her short hair. Turning slightly, she said over her shoulder, "G'night then, Merryn."

Part 14

Muttering to herself, Merryn rolled over again. Never had her bed felt so huge. Normally she loved the expanse of the bed, similar to having all the room she'd loved during her times of sleeping on the ground without the discomfort. Such nocturnal freedom seemed far more like a hindrance than a privilege this night.

Giving up on rest, she got to her feet, tugged on her boots, then grabbed a cloak to wrap snugly around her body. The fire had recently been rebuilt. Standing before it for a moment, she warmed her chilled body then strode out of the darkened rooms, grabbing one of her swords as she did.

As was expected, Saoirse was quiet. A few rats could be heard running along the walls, sniffing in their partial blindness for anything edible. The Donal walked down the stairs that led from her personal suite of rooms to the next floor, where guests and those of importance slept. She found her way to Paul's rooms. He had been in bed most of the previous day, and she had checked on him from time to time. Cara had assured her that he would be fine and just needed some rest. He would be more sore than anything.

Pushing open the double doors leading to his rooms, she saw his fire was just about burnt out. Quietly walking over to it, she quickly stoked it back to life. Turning to the bed, she saw him watching her. An instant smile lit up her face, far more than any fire could do.

"How are ya, lad?" Walking over to him, she perched on the side of his bed. He pulled his hands from under the covers and, with quick movements, told his mother that he was fine, though he still had a headache. He also told her that the Healer had been there not long ago. Merryn smiled with a nod. "Aye. She is wonderful." More movement of his hands. Again, she nodded. "Aye, son. I'd like her ta stay, as well."

Merryn looked away for a moment, indecision pulling her lower lip into her mouth. She felt Paul's eyes on her. Glancing back at him, she decided to tell him the truth.

"Son, I need ta tell ya somethin'." The boy nodded, giving her his full attention. She knew that if Cara were to stay in the castle, perhaps become the official healer of the Donal, Paul needed to know the truth. Meeting his curious gaze, she began her tale. Paul listened, nodding from time to time to acknowledge that she still had his full attention. As the story progressed, his eyes got wider as realization dawned on him of just what his mother was telling him, the exact nature of Merryn and Cara's relationship at one time. Merryn swallowed hard as she got to the point in the story of Cara's illness at the cabin. She described to him what it had been like to leave her, unable to burn or bury her. There was no way her heart could have survived watching such destruction. She ended her story at the night when she'd run into Tamara and her young son, Paul, and how she had happened to be there to save their lives.

Nervous, Merryn finally met her son's eyes, waiting to see what he would say about the whole thing. She knew the lad was clever and wise beyond his years, and she could only pray that he would use that wisdom in reconciling what he'd just been told.

After sitting there for long moments, the boy reached for the parchment he often used to write on when he was communicating with someone who did not understand his silent language. Bent over the parchment and scribbling a few words, he showed his writings to her.

Ye really do like to anger the Bishop, don't ye?

Merryn broke out in relieved laughter, especially when she saw the twinkle in the boy's eyes. She watched as he began to scribble furiously again.

I do not understand such a love, but I do see what a wonderful person Cara is. She makes ye happy?

"Aye, Paul. That she does."

Do ye know her again? As in what t' bible says of know?

Merryn read the words then shook her head. "No, son. I dona know if we'll ever be that way again. But I do love her, 'n want her in my life." Paul nodded, tapping his own chest. "Ya, too, eh, lad?"

The boy grinned, turning back to his parchment.

I don't have a chance now, do I?

Again, his dark eyes twinkled. Throwing her head back in thunderous laughter, Merryn took her son in her arms and squeezed him. Giving him a quick kiss on the forehead, she grinned at him. Shaping her thumb and forefinger into an L, she placed them over her heart. The boy returned the gesture. It had always been something between them.

Gaining her feet, Merryn took the parchment and quill from the boy. "Sleep now, lad." After making sure he was warm and comfortable, she left him.

She felt better but no less awake. Gathering her cloak a little closer around her, she walked on, heading down out of the residence suites, and deeper into the guts of the castle.

In some ways she hated being at home. On the battlefield, and in camp, she was typically so exhausted from fighting that she fell right to sleep. Out in the field, she got a better sleep in five hours than she did in a full night at home. Tonight she was restless. She'd had longer stints at home between battles before, but none that had been so taxing on her emotions.

She was glad to see the preparations for the festival that was approaching. It was time to celebrate. All the townspeople were invited to Saoirse to partake in food, wine, and good ale, and to buy any goods merchants wished to sell. It would be great fun.

She made her way toward the castle library. About to go in and fetch one of the hand-printed books to take up to her rooms, she noticed something, a flicker of light. She walked across the massive hall, her steps echoing against the high ceiling.

The chapel door was closed, though the very faint flickering of candlelight within licked under the crack.

Taking the handle in her hand, she gently opened the door, hoping the hinges would not creak. She was lucky and they held silence. The stone floor of the small room was bare; worshippers came in to kneel. At the front stood a small altar for the castle priest to say Mass.

A single tall candle burned at the center of the room, and the flame flickered in the constant breeze that weaved its way through the stone halls and rooms. Kneeling before this candle was Cara, her back arched as her forehead nearly touched the floor. She was completely silent.

Undecided whether she should leave this very private moment or not, Merryn's eyes were locked on that golden hair, which shimmered in the equally golden candlelight. She watched, enraptured by the gentle way Cara's body moved, almost as though she were rocking, raising just enough for her profile to be visible. Merryn could then see that her lips were moving, though no sound came out. Her clasped hands rested under her chin as she rocked back down, her forehead nearly against the floor once more.

Deciding it was a moment too intimate for her to be witnessing, Merryn slowly backed out of the room.

"Don't leave," she heard whispered. She saw Cara rock a couple more times before she sat up fully on her knees. Head bowed, she seemed to be closing her prayer, then she got up. Turning to Merryn, she smiled.

"'M sorry. Shoulda gone."

"No," Cara said softly, walking over to her. "'Tis alright. I was nearly done."

Merryn nodded acknowledgement.

Cara's head tilted slightly to the side. "Why're ye not sleepin'?"

Merryn shuffled her booted feet and fidgeted as she tried to avoid eye contact. Finally she felt a gentle touch to her cheek. Her face was directed toward Cara's amused one. One shoulder shrugged, almost like a child.

"Canna," she muttered in explanation. She melted at the smile that received from her answer.

"Do ye need somethin' ta help?" Cara was amused, but half serious all the same.

Merryn shook her head.

"Well then, let us get ye back ta bed." She took one of Merryn's hands in both of hers. "The Donal needs her rest."

"As does t' great, all-knowing Healer."

Cara smirked, walking past her, still holding her hand, giving her no choice but to follow.

"Paul said ye were by ta see 'im," Merryn said at length, stepping aside to allow Cara to enter a narrow staircase before her.

"Aye. He heals quickly." Cara glanced behind her, amused when she saw Merryn's eyes dart away from contemplation of her behind. "Like his mother." Merryn smiled up at her.

As they reached the top of the staircase, Merryn had to make a quick decision. One way would lead to Cara's rooms, the other to her own. Taking the lead as they reached the landing, she tugged lightly to the right. Looking down into twinkling green eyes, she smiled sheepishly and moved them toward the staircase that led to her bedchamber.

"Where is Paul's birth mother, Merryn?" Cara asked, her voice soft as they made their way through dark, cold hallways.

"She died when he was just a boy. His da, too." Merryn pushed open the doors to her chambers. The fire warmed the room nicely after the chill in the halls they'd just traversed.

"He adores ye." Cara smiled at the pride that reflected plainly in Merryn's face.

Merryn nodded. "And I him." *And ye.*

Cara looked around then turned back to her. "Why did ye bring me here?" she asked, her voice soft. She thought she had an idea; she too had had trouble sleeping, but she wanted to hear Merryn's answer. *Needed* to hear it.

Swallowing, Merryn took Cara's hands in hers. She knew that if she were to get Cara fully back into her life, she needed to be as honest as she could with the beautiful healer. She began to speak, her voice soft, slightly shaky.

"I couldna sleep because ya're not here. Will ya stay?"

Cara looked up into the beseeching face that was once again becoming so important to her. Lifting a hand, she cupped Merryn's cheek. She could feel the softness of the tanned skin, her thumb gently caressing the defined cheekbone. Nodding, she smiled. "Aye."

The tension in the air suddenly grew thick, as they gazed at each other. Cara could feel her heart rate quicken, and her breathing hitch slightly. Knowing she was not ready for anything more than sleeping, she dropped her gaze and took a step back.

Merryn swallowed hard, taking several deep breaths as Cara moved away from her, readying for bed. No other had touched her since Cara, and she knew not what to do with her body's sudden awakening. Deciding this night was not the time to think about it, she, too, got ready for bed.

The castle and grounds were abuzz before the sun had risen. Just inside the gates of Castle Saoirse, booths were being set up as merchants displayed their wares to their best advantage for sale: pots and jugs, instruments, herbal mixtures, various food stuffs, and carved, wooden toys, to name but a few. Excitement was in the air, and children were running around trying to help their parents and joyously playing with each other.

Every member of the household, including Evela and Angus, was helping to get ready for the festivities. There was no one that hadn't been bitten by the bug of excitement and anticipation for a wonderful day.

Giddy as a schoolgirl, Merryn crept back into her rooms. She was fully dressed and bathed, and had been busy with state affairs already, as the sun was beginning to smile upon the land. She walked over to the bed, where Cara was still very much asleep. Cara lay on her side, hands tucked up under her chin.

Snatching her full circle cloak from where she'd left it heating by the fire, Merryn passed the overheated garment from hand to hand as it cooled slightly. Finally able to handle it, she tossed it over her arm and gently woke Cara. Her eyes opened, then closed tightly, as their owner groaned in displeasure.

"Come on, now, lass. I've got a surprise fer ya." Merryn couldn't keep the grin from splitting her face wide open. She wrapped the warmed cloak around Cara's small frame, making Cara moan in pleasure as she was enveloped in soft warmth. This made her far more willing to follow Merryn out of the chamber.

Getting no answer to her request for information, Cara became silent, trusting Merryn, and attempted to keep her early morning temper in check. She was led down the stairs, toward her own rooms before being suddenly tugged through a door. Merryn gently nudged Cara before her.

Cara's eyes widened as she took in the beautiful room before her. Gone was the stone of the rest of the structure. The walls of this room were lined with marble, and the floor was beautiful tile forming a decoration of a rising sun. At the center of the room, which was hot and somewhat steamy, was a marble tub, of the likes that the Healer had seen in Rome — large and square with ornate carvings along the sides. There were two steps on each of the four sides.

Along one wall were pottery jars, labels scribed into the fresh clay before they had been baked. Cleaning pastes and herbs waited inside, as well as soaps made of lard and rose petals. Cara noted a complex network of piping that led into the floor, as well as a pump that sat about waist-high.

"What 'tis this?" she asked, stepping further into the room. She saw that the tub was filled with warm, inviting water.

"Yer own private bath," Merryn said, pride filling her voice. She was amazed that her people had managed to get it all done so quickly for her. She'd reward them greatly for it. Cara turned toward her, eyes wide in shock and disbelief. Merryn grinned with a nod. "No doubt yer still as much o' stickler as ya were before," she said with a wink.

"Thank ye."

Merryn was nearly bowled over by a very enthusiastic Cara. Giving her a tight hug, she pulled away a bit.

"Bathe now, lass. I'll send Carla in with clothin' fer ya." A quick kiss to her flushed cheek, and Merryn hurried out of the chamber.

Once alone, Cara walked further into the room, in awe and deeply touched. Her eyes lit upon everything, not wanting to miss any of the precious details that had been added just for her use. She uncorked each jar, inhaling the fragrant scents, recognizing each without having to read the label. Merryn had gathered all her favorites, and she was stunned at the thoughtful gesture. How had she remembered everything that she loved so much? It seemed that daily Merryn was surprising her all over again with her thoughtfulness.

Looking down into the tub, she smiled when she realized that the surface of the water was covered with floating rose petals, their deep red in sharp contrast to the white marble. Sitting upon the wide ledge that wrapped around all four sides, Cara leaned over, dipping her fingers into the water. She moaned at the warmth, imagining what that would feel like over her entire body. The best she'd ever had was a semi-warm bath in large wooden tubs, with buckets of heated water thrown in. That particular bath was semi-warm because the bath was in a much cooler room or had been outside. This was truly decadent.

Reaching up, Cara unclasped her cloak, hanging it on one of hooks that dotted one wall. As she worked the laces of her dress, there was a soft knock on the chamber door.

"Come!" Cara called. She watched as Carla entered, giving a smile and slight bow to the Healer as she set a new dress of white and green upon a small stool, as well as several soft, thick drying cloths. As soon as the young servant left, Cara walked over to the dress. Holding it up, she smiled as she shook her head. She'd been given more new garments in her past weeks at the castle than in her entire life.

She stepped out of the under gown she had slept in and moved over to the bath. She was almost giddy with anticipation. Holding onto the ledge, she carefully dipped a toe into the warmth, then her entire foot. As she continued, the water rose all the way up her leg to her upper thigh. Soon she had waded out to the center of the bath, glancing behind her to find the seat that would keep her head above the depths. Slowly lowering herself, she closed her eyes with a deep, throaty groan. Her nipples instantly tightened from the contrast of cold to hot, her skin prickled with goosebumps. It sent a shiver down her spine that she hadn't felt in years.

Looking down at her body, pale and distorted under the water's surface, she saw her breasts. Their slope was just above the water's ripple, which caused a rose petal to float by and hide her right nipple for a moment before moving on. It had been so long since Cara had looked at her body with any thoughts of pleasure. Not since Merryn. For a long time during her studies, she thought back to what they had done and the love they shared. She thought that perhaps the wickedness of what they'd done together was why God had punished them, separating them — why Merryn had left her.

But now...

They had been brought together again. Surely, if what they had shared together was so wrong, they never would have been reunited. And surely if it was so wrong, it wouldn't feel so right.

Closing her eyes, Cara leaned her head back against the edge of the tub, a deep sigh slipping from her lips. The water pulsed around her body, caressing her long neglected skin. She felt the soft, velvety touch of her thighs as her fingertips rested there, the tiny hairs tickled slightly by light touch.

Cara couldn't deny that Merryn still affected her, bringing her body to life when she thought her body, like her heart, was long dead. What was she to do? Dare she open herself up again? Though the logical side of her understood what had happened, how it had happened, and that through these past ten years Merryn had been tortured more than she, the other side of her, the lost, angry, devastated young girl, still cried and was terrified it would happen again.

Sighing heavily, she decided not to think about it nor analyze it too deeply. She was bonded to the ruler in a way that she could never break or deny. As she relaxed further into the water, she decided to simply allow things to fall out as they would. No conscious thought had been made the first time, so why now?

It had been nearly half an hour since the aleconner had sat on the bench in a puddle of ale. The crowd gathered around him watched, almost holding their breath. He swished a bit of the sweet ale around his mouth, his enormous belly resting on his leather-clad thighs. A heavy brow drew and released in concentration, some of the liquid darkened his red beard.

Swallowing what was in his mouth, he took the wooden mug into one plump fist and then began to wiggle his backside on the bench before finally standing. There was no sticking, his leather pants coming easily off the wood.

As he raised the mug high into the air, the crowd erupted in a cheer, particularly Jason, who had brewed the ale. If his ale had been "short-measured", bad quality or quantity, the punishment would have been severe. Breathing a sigh of relief, he enjoyed the good wishes of those who slapped him on the back with gratitude.

People continued to pour through the castle's inner walls as the morning lengthened with the shadows, merriment abounding as they perused the exhibits and ate the good food, all provided by the Donal. Her people stood at the outside fire pits, roasting meats and handing out bread and bowls of stew.

Games were set up: a line of targets for archery contests, a course for horsemanship, boccie, and of course, the crowd favorite, jousting.

"What?" Cara asked, exasperated. Glancing up at her companion, she saw Merryn look shyly away. Stopping their progress through the crowd, she put a hand on the Donal's arm. "Nay. Why do ye keep lookin' at me?"

Merryn gave her a sidelong glance then looked down at her boots. Finally raising her eyes again, she looked squarely at her. "Ya look stunnin' in that dress, lass. 'N this," she brushed her fingers over the crown of flowers in her hair, a smile tipping her features. Her eyes shone with such an intense shade of blue, Cara had to look away.

"Thank ye," she whispered, her cheeks turning every shade of red.

"Come, lass. Let us celebrate!" Grabbing her hand, Merryn tugged Cara into the excited throng. Music wafted through the air, making it impossible not to dance, and Merryn led Cara in an enthusiastic Grocheio. Both the Donal and the Healer had irrepressible smiles on their faces, as they clapped with the rest of the dancers, turning and joining again to make a tunnel for others to pass under. Cara felt the light material of her dress swishing around her legs. She whipped around again, clapping once before whipping the other way, again her palms coming together to join the round of claps. She watched Merryn over her shoulder, doing the same moves, their eyes catching again and again, only for one or the other to look away, then finding each other's gaze again.

Merryn couldn't keep the smile from her lips as she swung around with other dancers, watching Cara do the same. As they came back together, never touching, their gazes met once more, both flushed with the excitement and exertion of the dancing.

Dancing was something the Church strongly forbade, lest it incite urges of the Devil. Dancing was something Cara enjoyed very much, but had had little reason to do for a long time.

The music came to an end, and the dancers clapping enthusiastically in appreciation with a sense of camaraderie and accomplishment. Many of the townsfolk hurried over to the Donal, not often having such a chance to speak with her and thank her.

Cara stepped back out of the gathering throng, pride and wonder filling her. How on earth had a scrappy pickpocket end up ruling England? As she watched the way Merryn interacted with her people, it wasn't hard to see. She was confident and self-assured, stern and fair, yet kind and caring. It was obvious that she loved these people, and even more obvious that they loved her.

"Ye've managed what we've been tryin' ta do for years."

Cara turned to the amused voice. Evela gave her a smiling glance before turning to watch the Donal.

"'N what 'tis that?" Cara asked, her own smile returning.

"Ye've somehow convinced her to enjoy herself. She usually stays in a corner, watching, but never joining in the festivities."

"'N why not?"

"I know not." Evela sighed, plucking a flower from the basket she carried and handing it to Cara. She gave the Healer a smile of genuine gratitude. "Ye've given a ruler her heart back, young Cara," she said softly. "All of England and her far reaching empire thanks ye for it."

As Evela walked away, Cara twisted the flower between her fingers and let those words sink in. Vaguely she heard the music start up for another dance, then felt a tapping on her shoulder. She turned to see Paul bow deeply before her, his dark eyes twinkling with mirth and the health of a young man. He wiggled his brows, and she knew just what he was asking.

"I'd be delighted, Paul."

His grin was blinding as they began their dance.

Merryn flexed her knees, bringing her leg up to make sure the mail moved as she needed it to yet did not catch the aketon. Even though the aketon was worn beneath the mail to make it more comfortable, it could still be trouble if it did not allow the mail to move properly.

"Alright," she said, giving her squire permission to continue. The boy knelt as he attached the cuisse, protecting her thighs. The heavy plates clinked together as he attached them with leather straps. While he did this, Angus helped by putting her pauldrons into place, the rounded shoulder pieces fitting nicely over the couter.

"Bend," he ordered, watching as the Donal flexed her elbow, the metal moving as it should. Patting her on the shoulder, he turned to the cuirass with attached tassets, which reached to mid-thigh, neatly blending with the cuisse, which the boy had finished with. He was moving on to the greaves, making sure the armor fit properly over the Donal's boots, then strapping front and back together.

The boy stood out of the way, letting Merryn walk around the small armor chamber, flexing her legs and elbows, raising her arms, and moving her shoulders. Once this ritual was complete, Angus pulled the coat-armor over her head, her colors and coat of arms displayed brightly over the tournament garment. Grinning at her, he helped her with the mail coif, making sure it wasn't caught in her hair.

"I still say ya should be tournamentin', too," she grumbled, accepting her mail gauntlets from the squire and giving him a small smile of thanks.

"Nay," Angus said, taking her helm from its wooden stand and tucking it under his arm. "'Tis fer ye to cause the oohs 'n ahhs." He winked, making his Donal roll her eyes. "Been too many a year, lass. 'M outta practice." Merryn flexed her fingers into the gloves of mail and the wrist guards steel plate. "Excuses," she muttered, sliding a single hand-and-a-half blade into its place at her side. They walked out of the chamber into the yard where her warhorse had already been saddled and harnessed, his armor glinting in the sunlight.

With the help of a complicated crane-like contraption, and an "alley-oop!" she was up on horseback. She settled in the saddle for a moment, allowing her mount to get used to her weight, which was increased by her armor. Reaching down, she took her helm from Angus and rocked it into place, then lifted the visor with a mailed finger. She took her shield in her left hand and the lance, painted in her colors of black and gold, in the other. Tucking the weapon into her saddle, lengthwise along the beast, she nodded to her second-in-command, accepting his words of good luck. With a click of her tongue, her horse was on his way.

Cara moved with the excited crowd toward the jousting grounds. The crowds were gathering around the long, dirt field. Many of the wooden benches were already filled with spectators, some murmuring happily amongst themselves, others caught up in the antics of the two fools in the field who were providing amusement until the joust began.

Cara sat with Paul, Evela, and Ezra. The blacksmith stroked his dark beard as he chuckled at the antics of the men on the field, chasing each other and slinging barbs and insults.

Cara lifted her face to the warm, cloudless sky. The sun beat down, but a gentle breeze helped to keep the temperature comfortable. It was a perfect day.

She opened her eyes when she heard loud trumpets announcing the arrival of the competitors in the day's jousting match. The fools dashed off the field to be replaced by one of the castle criers.

"Hear ye, hear ye!" he called, all eyes on him. "T'day we have a treat of special care fer ye!" He threw his arm out with a flourish, as the two war horses pranced onto the field, proudly carrying their armored riders, each holding their lance at attention. Merryn was easy to spot, the sunlight glinting off the golden visor of her helm, showing her rank and position.

"Our Donal rides to t' field," the crier continued as Merryn raised her lance to deafening cheers from her people. She smiled as she heard the stomping of feet. She could hear her own breathing echoing inside her helmet, making her skin feel moist and warm. Looking through the slatted visor, she searched the crowd trying to spot Cara. She smiled when she saw four people standing near the middle of the first section. They were too far away to see clearly, but she caught the three dark heads and one golden, knowing exactly who was waving and yelling to her. Nodding her helm in honor to them, Merryn turned her attention back to the competition at hand.

Angus watched from beside the stands, where the riders had entered the field from the stable yards. He leaned against the wall, arms crossed over his chest. He ran a hand through his thick hair, much filtered with gray now.

Watching the two opponents on the field, he smiled, knowing it would be a good match. Lord Handon from Kent was on very good terms with the Donal, and they enjoyed each other's company. Handon was a good fighter and an equally good showman — just like the Donal.

"Warring against our Donal this day is Sir Henry of Maidenshire! First Knight of Lord Handon of Kent!"

The crowd cheered once again politely, though some began to boo good naturedly. The other horseman raised his lance, pumping his armored arm to taunt those in the crowd.

Frowning, Angus pushed off the wall, his eyes trained on the Donal, who glanced at him over her shoulder. Angus shook his head in confusion.

"Let t' games begin!" The crier ran off the field, allowing the opponents to find their positions.

Cara was beside herself with excitement. She had heard so much of the Donal's prowess with weapons and was anxious to see her in action. She smiled as she thought back to the days they traveled together. Merryn had been able to hold her own with a sword, but much of that had been bumbling luck.

She felt her fingers tense around the flower Evela had given her earlier, intent on offering it to Merryn as a gesture of victory. From beside her, she could feel Paul's excitement, nearly matching her own. She grinned over at him to find he was already grinning at her.

"Will she win?" she whispered. His dark eyes widened as he nodded vigorously. She giggled, linking her arm with the lad's, her legs bouncing with nervous energy.

Merryn grasped the reins of her horse tightly in her mail-clad fingers. She could feel beads of sweat rolling down her spine, the heavy, quilted material of the aketon absorbing it. She became focused solely on the mounted man down the field from her, seeing his own gauntleted hand flexing on his lance and, no doubt, behind his shield, just as hers was. She pushed her boot more snuggly into the stirrups, giving herself a more planted, solid stance in which to absorb a blow, or to plant her own.

Camulus, Merryn's massive black mount, stomped one of his front hooves, feeling the tension and anticipation of his rider. Bucking his head slightly, he let Merryn know that he was as ready as she.

She focused in on the other rider, seeing his thighs beginning to clench around his mount, as hers did around Camulus. She could feel the blood and excitement begin to sing through her system, her sight turning to tunnel vision as she focused her sole attention on her opponent. Though these were games, she had to focus as if it was battle.

The horses snorted, both ready to charge at the first indication from their masters. The cue was given and the beasts did just that.

The crowd was on its feet, cheering for their Donal as she raced toward her opponent, lowering her lance as she neared. There was a marvelous crack as the Donal's lance was turned away by that of her opponent. The horses passed each other and galloped on to the end of the course where the riders turned them around, effectively taking each other's starting position.

Bringing her lance up, Merryn studied the knight downfield. His horse was pawing at the dirt. Her horse breathing hard from exertion and excitement, Merryn patted his neck, murmuring to him to settle him a bit. Grabbing the reins again, she got ready for another pass.

"Ha!" she encouraged her mount, sending the beast speeding off back down the field, her opponent doing the same with his mount. Lowering her lance, she held it tightly against her side, holding it in position with her arm. She zeroed in on the oncoming knight, eyes widening when the sun glinted off an arrowhead that had been mounted to the end of his lance, painted dark red to match the rest of it.

"Bloody hell!" she cried as she lost her focus in her shock.

Cara gasped loudly, as did the crowd, as the two jousters collided. Merryn flew from her horse with the lance sticking out of her body. Cara held her breath until she saw the pole fall over harmlessly, thinking all was well. The Healer felt her heart begin to beat again. That is until Merryn didn't get up.

Merryn tried to catch her breath, desperately clawing at her breastplate. She felt the jagged hole in the steel, but no wetness. Opening her eyes as she sensed danger, she saw her opponent coming back at her. With a cry of intent, the man raised his bastard sword, intent on bringing it down to finish the job.

With eyes about to pop from their sockets, Merryn grunted as she forced her steel-encased body to roll out of the way.

Cara was about to run onto the field when she saw Merryn moving, her hands feeling around her breastplate. She was stunned to see the other jouster returning, his blade raised high above his head.

The crowd didn't have time to react as cries from the archery range rang out and people began to fall where they sat or stood, wooden shafts sticking out of their chests, backs, necks, and legs.

Realizing what was happening, the Healer made sure none of those sitting with her were hit, then she took off, jumping over some, crawling around others. Her healing instincts took over and, hiding behind fallen bodies or the stands themselves, she began to try and calculate where the worst wounded were.

Merryn had to use all her strength to pull herself to her feet in enough time to miss the third pass. Keeping her wits about her, she used her own lance to crack the front legs of the knight's horse. With a pained whinny, the beast went down, dumping his cargo on the ground. Like the Donal, the knight rolled, mindful of the felled horse and his opponent coming towards him.

It hurt to breathe, but Merryn knew she had to stay lucid as she looked at the knight. She heard the commotion from the stands, but did not dare look. She watched as the knight got to his feet before reaching him. Pulling her own blade, she met that of the knight, the clash of steel adding to the cries of fear and pain all around her.

Enraged beyond human capacity, Merryn felt extra strength rush through her. She had a good idea what was happening. She heard her men rushing onto the scene. She used all her might, all her skill and protectiveness of her people, to fight the highly trained knight.

She grinned with venomous satisfaction as his sword went flying out of his hands and onto the field, the sun glinting blindingly on it for a moment. The knight began to back away from her, but it was too late. With a cry of rage she thrust forward, aiming underneath his tassets. The sharp point of her blade sliced through his mail and into the tender flesh of his groin.

The knight cried out, the sound muffled inside his helm. Not bothering to run him through completely, Merryn kicked him off her blade and he fell with a loud clang of steel.

She reached up, unbuckling her helm, tugging it off her head and tossing it to the field. Hair glued to her scalp and face, she ran over to the knight's sword, snatching it up as she passed. Both blades in action, she ran into the fray, chopping at anything in her path that was aggressive. She looked around frantically for any sign of Cara but soon returned her focus to an enemy.

Looking out across the field, she saw Angus being attacked by two men with swords. He was doing his best to keep them off him.

Merryn ran to him, her armor and the two heavy swords in her hands slowing her progress. Baring her teeth, she sliced one of the attackers from behind with one blade then swirled around to slice his throat with the other. The man fell before he even knew what had hit him. Turning her attention back to Angus, she saw him sweating profusely as his other attacker went at him with quick, frenzied thrusts. Angus was doing what he could to defend himself, completely on the defensive. He had not fought in years, and he was not keeping his breathing under control.

Merryn heard someone come up behind her and turned, raising one of her swords to catch the blow her attacker had tried to bring down on her head. Her eyes burned with hatred of the coward who would dare attack from behind. A swift slap from her mail gauntlet had her attacker staggering backward; Merryn followed showing no mercy. She met his every blow, becoming the aggressor as she brought the other blade to bear.

She was not used to the weight of two long swords, and she could feel the strain in her forearms at the effort. Undaunted, she swung low with her left hand, taking the man's leg at the knee. Crying out in excruciating pain, he stumbled on his remaining leg, his cry cut short when he had a sword stuck into his gullet.

Not even bothering to tear the blade from his body, Merryn turned to help Angus but cried out in anguish. Angus stood motionless, his eyes as wide as his mouth as his opponent struggled to pull his blade out from the dark man's chest.

"No!" Merryn roared, her vision turning red as she used all her strength to whip her body around as she swung her sword, catching the terrified fighter in the soft tissue of his neck. She didn't even watch to see where his head fell as she threw herself to her knees. "Angus, no," she breathed, gathering her oldest, dearest friend in her steel embrace.

He looked up at her, a sickening gurgle coming from his chest. He reached up with desperate fingers, trying to find purchase. His fingers slid uselessly down the cold steel of Merryn's armor. With one final gasp, a word, he stopped moving, his body sliding down until he lay half on Merryn's thighs and half on the ground, eyes open, blood pouring from his mouth.

Teresa.

Feeling her eyes stinging with overwhelming emotion, Merryn leaned down, holding Angus close, the tears threatening to override her control. Glancing up, she saw a man coming at her with a dagger in his hand. He looked afraid but determined.

Gently setting Angus aside, Merryn felt her jaw muscles contracting as she got to her feet. The man faltered just a moment as he realized that he may be in trouble, but he kept his momentum, to his mortal detriment.

With the roar of a lion protecting his pride, Merryn drew her arm back and hit him as hard as she could with the steel of her gauntlet. The impact knocked the man off his feet, the side of his head crumpling like parchment. Dead before he hit the ground, Merryn looked down at him, spitting on his corpse.

About to walk away, she noticed something gleam in the sunlight. Bending, she brought her fingers to his throat, seeing the pendant attached to a leather thong. She tugged it off with a small grunt.

"Bastard," she hissed, recognizing the Bishop's seal.

Bodies littered the yards, some alive but many dead. Children, women — all gone. The attackers had left no one untouched in the slaughter.

Heavy, steel-covered boots picked lightly through the carnage, their owner not wanting to step on anyone, dead or no. Merryn scanned the dead, praying she'd find Cara but hoping to God that she wouldn't. Not here. Not in this field of death.

Merryn had given up asking anyone if they had seen her. All who survived were dazed and stunned, grieving not only for the dead but for what had been such a wonderful celebration of life. The *Donal's* life. Guilt was eating through Merryn like a ravaging monster. If only she had not spoken against the Bishop, if only she had treated him with diplomacy and grace...

Evela nearly jumped out of her skin as the double doors exploded inward. Her heart began to beat in relief when she saw Merryn storm in. She was looking around frantically, her armor dented, a hole at the center of her breastplate that went all the way through to the aketon. Her hair was flat to her head, blood and dirt streaking her features.

She was hurrying from group to group of the wounded, becoming more frantic by the moment.

"Donal..." Evela began, not daring to use the ruler's real name in front of so many of her subjects. She was cut off by a wild stare. She whimpered in fear when her upper arms were grabbed in a harsh hold.

"Where is she?" Merryn demanded shaking Evela with each word. She had never seen fear in the Donal's dark eyes before, but it mattered not. "Where?"

"She's alive, Merryn," Evela breathed, "gettin' more supplies..." She had not finished her sentence before the Donal was gone, armor clanking as she ran.

"Cara?" Merryn called, running down the hall, her voice nearly hoarse from fatigue and from swallowing a great deal of dust. Nearly passing the physician's supply room, she stopped, pulling herself back to the room with her hand on the doorframe. A stunned Cara stood inside, her white dress covered in patches of blood, her hair disheveled and her face smudged.

At the realization of who stood before her, Cara's face crumpled. She dropped everything in her hands, not caring as jars shattered against the stone floor. She threw herself at the Donal, nearly bowling her over.

The hard steel of Merryn's breastplate rammed against Cara's sensitive breasts, but she didn't care, thanking God over and over again that Merryn was alive.

Merryn heard Cara crying and held her tighter. Suddenly she was pushed away slightly, her face taken between two soft hands. She barely had time to react as Cara's lips pressed desperately against her own. Wrapping her arms more tightly around Cara, Merryn returned the kiss, both their mouths opening in hungry desperation born of fear and relief.

Out of breath, Merryn pulled back, resting her forehead against Cara's. "I was so afraid ya'd be dead," she whimpered, the full weight of her loss this day crashing all around her. She saw Angus in her mind's eye, and she lost control of her emotions at the gentleness of the woman in her arms.

Cara held her, whispering soft words of love into her ear, leaving little kisses along her cheeks, trying to kiss her tears away, noting how the emotion left a trail of skin through the smudges on the warrior's face. Soon Merryn calmed, the initial impact passing. She gathered herself together and pulled back.

"I need ta meet with me men," she said softly, bringing up a hand and caressing the side of Cara's face with her fingertips. Cara covered Merryn's mail-covered hand with her own. She nodded in understanding.

Merryn leaned her head down, placing a soft kiss on Cara's soft lips. "I love ya."

"And I love ye," she whispered, returning the kiss. "Go now."

"How did this happen!?" Merryn bellowed, her voice echoing throughout the Great Hall. Her men stood around, broken and bloody, just like she was. It pained her every time she realized Angus wasn't at her side. George and Aaron would never be joining them again either. "This," she hissed, walking around the room making sure that each man looked her in the eye as she passed, "is unforgivable." Heads drooped lower. "We're here ta protect these people, not get them slaughtered like sheep," she finished. "Get yerselves cleaned up."

Reaching out, she took the arm of one of her soldiers. He stopped immediately. The Donal looked away for a moment, her eyes squeezed tightly shut. Taking a deep breath, she turned to the man.

"Thomas, I need ya ta do somethin'."

Cara sighed, again, as she turned from one more who had succumbed to their injuries. Placing a bit of cloth over the child's face, she moved on. There were too many covered faces.

Out of the corner of her eye, she saw Merryn enter into the makeshift hospice. Turning, she walked over to the exhausted woman. Merryn's armor was gone, leaving her in the ruined aketon and mail leggings.

The pair embraced. Opening her eyes, Merryn saw Evela, trying to treat an elderly man who had broken his foot in the chaos.

"I'll be back," she muttered, walking over to Evela. "Forgive me t' outburst, Evela. 'Twasn't right," she said, resting a hand on the woman's shoulder.

Evela looked up, a sad smile upon her lips, and nodded. "Nothin' ta forgive, Merryn."

Merryn nodded, grateful for her friend's understanding.

"She was devastated," Evela said, nodding toward Cara, who was stitching up one of the last injured. "Be with her. Calm her." She reached up, placing a soft hand on Merryn's cheek. "And yerself."

"But..."

"Go."

At the gentle urging, Merryn walked back over to the Healer, standing behind her, watching as she spoke softly to the man, finishing up her stitching by holding the catgut tight in her teeth as she cut it with a small dagger. Cara turned, nearly walking straight into Merryn.

"Come."

Glancing over at Evela, who nodded, the Healer left her, Paul, and a few other helpers to finish tending the wounded.

Cara glanced up at Merryn from time to time as they made their way up further into the heart of the castle. Finally they arrived at the narrow staircase, turning right, then climbing the last staircase to Merryn's chambers. Merryn led the way in. The huge chamber was cold; there was no fire this night. Merryn's head fell, thinking that Matthew had probably been killed.

"Sit. Let me have a look at ye," Cara said softly, pushing her to sit on the side of the bed. She reached behind to unlace the aketon, peeling the quilted garment off the Donal and tossing it aside. She grimaced when she saw the massive bruise at the center of her chest, where the arrow tip had crashed into her body, shredding her armor and miraculously stopping just before penetration. "Let me get..."

"Nay." Merryn stopped her with a hand to the Healer's wrist. Cara willingly went to stand between the Donal's legs and ran her fingers through the sweat and blood-hardened strands of dark hair, gently untangling it.

"Ye should wash, Merryn," Cara whispered, her fingers running down the side of her face. With Merryn's forehead resting against her breastbone, Cara felt her nod. "Ye can even use my bath." Cara smiled at the chuckle from Merryn. Merryn raised her head, a smirk on her lips.

"'Re ya sayin' I'm disgustin', lass?"

Cara looked her over, slowly nodding. This time an all out laugh burst from Merryn's throat.

"I see."

Cara grinned, but it faded as Merryn sobered. "What 'tis it?"

"We lost so many today, lass," Merryn whispered. "So many. And Angus..."

"I know. 'M so sorry. Ye did what ye could, Merryn. Ye have ta know that." Soft fingers traced down along her jaw, then butterfly touches along her strong shoulders. "T' people don't blame ye for this."

"How many were lost, Cara?"

"Fewer than were saved." She leaned forward and placed a gentle kiss on Merryn's forehead. "Come." Wrapping a cloak around the Donal's naked shoulders, Cara led her down to the private bathing chamber. Soon the tub was being filled with steam-heated water, in which Cara added herbs that would help soothe Merryn's muscles and help her relax.

She stripped out of the rest of her clothing, the mail leggings falling to the floor in a loud clump. She had to peel her hose down her thighs; the garment was stiff with dried sweat and blood.

Cara tried to keep her eyes averted, but found it difficult. She caught a glimpse of Merryn out of the corner of her eye, and her breath caught. Gone was the tall, lanky girl of their youth. Before her now stood a strong, proud warrior, the skin of her arms and face tanned a deep brown, a testament to Merryn's strong belief in protecting her people by her own blade. It was thought that people with a pale and pasty complexion were more wealthy, as they sat fat and happy in their large homes. Tanned skin was for the peasants who actually had to make a living out in the harsh weather.

The years had placed lines of maturity and concentration on the already beautiful face, giving Merryn a look of strength and authority. Her body had grown strong and firm, rivaling just about any noble male in the realm.

Cara thought Merryn was stunning.

Merryn was completely oblivious to Cara's surreptitious glances as she climbed into the heated water, eyes instantly closing as a moan escaped her. It was pure bliss. She felt soft fingers on her shoulders.

"Let me wash yer hair, Merryn," Cara whispered, sitting on the ledge near her head. At the nod she received, Cara gently pushed on the shoulders, urging her to wet her tangled locks. She rubbed a generous amount of the most potent washing paste between her palms, feeling the thick, grainy substance squish between her fingers.

"Cara?" Merryn said

"Hmm?"

"Do ya think 'tis a sin ta murder a man o' t' cloth?" She waited as the silence grew longer. She dunked her head under the water.

"Do ye believe the Bishop was behind this?" Cara asked finally, her voice troubled. She rubbed a second lot of the cleaning paste between her palms, this time one made from rose petals. It smelled wonderful.

"I know he was. I found his seal on one o' those bastards." Merryn couldn't keep the hate out of her voice. Never had she felt such deep loathing for an enemy. Any battle she'd ever fought before had been a matter of politics and business as usual. The attack today had been simply cowardly and brutal. It had been a massacre and it was unforgivable.

"Then I say His Grace should live by the Word — 'an eye for an eye'," Cara said, her voice deceptively soft. "Rinse."

Merryn wiped the water from her eyes as she broke the surface. She glanced over her shoulder at Cara who was still perched on the ledge of the tub.

"Join me now that I'm not so disgustin'?" she asked, a grin playing around her mouth. Cara smiled, nodding. She was nervous as she stood, pulling her dress from her body. She could feel blue eyes on her just as acutely as she could feel her own body trembling under the frank gaze.

Merryn felt as though she should give her privacy by not ogling her, but she couldn't take her eyes off the beautiful woman. The skin was so pale, that it was almost translucent in some places. The girl she once knew was gone, leaving the incredible woman standing before her now.

Trying not to stumble into the tub, Cara accepted the hand that was offered for balance. Murmuring a thank you, she sat down across from Merryn. Their gazes met for a moment.

Cara leaned back against the side of the tub, allowing her body to relax, only for her heart to start racing again when she felt Merryn's thigh brush her own.

"Relax, lass," Merryn whispered, caressing the side of Cara's calf under the warm water.

Cara tried, but the proximity of a naked Merryn was having interesting affects on her. It had been so long that she just wasn't sure what to do with all the feelings coursing through her, and part of her felt horrible for having them. It was one of the worst days of Merryn's reign, and here she was thinking of how much the Donal's nakedness was affecting her.

Merryn watched Cara, noting as she chewed on her lower lip, brows slightly wrinkled in thought. Perhaps she shouldn't have invited her to bathe with her? She was about to say as much when Cara beat her to speaking.

Leaning slightly forward, she looked at Merryn, her gaze strong, but her lip still tucked under her front teeth before being released. Very slowly, Cara pushed Merryn's legs open, then turned around, scooting back until her back came into contact with Merryn's front.

Merryn's eyes closed as the smaller body moved against her, her arms automatically moving to wrap around Cara's waist, pulling her tightly against her. Cara's head fell back against Merryn's shoulder and they both sighed in utter contentment. It amazed Merryn just how familiar the position still was, as if they had sat like this every day.

As soon as she relaxed back into Merryn, any doubts Cara might have had disappeared. Immediately her body remembered this, how it felt to be held, how safe she felt, loved and content. How had she lived without it for more than ten years?

Merryn had always been amazed at the way their bodies fit together. She allowed her mind to expand into every fiber of her being, closing her eyes as she concentrated on every place in her body that came into contact with Cara's skin. New tingles began to flow through her as deft fingertips began to drift up her arms before sliding back down, entwining themselves with Merryn's.

Merryn leaned forward, allowing her nose to move up Cara's neck, inhaling all that was the Healer, reacquainting her senses. Cara tilted her head slightly, feeling the feather light brushes of Merryn's cheek against her own skin. Her heart began to beat faster as her breath caught.

Suddenly, an unwelcome image came before Merryn's eyes: Angus, in pain and the life fading from his body. She squeezed her eyes tightly shut, holding Cara closer to her. Cara immediately felt the change in Merryn's touch from a gentle lover's caress to a touch filled with desperation and profound sadness.

"Merryn?" she said softly. Merryn clutched their joined hands almost painfully tight.

"Aye?" Merryn whispered, burying her face in short, blonde hair, trying to keep her emotions under control.

"This day 'twas not yer fault."

"How can it not be?" Merryn exclaimed, feeling her emotions rising despite her trying to keep a tight rein on them. She was surprised when she felt the Healer pull away from her, then turn and face her. She met the kindest gaze she'd ever seen as Cara slowly moved back to Merryn, gently climbing into her lap. Merryn held her gaze, looking into the lovely face of the woman she loved. Blue eyes closed as soft fingers gently brushed dark strands of hair away from her face, a palm coming to rest on her cheek.

"Ye did what ye could, Merryn," Cara murmured, placing a soft kiss to Merryn's forehead. She was hugged tightly to the ruler, a soft sigh escaping both of them. Finally, it seemed, everything had come full circle.

Merryn met with her advisors, discussing how the breach of security had been so gross, resulting in disastrous losses for the Donal's people. Throughout the entirety of the meetings, Merryn had tried to stay focused, listening to ideas and suggestions from her men, but in truth her mind was far away. For the first time in many, many years, she contemplated leaving everything — taking Cara and Paul and starting a new life somewhere else — somewhere away from the stress, away from the dangers. She could have lost both Paul and Cara in the attacks, and would have had to live with that for the rest of her life.

Later that night, she lay in bed with Cara in her arms and told her of her wishes. Cara pushed herself up so her cheek rested on her open palm.

"Ye could never leave yer people, Merryn," Cara whispered, brushing away an errant tear. "Nor Paul nor I will let ye." She leaned down, placing a soft kiss on Merryn's temple. Merryn looked deeply into Cara's eyes, making Cara's breath catch. Merryn's intense gaze was beginning to make Cara slightly uncomfortable. "What 'tis it?" she asked at length.

Merryn smiled, lifting just far enough to place a gentle kiss to Cara's cheek. She lay back down, pulling the startled woman atop her, hugging their bodies together. Cara held her upper body up on her elbows, her gaze studying Merryn's face.

"'M glad ya stayed," Merryn whispered, brushing soft, blonde hair away from Cara's face. The healer smiled with a nod.

"As am I." She allowed her gaze to trail over the face before her, noting the ways Merryn had aged since their time together on the road. She could see the small wrinkle that streamed from her eyes from far too many years squinting at the sun while on the road or the battlefield. She saw far too many nights worrying and planning, far too many nights alone. "I love ye, Merryn," she whispered, leaning down and placing a soft kiss on full lips.

"Dona leave again," Merryn whispered against the kiss. She felt Cara shake her head.

"Nay. Ne'er again." Cara lost all control of her feelings, and of the carefully maintained self-control she'd hidden behind for so many years. She deepened the kiss, answering Merryn's soft moan. She felt tentative hands on her back, rubbing soothing circles over the narrow expanse. "Merryn?" Cara whispered, lifting just enough to look deeply into Merryn's eyes. She saw the question there. "I want..." she wasn't entirely sure what she wanted, exactly. Well, she knew what she wanted, but wasn't sure how to voice it.

"Anythin'," Merryn said, her fingers brushing up along Cara's back until finally she tucked some blonde strands of hair behind Cara's ear.

Cara nodded, encouraged by the soft promise. "I want us ta be t'gether. Like before." She met Merryn's eyes, her own shy and uncertain.

Merryn swallowed, her body filling with heat. She nodded, only able to whisper her response. "Aye."

Cara found Merryn's mouth again, the kiss much different from the one shared moments before — it was slow, sensual, and meant to seduce. Merryn's hands returned to Cara's back, fingers slowly gathered the material of the sleepshirt until she felt the warm skin of Cara's lower back. Cara sighed into the kiss as she registered the touch. Suddenly, Cara pulled away and rose to her knees. She pulled her gown over her head, her naked skin glowing in the light of the fire. She helped Merryn off with her own gown, then lying back down, both groaned at the sensation of skin on skin.

Doing something she had never done before, Cara began to explore Merryn's body with her mouth, sucking a nipple. Enjoying the taste and reaction, her tongue flicked over the rigid flesh.

Merryn arched her back, needing more; though what, she had no idea. Burying her hands in soft, golden hair, she pressed Cara deeper into her breast, gasping as a hand cupped her neglected breast. She hissed as Cara's mouth switched to the other nipple.

Cara was amazed at just how arousing it was to pleasure Merryn. She could feel herself becoming wet once more. Lifting her head, she saw the most beautiful sight she'd ever seen. Merryn's eyes were closed, her lips slightly parted, her breathing erratic. Cara watched as Merryn threw her head back after pinching one of her nipples. Cara took that opportunity to latch on to Merryn's neck, using her tongue and teeth.

"Oh, Cara," Merryn moaned, her hands finding Cara's backside. Merryn pushed Cara into her own lifted hips, trying to find some purchase.

Cara never left her prize as she shifted her body, inserting one of her thighs between Merryn's legs. She felt Merryn's wetness painting her flesh.

Cara released Merryn's neck, raising herself up on her hands. She looked down into the flushed face, her own breathing uneven and shallow as she pushed her own sex down onto Merryn's strong thigh. She could barely keep her eyes open as she felt the pressure surge through her midsection.

Merryn reached up, needing Cara's mouth against hers. The kiss was deep, Cara's lips moving against her own.

Cara nipped at Merryn's full bottom lip before caressing her tongue, swallowing a desperate whimper. Cara began moving her hips in time with Merryn's.

"Cara," Merryn panted, "I want ta feel ya." Cara looked down at her, with a look of confusion. Merryn reached down, feeling the unbelievable heat they were both producing. Cara cried out as Merryn slid her long fingers through the saturated folds of Cara's sex. "I want ta be inside ya, Cara. Please let me," Merryn begged.

"Anything, my love. Anything." Cara's mouth opened and her eyes closed when she felt one of Merryn's fingers sliding inside her depths, where no one had been before. Stunned and amazed by the bond she felt with the other woman as the finger gently slid back out, then in again. Needing desperately to share the experience, Cara balanced herself on her forearm, her other hand reaching down, nudging Merryn's legs further apart. Merryn hissed as Cara's fingers found her wetness, crying out as they grazed across her clit. Cara followed the natural curve of Merryn's sex, so much like her own, gasping as her fingers sunk into moist velvet.

Merryn gasped, pulling Cara closer to her as she felt herself filled. She found Cara's mouth. She was breathing too hard to kiss her, but instead held their lips together, both panting into the other's mouth as they began to move as one.

Cara could feel her release coming quickly as small whimpers escaped her throat as she moved her hips in time with Merryn's gentle thrusting. "I love ye," she whispered as her eyes squeezed shut and her body began to convulse once again. Merryn was too far over the edge to respond, the blood in her body pulsing to the waves of pleasure that spread through her with the speed and damage of fire, leaving her singed and forever changed.

Holding Cara desperately to her, she tucked the golden head under her chin, feeling Cara's chest heaving as hard as her own as they attempted to regain control.

"Mo Shearc."

Cara smiled, nodding. "Aye."

The ruler of the English empire slept soundly with the woman, who would become the greatest healer in history, wrapped tightly in her arms.

A new mother gazed lovingly down at her daughter, tiny fingers wrapped around her smallest one as the babe suckled at her breast.

"Soon, little, Chloe," the young woman whispered, "yer da will be with us."

The candlelight burned brightly, the flame flickering slightly from the cool breeze that wafted in every now and then. A young man frantically scribbled the events of the past two days in his book, so as not to forget a single detail — the newest volume to the chronicles of the Donal being created.

With love and pride he wrote, describing to a future world the wonders and goodness that lay in the breast of a single woman. His mother, friend, and ruler.

A lone, cloaked figure walked the halls, crossing himself as he passed a huge, golden cross. Keeping his focus, he felt the hard grip of the dagger in his right hand as it remained hidden. Ducking quickly into a small alcove in the wall, he waited for a small group of priests to hurry past, then continued on his journey.

"NO!"

A household turned to chaos as terror spread like the hand of God as a dead Bishop lay in the arms of his squire. Small, beady sightless eyes looked up to the Heavens, a look of fear forever on his brow. His cold fingers remained wrapped around the crucifix at his neck, a dagger of black and gold pinning the chain to his chest.

Kim Pritekel was born and raised in Colorado. She is a full-time writer, working on novels as well as in the film industry. She is a writer, producer, and director, currently working to bring several of her novels to the big screen through her film compnay, Asp Films. She can be reached at XenaNut@hotmail.com or through Asp Films: www.officialaspfilms.com

Other works by Kim Pritekel:

First

ISBN: 978 - 1 - 933720 - 00 - 5 (1-933720-00-X)

Emily Thomas is a successful New York attorney who has left her childhood back in Pueblo, Colorado behind her. She lives well and is happy with her partner, Rebecca. All of that changes with a simple phone call from her brother.

Beth Sayers was Emily's best friend from the time they were children until the day Beth left Emily stunned, confused, and alone in a college dorm room ten years later.

Emily must delve back into her past and into a friendship that had fallen apart, taking her love and trust with it.

Lessons

ISBN: 978 - 1 - 933720 - 08 - 1 (1-933720-08-5)

Chase Marin is an 18 year old girl filled with more confusion than common sense. Daughter of successful parents, and equally successful big sister, Chase is expected to go to college at the University of Arizona and prove herself. How can she do that when she doesn't even know herself?

Dagny Robertson is everything that the Marin's would want in a daughter — too bad Dagny's own parents don't even know their one and only child, born from their intense love, exists. Now, Dagny works on her graduate degree while acting as TA in Psych 101.

Can this older woman, once worshipped babysitter of a lost eight year old girl, help her find herself?

Twilight

ISBN: 978 - 1 - 933720 - 30 - 2 (1-933720-30-1)

Christine Grey is one of the greatest musical talents of her generation, money, success, an army of doting fans, yet has never felt more alone. About to drown in a life of pain, secrets and excess, she is saved by an unlikely hero. Willow Bowman is a nurse, and happily married woman, with a life filled with love and security. The events of one night change both their lives forever.

Available at your favorite bookstore.

Printed in the United States
117998LV00007B/148-165/P